Secrets of a Summer Village

Secrets
of a
Summer Village

Saskia E. Akyil

ISBN-10: 1463740115

ISBN-13: 978-1463740115

Saskia E. Akyil

For Levent'im

Chapter 1

Do not be satisfied with the stories that come before you. Unfold your own myth.

- Rumi

Izmir, Turkey

July 15

Rachel was lightheaded from excitement and lack of sleep, and the suitcases going around the carousel at the Izmir International Airport were making her dizzy. She tried to figure out how long she had been traveling. Her watch said 8, and was still on Pacific Standard Time, but she had left home so long ago that she could no longer figure it out; was it 8am or 8pm? It had definitely been more than 24 hours since she had left home in Olympia, Washington and she hadn't slept even half an hour. In her backpack, she carried a guidebook on Turkey given to her by her best friend, Hanna, and three back issues of *Seventeen* magazine. She thought that her host sister might enjoy reading them, but then again, she didn't know her host sister at all, so who knew what she liked.

Rachel had flipped through the pages of the guidebook on the flight from Seattle to Paris, but none of it sunk in. It was the type of guidebook that had text but no photos, so she just couldn't imagine what Turkey would be like. Hanna was more of a reader than Rachel; of course she would pick a guidebook without pictures. By the time she got to Paris, Rachel had read all of the magazines, watched three movies, and perused the airline's duty-free catalogue. The food hadn't been too bad, but she really wanted a latte, and she didn't have any European money, so she couldn't buy a single thing. She could have converted some of her dollars to Euros, but her layover was only an hour and ten minutes and she didn't want to waste her spending money. Everybody talked about Paris as if it were the capital of everything cool, but Rachel had chosen to study Spanish, so a summer exchange in France hadn't seemed like an option. How, then, did she end up on her way to a Turkish summer?

From Paris, Rachel flew to Istanbul, where she waited for three and a half hours. Where are all the women in veils? She wondered. The guidebook had said that 99% of people in Turkey were Muslim. Didn't all Muslims have to wear veils? In all the movies and documentaries about Muslim countries, women were all in dark veils. Rachel looked around and spotted a few veiled women, but they were wearing tight-fitting jackets and pants, not the flowing black capes she had imagined. Most of the women at the Istanbul airport did actually look like something out of a movie, but a different kind of movie than the ones that took place in the Muslim countries. These women had perfectly coiffed hair and their makeup was so immaculate it could have been applied at the makeup counter at the mall. And they wore fitted, fashionable, revealing clothing like sexy fashion magazine models. They were nothing like the sweat-pants, t-shirt and flip-flop wearing people of Olympia, Washington. Rachel felt slightly grubby in her jeans, running shoes, and Olympia High t-shirt. Since she hadn't known how to dress for Turkey, she had tried to dress comfortably, but among all these well-groomed women, she felt less than comfortable.

Before she knew it, the hour-long flight to Izmir was over and there she was, at her destination. As soon she got her bag, she could go through the doors to the waiting area, where her exchange family was hopefully waiting for her. Every once in a while, the sliding doors opened and she saw a crowd of people excitedly greeting their loved ones. The airport was new, bright and clean – a huge improvement over the Seattle airport, which had been in renovation since Rachel was born. Parts of it were nice, but most of it was still more like a dusty construction site.

The sleek Izmir airport was not what she had expected of Turkey. She thought it would be like the one in Puerto Vallarta, Mexico, where she had once gone on vacation with her family. There, they had walked from the plane to the tarmac and then into the airport, where taxi drivers had surrounded them, each guaranteeing they had the best rates to the hotel. The airport there was hot, and the sea breeze went in one side of the airport and out the other. The Izmir airport was disappointingly modern, air-conditioned, and, well, not all that exotic.

Olympia, Washington

June 30 (Two weeks earlier)

Rachel, aged 17, was not sure whether or not she should apply for a summer job. School had been out for two weeks and July was only one day away, but Mother Nature had apparently not been informed that it was supposed to be summer; she still had to wear a sweatshirt when she went down to the Olympia marina to hang out with Hanna. It wasn't sunny, but didn't look like it would rain either. Olympia was the rainiest city in Washington State, so you never knew for sure. Rachel was proud to have been born and bred in Olympia. She wasn't sure why she was proud, after all she hadn't been to many places, but her mom told her it was something to be proud of.

Rachel walked down the hill from her parents' house on the West Side of town and across the new bridge. The old bridge had been destroyed in an earthquake. It had taken them 4 years to get a new one up and running, but it was a nice bridge, Rachel thought as she walked over it. It had good lighting and a wide sidewalk, things that the old bridge had lacked. It made Olympia feel like she lived in an important city rather than a small-town state capital with rickety bridges and a small, liberal state college. Hanna waited for Rachel in front of The Oyster House restaurant, which stood between 4th Avenue and the waters of Puget Sound. She wore a periwinkle polar fleece jacket and jeans, but still looked cold. Her hands were stuffed into the pockets of her jacket and her cheeks were pink.

"You look so cold!" Rachel said, once she was within earshot.

"Well, I only wore a tank top inside my fleece, in case the weather warms up when the sun comes out." With her very blonde hair, ice blue eyes, and always-pink cheeks, Hanna often looked cold. Her grandparents on one side were Swedish and on the other side, Finnish.

"You're really lucky that your grandparents moved to Olympia," Rachel said. "You would have frozen your butt off if you had to live in Finland. How would you have survived the summer exchange there? It's a good thing you changed your mind about going." Hanna was going to stay with her cousins in Helsinki for six weeks, to study Finnish and make her father happy. But since she was sure she wanted to be pre-med and become an orthopedic sports medicine doctor, the school counselor thought it would be a better idea for her to get a summer internship with either an orthopedist or a physical therapist, to help her get into a good pre-med program when she applied in the fall.

"I'm still going next year," Hanna replied. "Besides, it's pretty warm there in the summer. And there's daylight like 19 hours a day, my dad says. It sounds pretty decent to me. But I guess you're gonna be here this summer, after all, so I don't mind waiting until next year."

"We don't know that for sure," reminded Rachel. She had mostly lost hope that a place would open up for her on the summer exchange program to Mexico. Her family vacation to Mexico the previous Christmas had been perfect –warm, humid weather and floral scented air. She had played volleyball on the beach with other hotel guests. There had been a cute guy who played every day, but he never seemed to notice that Rachel existed.

"Do you really still think a spot will open up for you?" asked Hanna, rolling her eyes. "C'mon Rachel, face it, it's another summer in Olympia for you and me. You'd better find something to do with yourself."

"Yeah, I'm thinking of getting a job... maybe at Batdorf and Bronson again." Rachel loved how coffee smelled, and it felt very cool to work as a barista, even though the money wasn't good.

"Don't waste a summer working at a coffee shop, Rach." Hanna had a way of saying coffee shop as if it were a dirty word. She was much more ambitious than Rachel, and working at a café was a road to nowhere as far as she was concerned. Rachel thought that Hanna was probably right, but of course she couldn't admit it.

"I was thinking the same thing," she said. "I was just talking... you know, it would be cool. But I should get something maybe where I can earn as much as possible, maybe waiting tables or something. Even if I don't get to go, it would be good to have some pocket money..."

"Rachel, you're always thinking in the short term. You need to get something that's gonna look good on your resume. What do you want to major in, in college? Don't you know by now? You should get something that will help you out there."

"Time to change the topic," Rachel quickly replied. She was not interested in thinking about what she was going to be. She planned to go to college and figure it out there. This was the last summer of high school, and she didn't want to spend it worrying about the future. She just wanted to spend the summer somewhere fun and different. Why not? After all, Mom and Dad had always told her to enjoy her youth. For once, she was going to listen.

Neither Rachel nor Hanna knew that in fact there was a letter on the way to Rachel's mailbox from Mr. Finney the guidance counselor. A job at Batdorf & Bronson would be unnecessary that summer if Rachel accepted the unexpected proposition from the Summer Exchange Adventure Company.

Once the haze burned off, the sun was as bright and strong as it should be in July. Rachel had taken off her sweatshirt, and her arms had gotten slightly sunburned for the first time of the year. They were light pink, but she was slightly concerned that they would be closer to slightly red by the evening. She was worried because she had been wearing a t-shirt rather than a sleeveless top, and she was going to start out the summer with a farmer's tan.

When she opened the front door and walked into the house, her mom called to her from the kitchen, where she was preparing salmon for dinner.

"Rachel honey, there's a letter for you from school on the counter here... it's addressed to all of us. Is there anything I should know?" Even though she hadn't done anything wrong that she could think of, she instantly felt guilty and worried that she had forgotten something. Her cheeks burned and tensed until she walked into the kitchen and saw the letter, with Mr. Finney's name above the return address.

"Hey, this is from the guidance counselor, maybe it's about the summer exchange!" Rachel exclaimed, immediately forgetting any wrongdoing on her part, real or imagined. Her mom looked up and smiled one of those my-poor-baby-I-hope-she's-not-disappointed smiles.

"Hon, if there's no space for you we'll take a family trip somewhere fun, like to Vancouver," she offered. As if that would replace a summer exchange to Mexico! Rachel thought. Great, a week with weird Aunt Celia, the psychic who insisted on reading her tea leaves and tarot cards and made her wear crystals to ward off bad energy. The letter from Mr. Finney better have good news. She tore open the letter, sat down, and started reading it to herself until she got past the chit chatty greeting and on to the bad news, which she read out quietly to her mother:

"... although spaces have opened up in the summer exchange program to Guadalajara, Mexico, the waiting list was very long and unfortunately the Summer Exchange Adventure Company is unable to offer you a spot..."

Her voice trailed off, and she felt way more down than she expected to. She had been on the waiting list for months with no luck, and the exchange was set to begin in two weeks, how had she gotten her hopes up? Rachel's mom had by that point washed her hands, and come to sit next to her on the mauve leather couch that had been in their living room ever since she could remember.

"Mom, you smell like fish," she pointed out. Her mom didn't even notice the comment; she was absorbed in the rest of the letter, and began to read it aloud:

> "However, an unusual opportunity has presented itself and I hope that you will consider it. A spot has opened up in a summer exchange program to Turkey. The exchange lasts one month, from July 15th to August 15th, and has no language requirement.
>
> The host family has two daughters, one who is your age and another who is 24. Both have studied English extensively, and would like to practice their English with an exchange student. They live in Izmir, which is a major city on the Aegean Sea. Please talk the possibility over with your family and get back to me by July 4th so that travel arrangements can be made."

"Wow, Rachel, that's ... interesting," Rachel could tell that her mom didn't know what to say. "Hey, let's break out the map and see where Turkey is!"

"Mom, I know where Turkey is."

"Where is it, then?"

"It's next to Greece. There's all this stuff going on about whether or not it's going to join the European Union." AP European History was good for something, it seemed. The teacher, Miss Buckley, was insane and made them learn way more than necessary for the AP test, but some of it was interesting. Sometimes. And, truth be told, the class was mostly guys and some of them were actually cute.

"Wow, Greece!" Everyone had heard of Greece, even Rachel's mom. It had lots of beaches and gyros. "But that's really far away... I bet it's expensive to get there..." her mom had already started to worry. Both of her parents worked for the State government. Her mom was a receptionist at the Department of Transportation, and her dad was a traffic engineer. They had a house (ranch style, built in 1956), a yard (mostly grass), and two cars (Rachel was allowed to drive them on weekends and in the summer). They had everything they needed but were definitely not rich. Going to Turkey was not likely. After all, her parents were trying to save for Rachel to go to college.

Going to Mexico or France sounded cool, but Rachel couldn't gather much excitement for going to a country so much on the edge of Europe that there were huge debates as to whether or not it could be counted as part of Europe. She may have been able to find it on a map (after all, they had to take a map quiz every other week) and she knew it was being considered as a member country of the European Union (that was on the final exam), but she knew nothing about it, so how could she want to go there? She didn't know what language they spoke, what they ate, or what kind of music they listened to. It would be just fine if she didn't go on a summer exchange there because she couldn't imagine what it would be like, even for a minute.

"That's ok, mom, I won't go. I put in an application at Batdorf and Bronson's today anyway, and they told me that my chances were good because they had openings at their new branch." Rachel could tell that her mom was not listening to her, again. She was staring out the window at a bird that was sitting on the power line.

"I think something came across my desk about a state scholarship for study abroad. I wonder..."

"Mom, you're not listening to me! I said I won't go, it's ok, don't worry. Hanna's not going anywhere this summer, either, we'll have fun." Suddenly, her mom heard her and she looked unexpectedly upset.

"No you don't, young lady, don't you give up so fast! You want to go on an exchange and we will find a way. I never got to

13

go anywhere growing up, and here I am, still living 14.2 miles from where I was born. You are going to Turkey." Great, Mom is living vicariously through me, again. Her mom had forced her to go to Junior Prom completely against her will, because she had not gotten to go herself. And now she was going to have to go to Turkey when she really wanted to go to Mexico and lie on the beach and learn Spanish better and then take AP Spanish next year so she could get credit for it in college. Going to Turkey was not part of the plan.

"Mom, I'm 17. You can't make me go to Turkey if I don't want to." It was the best she could come up with on short notice. She could have thought of a better comeback if she had anticipated this situation. But it's not every day that your mom threatens to send you on a summer exchange to Turkey. Rachel's mother took a deep breath, something she had started doing a lot since she started a yoga class at the Y.

"Can you at least think it over and sleep on the idea for one night before poo-pooing the idea?" The terminology made Rachel laugh.

"All right, Mom, I'll humor you," she said, and walked to her bedroom to Google Turkey on the computer she had bought with last summer's savings.

The search brought up some news results first… something about the European Union, and then something about the bird flu in turkeys in England. Then there was a Wikipedia article, but she was tired of Wikipedia because she had to write an article for it for Miss Buckley's final class project, and after all, it was not always reliable. The next link was for the official tourism site, which she clicked on (after all, she would be a tourist). The homepage had images of stone head statues, a mountain, a city on the water, a balloon ride over a desert, and some small boats on the sea. It looked pretty, but it was too close to the school year. Rachel was burned out from all the research she'd done for final papers. She closed the browser and opened up her chat program. As she suspected, Hanna was online. Their usernames were their first names in Pig Latin.

ACHELRAY: what's up?

ANNAHAY: reading e-mail.

        got an internship

        (unpaid) with an orthopedist

        dr. wheeler

ACHELRAY: jenny's dad?

ANNAHAY: yeah.

        i know.

        she's a snot, but her dad is nice.

ACHELRAY: cool.

ANNAHAY: any news about Mexico?

ACHELRAY: yeah…

ANNAHAY: AND!??

ACHELRAY: nope. no hope.

ANNAHAY: sorry.

ACHELRAY: it's ok.

ANNAHAY: we'll hang out, it'll be fun.

ACHELRAY: maybe…

ANNAHAY: ?

ACHELRAY: they want to send me on exchange

        to Turkey.

ANNAHAY: what?!

ACHELRAY: I know…

ANNAHAY: u gonna go?

ACHELRAY: dunno… mom says I have to

ANNAHAY: ?

ACHELRAY: whatever

        doubt we have the money…

ANNAHAY: u wanna go?

ACHELRAY: dunno

don't know anything about the place.

ANNAHAY: sounds exotic...

ACHELRAY: u know anything about it?

ANNAHAY: muslim country...

ACHELRAY: as in wear a veil?

ANNAHAY: ??... i guess

ACHELRAY: that would be weird ...

ANNAHAY: gtg, dinner, chat later

ACHELRAY: bye

ANNAHAY: cya

Rachel went to lie down on her bed. It was comfortable and she sunk into the comforter. She closed her eyes and thought about her options. It was stay in Olympia and work in a coffee shop, or go on a summer exchange program to a country she knew pretty much nothing about, where they spoke a language she didn't even know the name of. The answer was obvious. Go to Turkey. Adventure. After all, it was only a month. If her parents could come up with the money for the plane ticket and fees, she would go... people always said that youth was a time to be reckless. Didn't they? Or something like that. She was usually careful about her plans (the few times she had actually planned anything), but here she was deciding to go somewhere she didn't even have the energy to research. Maybe that's why I decided to go. I don't have the energy to argue with Mom again.

Rachel got off her bed and went out to the kitchen, where she could smell the salmon sizzling on the grill on the deck.

"Sorry I argued with you, Mom," she began. "I think you're right..."

"Oh, no, I am sorry," her mom interrupted. "I just talked to Aunt Sharon, and she... well, maybe you're right." Sharon was her dad's sister. She worked at the Lancôme counter at the mall in Seattle.

"Why, what did she say?"

"She said that Turkey was in the Middle East and that when she went to the Lancôme training, her boss was from the Middle East, like Iran or Iraq or something, and said that makeup was really important there because the women had to wear veils and so only their faces showed."

"So?" Rachel didn't see why this should matter for one month. She had already decided that she would go, though she couldn't think of any reason other than it sounded more interesting than "Decaf soy latte with a vanilla shot. Grande or tall?".

"What do you mean, so!? Isn't that scary? Maybe they won't even let you leave the house! What if…"

"Mom, you're getting carried away. It's a one month exchange program. They must screen the families. It could be fun."

"Rachel, half an hour ago, you said you didn't want to go and now you want to go. What changed in that time? I shouldn't have encouraged you to go without learning about where it was. Mexico was fine, Europe would be fine, but not the Middle East."

"Mom, you're being so unfair! Half an hour ago you told me I was going and now you're all against it. I could go on an adventure but instead you just want me to serve coffee all summer! Thanks for your support!" Ugh, sometimes it was so hard to be reasonable when her mother was being unreasonable.

"I doubt we have the money, anyway," said her mom, softening her voice after taking a yoga breath. "Baby, maybe next year. And we'll get your application in earlier." Rachel knew that if she wanted permission to go, she'd have to somehow prove it to her mom.

"At least can we meet with Mr. Finney and get some more information about the family and stuff?" Wow, she thought. That was a good comeback. She sounded more like the mom than the kid for a second.

That's when her dad walked in. Dad was quiet. Not just today – Dad was always quiet. Wasting words wasn't something he did. Unless it came to talking about the flow of traffic in Olympia and the need for more traffic circles. Then he had plenty to say, but for the most part, he listened. He was actually cool. She could tell him things and she knew he would keep her secrets. She was the only girl she knew who could confide in her dad more than in her mom.

"Hi Dad, how was your day?" Her dad smiled and winked.

"Fewer accidents on Lacey Avenue this month," He replied. "Helen, the fish smells good," was his greeting to her mom, who smiled back. They didn't seem to talk to each other much, but somehow they were still a nice pair. Helen's mom thought he was the greatest man to ever walk the Earth, which was one thing that Rachel and her mom agreed on.

"Dad, we got a letter from Mr. Finney today," Rachel said as she handed him the letter, hoping he would instantly declare sending their only child to Turkey for a month a brilliant idea, and therefore getting mom's approval. He took the letter and read it standing like a marble statue at the kitchen counter. He didn't look up when he had finished reading.

"Mom and I will have to talk this over a bit. Rachel, what's your take?" He finally looked up from the letter. His face didn't give away what he was thinking. Hmm, that hadn't gone as Rachel had expected, or at least not how she had hoped. No instant proclamation that it was a brilliant idea. But at least he hadn't said no. Yet.

"I want to go, it sounds cool." was all Rachel could come up with in response. Not very convincing, but she really didn't have any facts to present her dad with. He was a facts person. Ugh, I should have read the Wikipedia entry.

Chapter 2

And you? When will you begin that long journey into yourself?

-   *Rumi*

-

Nobody talked about the exchange at dinner. Rachel's mom talked about how she was planning to apply to the nursing program at South Puget Sound Community College, and how popular it was and how she would have to take lots of prerequisites before she could even apply. Rachel's mom had quit college after Rachel was born. That was a long story.

After dinner, Rachel went to her room and wrote an e-mail to Mr. Finney.

Hi Mr. Finney,

We got your letter today. The exchange to Turkey sounds like a cool idea, but I have some questions. Do you have office hours this week? I might come with my parents. Please let me know.

Thanks,

Rachel Guo

She felt like it was way too short of an e-mail, but she didn't want to go into detail about maybe not having the money or about her mom's fear of the Middle East or about her (lack of good) reasons for wanting to go.

Somewhere between Izmir and Denizli, Turkey

July 2

Aylin (pronounced Eileen) sat in the back seat, behind her dad, who she called Baba (which means "daddy" in Turkish). Sitting behind him was pretty much the worst place anyone could sit, because he pushed his seat back so much that there was no room. She complained every time she got into the car, even though it made no difference, and her father ignored her every time, because it made no difference. He was six foot two and needed the legroom. She could have sat behind her mother, Annecim (pronounced Ah-nay) in Turkish, but that seat was taken by bags of tomatoes, apricots, and cranberry beans that they had bought at roadside stands. Aylin was being strategic. The seat behind her mother always went to her sister, Leyla, who was the same height as Aylin but was older and thus had gotten there first. When Leyla wasn't in the car, Aylin could have sat there, but the strategy this year was for Aylin to sit in her normal seat and get all the fruits and vegetables piled up on Leyla's seat so that hopefully Leyla would end up with them at her feet. Aylin had already claimed the space by her own feet with her duffel bag of clothes, which was much more comfortable to have by her feet than eggplants.

They were driving from Izmir, where they lived most of the year, to their summer house in Didim, which was a summer village on the Aegean coast south of Izmir. Since Leyla's father was a tenured professor, he had summers off and the whole family spent the summer at the beach. Most of her friends' families also had summer houses, but not in Didim. Aylin's mother, who was from Denizli, had inherited their summer house from her aunt, who didn't have any children. Denizli is an inland city about three hours by car from Izmir, and they were on their way there now to pick up Aylin's sister, Leyla, who had just finished graduate school there.

"Annecim, are we going to stop and see Aunt Ilkay in Denizli?"

"No, Aylin, not this time... she is at her friend's summer house in Marmaris. In fact, almost all the aunts and uncles and cousins have gone to their summer houses already." She looked at Aylin's father.

"Don't look at me," he said. "I had to finish my end of the year paperwork. You can't complain! Most husbands are only there on the weekend and I stay with you the whole time, my love." Just then, Aylin's dad quickly pulled his car over to the side of the road, where there was a fruit stand selling peaches. There had been at least five identical stands before it, all selling peaches, but this was the one they stopped by every year when they drove to Denizli. The woman who sold the peaches there was the wife of the farmer who grew the peaches. She wore a green flowery scarf loosely over her hair. When she saw Aylin's father, she grinned widely, exposing a few gold teeth among the white ones, themselves yellowed by years of drinking tea. He bought a large bag of peaches, and the farmer's wife followed him to the car, carrying peaches she had washed in a bucket of water. Aylin's mother opened her window and the farmer's wife spoke.

"*Hos geldiniz*, welcome Hanim, how are you this year? Oh, and look at Aylin, *masallah*, God protect her, she has grown up so much, why don't you all stop and have some tea with me? I also have some pastries that my daughter made..." It was the same conversation every year, and it was a sign that summer was here and that they were getting close to Denizli. It would have been only a three hour drive directly from Izmir to Didim, but every year there was a reason to stop by Denizli on the way. They had to visit a relative, go outlet shopping (Denizli is famous for its textiles), check on the tenants in their rented apartment... this year, it was to pick up Leyla. So what could have been a three-hour drive was doubled because of the detour to Denizli, and tripled because of all of the stops, to buy fruits and vegetables, to eat, to stop by relatives' homes and drink tea. So what could have been a three-hour trip was an all-day trip. When they were younger, Aylin and Leyla were always annoyed because they were so excited to get to the beach and see who would be there. But this year, everyone was already gone and Aylin missed visiting her cousins, second-cousins, aunts and uncles. Everyone was spreading out. Many of Aylin's older cousins had gone to college in Istanbul and Ankara and stayed on to work.

"*Tesekkur ederiz*, thank you, Aylin's mom politely refused, but our other daughter, Leyla, is waiting for us and we don't want her to wait. The peaches are wonderful, *kolay gelsin*, may your work be easy!"

"Have safe travels" She called after them as they drove away.

"I have to start thinking in English!" Aylin announced. "We might have an exchange student!"

"Do you think so?" Aylin's mom said with a slightly disappointed sound. "The agency has not sent any news. They said that with the things happening in England and the United States, not many families want to send their children to a Muslim country. Well, *hayirlisi olsun*. They don't know what they are talking about, they have not been here and they are afraid of here. Humpf." Aylin's mom was insulted by the idea that nobody in America wanted to send their child to Turkey for an idyllic month by the sea.

"Ok, for example, *hayirlisi olsun*, how do I say that in English? Why don't they teach us this in school? I can talk about 19th century English literature, but I cannot say something useful like *hayirlisi olsun*." Aylin wondered how her teachers could leave such huge knowledge gaps in their lessons. Aylin's mom smiled at the comment, but her eyebrows did not lose their worried look. Aylin knew what this was about, and it didn't have anything to do with a hypothetical exchange student. Her sister Leyla's heart had been broken six months before, and since that time she had barely called and had come home only once. They got all their news from Aunt Ilkay, who was suspiciously quiet, but promised them that Leyla was really going to be ok and just needed a little time. Aylin tried to keep them off the subject.

"Well, since we won't be stopping off to see anyone in Denizli this time, can I just run into the computer lab at Leyla's university? I want to check my e-mail, maybe there's news about the exchange student... and the dial-up in Didim is so slow. Babacim, pleeeeeeeeease?" Aylin's father's smile broke through his worried look.

"I can never say no to you, Aylin'cim," he said. "You always have reasonable requests."

When they approached Pamukkale University, it was just past noon, three and a half hours after they had left Izmir. Although Leyla lived with Aunt Ilkay while she was in school, they had agreed to meet her at the University to pick her up because she'd had to turn in her final project that morning. She was wearing red capri pants and a crisp white form-fitting polo shirt. Her long chestnut hair had been highlighted with auburn streaks in the front. She looked way better than Aylin had expected for someone who was heartbroken. Aylin was happier than usual to see her sister, maybe because of her absence the previous six months. Even though Leyla was seven years older than Aylin, they had always been partners in crime.

Aylin kissed Leyla on both cheeks and then hugged her fashionable older sister, who smelled of a floral perfume.

"I missed you so much," said Aylin, and she meant it. "We've been so worried about you..." she said, and before their parents reached them, Leyla kissed her on the cheek again.

"Don't worry, I'm in love," she whispered in Aylin's ear, then stood back and winked. Aylin was sure she wouldn't get the story until they were in private, but she sensed that it was going to be a great summer.

They decided to eat at the University's faculty cafeteria, which had outside seating overlooking the city, and to which they had access because of their father's connections. After she ordered her food, Aylin escaped with Leyla to the computer lab, to check her e-mail.

When they were out of earshot, she squeezed Leyla's hand and said, "Tell! Explain everything!" But Leyla was going to be suspenseful.

"It's too long, I'll tell you later. I'll just get you logged into the computer and you can check your e-mail. Then I'll go sit with our parents or they'll suspect something; this time I want to be discreet." With the excitement of Leyla's odd secrecy, Aylin almost forgot about the exchange student. But not quite. A sister's new romance plus an exchange student in one summer, this was going to be a summer to remember. If, that is, any parents of an English-speaking daughter her age were going to let the said daughter travel to Turkey for a month.

Apparently, there was one, and that was all it took. Aylin read Rachel's e-mail excitedly... and maybe a bit disappointedly because it was very short, revealed almost nothing, had no picture attached, and made Aylin wonder if Rachel were a very boring girl and if maybe she had made a mistake.

Dear Aylin,

My name is Rachel Guo and I will be your exchange student. I still don't have my ticket, but I think I will be there about July 15th. I'm from Washington State and I'm 17. I'm a junior. I've never been to Turkey before. Please tell me what I should pack. I look forward to meeting you and your family.

Sincerely,

Rachel Guo

Well, try not to judge too early, she told herself, it's just an e-mail, and immediately wrote back as fast as her hands could type in English.

Dear Rachel,

I am soooooooo happy to receive your message. My name is Aylin, pronounced like Eileen in English. I am also 17 years old and I am waiting for you with four eyes. We will wait for you at the airport! This summer will be veeeeeery beautiful. Pack your normal summer clothes. The weather will be very hot. Definitely do not forget your bathing suit! What is your favorite food to eat? I will make it for you when you come.

I am studying English since I was 8 years old but I never practice outside the school so I hope we will practice. I want to travel to the United States or England to practice but my father says nooooooooooooooooo. I will fall in love there, he is afraid. Hahaha. Now we go to summer house in Didim, and our internet is slow. I will check my e-mail there, but not every day.

Take care and please say many hellos to your family.

Kisses,

Aylin

Olympia, Washington

July 1 (The Day Before)

Unlike Rachel and her friends, Mr. Finney apparently didn't check his e-mail every five minutes; she didn't get a response until the next day, after her parents sat her down and told her that if the trip cost more than eight hundred dollars, they just couldn't afford it right now. And they didn't want to ask Grams because she was already paying for mom's nursing school. Rachel knew that was not the real reason they couldn't ask Grams – she had heard her mom complaining before that Grams thought they were still kids who couldn't take care of themselves. So the $800 they could come up with was the maximum available for Rachel's study abroad.

After the money talk, Rachel wished she hadn't spent last year's summer savings on a computer. But then she wouldn't have been cut off from all of her friends and would have to type her papers in the computer lab at school or at the library. Or write them out by hand and have her mom type them out at work. And then she couldn't do anything at the last minute, so it was really good to have the computer. Plus, now she had an easy way of finding out how much airplane tickets cost.

Or maybe it would have been better not to know. The cheapest flight she could find was $1,990. Plus tax and a fuel surcharge. Maybe I shouldn't bother meeting with Mr. Finney, she thought. No point in getting excited anymore, if I can't go. But by the time she had found out that she couldn't afford to go, her choices were race to catch the bus, or call and tell Mr. Finney that her parents didn't have the money. Ah, what the hell, she thought, and raced out the door.

Mr. Finney was a decent guy. He had longish dirty blond hair and his trademark outfit was colorful t-shirts underneath a blazer. It was a strange outfit but was almost like a uniform for him. Everyone expected it of him. And even though everyone knew he used to be a professional skateboarder and was probably pretty cool in his time, the blazer made him seem old and gave him some authority, which was probably what he wanted. He was really smart, but he still spoke like a skater.

"Hey, Rachel Guo!" he said when he looked up from his desk and saw her. "Glad to see you!," he said, like he didn't know she was coming.

"I'm here about the exchange program to Turkey," she began, to remind him, in case he had forgotten.

"Totally!" he replied. She wasn't sure if he really remembered or if he was just pretending. "So what do you think? Can't pass it up, right?" He was so enthusiastic, she felt bad she would have to tell him that she couldn't afford it.

"Yeah, pretty awesome," she said. She'd save the bad news for later.

"Great, then, I'll get you the details." Wow, that was too quick. She'd have to tell him.

"Look, Mr. Finney, I really really want to go, I mean this is totally exciting and stuff, but I can't come up with the money. I mean, I was looking online and the cheapest ticket I could find was almost two thousand dollars. So I'm sorry." Amazingly, Mr. Finney didn't look too upset.

"But you really want to go?" He was like a kid. How could she explain this to him?

"Of course, but I don't have the money," she repeated.

"It's not that much," he said.

"Mr. Finney, my parents aren't rich!" Rachel blurted out. What was his problem, why didn't he get it? Mr. Finney took out a green file folder from his drawer.

"Money's no problem, Rachel, it's your attitude that matters." He made no sense at all until he elaborated. "This

Dear Rachel,

I think you are very funny! I have only two eyes but when we say we wait for you with four eyes it means we are very excited to see you. But now when I think about it, it is very funny!

Of course, any kind of bathing suit is ok but it should have a top because our beach does not allow topless. I think you must bring some shorts and tank tops because it is very hot in the daytime, but also bring jeans and regular shirts because at night we go out and you shouldn't get cold. I don't like to wear skirts, but if you like skirts that is fine. In Turkish culture we all dress as we like but I watch American movies and TV and I think we dress the same as you.

You have never eaten Turkish food! I cannot believe! Turkish food is great. My mother can teach you how to cook Turkish food and you can make it for your family! We won't find strawberries in July but we will eat watermelon and French fries every night if you want! By the way, why do you say they are French? We call them fried potatoes here.

One thing I must tell you which is very important: we don't speak Arabic here. Arabs speak Arabic, but we are not Arabic... we speak Turkish. I think you will learn some Turkish words here.

The guys here are very handsome, but we don't tell them and also don't tell your father!

Take care,

Aylin

Olympia, Washington

July 12

Rachel's departure was two days away. In order to arrive in Turkey on July 15th, she had to fly out of the Seattle airport on the 14th. On the 13th, her parents were putting on a pizza party for her and her friends. But on the night of the 12th, Rachel's mom had to help out at a conference, so it was just Rachel, her dad, and a pizza.

"Rachel, I hope you have a wonderful time in Turkey," her dad said, in a rare departure from talking about traffic patterns. Rachel sensed he had something important to say to her because he looked slightly less calm than usual.

"Thanks, Dad," she replied. "I promise to take lots of pictures, and to take really good care of your camera," she said. Maybe he was worried she would damage his new digital camera, which had been a gift from mom for his birthday. Dad was getting into photography and went out almost every weekend to take pictures in and around Olympia. But he had offered it to Rachel for her trip because it was just too important of a trip not to document.

"Oh, I know you will Rach," he said. Hmm, that wasn't it. He didn't seem to have a second thought about the camera.

"Now, you're going to be representing America over there so I know you'll be polite and kind and basically act like the perfect guest. Help out and so forth."

"Of course, Dad." This was weird. So unlike her dad. He knew she was good and respectful. What was this about?!

"And I, I" he stuttered. "I want you to make good decisions." He was getting somewhere but Rachel still didn't know exactly what he was alluding to. However, he didn't offer any clarification and seemed to expect her to know what he meant.

"Dad," Rachel was direct. "I don't know what you're trying to say here. I mean, of course I should make good decisions." Her dad sighed.

"I mean about boys. You're 17 and, well, you'll be far away from home. Be careful and make good decisions." Aha, this was the birds-and-bees talk that she had gotten from her mother three hundred thousand times, but it was so embarrassing getting it from Dad. She felt her cheeks turning hot as her mouth froze.

"Dad, I, I, um, you don't have to worry. I'll be good. I am good. I've never done anything to make you not trust me about stuff like that. And even if I wanted to, guys don't seem to like me." How could Dad do this to her? He had no reason to doubt her! Her father took a sip of his Coke, smiled, and shook his head.

"First of all, you are beautiful, and I don't believe that boys don't like you. Second, I trust you 100%, Rach," he said, easing up slightly. "It's not about trust. It's about decisions. Nothing more than decisions. Every time you do something or don't do something, you are making a decision. So I just want you to think about that and ask yourself if you're making a good decision, when decisions are being made. That's all." That was as specific as he was going to get. Whew!

"Ok, Dad, thanks," Rachel said. She knew all too well that Dad had reasons for having "a talk" with her. But she also knew that he had no reason to be worried.

Olympia, Washington

July 13

Dear Aylin,

I'm leaving tomorrow morning! I'm totally excited now. My suitcase is packed and my family had a party for me tonight.

Don't worry, I don't plan to go topless on your beach. That is crazy! We never do that here. It would be so embarrassing!

You still haven't sent me a picture of you, so I'm sending you one of me so you know who I am when you see me. It's a new picture, and I still look the same – my hair is dark brown and my eyes are dark brown. I will be wearing jeans, running shoes, and a navy blue t-shirt that says "Olympia High School".

Sorry about the confusion about Arabic. I just assumed that all Muslims spoke Arabic but obviously that was pretty stupid of me. I googled Turkish Language and read about it a little. It looks pretty hard, but I'll still try to learn some. I'm glad to hear that it's written with the same letters as English. That's a huge relief.

I didn't tell my dad that the guys there are cute, but he's worried anyway.

I hope you get this e-mail before I get there! If not, I hope we can find each other at the airport.

Hugs,
Rachel

Chapter 3

On a day
When the wind is perfect,
The sail just needs to open and the world is full of beauty.
Today is such a day.

-    *Rumi*

Izmir, Turkey

July 15

Rachel spotted her giant orange duffel bag the instant it exited onto the carousel. It had been a gift from Hanna, who had traveled a lot and knew that most people had black or navy bags, which were hard to distinguish. Hanna, as usual, was right. When it was Rachel's turn to go through the sliding glass doors with the noisy crowd on the other side, she was more than nervous. What if Aylin didn't like her? What if Aylin wasn't there? What if Aylin didn't know how to speak English as well as she wrote it? Rachel's heart was beating rapidly as she stepped towards the door. Other people walked by her, obviously in a hurry to get out to their friends and family.

Once on the other side of the door, Rachel didn't even have time to look around before she heard a girl's voice call out to her excitedly.

"Rachel, Rachel, Rachel!!!!!" A girl her height with curly-frizzy medium-brown hair and blue eyes ran towards her and threw her arms around her, then kissed both of her cheeks. Next came a woman who looked just like her, but about twenty years older, who didn't hug her, but kissed her on both cheeks. Then came a man, about her father's age, who shook her hand (thank goodness, because it would have been extremely weird to be kissing some man who she'd never met! Cheeks or not!). The girl didn't introduce herself, but Rachel assumed she was Aylin.

"Aylin?" she said, just to make sure she wasn't going home with the wrong family,

"Of course, it's me!!" said the young girl, excitedly. "Welcome to Turkey, we are so happy! I am too excited, I am forgetting my English!" Rachel forgot her fear and felt her toes relax in her shoes. Aylin was totally friendly, her parents seemed nice, too. Rachel smiled and then, to her surprise, started to cry. "What happened, is something wrong? Are you good?" Aylin immediately asked, as her mother stroked Rachel on the back. Rachel started crying harder.

Stunned and embarrassed by her reaction. "I guess I am just relieved to be here and tired and you seem so nice, I'm just really happy, I think."

Aylin put her arm around Rachel's arm and squeezed her. "You must be part Turkish! We are so emotional here, you will love here!" she said as her mom handed Rachel a tissue. Once Rachel had wiped her eyes clean, she realized that Aylin and her mom had joined in the crying party and she didn't feel as lonely in this faraway place as she had expected to. This is going to be a great summer, she thought.

* * *

Rachel woke up in the car with her cheek resting on the door. She was confused for a few seconds, but quickly remembered that she was in Turkey with her exchange family. She felt badly for having fallen asleep, but then she looked to her right and saw that Aylin looked like she had just woken up, too. Her hair was flat on one side and she had a red mark on her cheek from where it had rested on something. In the middle seat were bags of what looked like apricots, tomatoes, and cucumbers. The bags hadn't been there when she had gotten into the car, but she didn't remember them being put in. She must have been sleeping very deeply.

"You slept only five minutes after we left the airport!" Aylin said, teasing as if she and Rachel had grown up together.

"How long did it take you? Six minutes?" Rachel replied, an unusually quick comeback. Aylin laughed.

"Maybe seven. My sister and I stayed up talking so late last night and then I got up early to help my mom make everything ready for you."

"Sorry," Rachel said, "I hope you didn't go to too much trouble…"

"What trouble? We do this happily. Now you even slept so you are not too tired to taste Turkish food tonight! Look!" she said and pointed out of her window. "We are almost there. In one minute, we can see the Aegean Sea!"

Rachel looked in the direction Aylin had pointed. There was a hill covered in rows of small trees with greenish-grey leaves. The land looked dry, much drier than Olympia, and there was no grass on the ground below the trees. "What kind of trees are those?" she asked Aylin.

"Olive trees!" she replied. Aylin seemed so excited about everything, and the excitement rubbed off, even on tired, calm, still-slightly-nervous Rachel. "Do you like olives?" It was a hard question to answer. Rachel had eaten an olive once. She remembered it vividly. It was a green olive stuffed with a red pepper sliver and an almond sliver. It was at restaurant when she was ten. She remembered it being very salty and bitter, and she had thus avoided olives ever since.

"I've only tried an olive once" Rachel admitted.

"Really!! Well you can eat many olives here in Turkey. We love to eat olives at breakfast, and we use olive oil for all of our food. We have our own olive tree!" Rachel decided not to divulge the details of her negative first and last experience with olives, since Aylin clearly loved the things.

"You eat olives for breakfast?" Rachel couldn't imagine such a thing. Olives were for pizzas, sandwiches, and fancy alcoholic drinks in movies.

"Yes, of course! This is a classic Turkish breakfast food. You will see. But not today. Today it is already close to dinnertime. We will try Turkish olives tomorrow morning. But if you cannot wait, we can try when we get home!" Aylin was enthusiastic about everything. Is she always this way? Rachel wondered.

"That's ok... I can wait until the morning," Rachel said, and let out a little giggle.

"Oh, there it is, do you see it?! The Aegean Sea! Do you see the water, Rachel? Welcome to the sea!!" Aylin had an enormous grin and her eyes sparkled as she pointed out the sea to Rachel. "We will swim there every day. Now we are almost coming home. We turn right now and then five more minutes and we are home. My sister Leyla is waiting for us there. You will see she is not crazy like me, she is quiet and very neat and beautiful. Oh! You see this building? This is our mosque." Aylin pointed to a small white round building with small, high windows and a tower on one side. Rachel had never seen a mosque before, but they talked about them sometimes on the news.

Rachel turned to look out of her own window and saw rows of white houses. They looked so different from the houses in Olympia, which were mostly wide single-story ranch-style houses made of wood. These were all narrow two and three-story houses made of cinderblocks and mostly painted white, though there were a few yellow houses. Some were unfinished, and you could see the unpainted bricks with steel support bars sticking out of the top. On their flat roves, the houses each had a metal tank with a shiny glass panel leaning against it, all facing the same direction.

"Aylin? What are those things on the top of the houses?"

"What things?" Aylin didn't seem to understand what Rachel was talking about. "Which houses?"

"Every house. Those tanks and the glass things."

"Oh!" Aylin laughed. "Do you not have that in America? That is for making hot water with the sun. They are for sun energy and the metal cans have water inside. When we take a shower, the hot water goes down from the tank." What a good idea, thought Rachel. She wondered if they had enough sun in rainy Olympia for those. The environmentalists would definitely like that. She had heard of solar energy, but had never seen it in action.

"Solar energy," Rachel said, as much to herself as to Aylin. "I'm sure we have them in the United States, but it's really not very sunny where I live." Before she could go on, they turned into a narrow road of houses. The houses didn't all look the same when you were so close to them and couldn't see the   roofs. They were tightly packed, with only five or ten feet between each one, and every inch of ground was covered with either tile paths, trees, or plants. Some people had small gardens and all of the houses had some sort of vine or flower or plant growing up the walls.

Aylin's father drove extremely slowly down the road, which was barely wide enough for two small cars to pass. Kids of all ages were playing in the street, and adults sat on their balconies and waved as they drove by. The car stopped at the seventh house on the right. It had three small fruit trees in the front, and behind them was a large balcony with a large table set up for dinner. A thin woman with long brown hair wearing a polo shirt-dress came down the three steps from the balcony towards the car.

"That is my sister, Leyla!" said Aylin, with the same enthusiasm she showed everything. Then, for the first time she said something in a whisper. "She has BIG secret that she doesn't tell me but I am sure it is about a boy and we will learn it, I know." Aylin winked at Rachel and her eyes sparkled. Just then, Aylin's door was opened from the outside. A rush of hot air flushed into the car. A boy about their age bent down and said something in Turkish to Aylin's parents. He then smiled at Aylin and nodded his head at Rachel.

"Welcome!" he said. "You must be Rachel," he said in a British accent. "I'm Aylin's friend, Emre." Emre had dark hair and long eyelashes, was very tan, and wore an ironed dress shirt and jeans despite the heat. Aylin blushed and smiled and for the first time didn't have anything to say. For just a few seconds.

"Emre spent last year in England so he thinks you want to be his friend," said Aylin jokingly as she poked Emre in the arm.

"Pleased to meet you," said Emre. "Shame that your host sister is such a chatterbox," Emre teased and yanked at one of Aylin's curls. Rachel caught Aylin's father watching the scene in the rear-view mirror, his eyebrows furled.

"Emre, you can help me bring the suitcase into the house," he said in English. It was the first time Aylin's father had spoken at all, and Rachel was surprised that he spoke English, too.

"*Tabii, tabii*, of course Timur Amca," Emre said and went to get the bag out of the trunk. Aylin's mother and father got out of the car and Rachel's door was opened from the outside. Rachel got out, and Leyla stood there quietly, smiling warmly.

"I am very happy to meet you," she said in a timid voice, still smiling. "Are you very tired? Are you hungry?"

"We are very hungry, Ablacim!" replied Aylin to her sister.

"Nice to meet you," Rachel said. "We slept in the car, so I think we're ok." Rachel was still dizzy and her eyes felt puffy, but since she had figured out it was morning in Olympia, she was starting to wake up.

"We must put the olives on the table, Ablacim, Rachel doesn't know olives!"

"Come," said Leyla, putting her arm around Rachel. "You sit down and I will bring you tea. You like tea?" Leyla and Aylin were so different, Rachel thought. Both were kind, but Leyla was slow and gentle while Aylin was active, talkative, and jumpy. Rachel wondered what it would have been like to have a sister. She couldn't imagine it. It had always just been herself, Mom, and Dad.

They walked up the stairs, and Aylin's mom was already on the balcony, putting food on the table. She handed Rachel a pair of plastic slippers. She motioned for Rachel to take off her shoes and smiled. Rachel took off her shoes.

"I don't need slippers, it's ok, it's hot, I'll go barefoot," Rachel explained.

"Yes, yes! You wear," she said, putting the slippers on the floor by Rachel's feet. "You no wear, your feet cold, your stomach hurts." Rachel did not want to insult Aylin's mother, so she put on the slippers. Maybe it's some kind of cultural thing, she thought.

* * *

There were so many different dishes at dinner that Rachel had to count them so she could write home about it. There were eight dishes, plus a few little plates with pickles, raw onion quarters, and fried cayenne peppers like they had at the Chinese restaurant but nobody ever ate. Before they could get to the dishes on the table, Leyla brought out a pot of pinkish-colored soup and served everyone a bowl. The soup tasted sour and salty and garlicky, but Rachel could not make out what it was made of. She was afraid to ask, in case it was something weird, so she just finished her bowl and said it was good.

"*Afiyet olsun!*" said Aylin's mother.

"That means may you enjoy it," said Aylin. "Hmm, I don't know how do you say that in English. What do you say after somebody is eating in English?" Rachel thought but nothing came to mind.

"I don't think we say anything in English," Rachel said, herself confused because she wasn't sure if they didn't say anything or if she just couldn't think of anything. "Some people say *bon appetit*, but it's not English. I think it's French. And people don't say it that much, actually."

"Well, here we say *afiyet olsun* always to a person who is eating. And what do you say in English to the person who made the food?"

"I thought you were studying English every day, my girl. Why do you not know these things?" Aylin's father said, laughing, as he sat back in his chair. Aylin didn't appear at all insulted.

"Babacim, I told you they are not teaching us important things!" She replied, then turned back to Rachel. "What do you

39

say to the person who made the food?" Rachel wondered if this was a trick question.

"Thank you, I guess." Everyone must have understood because they all laughed. When Rachel didn't laugh, Aylin's smile faded.

"Are you serious?" she asked. Then Rachel laughed at the weirdness of the whole situation. Of course she was serious, and what was so strange about saying thank you for a meal? "Here, we say *elinize saglik*. It means health to your hands, to the hands of the person who make, I mean made, the food." Rachel tried to pronounce the strange words but she could only get the first one out before she forgot the expression. Still, everyone smiled and congratulated her for trying.

Rachel was starting to feel very groggy. Between the heat and the food and the new people and new language all around her, it was tiring to soak it all in. The rest of dinner was a blur of new tastes, some good, some strange. Every time she tasted a new dish, all eyes were on her and she was hoping she wasn't doing anything wrong. After dinner, Aylin's mom wanted to serve her Turkish coffee, but Rachel had to say no to that one, she could barely keep her eyes open and all she could think about was lying down and going to sleep.

"Everything was delicious," she said to Aylin's mother and Leyla. "*Elinize*... what was I supposed to say again, Aylin?"

"*Saglik*," said Aylin's mother. "*Afiyet olsun, kizim*," she said and patted Rachel on the back.

"I'm so tired, I want to stay up and talk to you all but I am afraid I'll fall asleep in the middle of a sentence. So is it ok if I go to sleep?"

"Sleep! But I want to bring you to the beach, my friends are waiting for you tonight! They will be very sad if you don't come to meet them."

"Aylin, poor Rachel is very tired, see her eyes? She can meet everyone tomorrow. Now, come, we must show Rachel her bed. Rachel, come upstairs, your bag is already there." Leyla took Rachel by the hand and led her up some stairs.

The next thing she knew, it was sometime in the middle of the night. There was a sound of somebody chanting or something, but it was pretty loud, as if it were being broadcast over a megaphone. Rachel sat up and looked out the window. She had been so tired the night before that she hadn't noticed the sea view from her window. It was partially blocked by the roofs of some houses here and there, but she could definitely see it. The water was calm, and she could see the reflection of the moon in it. The chanting stopped, and everything was quiet again. Rachel lay back down, and didn't wake up until she heard the clattering of plates and clinking of glasses.

Chapter 4

Speak a new language
So that the world
Will be a new world.

    -   *Rumi*

Didim, Turkey

July 16

        Rachel sat up in bed and looked out the window at the sea. The sun wasn't too high in the sky, so Rachel figured it was still pretty early. She had forgotten to change the time on her watch, so she didn't know what time it was. The room was neither hot nor cold, and Rachel decided to put on her jeans again, and a t-shirt, until she knew what Aylin was going to wear. She looked around the room. There were two twin beds, one in which she had slept and one in which Aylin was still sleeping. There were only about six inches between the beds, which had bottom sheets but no other sheets. A thin blanket covered the sleeping Aylin, and another was crumpled at the foot of Rachel's bed. It must have been a fairly warm night for her not to have been cold with just a thin blanket. It felt funny to not even know how to dress. She thought about staying in the room until Aylin woke up, but she was so wide awake that she couldn't help but go downstairs. She was also hungry, and hoped she could find something to eat. Even though there had been so much food at dinner, a lot of it had been so strange that she just tried a small amount of each thing, and wasn't able to really fill up.

Downstairs, Aylin's mother and Leyla were sitting at the table on the covered balcony, drinking something out of small tulip-shaped glasses. Rachel went up to them and smiled.

"Good morning," she said. "Sorry, I don't know how to say that in Turkish." They must not have seen her or expected her because they both startled.

"*Gunaydin!*" they said in unison and then laughed.

"*Gunaydin,*" Rachel repeated, and both Aylin's mother and Leyla laughed.

"Come, have some tea with us," said Leyla, who got up and went into the kitchen. Rachel followed her into the kitchen, which was a tiny room, maybe five feet by ten feet. Nothing was built in except the sink; there was a four-burner gas range on top of the counter, but no oven. A toaster oven was next to the range, and a dishwasher in the corner. On top of the dishwasher was a small refrigerator. Rachel wondered how so much food had been produced in such a tiny kitchen. Leyla noticed Rachel looking at the fridge.

"This is just the small one," she said. "Our big icebox is in the sitting room because we don't have space in the kitchen!"

"Oh, I see," said Rachel, slightly embarrassed that Leyla had noticed her staring. She knew that Leyla meant "refrigerator" when she said "icebox" because she had seen it called that in the old sitcoms she watched on TV with Grams. "We usually call that a refrigerator now," she explained. "But my Grams sometimes calls it an icebox."

"That is hard! Can you say it once more?"

"Re-frig-er-a-tor."

"Re-frig-ate..." Leyla sighed. "I think icebox is much more easy! They should not have changed this word," she said with a defeated look in her eyes.

"Oh, you can say icebox, I'm sorry, that's totally ok!" Rachel felt so nervous and worried that she was going to offend or upset somebody the first day. Leyla immediately sensed her discomfort and put her hand on Rachel's back.

"You must not worry, Rachel, we already like you so much," she said. "Of course I want you to tell me my mistakes. Maybe every time I can't say everything right but you must tell me or I can't learn, ok? Please, now forget about the modern icebox and I will show you Turkish tea." Leyla was very perceptive, Rachel thought.

The Turkish tea kettle looked like Grams' silver coffee service pot with a smaller silver teapot on top.

"In the bottom," explained Leyla, "there is boiling water, and in the top there is strong tea." She poured a small amount of the tea into a little tulip-shaped glass and then topped it off with boiling water. "Do you use sugar?" she asked.

"I don't know, I don't usually drink tea," Rachel said. "But sure, I guess I could try it with a little sugar."

"Sorry, you don't like tea?" Leyla asked.

"It's not that, I just almost never drink it, except maybe iced tea. And maybe like fruit teas, if that counts. We drink a lot of coffee in my family." Leyla's eyes got wider, but she otherwise didn't make her shock obvious.

"Now you try Turkish tea and tell me what you think," Leyla said, still in disbelief. Just like the night before, Rachel felt under pressure to like something new. She stirred in a cube of sugar and picked up the glass, only to put it down again before drinking the tea.

"It's so hot!" Rachel exclaimed, glad she hadn't spilled any.

"Oh, you should pick it up here, on the top," she said, pointing to the ridge. Rachel looked through the window at Aylin's mom, who was lifting the glass to her lips with two fingers on the rim. Rachel picked up the tea and sipped the hot liquid carefully. She wasn't sure if she was tasting the sugar or the tea, but it was a refreshing flavor.

"Hmm, I like it," she said, surprised.

"Annecim, Rachel likes Turkish tea!" Leyla called to her mother.

"Afiyet olsun," said her mother. "Come outside and sit with me now." Rachel followed Leyla outside and sat down at the table. They could see five other balconies from theirs, and there were a number of women putting breakfast onto the tables. "Are you hungry?" she asked.

"No, thank you, well, yes I am a little, but I can make myself breakfast if you show me where everything is," Rachel replied. Both Leyla and her mother looked shocked.

"What are you saying!?" Leyla said, more animatedly than usual. "No, you don't make for us, we make for you! Today you are new here, you are our guest. We will make for you now," she said and stood up at the same time as her mother.

"Sorry, I am really ok, I can make my own!"

"No, you don't, not in Turkey. Here it is very important, you are our guest. Later, you will be like our family and we will all make breakfast together, but now you sit and drink your tea and please relax."

Dinner had been good, but some of the dishes had been odd; for example, some things that would have been eaten hot at home, like green beans, were cold. Also, they put a sauce of garlicky plain yogurt on top of a lot of the veggies. Breakfast, however, was not strange at all, except for the olives. It was definitely different than breakfast at home, but it was good. There were hardboiled eggs, tomatoes, cucumbers, peppers, different kinds of cheese, garlicky pepperoni-type slices of meat, homemade jams, and fresh apricots. There were breads that looked like sesame bagels (but tasted slightly different), butter, and honey. There were also green and black olives, which both turned out to be way better than the stuffed olives Rachel had tried once upon a time. Aylin came down when breakfast was nearly ready, wearing shorts and a tank top, her hair frizzy on one side and frizzy on the other.

"Oh, good morning Rachel! My friends missed you so much, they want to meet you now at the beach. You're wearing jeans, you will be hot. You can wear shorts after breakfast. What do you think about Turkish breakfast? How did you sleep?" Aylin talked in paragraphs, not sentences. Rachel decided to answer in a paragraph.

"Good morning Aylin! I look forward to meeting your friends, I'll change into shorts after breakfast, I think Turkish breakfast looks delicious, I slept great, how about you?" Everyone laughed and Rachel was put at ease, thrilled that everyone had understood her humor. She almost felt like she was a part of this family, already, after less than a day.

At breakfast, Rachel decided that she needed to know what to call Aylin's parents, because until that point she was still trying to avoid talking to them because she didn't know what to call them in order to get their attention or direct questions at them.

"What should I call your parents?" she asked Aylin in a whisper when Aylin's parents and Leyla were speaking to each other in Turkish.

"Good question!" said Aylin. "Hahaha, this is what my teacher always tells us. You should call them Timur Amca and Bahar Teyze. Timur is my father's name and *amca*, well you pronounce /am-dja/, means uncle. Bahar is my mother's name and *teyze*, you pronounce /tay-zay/, means aunt. Timur Amca and Bahar Teyze." Rachel said the names over and over in her head until she could say them.

"Everything is delicious, Timur Amca, Bahar Teyze" she said. "Elinize.... What was that again I was supposed to say?"

"Saglik," everyone said in unison.

"Yes, thank you, I'm gonna get that one day!" Aylin hugged Rachel around the shoulders.

"Of course you will!" she said, and stood up from the table. "Now, I help to clean up and you put on shorts, then we go to the beach!" It was unbelievable. Four weeks of lazy breakfasts and going to the beach, and she was going to get school credit for it if she wrote a 15- page report. And to think she almost spent the summer dressed in black behind a coffee shop counter.

After breakfast, it was finally time for Rachel to see the beach. Rachel had spent a few days here and there at the beach in Washington, where her family rented a room at an inn. The beaches there were windy, vast and flat, with the rough, cold pacific waves on one side, and tall grass-covered dunes on the other side. They would often build a fire and drink thermoses of hot cider along with their picnics, even in the summer. Every year, Rachel jumped in the water and swam for a few minutes, just once so she could say she had. The water was so cold that her feet would hurt and she would run back to the cabin afterwards to jump into the hot bath her mother had prepared for her. She thought about the Washington beaches as she walked down to the beach with her new friend Aylin, slightly homesick for her parents and her friends. Not that she wanted necessarily to be back in Washington, but she wouldn't have minded them being here. She worried that Aylin's friends wouldn't like her.

The walk was so short that Rachel didn't have much time to worry. The beach was not large – only about 30 feet from the retaining wall to the water, and was a few hundred feet wide, down a set of cement steps from a sidewalk flanked with benches. It was sandy, but the sand was littered with cigarette butts, sunflower seed shells, and piles of dried seaweed. There was also an occasional shard of glass. The beach would have been entirely unappealing if it had not been on a quiet bay with a few small sailboats anchored in the turquoise water. Rachel and Aylin walked over to a group of three girls sitting on colorful beach towels. Grams had advised her to be conservative and bring a one-piece suit with a matching cover-up. As they approached the group, a girl in a red bikini noticed them and sat up on her towel. She had long, straight black hair and her eyes were exotic. Rachel thought she looked Hawaiian, but as she later found out, she was Turkish, as were most of the people she encountered in Didim.

"Hello Rachel, I am Elif. Pleased to meet you," Elif smiled and her dark eyes sparkled.

"Elif is my bessssst summer friend," explained Aylin. "Our families come to this beach every summer since we were babies so we are like sisters. Right sister?"

"That is right," Elif replied with what seemed like a sigh of relief. Maybe she was worried that Rachel was trying to take over her role, Rachel wondered.

"Thanks for sharing your sister with me this summer," Rachel said.

"Oh! I don't share her with you! Now we are all sisters together," Elif said, and then she introduced the others. Rana had shoulder-length curly dark brown hair, blue eyes, and wore a blue tankini. Ela was short with wide hips and wore a black and turquoise striped one-piece. Her hair was dirty blonde and tied back into a ponytail.

"You don't look so American like I thought," said Ela, who it turned out was always very direct.

"What do you think Americans should look like?" Rachel asked, thinking that Turkish people also didn't look how she had expected.

"Well, of course in the movies there are so many blonde and black people. And everyone has very high fashion, but you are wearing old fashion." Ela looked very serious as she analyzed Rachel, but for some reason Rachel didn't feel offended. Rana, who it turned out was Ela's cousin, elbowed Ela. "What happened?" Ela exclaimed, looking at Rana.

"Ela, you shouldn't say Rachel is wearing old fashion. It's not nice. And it's also not true." Rachel was wearing a brown one-piece suit with a turquoise belt and a brown mesh cover-up dress. She had bought it with Grams, but they had gotten it from the teen section. Grams had said it was conservative but modern at the same time, and Grams knew about that kind of stuff.

"I am sorry Rachel," said Ela.

"That's ok, Ela, I agree it's a little old-fashioned. My grandmother picked it out but she said it was modern."

"Rachel, don't worry about it, it is really nice!" Aylin said protectively. "Leyla said that this morning when she saw it and Leyla knows more about fashion than Ela. Well, she also knows more than I do! If Leyla says something, it is true."

"Thanks, Aylin – it really doesn't bother me, though. I'm curious, though. If I don't look American, what do I look like?" There was a silence for a few seconds, as everyone thought.

"You look Turkish," Elif said, finally. Aylin, Ela, and Rana agreed with nods and comments in Turkish. The Turkish girls she had seen so far were quite pretty, thought Rachel, so she took it as a compliment.

"My mother has blonde hair," Rachel explained. "But my father is of Chinese origin. And I look way more like my dad."

"That's why you look Turkish!" Elif exclaimed. "Turkish people come from central Asia so we are Asian. But we mixed also with Europeans so we have also people with blond hairs."

"Interesting, I didn't know that. But it explains a lot. I thought you were Asian, Elif, but then Ela looks like she could be from somewhere in Europe."

"Let's sit down," suggested Aylin. She spread her towel on the sand next to the other girls' towels, and Rachel followed her lead. Everyone then sat down on their towels, and Rana took out a bag of unshelled sunflower seeds, which she passed around. Everyone took a handful of seeds and began to expertly nibble at the husks, eating the seeds and putting the husks into a second bag Rana placed on the sand. Rachel tried awkwardly to open the seeds, not being used to nibbling on unshelled sunflower seeds. Nobody seemed to notice her lack of skill. She wasn't even hungry, after the huge breakfast, but wanted to fit in.

"What did you think Turkish people will look like?" Ela asked. Rachel hadn't thought much about what the people would look like because she mostly imagined women wearing veils and long robes. She hadn't thought much about their faces or hair color. Should she admit this and look stupid?

"I had no idea," Rachel said, deciding it was the truth. I guess I thought everyone would be kinda darker, maybe like with black hair," she said.

"Aren't there Turkish people in America?" asked Ela.

"I don't know any," Rachel admitted. "I guess there aren't a lot in Olympia, where I'm from. I mean, we have people from lots of countries, but I don't know any Turkish people. We have lots of Koreans, Vietnamese, and Mexicans."

"You're not from Washington? But Aylin told us you are from Washington." Ela looked a little confused again. Everyone looked at Aylin, and Aylin looked at Rachel.

"I am from Washington," Rachel said, and Aylin looked relieved. "Washington State, it's a state in the northwest of the country."

"You aren't from the capital?" Aylin asked.

"No, that's Washington DC – I've never been there. It's like three or four thousand miles from Washington State."

"How far is that in Kilometers?"

"I dunno, we don't have kilometers in the US. My dad goes there sometimes for conferences, though, and I think the plane ride takes like 5 hours or something."

"That is so far!" exclaimed Aylin. I made mistake, I thought you are from Washington, where the President lives."

"Nope, sorry – I'm from a small town with less than 50,000 people. Hope you're not disappointed!" Rachel felt like she had betrayed Aylin, even though her application had all the correct information on it. But Aylin didn't look upset at all.

"Oh, Rachel I am so happy! I thought, you are from a very big and cosmopolitan city and you will find our summer village so small and boring but you are from a small town so maybe you are not disappointed with here. And my father will never let me go to a big and dangerous city but maybe one day he will let me visit you in your small town!"

"Should we play volleyball in the water?" Rana suggested. "Let's go and see if the boys will want to join us." Rachel looked in the direction that Rana indicated with her eyes. A group of boys their age pretended not to be watching them. One of the boys was the one who helped carry Rachel's bags into the house.

For a second, really just for as long it takes to blink, Rachel wished she had grown up in Turkey and had beach vacations every year. She had spent her entire life in Olympia and yet still had only one close friend and a few so-so acquaintances who came in and out of her life. She had been in Didim for less than a day and yet she was already part of a group of friends. Well, sort-of friends. After all, they didn't really know each other yet, but it was like they had some sort of promise to like each other and were all trying hard, which was way more than could be said for the vast majority of kids she knew at home. And if they thought she looked Turkish, that was huge. It meant that they accepted her as one of them, which was exactly, she decided, what she wanted to be this summer.

Chapter 5

THROUGH LOVE all that is bitter will sweet
Through Love all that is copper will be gold.
Through Love all dregs will turn to purest wine
Through Love all pain will turn to medicine.

- Rumi

Didim, Turkey

July 18

It didn't take long for Rachel to get used to the daily
rhythm. Get up late, eat breakfast (with new delicacies appearing
every day), get into bathing suit, go to the beach, go home, eat
lunch, take a nap during the hottest part of the day, wake up
groggy and sweaty, go back to the beach for a few hours, go home,
take a shower and get dressed up, eat dinner, go out. Actually,
Rachel didn't make it to the go out part of the day for the first few
days. She was too exhausted. Between the jet-lag, the heat, the
volleyball, the swimming, and trying to learn words in Turkish
here and there, Rachel was too tired to go out at night. She was
also a little nervous. She was very comfortable with Aylin, Rana,
Elif and Ela, but she was nervous about meeting "the boys".

After a few days there, Leyla suggested that the three of
them walk to the next "summer village" and eat dinner there
together, just the girls. Apparently, it was Bahar Teyze and Timur
Amca's wedding anniversary and Leyla wanted them to have a
nice evening together, so she made them dinner and the three girls
got ready to leave. It was going to be Rachel's first evening out
and she had no idea where they were going or what to wear. After

her shower, she kneeled by her suitcase wearing a bathrobe, and looked through the clothes she and Grams had bought together. Were they too conservative? Where they old-fashioned? At home, Rachel wore the same "uniform" as everyone else – jeans and t-shirts, flip-flops or running shoes. But it seemed like the rules here were different. After showering off the day's accumulation of suntan lotion and salt, Aylin came into the room, too.

"What should I wear?" Rachel asked, feeling very childish not to know.

"You are asking the wrong sister!" Aylin laughed. "Everyone laughs at my clothes and my hair and they say I should not dress myself. Let's ask Leyla. By the way, *sihatlar olsun.*"

"What was that?"

"Sorry, I don't know how you say it in English. We say it after somebody takes a shower."

"What does it mean?"

"It means like we hope it makes you healthy. What do you say in English?"

"Nothing."

"Nothing?"

"Yeah, You mean you say it to everybody after they take a shower?"

"Yes we do! You are missing so many things in English!"

"You have so many extra things in Turkish!" Both girls laughed. Leyla came into the room looking elegant, as always. She was wearing khaki linen pants, a white blouse, and had a long fuchsia scarf wrapped around her neck a few times. She wore four silver bangles on one wrist, and she smelled of floral perfume.

"What should we wear, Abla? You must dress us, maybe there are handsome boys out there this summer!" It was obvious that Aylin looked up to her sister. Rachel had always wanted a sister, but her mom couldn't have any more children after Rachel.

Leyla picked an outfit from Rachel's clothes – a flowery peasant-style dress and sandals.

"Your clothes are very nice," Leyla remarked.

"Oh, thanks, my grandmother helped me choose them and bought them for me as a gift before I came here. They're almost all new to me, too."

"Wow, your grandmother helped you! What a modern grandmother!" Rachel's opinion of Grams, already very high, increased significantly. "You need to get a sweater, though."

"But it's so hot outside!"

"You might get cold," Leyla warned. "You were in the sun all day and now evening is here and it will maybe be windy where we will sit. I don't want you to get sick!"

"Oh, I won't get sick from the wind," Rachel said, wondering why they were so concerned about the cold. It was way colder in Olympia.

"Ok, you know yourself," Leyla said, tilting her head in apparent disapproval.

Leyla chose tight jeans and a t-shirt with a sequin butterfly for Aylin. She put her own necklaces on both Aylin and Rachel, and finished them off with makeup and perfume. Rachel rarely wore makeup or perfume. She just wasn't in the makeup-and-perfume crowd at school.

"I almost never wear makeup at home," she explained as Leyla applied mascara to her lashes.

"Why not?" asked Aylin and Leyla in unison. Rachel giggled, as if it were so hard to believe.

"Just don't. Most of my friends don't, either. I don't even know how to put it on, except for lip gloss and maybe blush."

"Turkish girls all know about makeup," Leyla explained. "We won't go out in the evening without our makeup and our perfume and our jewelry. Everything in Turkey was just way different than Rachel had expected. Hanna was probably at home picturing Rachel in a veil stuck in a house somewhere for a month. Where on Earth had they gotten these weird ideas about Turkey? She needed to send out an e-mail. She had called her parents upon her arrival to let them know she'd gotten there ok, but since then hadn't given any news. Her parents didn't have an international calling plan, so they had agreed to e-mail. Rachel had just been too busy settling in to write one. She promised herself she'd write one once they got back.

The three walked downstairs together, where Timur Amca and Bahar Teyze were reading the evening newspaper. Timur Amca looked up over his newspaper distrustfully.

"You are very dressed up, girls. Who are you meeting?"

"Nobody, Babacim," said Leyla confidently because it was true. "We are going to eat pide in the next neighborhood and then we will eat lokma at Mavisehir."

"Enjoy your food," said Bahar Teyze with a kind smile. "Thank you for your beautiful food, Leyla'cim."

"I hope everything is delicious. Bon appetit to you, too." Leyla had stayed home all day to prepare the meal for her parents. She had prepared more dishes than Rachel even knew how to make.

"Oh, that's right, happy anniversary!" said Rachel.

"You wear something on top," said Bahar Teyze. "You will be cold, you will be sick!" Rachel decided to stop ignoring the advice about wearing a sweater. Maybe they knew something she didn't. She went upstairs to get her cardigan and tied it around her waist. When she went back downstairs, Leyla approached her, clicking her tongue in disapproval, removed the sweater from Rachel's waist, and draped it over her shoulders.

"You have nice clothes but you don't know how to wear them," she said in her gentle, smiling way that made the comment harmless rather than insulting.

The three girls walked for 15 minutes along a dusty dirt road over a hill to another bay, where the restaurant consisted of 20 tables or so on a concrete terrace about ten feet above the water. It was breezier than the other bay, and Rachel was glad her sweater had come along. Aylin and Leyla ordered the food. The restaurant had no menu, and even if it had, Rachel wouldn't have understood it.

"If there's no menu, how does everyone know what to order?" Rachel wondered how a restaurant like this could survive in the US, where menus were so detailed, explaining every side dish, every sauce, and practically every spice used in each entrée.

"Everyone knows what can be on a pide," Aylin answered.

"What is pide?"

"You will love it so much, if you like pizza."

"I love pizza."

"Then you are lucky tonight, this is better than pizza." Ten minutes after Leyla spoke to the waiter, four pides arrived at the table. They were long, canoe-shaped breads that were cut into manageable rectangular slices. The crust was folded over on the sides, and they each had different fillings. One had cheese, one had ground meat, one had pepperoni-like sausage slices like the ones that had appeared at the breakfast table, and one had egg. Leyla put a slice of each on Rachel's plate. Rachel took a bite of the cheese pide first, and the hot, thin, crusty dough warmed her up enough to forget about the breeze.

The girls must have all been hungry because they ate quickly and in relative silence as they watched the moon rise over the sea. When they had finished the last of the pide, Leyla wiped her mouth with a napkin and quietly cleared her throat.

"I will now tell you both something very important and very special." Aylin looked at Leyla with a huge smile before Leyla had explained anything. "I have a, a friend. And we want to get married. And Aylin, my dear sister, I could not tell you before because, I love you so much but you cannot keep secrets and this one is too important. I am sorry."

Aylin squealed. "Ablacim! I want to jump up and put my arms around you and squeeze you but then everyone here will know what has happened and then as you say I would ruin your secret. So I will do it when we are not in the restaurant, but now I will say you must explain everything."

Leyla's tenseness relaxed. "You are not angry that I did not tell you before?"

"No, because I know me and you know me and of course I cannot keep a secret, but this is so beautiful and I am so happy! Do I know him? What is his name? How did you meet him? When will you marry? How does he look? Do our parents know yet? They don't know, right?" Leyla smiled at Aylin's enthusiasm, and for the first time since Rachel had met her, she showed excitement, herself.

"Congratulations," Rachel said, not knowing exactly what else she was supposed to say and not wanting to interfere in what seemed like an intimate family moment that she was imposing on. "Do you want me to just go for a walk so that you two can talk?" she asked, thinking that maybe she would feel more comfortable herself. She really felt like she was intruding.

"No, you stay here," Leyla said. "I like you. Aylin likes you. I want to share this moment with you, too." Wow, Rachel thought. That made her feel really good about herself. She made a mental note to save the sentiment and share it with somebody one day, when she had something special to share.

"His name is Kerem. He is an architectural engineer and his family is from Denizli, but he is working in Ankara now."

"Wait," Rachel interrupted. "I know English is my native language, but what is an architectural engineer?"

"Kerem helps design buildings that are safe in earthquakes," Leyla answered proudly. "You know, we have a lot of earthquakes in Turkey."

"We have earthquakes in Olympia, too," Rachel explained, herself very interested in earthquakes since a large one shook Olympia when she was 10 years old. "Sorry for interrupting."

"It's ok. Kerem will be happy to talk about earthquakes with you," Leyla continued. "Ilkay Teyze introduced us soon after the disaster with Hakan. I didn't want to like him, because my heart was broken and I thought 'I will never love again', but actually I think maybe I didn't love Hakan completely because I quickly fell in love with Kerem. And Kerem also loves me and is so kind to me, so I cannot wait to marry him." At this point, Leyla was twirling her necklace and staring off at the moonlit cliffs beyond the bay.

"Ilkay Teyze is our mother's mother's sister's daughter," Aylin explained. Rachel thought about the family tree for a few seconds before it clicked.

"Ok, so she's your mother's cousin."

"Yes, ok. You can say that," Aylin continued. "And she is born in the same month and same year as our mother, and they were raised in the same street so they are like sisters. Ablacim, can I tell Rachel about Hakan?"

"Oh, you can tell but don't waste your voice too much." Leyla looked slightly annoyed for a second, but was quickly lost in daydream again as Aylin explained.

"Hakan was Leyla's boyfriend for three years. She did her graduate studies in Denizli just to be close to him. But this was a secret, our parents of course did not know. Ilkay Teyze knew, but she promised to not tell our mother if Leyla promised to always be honest with her and to not do anything wrong to make my parents ashamed. So six months ago, Hakan decided to move to Istanbul to follow his dream to become a suit designer for a famous Turkish company called Vakko. You know this company, right?"

"No, sorry. I don't know much about fashion,"

"Unbelievable. Vakko is such a famous company. Anyway, Leyla knows about fashion and Hakan was interesting for her because he also knows about fashion. But of course she could not move to Istanbul without a job or an education excuse. So they decided they must get married."

"Wow, Leyla, you were engaged before?"

"No," Leyla answered, her voice somewhere between sadness and relief. "We never became engaged." Rachel was confused, and turned to Aylin for further explanation.

"They could not become engaged. Our parents met with Hakan's parents and they did not like each other, they could not agree on anything. Hakan's mother was covered. They said they wanted Leyla to cover also after marriage. Hakan for many months before told Leyla that he did not think she must cover, but when his parents said this, he did not argue. After that, everything went bad. It wasn't only about covering, but the story is long and it did not finish happily." Aylin seemed to feel that she had explained everything, but Rachel was left feeling very confused. Because she felt like she had missed a major twist in the plot line, she decided to take the risk of looking stupid and ask for clarification.

"Ok, this might sound stupid to you, but what was Hakan's mother covered with?" Leyla broke out of her daydreaming spell and started to laugh hysterically until tears trickled from her eyes. Aylin tried a few times to explain, but Leyla's laughter drowned out her attempted explanations. Aylin rubbed her sister on the back for a few minutes, and Rachel was unsure whether the tears were happy or sad ones.

"Thank you, Rachel," she said finally, pulling herself back into a state of calm by breathing deeply. "I really needed to laugh, now my stress is gone and the unhappiness of that day is finished." Leyla inhaled deeply and then released her breath slowly.

"Hakan's mother wore a scarf on her head," Aylin finally explained.

"Oh! A veil!" Rachel exclaimed in spite of herself. "I didn't realize many people in Turkey wore headscarves. I mean, I haven't seen anyone here in Didim except maybe a few old people."

"Didim is different, it is just a summer place," Aylin explained. "And 50 years ago or more, most women in Turkey were not covered. The founder of our Republic told women they had to remove their head scarves. His name was Ataturk. You know about him, right?" Rachel felt like this was one of those times it would be best to not reveal the Complete Truth.

"Uh, I don't know much about him. Maybe you can tell me about him later?"

"Of course," Aylin continued. "So this is a big topic, I don't want to talk too much now because I want to hear more from Leyla's story. But I will say that here there are now many people who do not wear a headscarf and many people who do wear a headscarf. But the people who don't wear a headscarf don't want their daughters to wear one. And the people who wear a head scarf normally don't want their sons to marry a girl with an open head."

"Not always, Aylin," Leyla corrected. "It's not so simple."

"That's ok, I think I get the point. I interrupted your story, Leyla. Sorry."

"No, it's fine. You made me laugh, it feels so good to laugh. Anyway, my parents did not like the situation and they told me we cannot become engaged. And actually I agreed because Hakan did not argue with his parents about the headscarf and many other things that were discussed, he just told me 'well, it is over now. May it be for the best.' My heart was dead, I thought. I spent almost two years in Denizli only to be close to him and he just dropped me so easily. I thought no boy will want me now and I cannot trust anyone. But Ilkay Teyze took me with her one day to drink coffee with her friend, and the friend's son was there. Kerem. They organized everything for us to meet. And they disappeared a few times into the kitchen for us to talk. And when Kerem's mother read my coffee grounds, she showed that she liked me for her son."

"What did she see in your coffee grounds? Hurry, tell us!" Aylin said, wanting more detail.

"She said I see two roads. One road is short and finishes in an empty space, but the other road is long and I see two people walking on that long road. A bird is flying above them. I see that you were so upset, Leyla, but that now everything is clear for you. Beautiful, all good things. I remember this so well, I wrote it in my diary."

"Soooooooo beautiful," Aylin said, resting her head on her hands and smiling warmly at her sister.

"So you're engaged," Rachel said. She hadn't understood about the coffee grounds, but decided to ask that question later. "Congratulations!" Both Leyla and Aylin looked at Rachel with their eyebrows raised.

"Engaged, no, not yet! I haven't even told my mother yet," Leyla said.

Rachel had felt confused all night, why should things change now? "But didn't he ask you to marry him?"

"Yes, but we are not engaged until we have an engagement ceremony."

"Oh, I see. We don't have that in the States. So I guess you must have a promise ring or something?"

"No, we are also not promised yet." Rachel thought maybe she should just stop asking what appeared to be stupid questions, but it was too interesting and she couldn't help herself.

"I guess maybe you need to explain to me how it works here because I think it's really different from back home."

"I think you are right, Rachel," Aylin agreed. "But it is not so complicated. First, a boy and a girl talk and decide that they want to marry. Then their parents meet and if that meeting is good, then the marriage is a promise. We say *sozlendik*. It means "we promised". After that, there is an engagement ceremony made by the girl's family. The boy's family gives the girl an engagement ring. After that, there is a wedding. First the wedding is at the government and some people also make a religious wedding. And usually people make a dinner party, too. The wedding part is organized and paid for by the boy's family."

"That is pretty different from the United States. In the US, the boy proposes to the girl usually. He asks her to marry him and gives her a ring. Then they get married. The parents don't have much of a say in the whole thing."

"Really?" asked Leyla.

"Yep. Do you wish it were like that here?" Rachel asked.

"Oh, no," Leyla said, clearly having thought before about her parents' role in the marriage. "If our parents were not important in the wedding then perhaps I could be married to Hakan now and that would be terrible. Now I see so many things wrong with him. My parents knew more than I did."

"I guess you have a point," Rachel said, wondering if fewer American marriages would fail if parents were involved in the choice. Then again, she wasn't sure if she'd want her parents involved with such a delicate matter, even though they were great parents.

"Who organizes the wedding then?" Leyla asked.

"The girl's family usually does the wedding, but so many people get married late now that a lot of times the people getting married organize and pay for their own wedding."

"So different," Aylin said. "In this case I think Turkey is better. The young people don't have to pay."

"Should we drink some coffee?" Leyla suggested, and caught a waiter's attention. She ordered three coffees, and while they waited for the coffee, they returned to talk of Leyla's wedding.

"So will you get married next summer?" Rachel asked.

"Oh no!" Leyla exclaimed. "Why next summer? Of course we will be married as soon as possible." Rachel decided not to ask the delicate question of when the baby was due. "I see," she said instead.

"What do you see?" Leyla asked, slightly offended.

"Oh nothing, I just, I mean in the US people are usually engaged for like a year because it takes a long time to plan a wedding and save the money and stuff. But some people get married quicker, you know, when they have a reason."

"Well," Leyla said, not sure if Rachel was implying what she seemed to be implying. "Here, people usually get married a few months after the engagement. It does not take so long to plan a wedding."

"Here, we are afraid that they will change their mind so they have to be married fast," Aylin said, attempting to break the tension.

"Good point," Rachel said, smiling but knowing she had said something wrong.

The coffees arrived in small espresso cups.

"This is Turkish coffee," Leyla explained. "The coffee is in the bottom of the cup so be careful you don't drink it. When you are finished, I will show you what to do so we can read the coffee grounds."

Rachel was worried that she wouldn't be able to sleep after drinking espresso, but she sipped the coffee and found that it wasn't as strong as the coffee served in tiny espresso cups at Batdorf and Bronson. It was already sweetened and didn't need any cream. She forgot about the grounds until she got some in her mouth. "Oops, I drank some of the grounds. Is that ok?" she asked.

Aylin giggled. "Oh, no, your future will be changed now!" Rachel was confused yet again, but it was quickly cleared up this time. Leyla looked into Rachel's cup, nodded that she had drunk the right amount of coffee and left the grounds, and explained that Rachel had to put the small saucer on top of the cup, then to swirl it around three times and flip it over so that the cup was upside-down on the saucer.

"We can see the future in coffee grounds," Aylin explained. "I know you don't have this in America, but maybe you can learn and you can show your friends when you get back," she continued. Definitely a cool talent to pick up, Rachel thought. She could use it in her career working at coffee shops. Since she was no closer to figuring out what she wanted to do with her life. Once the cup had cooled to air temperature, Leyla read Rachel's grounds, then Aylin's.

"Rachel, you have so many paths. Some of them are long and some of them are short, but all of them are open. There are two fish looking at each other, that is a good thing. Fish are good. It could mean love. I think you have so many possibilities in your future, but you cannot decide which ones to follow. You don't know who you are and you don't know what you want. But your future will be good. You have many choices." Rachel felt slightly spooked at how accurate the fortune seemed. She didn't know which college she wanted to go to in a year and she didn't know what she wanted to major in. She wondered what the fish represented. Leyla continued with Aylin's fortune.

"My dear sister, you have one road, a very curved and wide road. Next to the road there are many mountains, and over the mountains are many birds. But I also see an eye. This could be *nazar*, so you must be careful."

"What is *nazar*?" Rachel felt like she'd asked too many questions tonight.

"It is the evil eye, the bad luck that can happen to you because someone is jealous of you." Aylin said, looking uneasy.

"Won't you read Leyla's grounds?" Rachel asked.

"I don't want to know my future right now," Leyla said, standing up and motioning to the waiter that she wanted to pay. "I just hope that Kerem's mother's reading was true."

* * *

When Rachel finally checked her e-mail for the first time, hidden in the dozens of spam messages were three messages from Mom and Dad, one from Grams, and six from Hanna. They were mostly questions, and none had any interesting news.

Dear Mom, Dad, Grams, and Hanna,

I'm sorry I didn't write sooner. I've been really jet-lagged and busy, and this is a dial-up so it's slow. I hope you're all doing fine. Everything here is great. I can't even explain how interesting it is and how much fun I'm having. Everyone is so nice, the food is delish (but I do miss microwave popcorn, peanut butter, and instant oatmeal), and the weather has been hot and sunny every day. Tonight we tried this thing called pide which is sort-of like pizza. It was really good. My host sister's name is Aylin and her sister's name is Leyla. Leyla just got engaged, well sort-of, that is a long story too and it will take too long to explain here so I'll tell you all about it when I get back. I wish you guys were all here, you'd love it. By the way, almost nobody is wearing a veil here like we predicted, but apparently some people do, I just haven't seen them. Also, the coffee here is pretty cool, you read the future in peoples' grounds, I guess like Grams Ming talks about her grandmother reading tea leaves. I want to learn. I guess they have to pay by the minute for this connection so I don't want to write too much. Ok, gotta go, I'll just post on my blog in the future, and I'll try to put up a few pictures. Send me the news from Olympia.

Love and hugs,

Rachel

Chapter 6

Reason is powerless in the expression of love.

-Rumi

Didim, Turkey

July 19

Aylin and Rachel went to the beach earlier than usual the next morning. Eager to talk to her mother about Kerem, Leyla had rushed them out of the house. The beach was quiet and mostly empty, and the chill of the night still hung in the air. Elif, Rana, and Ela weren't there yet, but Aylin and Rachel set up their towels in the usual place.

"It's really exciting about Leyla getting married, don't you think?"

"I hope everything is for the best. Leyla seems happy, so I hope that my parents like him and like his parents. I cannot be excited yet."

"Do you always have to get your parents' approval to get married here?" Rachel wondered what her future would be like. Would someone ask her to marry him one day? Would her parents like him? It all seemed so far off in the future.

"Well, you don't have to but if you don't then it is very bad and you are starting your family life with bad things so I think it's better if the parents like each other. Don't you think so?" Rachel had really never thought about it before.

"I guess, in the United States, the parents are not that much involved in the decision. I mean, in the old days, in old movies and books and stuff, the guy asks the girl's father for permission. But not anymore, well, maybe somebody's family works like that, but not the people I know. Now it's more like the people get engaged, then they tell their parents."

"And your parents, didn't they ask for permission from their parents?" Uh oh, Rachel had led the conversation here herself. She was hoping to avoid the topic, but decided that Aylin could handle it.

"Well, no. My parents' story is totally different." She had opened a can of worms and now she could only hope that Aylin would be understanding.

"Tell me how they met! I love to hear stories like this," Aylin said, eagerly propping her chin on her hands as she lay on her stomach. Rachel inhaled deeply before she began to tell the long version.

"My parents met in high school. They were my age I guess, wow, I haven't thought about that recently. But my mom's mom didn't want mom dating anyone, so they kept it a secret."

"Like here," Aylin commented. Most people don't tell their parents when they are dating someone."

"Really? Like no matter how old they are?"

"Yeah, most of the time."

"Well, in the US I think most people tell their parents. Unless they're really religious or something. Like my Grams. And my mom was also afraid Grams wouldn't like Dad because he's Chinese."

"It is very interesting that your father is Chinese! I don't know anyone with a Chinese parent. It is very exotic."

Rachel laughed at being called exotic.

"That's funny, I think you're exotic, but you're calling me exotic."

"Why did your father come to America? Do you speak Chinese?"

"My dad's parents escaped from China to get away from communism. My grandfather was an English professor in China, but got a job teaching Chinese at Evergreen State College in Olympia and he basically never went back to China. My dad was born the year after they came. So anyhow, he was born in the US and is an American citizen and speaks perfect English of course. He speaks Chinese, too, but he didn't speak it with me. I wish he had."

"But they still got married, how? Did they run away, like in the movies?"

That would be easier to explain, thought Rachel. Maybe she should just say they had run away. But then that would have been lying. Aylin could handle the truth, couldn't she? Weren't they friends?

"They didn't run away." Rachel paused. She thought about how to explain it to Aylin. Then she just started talking, and it came out way easier than she had expected. "They both went away to college, to the same college. And they kept dating. And then when they were juniors, Mom got pregnant." Rachel looked at Aylin, who didn't gasp. She didn't actually seem to be breathing at all. "Breathe, Aylin, I know it's kinda shocking but it's not like they're the first people in the world to, you know."

"Yes, yes, I just don't know anybody who has this situation. Did they get married then very quickly?"

"No, they didn't tell anyone for like five months. They didn't know what to do, so they decided to wait a little. Then Mom started to look pregnant and she felt the baby, well me, kick and she realized she couldn't have an abortion."

"Wow. So then they got married?"

"No, then they decided to not tell their parents until I was born, and then they thought their parents would fall in love with me and not be mad."

"This is exactly like a movie, Rachel!" Aylin didn't look shocked in the whoa, they are so wrong kind of way, but in the that is pretty cool that your parents did something like that kind of way. "What happened after you were born?"

"Secrets like that can't be kept. They found out before. When my parents didn't go back to Olympia at spring break, my dad's parents went to visit him as a surprise and, well, they saw my mom. His parents already knew they were dating. She was like six months pregnant then. They were surprised but actually they were really cool. They told my parents they should get married, but my dad said he didn't want to do it that way. He didn't want anyone to think they were only getting married because Mom was pregnant."

"When did they tell your mother's mother?" Aylin asked, completely absorbed in the story. Just then, Rachel heard a man calling out something loudly over and over again. It sounded like he was saying smeeeeeeeeeeeeeetjeee smmeeeeeeeeeeetjeeee. Startled, she looked around until she saw the man walking along the beach carrying a tray stacked with the same sesame bagel things they had eaten at breakfast. Hanna would have said, "that is so surreal," Rachel thought. Why is a man walking along the beach with a tray of sesame bagels? This would never have happened in Olympia. Even if it had a beach.

"What is he doing?" Rachel asked, forgetting the story about her parents.

"Who? What?" Aylin didn't seem to notice the bagel man.

"Him," Rachel pointed to the man who was so obvious that she couldn't believe Aylin had to ask the question. Aylin looked around until she saw the man wearing jeans and a shirt on the hot beach with his tray of bread.

"Ah, he is selling simit. We ate it at breakfast, do you remember? Do you want one, are you hungry?" Everyone here always worried that Rachel was hungry even though she had never eaten so much in her life.

"Oh, no, it's just weird that he's selling them on the beach!"

"Here, it is quite normal. There is also a man who sells corn. But usually he comes in the afternoon. Did you not see him yesterday?"

"I must have missed him, or I thought he was selling ice cream or something appropriate for the beach."

"Ice cream is a good idea, but on our beach we only have simit and corn. But if you are not hungry then you must finish your story!"

"Yeah, where was I?"

"Your mother did not tell her mother that she was pregnant?"

"No. She was actually so afraid of her mother's reaction that she waited until I was born."

"And then?"

"My grandmother was really sad. Mom is her oldest child and she had really high hopes for her. Mom wanted to be a counselor for troubled teenagers. She was studying psychology and she was doing really well. But she dropped out and stayed home to raise me. Anyhow, that's the story. They got married when I was one year old and they're still married and they're really happy together and I think they're great parents. But it started hard." When Rachel had finished, Aylin was pensive. Rachel looked out at the water, still calm under the early morning sun. A light, warm breeze blew her straight, dark hair away from her face. It felt as though it was going to be a hot day.

"Your parents must be very strict with you," Aylin finally said.

"Why?"

"Because they know what can happen if you, well, you know, if you do things you should not do."

Rachel tried not to be hurt by Aylin's comment, but it did hurt.

"I don't see it like that and neither do they," she said, with some resentment showing through in her voice. Aylin looked at Rachel, understanding that she had said something wrong, but unsure of what she should have said or what she could say to correct her mistake. "If my parents hadn't done what they did, I wouldn't have been born, and I love my life. And if they didn't have sex before marriage and get knocked up, maybe they would never have gotten married. Maybe they would have given in to the pressure from my grandmother and found people their own race. And that would really suck because they have a totally happy marriage, unlike lots of my friends' parents. They were meant to be. Their pregnancy was fate bringing them permanently together. Who cares about weddings anyway? What difference do they really make?" Rachel didn't know where her outburst had come from. She had never defended her parents' decisions before – she'd never had to.

"I am sorry, I didn't mean anything bad, I just, I mean, in our culture," Aylin began, but she did not go on, even though Rachel waited for her to finish.

"Look, in my culture it's not so great either. Tons of people have sex before marriage. The only thing different with my parents is that they got pregnant and chose not to have an abortion. Only people who don't know how great my parents are would judge them. Of course, you don't know them so you can't possibly know. My parents always tell me that I am not a mistake, that I am a gift from God. They say that they are so happy they had me. My mom had this thing two years after having me, endometriosis, and so she couldn't have any more kids. So if they hadn't had me when they did, they wouldn't have had any kids at all."

Aylin looked down, clearly ashamed.

"I am sorry Rachel, I really am sorry. You are right, I judged you and I didn't think I would do such a thing. I don't like what I said."

"It's ok," Rachel said, not really feeling like it was ok, but she knew Aylin had meant her apology and what else could she say? "Anyway, my parents aren't strict. Not at all. They're the opposite of strict. They say that they made some really bad decisions because my Grams was so strict. Like, if she had let them date in the first place then, well, they wouldn't have hid the pregnancy, they wouldn't have hurt their parents so much, stuff like that. So they always want me to tell them everything and they are constantly telling me to make good decisions."

"Wow, you are right. Your parents sound super." Aylin sounded so sincere that the hurt of her previous comments were mostly forgiven. Rachel laughed and wiped away the wetness that had formed in her eyes.

"Actually, it can be kinda annoying!"

"What? How is that possible?"

"Well, for example I don't have a boyfriend. I've never had a boyfriend. And they keep asking me and I'm telling them the truth even though there really isn't much to tell. But I'm pretty sure my mom thinks I'm lying and that there's someone that I'm not telling her about. So I tell her 'there's really nobody' and she says, 'there must be, you are so beautiful and smart, why don't you share with me? I promise I won't judge you' and I'm like, "mom, there really isn't anyone' and so the conversation is never-ending."

"I think all types of parents must be difficult," Aylin said reflectively, and Rachel nodded in agreement.

"If you don't have a boyfriend and your parents want you to have a boyfriend, maybe we can help," said a voice from behind. Rachel and Aylin turned around to see Elif in her red bikini. Rachel had yet to see her in street clothes.

"How long are you standing there?" asked Aylin.

"I just arrived to hear about Rachel and her no boyfriend status.

"Do you have boyfriends?" Rachel asked the question openly to whoever would answer. Elif spread her towel next to Aylin's and sat down.

Elif answered in a whisper. "I had one last year, but this year his family goes to their new summer house in another village so I don't see him anymore. Sorry, many people here understand English so I must be quiet."

"It's a secret?"

"Oh, of course. My parents would be so angry and say I am much too young."

"How old are you?"

"I am 18 in September."

"Wow. Your parents are really strict, huh?"

"No, I think they are normal for here."

"What about you, Aylin?" Rachel asked her host-sister, who had never mentioned a boyfriend. Looking towards the group of boys who had begun to kick around a soccer ball on the beach, Aylin blushed.

"You met him, he brought your suitcases into the house. Do you remember?" She smiled and turned toward Rachel, still smiling.

"Oh yeah, what was his name?" Rachel had thought he was cute.

"Emre," Aylin said. She was apparently in some sort of daydream because she was not normally so speechless.

"Have you been together long?" Aylin awoke from her dreamland and returned to her chatty self.

"We were friends last summer, and it was a beeeeeeautiful summer. We made picnics and we watched the birds and went dancing in the disco on the beach. And then he went to England for one year, with his parents because his father is also a professor and he taught in an English university for one year. And he wrote me many e-mails. And now it is summer again and we are together again, but he is a little changed and I miss him from last summer. Last year, he told me he loves me and now this year he says we are too young for love. How is this possible? But I think he is just maybe confused. He is still very nice with me. And also I don't know if I love him, so maybe I should not care if he loves me, you know?"

"I guess," said Rachel. "I mean, I don't have any experience to compare you to except my friends and my parents. Do your parents know?"

"Of course they do not know!" Aylin said, laughing. "My father will drown him if he knows that Emre kissed his daughter!"

"Really?" Rachel didn't think Timur Amca seemed that violent.

"Haha, no, I am making a joke. But of course they do not know. Well, I mean probably they know, maybe even they spy on me at the disco, but we do not talk about it. They do not ask and I do not tell. It is better that way."

"I guess," Rachel said, not sure of the best way to handle the subject with parents. If she had a boyfriend, would she really want to share that information with Mom and Dad? "What would happen if you told them? I mean, has anyone tried it? Maybe parents are more reasonable than we're giving them credit for." Aylin and Elif shook their heads and clicked their tongues in unison.

"Then they lock us in the house until they find us husbands," Elif said, laughing. This time, Rachel understood it was a joke.

"Do not worry about a boyfriend for Rachel," Aylin announced to the other girls. "I think I know the perfect boy."

"Oh? Who? And why did you not share him with us?" asked Elif, who seemed genuinely offended.

"I did introduce him to you, Elif, and you were not interested."

"Great! So Elif didn't like him but you think I will?" Who were they trying to pawn off on the boyfriend-less American?

"Elif hasn't good taste," Aylin teased, but Elif didn't find anything funny about it. "He is my cousin, and if he were not my cousin, believe me he would not be available for you."

Rachel looked around the beach for someone who might be Aylin's cousin.

"Is he here?"

"No, he is in Antalya, which is a very long drive from here. But I will figure out something, don't worry."

Rachel was relieved. She wasn't ready to meet him yet.

* * *

When they went back to the house for lunch, Leyla's parents were sitting at the table talking in hushed tones. They didn't notice Aylin and Rachel approaching, and both startled when the girls walked up the stairs to the balcony.

"Welcome, we have lunch in ten minutes, Leyla is upstairs," Bahar Teyze said, clearly indicating to the girls that they should go upstairs, too. They walked through the bead curtain hanging from the doorframe to keep out flies and mosquitoes, and the rattling beads alerted Leyla that someone had entered. She ran down the stairs, and stopped when she saw Aylin and Rachel.

"It's you," she said, looking slightly nervous. She turned and went back up the stairs. Aylin and Rachel followed her.

"How did it go with our mother?" Aylin asked.

"Oh, fine, I think. She seemed happy but I think she is nervous, you know, after last time. But I told her what I told you, and she said it sounds good, but she does not know until she meets Kerem and his parents. And I am worried what Babam will say. If he says ok, then Kerem and his parents will come in two days to meet." Aylin played with her necklace.

"Your necklace is pretty," Rachel said, thinking maybe she could distract Leyla and help her forget her nerves for a few minutes. Leyla's necklace was gold with blue, yellow, and clear gemstones in a pattern that looked like an eye.

"Oh, thank you Rachel. It is an evil eye, remember I told you about that? It is a gift from Kerem. To protect me."

"I also wondered from where this necklace came. Wooooooow, this is beautiful Ablacim, I am soooooooo excited to meet Kerem. He makes you very happy, I think." Even Rachel, a relative stranger, could see how much Aylin looked up to Leyla. Again she wished she could have had a sister.

"Leyla'cim, come," came Bahar Teyze's voice from downstairs. Aylin kissed her on both cheeks.

"Good luck, Ablacim," she said. Leyla went and kissed Rachel on both cheeks, too. Rachel felt thrilled to have been included.

"Good luck, Leyla," she said. All the smiling and warmth was rubbing off on her and she couldn't help herself but to be nervous for Leyla. Rachel and Aylin waited at the top of the stairs and listened for signs of how things were going. After a few minutes, she heard kisses being given, and a few minutes later, Leyla came to the top of the stairs, her eyes sparkling and smile on her lips.

"They will meet with Kerem's parents, I will call them now, oh, maybe this time everything can be ok!"

Chapter 7

When you do things from your soul,

You feel a river moving in you,

A joy.

- Rumi

Didim, Turkey

July 20

For the first time since Rachel had arrived in Turkey, Aylin got up before her. Rachel heard rustling in their room, and rolled over to see Aylin, already dressed in shorts and a t-shirt, tying her hair into a ponytail.

"Gunaydin," Rachel said, finally remembering how to say "good morning" in Turkish without thinking too hard.

"Ah, *gunaydin* Rachel! I am sorry, did I wake you? I tried to be quiet. But I am so clumsy and I fell when I tried to put on my shorts. If you could be awake at that time, you would laugh so much!"

Rachel laughed, "well, we won't tell anyone until after Emre and you are married. If they think they're getting a clumsy girl, maybe they won't accept you."

"Oh, your thinking is becoming more Turkish! But unfortunately my clumsy nature is not so easy to hide. Perhaps I must find someone more clumsy than me, then to compare us I will not seem so clumsy." Aylin was always full of quick comebacks.

"That's a really good idea. I hope we can find someone," Rachel said with a smile. Aylin punched her in the arm.

"You earned that," she said, laughing. "Rachel, today I cannot come to the beach. I really should stay and help my family clean the house and prepare some things for tomorrow. Kerem and his parents are coming for lunch. But you should go and have fun with Elif, Rana, and Ela. Rachel thought about it for a few seconds before deciding she didn't like the idea.

"No, Aylin, I'll stay here and help you all. That would be really rude for me to just go to the beach while you clean and cook here."

"Rachel, it is not rude. You are here for your vacation, you must go to the beach. Really, this is no problem. Maybe I will come in the afternoon if we can complete everything quickly."

"Aylin, seriously, I want to stay and help you all. I didn't come here for vacation, I came to be a part of your family and learn about Turkey. And if you don't let me help then I won't feel like I'm part of your family." Wow, that was good, she thought to herself, Aylin can't say no to that.

"I cannot say no to you if you say that, Rachel! Ok, so you help us too. First we will eat breakfast for energy and then we will make this house perfect for our important guests tomorrow, Leyla's prince on a white horse and his parents."

It was the most fun Rachel had ever had cleaning. In the morning, Rachel and Aylin were given the job of cleaning the bathrooms. They used old toothbrushes to scrub the hard water deposits around the faucets and tiles, and bleach to whiten the toilet. They took all of the toiletries out of the cabinet (mostly suntan lotion, some of it ten years old, moisturizing lotion, and a bowl full of soap bars) and threw out the ones that were empty or dried up. They sang the popular songs that they both knew

(American ones, of course, because Rachel hadn't learned any Turkish ones yet). They discussed whether to rearrange the lotions according to content, color, or size. When they were done, they stood in the doorway and admired their work.

"When "Prince Kerem's" mother sits on this toilet, she will look around at this perfect bathroom and think, "my son should marry the girl whose family has such well-organized lotions," Rachel said.

"And when she has finished her toilet business, she will ask if Leyla has two younger sisters for Kerem's younger brothers to marry." Both girls laughed at the thought. "I wonder if Kerem has any younger brothers?"

"For you or for me?" Rachel asked.

"Well, at the moment I have a boyfriend, but still, who knows if we will get married!"

"You know, I never in a million years thought I'd spend a day of my life cleaning bathrooms in a house on the beach in Turkey. But it really has been a cool day. It's one of those days I think I'll never forget, you know?" And she really meant it.

At lunchtime, Bahar Teyze ordered them to finish all of the leftovers in the refrigerator so that it would be empty enough to clean properly and fill with the food they would make that afternoon. While they were eating, a few small pickup trucks full of fruits and vegetables drove by at a snail's pace, each with one or two scruffy guys sitting in the back shouting loudly.

"What are they saying?"

"They are saying nonsense," Aylin answered. "They are selling those fruits and vegetables in the truck, and they should just call out the names of the foods they want to sell, but they have fun to shout these names in a funny way and wake up anyone who might sleep. You should listen, every time a truck passes by, you can hear a baby crying." Timur Amca bought watermelons, figs, peppers, tomatoes, cucumbers, green beans, eggplants, zucchini, okra, and onions from the "mobile" vegetable stands.

"Easier than going to the store," Rachel said. "That's cool, I think they should do that in Olympia." She thought of mentioning it to her mom, whose second cousin managed the Olympia Farmer's Market.

After lunch, it was time to help prepare the next day's meal for Kerem and his family. Aylin and Rachel followed instructions for prepping the food, while Bahar Teyze and Leyla did the cooking. First, Leyla showed them how to properly trim the okra stems into a cone shape without making them go slimy. Next, they diced a large amount of onions and tomatoes, since lots of the dishes that would be made had both ingredients. They also hollowed out halved zucchinis to be stuffed, and took the ends off of the green beans. After Leyla prepared the rice, meat, onion and mint filling for the zucchinis, they stuffed those as well. Bahar Teyze and Leyla were going to serve stuffed grape leaves called *sarma*, but they didn't want Aylin and Rachel to help this time, because they didn't want the grape leaf rolls to look like clumsy, untrained hands had made them.

Once the vegetables had been stuffed, Rachel looked at her watch. It was six o'clock. The time had passed faster than she'd thought.

"*Tesekkur ederim*, thank you, Aylin and Rachel," Leyla said when the girls handed over a pot filled with stuffed zucchini. "You did great work today. Why don't you relax now, and go out tonight with your friends? Have fun. I will stay home this time." Leyla's eyes looked tired and excited, young and wise all at once. "Tomorrow, after breakfast, we can prepare the table together." She winked, and Aylin and Rachel went to get ready for her first evening out in Didim.

Rachel had never been to a disco before. Had there been one that allowed people her age, her parents would have let her go, but there was nothing like that for people under 21 in Olympia. Rachel wasn't sure if she was scared or excited, because both emotions made her hands shaky. The weather was as hot as always, but the unusually high humidity of the day meant that the evening wasn't cooling off as much as it usually did. Rachel decided to wear a black short-sleeved dress that Grams had picked out for her. It was neither short nor long, hitting her just above the knees. Even though she wasn't used to wearing dresses, it was comfortable because it felt like a t-shirt, and it was black. In spite of the heat, she didn't put her long, straight hair in a ponytail, since Hanna had always said it looked better down.

She wondered what Hanna was doing. 7pm. Ok, 10 hours earlier in Olympia, which meant it was 9 in the morning. Rachel couldn't remember if it was a weekend or weekday. What a luxury, she thought, not knowing what day of the week it was. If it was a weekday, Hanna would be at her internship already, dressed in office-type clothes, probably with uncomfortable shoes (not that Hanna minded that kind of thing). If it was a weekend, Hanna was probably having breakfast, wondering why Rachel hadn't written. They'd probably be back too late tonight to write, and tomorrow would be a busy day with Kerem's parents coming and everything. Hopefully, she'd get a chance to write tomorrow night.

"Ready?" Aylin asked. She was wearing tight jeans, a white t-shirt, and a turquoise and silver necklace. "Aren't you going to wear any makeup?"

"I don't even have any makeup. And even if I did, I don't have a clue how to apply it."

"That's right, I forgot. Come here, I will do it for you. I am not good like Leyla, but also not terrible. Of course, she is teaching me for many years!" After Aylin applied some eyeliner and mascara to Rachel's eyes, she brushed on some blush, then handed Rachel a tube of reddish lip gloss. "You put on this by yourself," she said, and watched as Rachel applied it. "Good, now some perfume," she said, and sprayed it all over Rachel's neck and arms before Rachel could protest. "Now, we are ready," she said, and they headed downstairs where Leyla and her mother were still in the kitchen, cooking.

"Have fun," Leyla said with an exhausted smile. Bahar Teyze also smiled a tired smile.

It took quite a while to walk the hundred and fifty yards from Aylin's house to the disco. The first stop was two houses down, where a woman Bahar Teyze's age but quite a bit wider and with a lot of mascara, came to the edge of her balcony and greeted Aylin.

"Merhaba, Rachel, I'm Aylin's Gül Teyze, I have heard so much about you from Bahar, she says you are such a nice girl, not like she thought Americans would be. But I told her Americans can be very nice, of course, I know many. I am so pleased to meet you, I wanted to come and meet you before, but Bahar said you were tired from the jet lag and I should wait. How are you feeling now, how do you like Turkey?"

"Nice to meet you too," Rachel said, not knowing whether she should reach out her hand to shake hands or what.

"Come, you can kiss my hand," said Gül Teyze, extending her hand to Rachel. "This is how we greet special older people here in Turkey." It felt a bit funny to be kissing someone's hand, but she looked at Aylin, who had an unusually uncomfortable smile on her lips.

"You don't have to actually kiss her hand, you can just touch it to your chin, then touch it to your forehead," Aylin instructed loudly. Rachel made the greeting, feeling badly that she hadn't done so to Aylin's parents.

"Please do come and visit me anytime, sweet girl, and we can chat in English."

"Thank you," Rachel said, feeling a little like she had made a friend, but not sure if simply speaking English was reason enough to talk to the woman who talked so much and didn't ask any real questions.

Once they were out of earshot, Aylin whispered to Rachel, "My mother really really does not like Gül Teyze. She is a little bit crazy."

"Really? How?"

"Well, she spends most of her time flirting with the boys our age. My mother does not like her."

"But she said she talked to your mother, didn't she?"

"Yes, but my mother has no choice, she talks to everyone. She doesn't have any real friends, but she goes around to visit everyone always at mealtime and so they have to then invite her to sit down. She always accepts, so I don't think she cooks anything herself! She just goes around town and finds somebody to feed her. Then she talks until they make an excuse to make her leave. Anyway, if you see her again, you don't have to kiss her hand. She took advantage of you because you don't know the rules. She of course wants everyone to kiss her hands, but only the younger close family and friends should do that. And she doesn't have any friends so she is looking for people to kiss her hands. "

"Is she married or anything?" Rachel didn't need to know, but she was curious and thought, correctly, that Gül Teyze was part of an interesting story.

"Yes, her husband is very rich, I am actually surprised she did not mention that because she usually says something about his money whenever she can. He is a famous film director. He was not famous always, he was a film teacher, but about five years ago he became famous. Then he was always in the newspaper. Pictures of him and the young actress who is in all of his movies. So everybody knows..."

"And they're still married?"

"Yes, and so she gets all of his money and she goes to the official big parties and everything with him, and she spends months every year in the summer house. I am not sure why she is here in their old summer house and not someplace more fancy. But my mother says that he is with the actress in a fancy new summer house in Bodrum."

"Wow, kind-of like a movie."

"See that house there?" Aylin motioned to a pale green house with a tidy rose-lined patio. "That is Emre's house." It hadn't seemed like anyone was home, but something rustled behind a hibiscus bush with yellow flowers, and a man who must have been Emre's father appeared from behind the moving hibiscus. He was a handsome man with his black hair graying at the temples. He wore madras shorts and a white undershirt.

"Merhaba, Hakan Amca," Aylin said as she took his hand and bent down to kiss it. Hakan Amca held his hand down and shook hands with Aylin instead. "This is our American exchange student, Rachel," she said, putting her hand on Rachel's back and bringing her towards them.

Hakan Amca held out his hand and Rachel didn't know whether or not to kiss his hand. Aylin had clearly tried to kiss his hand, but he hadn't wanted her to for some reason. It was so confusing. The rules were all different here. Aylin didn't want to offend anyone but she didn't know what to do in order to be polite here. It was like playing a board game without knowing any of the rules. She was trying to guess them as she went along, hoping she wouldn't be penalized for breaking a rule she hadn't yet deciphered. Rachel tried to kiss Hakan Amca's hand, and he did the same to her as he did to Aylin.

"Pleased to meet you," he said in his confident English accent. "I can see that Aylin has been practicing a lot with you, her English seems to be improving," he said, smiling at both. "
"Emre's not gotten himself together yet for the evening, I'm sure you'll meet up with him later, then." Aylin blushed. And Derya Teyze is just having a nap, I'll tell her you stopped by. Have a lovely evening, ladies," he said, and turned back to trimming the hibiscus bush.

When they were a few houses away, and Rachel knew they could not be heard, she tried to figure out the hand-kissing game rule by asking another question.

"So why did Hakan Amca not let you kiss his hand?"

"Some people just don't like it, or something, I don't know. But they are very close friends of my parents, so I always try even though Hakan Amca never lets me."

"They're close friends of your parents?!" Rachel was amazed.

"Yes, they have come here like us, since we were maybe five years old."

"Oh, come on. They must know that you are dating then." Rachel couldn't believe that Aylin's parents didn't know that their daughter was dating their good friends' son.

"I think they all maybe think something, but they don't talk about it. We don't talk about it. It is like that." Rachel didn't really get it, but she didn't have time to press the issue, because Aylin was saying something to a petite woman who was setting the table on a balcony. After what seemed like a friendly exchange, they moved on.

"That was Elif's mother. Elif is already at the gazino waiting for us." Two houses later, the road turned right at the beach. The girls followed the road, beach on their left, houses on their right. The houses on the beach were larger than the ones on the back road. Finally, they came to the disco. It was a little wood building at the end of the beach.

Chapter 8

There is a candle in your heart, ready to be kindled.
There is a void in your soul, ready to be filled.
You feel it, don't you?
- Rumi

Even though she'd never been to a disco before, the gazino didn't look as she expected it to. Perhaps she'd been affected by TV, where nightclubs had glass shelves with liquor bottles, flashing lights, and sometimes some of that dry-ice smoke around people's feet. This place was in a building that was something between a cabin and a tumbledown shack that went on and on. It was a large room with a trail of four more rooms off of one corner. Maybe it used to be a house, Rachel thought, or maybe they just kept adding on rooms because it was cheaper than making the big room larger. The floor was concrete, and the windows had wood shutters that were open, but no glass. There were dusty, lanky geranium plants reaching up to, and sometimes out of the windows. Other potted plants filled the corners, and one of the rooms had a giant tree in the middle of it. Rachel wondered if the tree or the room had existed first. Another of the rooms had six wobbly tables filled with boys, some younger and some older, playing some kind of game that looked something like Scrabble but with numbered tiles instead of lettered ones. At a few tables, they were playing backgammon (which Rachel recognized, even though she didn't know how to play). The boys were munching on sunflower seeds, a skill Rachel was still perfecting, and quite a few of them looked up when Aylin and Rachel walked in. The only thing about this "disco" that was as Rachel had expected was the music, and she even recognized some of the Turkish songs because they played on the stereo at Aylin's house day and night.

"This doesn't look how I thought a disco would look," Rachel said.

"It is not really a disco," Aylin confessed. "We call it Gazino. It is everything. They sell newspaper and bread in the morning, they have some games and they have football games on the television, they have music and dancing in the evenings."

Rachel decided she liked this Gazino concept. If it had been like the places she'd seen in movies and on TV, she would have felt out of place, but this place was laid-back, and the crowd was young. Guys weren't coming up to them and offering to buy them drinks, like in the movies, and in fact nobody was smoking, either.

"Do any kids our age smoke here in Turkey?" Rachel asked. Aylin laughed.

"Of course, some people do."

"Nobody's smoking here," Rachel commented.

"Oh, not here in the gazino, of course not. Ali Amca will tell their parents. He is smoking a cigar himself, but he always tells the parents if the kids smoke cigarettes. It is like a rule that nobody says."

"An unspoken rule."

"Yes, I like that word, unspoken. We don't have that word in Turkish. But we have mannnnnny unspoken rules!" Aylin always did that, made the words longer to emphasize them. Even though Rachel couldn't understand much Turkish, she could tell that Aylin did it in Turkish, too.

Rana, Elif, and Ela were already at a table, and Rachel and Aylin went to join them. A man, who must have been Ali Amca because there didn't seem to be anyone else working at the place, came to ask them what they wanted to drink.

"Ne icersiniz?" Rachel had learned that in her Teach Yourself Turkish book, and only knew a few possible answers, so she asked for Coke.

The other girls also ordered either Coke, Fanta, or Gazoz, a drink that tasted something like tonic water. Grams had always given her tonic water because for some reason, she thought it was the only soda acceptable for kids. Coke would be good for a change.

"Will Emre come to the disco tonight?" asked Elif.

"I think so, he sent me an SMS today and asked if I will come because he wants to talk to me," said Aylin.

"You did not tell me before!" said Elif.

"She didn't tell me either," Rachel said. Elif seemed pleased that she wasn't the only one who was not informed.

"Now you have so many secrets, Aylin," Elif said with irritation.

"No, we were just really busy today," Aylin explained, looking at Rachel for support.

"Yeah, it was a busy day. We cleaned all morning and then we helped all afternoon with cooking. Leyla's fiancé and his parents are coming tomorrow."

"NOT fiancé!" Aylin corrected. "Maybe one day fiancé!"

"Sorry, yeah, it's just so much more complicated here. Anyway, it was a busy day."

"Will we all see days like Leyla?" Rana wondered out loud. "Will we all find boys who want to marry us?"

"If you don't, your parents or aunts or whatever will help you," Rachel said. "If I don't find anyone, I'm out of luck. Or I have to use online dating or something."

"Why?" asked Ela. "Don't you have parents or aunts?" Everyone laughed.

"No, Ela," Aylin explained, now an expert on how things worked in America. "They don't ask their parents or aunts or anyone for help to find someone usually. They find someone to marry by themselves. Right, Rachel?"

"Yep, I mean, sometimes parents help to introduce someone but I don't think it works like it does here. I mean, usually in the US if someone's parents get involved, they get annoyed."

"And in America, they become engaged alone, just the boy and the girl, no parents! And sometimes they are engaged for one year or longer!"

"Then I think things are better here," Elif said, crossing her arms in front of her. "I want my parents to find someone for me. It is better that way." She looked at Rachel. Aylin, Ela, and Rana also looked at Rachel. This was a challenge.

"Well, then it's good news that you live here. I guess in some ways, you actually have more options than I do. You guys can find someone by yourselves or you can have your family do the matchmaking."

"Don't worry. I can also be your matchmaker. I already decide you should marry my cousin," Aylin said enthusiastically.

"So, it's already been arranged, before I even meet him?" Rachel said with a giggle. "That was way easier than being in the dating scene, maybe you're right!"

"For our great-grandmother, it was like that!" exclaimed Ela.

"Actually, for my great-grandmother it was like that, too, back in China," Rachel said, feeling suddenly less strange because of it. When she had told her friends at home, she had felt weird, but here it made her feel like a member of the arranged-marriage-ancestors-club.

"You see, you are like Turkish people. This is good," said Aylin.

"Can I at least know your cousin's name?" Rachel asked.

"I don't know if I tell you. I have not yet received payment for my services," giggled Aylin.

"Please, oh please. I promise you my father will pay my dowry," Rachel pleaded. She knew how it had worked for her great-grandmother.

"Oh, no, no! Why will your father pay? Is something wrong with you? Here in Turkey it is the *boy's* family who must pay a dowry! But I think I can tell you anyway, since I trust the honor of my cousin's family," said Aylin, batting her eyelashes and smiling mischievously. "Your future husband's name is Cem."

"Gem? Like gemstone? That's not bad. A Turkish name that is easy in English. I like gemstones." Rachel said with approval.

"The difficult thing for you is that we spell it c-e-m. Our "c" has your "j" sound."

"Yeah, I read about that in my book. I can handle it, though." Rachel wondered what Cem would be like. If she ever met him, Aylin would be really disappointed if she didn't like him. Well, she'd probably never meet him anyway, since he was apparently not in Didim.

"Good, the contract is done. I will not tell you his last name yet or perhaps you will change your mind!"

Elif dropped her crossed arms and let out a sigh. She exuded more tension each day that Rachel saw her. But every time that she made an obvious jab, Rachel was able to diffuse it. Rachel knew that this was a talent she had, but she didn't like the increasingly strained conversations. She didn't know what to do, but she felt that eventually there would be some sort of argument. Elif wasn't as warm and welcoming as she had seemed at first.

Emre arrived just in time to end the awkward moment. He was with two other guys, one that looked a lot like him, tall, skinny and tan with black hair. The other boy was a little on the chubby side, with high cheekbones, straight dirty blond hair, and a straight nose. They had all sprayed themselves liberally with cologne, and their scent had preceded them. Aylin smiled at Emre and forgot to introduce the other boys to Rachel.

After a minute of everyone else saying their hellos and kissing each others' cheeks, Rachel stood up to introduce herself.

"Merhaba. I'm Rachel."

"Oh, I am sooooo sorry," Aylin interjected. "You remember Emre, I think. And this is Hasan, his younger brother," Aylin indicated towards the tall boy that looked a lot like Emre. "And this is Murat." Rachel nodded as she said their names, just like she would have done at home when meeting someone her own age, but they reached out to shake hands. She shook hands with each one, but it felt a little grown up and formal to be shaking hands, like it was an interview or something. Meanwhile, the other girls had kissed each of the boys on both cheeks. Emre shook hands with Rachel and then pulled her in to kiss her on both cheeks. A burst of electricity rushed from Rachel's cheeks to her fingers, through her spine to her toes. She felt violated and exhilarated. No boy had ever kissed her, even on her cheeks. It felt wrong to be kissed by Emre, in front of his girlfriend no less! Rachel pulled away as fast as she could. She could feel Emre looking at her, but she looked at Aylin uncomfortably. Aylin smiled, clearly undisturbed.

It didn't take too long before Emre asked Aylin to go off with him to talk privately.

"I will come back soon," Aylin said, mostly to Rachel.

"I'll be fine," Rachel responded, but Aylin was already walking away from the table, Emre's hand on her waist.

"What are they going to do?" asked Ela, and everyone laughed. Rachel laughed, too, even though the same question troubled her.

"You will know one day," Elif answered Ela with an air of authority.

Aylin and Emre were only gone for five minutes. When they came back, Rachel thought Aylin's cheeks looked flushed, but it was pretty dark and they had put on makeup before going out, so Rachel couldn't be sure. The rest of the evening, they just sat around and talked about pretty normal stuff. Emre's English was perfect, just as Aylin said, but his British accent was sometimes hard to understand. Hasan and Murat both asked questions about the US, mostly about basketball stars that Rachel was unfamiliar with. They were all curious about life in the US. It was a fun night. Much to Rachel's relief, nobody danced. They stuck together as a group and drank their soft drinks, nibbled at sunflower seeds, and talked. Emre looked at Aylin a lot, but Aylin didn't look back at him much. He also looked at Rachel, straight in the eyes. After it happened a few times, Rachel realized she had been looking at him, too, so she stopped. Something was definitely going on. Rachel decided not to pry on the way home. Aylin was open about sharing things when she wanted to.

Chapter 9

In the house of lovers, the music never stops
The walls are made of songs
And the floor dances.
- Rumi

Didim, Turkey

July 21

Kerem's parents were supposed to arrive at around 1:00 for lunch. If they had been driving from their home in Denizli, it would have taken them about three hours, but they were both retired and spending their summer at their beach house in Kusadasi, a port town where cruise ships often docked, a 45-minute drive away. Kerem was apparently staying with them for the weekend, and would come with them. At 9 in the morning, Bahar Teyze and Leyla were getting ready to leave the house. Since everything had been prepared the day before, Rachel had thought it was going to be a relaxed morning for everyone. But, as she had already found out, many things were different in Turkey. Leyla and Bahar Teyze were going to have their hair done at a salon in Altinkum, a nearby town that was, according to Leyla, not much more than beachfront, restaurants, bars, discos full of British tourists, and endless apartments.

"My mother is not happy that they will have their hair done here and not at their known salon in Izmir, but they have no choice. They are leaving early because if the hairdressers make their hair ugly, they still have time to go to another hairdresser or to come home and fix it themselves."

"Wow, that sounds dangerous, having your hair cut the day of the lunch," Rachel's own hair had always been the same – long, straight, one inch off the bottom, please – but she remembered some hair disasters her mom had experienced in the past. Those included "going a shade lighter", "a little more layering", and "a gentle perm".

"They will not cut their hair," Aylin said, horror in her voice. "Only make a nice style."

"Oh, I see. Wow, just for a lunch they're going to the salon? My mom only goes to get her hair cut or colored."

"Here, the women go for every event, even sometimes just for going to dinner at somebody's house. You mean you never do that?"

"No. Actually, some girls do that for prom, but my mom did my hair."

"What is prom?"

"Oh, it's this dance that they have in your last year of high school. You get dressed up, you go with a date. Unless you're me, then you go with your best friend. Actually, I went to junior prom. That's the one that happens junior year. Lots of kids rent limousines and go to really fancy restaurants. They spend a lot of money on prom. I only went because my mom made me."

"Your mom sounds so interesting," Aylin said in awe. "She makes you do the things that other parents say "no, you cannot do that."

"I guess either way it's not fun. Why can't they just let us do what we want?" Both girls reflected on this unanswerable question.

While Bahar Teyze and Leyla were at the salon, Rachel and Aylin set the table according to strict instructions left behind by Leyla on a pink sheet of stationary in neat handwriting. An hour and a half later, Aylin's mother and sister returned with their hair shiny and stiff. Bahar Teyze's usually curly-frizzy dark-blonde hair had been blown straight and though usually chin-length when curly, it fell to below her shoulders. She looked far too young to have a daughter who was getting married (well, maybe getting married). Leyla's long, and normally straight, chestnut hair now had loose curls and was swept away from her face with a sparkly barrette in the shape of a butterfly. At home, such a clip would have looked really juvenile to Rachel. She would never have thought of an adult wearing it, but it looked glamorous on Leyla. Both Bahar Teyze and Leyla looked ready to walk down the red carpet, except that they were in their regular clothes. But about when Kerem and his parents were probably leaving Kusadasi, Bahar Teyze and Leyla went upstairs to change, and later came back down looking like something from the glossy pages of a magazine. Bahar Teyze wore a butter yellow linen skirt with a matching linen blazer. Kerem's parents would surely be impressed by Leyla in her lavender linen pants, and a white tunic with lavender and turquoise sequins along the bottom. Bahar Teyze hurried Timur Amca, Aylin, and Rachel upstairs to change.

"They look so fancy, what are we supposed to wear, Aylin!?" Rachel felt truly panicked over what to wear for the first time since – ever. She was not one to worry much about clothing. But this time it mattered. She didn't want things to go wrong for Leyla today, but Leyla seemed too preoccupied and busy to be asked for advice.

"Wear what you wore when we went to the pide restaurant," Aylin said, making it easy. But Rachel questioned her suggestion.

"But that's not fancy at all. Your mom and Leyla are dressed up so nicely,"

"This is about them," Aylin said. "They will notice me a little, but maybe they will not notice you at all. They will watch Leyla closely and make sure they like her, and my parents will watch Kerem closely and make sure they like him before they allow their daughter to spend the rest of her life with him. Today, if we are quiet, it's ok. We must do everything to help Leyla and make her look good." Rachel wasn't sure if she should be offended about her insignificance or honored to be a part of this special day.

In some ways, it felt more important than a wedding. At a wedding, the two people have already made their decision (at least in theory), and the wedding was just a ceremony and party. Aylin was certainly more serious, and less clumsy, than usual.

When they got downstairs, Leyla was sitting nervously on the sofa, looking at her watch. Without paying too much attention, she looked up when they entered the living room.

"You look nice," she said, before she could have possibly taken much of a look at them.

"Thank you, Ablacim! You look beautiful," Aylin said, like the maid of honor. "What can we do to help you?"

"Actually, you can put the crystal dessert bowls in the kitchen, I think you forgot that."

"Sorry, Ablacim! We'll get them now," Aylin said. Rachel knew it had been left off the list because they had crossed through each instruction as they went along, but this wasn't a time for arguing petty details. Aylin and Rachel each took four bowls from the buffet. They didn't stack, so Rachel held them against her body with her hands. And then a terrible thing happened; Rachel tripped on the threshold of the kitchen door, and a bowl fell out of her hand and onto the marble floor where it shattered, echoing through the unusually quiet house. Rachel would have very happily disappeared, and suddenly felt overwhelmingly homesick, wishing she were in her bedroom chatting online with friends, or working at the coffee shop, or anything other than being in a house in Didim surrounded by a thousand shards of crystal.

Until, that is, everyone had an entirely unexpected reaction. Whereas Rachel thought they'd be irritated but not want to show it, as in that's ok, don't worry about it, it was old anyway, Bahar Teyze looked genuinely relieved.

"*Allah'a sukur, nazar cikti,*" she said, wiping her brow and sharing the first unencumbered smile Rachel had seen from her since Leyla had shared that Kerem wanted to marry her. She then carefully wiped tears from her eyes with the corner of paper towel, before they could escape and run down her cheeks, ruining her makeup. In spite of the apparent released tension from everyone's faces, Rachel was still not sure what had happened. Everyone looked happy, but they all had eyes shiny with unshed tears.

"I am so, so sorry, I will replace that bowl, I am so embarrassed, oh my goodness," Rachel said, not knowing what Bahar Teyze had said and herself not knowing what else to say.

"Do not be sorry!" Leyla said, sounding as though she really meant it. "We are so happy!" Thoroughly confused, Rachel couldn't stop herself from asking for an explanation of that one.

"But I broke your beautiful bowl, why are you happy?"

"Like my mother said, the Evil Eye left. Remember I told you about the Evil Eye when I read your coffee? We say nazar?" Rachel did remember that, but hadn't given much thought to it since.

"When we have something that we want to be happy and important, we are worried that it will bring bad luck and something bad will happen. And we say that when something breaks, it is because the nazar left. My mother said, thanks to God, the Evil Eye left. And I think because this was a very nice bowl, it was even better because it meant there was a very big nazar. Now we can be comfortable. Sometimes, people break a glass or something by themselves but if it happens naturally, it is better of course."

Rachel looked at Aylin, who smiled and nodded her head in agreement.

"Good job, Rachel, you made everyone feel better!" Aylin said with approval.

"We definitely don't have anything like that in America, but that is really awesome," Rachel said, thinking that she had to teach this one to her mom, who would have been sulky about a broken crystal bowl. Together, Rachel, Aylin, Bahar Teyze, and Leyla, in their elegant clothes picked up the pieces of the bowl, laughing and chattering happily once again, so that they didn't even notice Kerem and his parents' arrival at the balcony.

Aside from the nice-to-meet-yous and how-do-you-like-Turkey's that took place in English when Kerem and his parents were introduced to Rachel, Rachel didn't understand much of the conversation during lunch. She observed the scene intently, trying to guess what everyone was saying, like watching a foreign film without subtitles, as her Spanish teacher had made them do at the end of the year.

Kerem's mother, Zümrüt Teyze, looked slightly older than Bahar Teyze. Like Leyla and her mother, she looked as though she had been to the salon that morning, and her burgundy chin-length hair was lacquered into place and barely moved. Rounder and shorter than Bahar Teyze, she had wide hips and wore a white suit with a beige design embroidered on all the seams, a sequined beige shirt underneath, and shiny beige high-heeled sandals. In spite of the stiffness of her hair, she exuded kindness and comfort. When she arrived, Leyla held Zümrüt Teyze's right hand, bent at the waist, and kissed her hand and put it on her forehead. Afterwards, Zümrüt Teyze pulled Leyla to her and kissed her on both cheeks. Bahar Teyze looked happy with maybe just a slight bit of something else. Was it jealousy that this woman could become her daughter's "other" mother?

Kerem's father, Efe Amca, was even rounder than Zümrüt Teyze, had white hair and blue eyes, and bore a resemblance to Santa Claus minus the beard. He wore a blue oxford shirt, a charcoal tie, and charcoal pants. He already looked too hot in the afternoon sun, but throughout the lunch he just kept on blotting his forehead, never loosening his tie.

Rachel tried to help as much as possible, following Aylin's lead by running back and forth to the kitchen to fetch things as they were needed (food from the stove, dessert, clean plates), and used the opportunity to ask Aylin about what was going on.

"It's mostly just normal conversation," she said when they brought the final lunch plates in and collected the dessert (rice pudding with cinnamon on top) from the refrigerator. "They are asking 'what do you do, who do you know, where were you born, where were your grandparents born' but actually there are some interesting things, too. Like my parents asked Kerem's parents if they think Aylin should work after she has a baby and Kerem's parents say only if she wants to, which is good because that is what my parents want for her. Something strange is that they are not asking my parents many questions about Leyla. It seems like they already know her and they already want her so they don't ask anything."

So, this really wasn't just a meeting. Rachel had thought maybe it was just a get-to-know-you type of the lunch and the decision had already been made, but in fact serious things were going on. She had understood enough at one point to know that a lot of discussion was made about what they were going to drink.

"What about the beer, Aylin?" she whispered. "I still barely understand anything in Turkish, but there was a weird vibe when they were talking about bira."

"What is vibe? What does it mean?" Aylin asked. Sometimes, Rachel forgot that Aylin was not completely fluent in English.

"Oh, it's like, oh how do you explain vibe? It's like a feeling like in the air or something." Aylin seemed to understand.

"Ah, yes, we say hava for that. It means air or can also mean weather. Yes, you are right, that was weird. I was thinking myself, what would I do if I were Leyla?" Aylin had not clarified anything.

"But what happened?"

"My parents decided on purpose to offer everyone beer or wine with lunch, even though normally they don't drink at lunch time. But they wanted to see what Kerem and his parents thought about women drinking alcohol, because some people think women should not drink or they also think men should not drink. Of course if somebody does not drink it is not bad, but in our family we drink alcohol and my parents do not want Leyla to go to a conservative family. So this was a test, you see."

"And what happened?"

"My father asked who will drink beer, and Kerem's parents chose to drink beer. Kerem refused, which is normal because young people would probably not drink alcohol at such an important meeting. Leyla also said, no, I won't drink beer, I will become sleepy, and our father was angry with her because he told her she must say she will drink beer to test their reaction. So then my father kicked Leyla under the table, but he really kicked Kerem's father by mistake! And Kerem's father thought that Kerem's mother kicked him, and then he said loud so everyone can hear, "Zümrüt my dear, I promise I won't fall asleep," and so everyone looked at everyone. Then everyone laughed and they talked to figure out what happened. And then Kerem's parents told Leyla she should enjoy her beer and we will all wake her up if she falls asleep and this will be a funny story one day."

"Wow, that is awesome. So everything is going ok?" Rachel was relieved. She had sensed that the laughter meant everything was going well, but you never knew if it was real or fake, especially when you don't understand any of the words surrounding it.

"Until now, everything is good. May everything be for the best. Wow! My oooooone big sister could be promised today, I cannot believe it! Will this happen to us one day, Rachel?" Rachel thought before she answered. She could not imagine it working out quite like this for herself.

"It will happen to you, Aylin," she answered. "And for me, I hope I meet someone one day and get engaged and everything, and I hope it's cool, but I doubt I'll experience a day like today."

Just then, Leyla came in. Rachel and Aylin, deep in conversation, had forgotten their task and had forgotten to whisper.

"Ooooo, sorry Ablacim! Sorry sorry, is everything ok?"

Leyla looked a hundred times more relaxed than she had at the beginning of the meal.

"It's going great, don't you think?" she said in a whisper. "May God protect us from the evil eye. I will make coffee and then, maybe..." Leyla didn't finish the thought with words, but she grinned more widely than she had since Rachel had met her. "I will make coffee now. You two please bring out the dessert before you forget again! Eat quickly and then maybe you can come back into the kitchen so we can drink coffee just our parents and Kerem's parents, with Kerem and me. You can spy on us from the upstairs balcony!"

The view from the upstairs balcony was partially obscured by the fuchsia flowers of a bougainvillea vine, which nonetheless offered good camouflage. Leyla went outside with a tray carrying six coffees in tiny cups that Rachel hadn't seen before. They were decorated with gold, blue, and red designs, Rachel could see that much.

"It is important that Leyla makes excellent coffee with nice foam on top. Of course it is always nice to have good coffee, but today it is very important," Aylin explained. Rachel liked coffee, but she couldn't imagine it really mattering how well someone prepared it. Then again, maybe it was more important than she gave it credit for. After all, Grams always joked that Dad made terrible coffee, and she really meant it as an insult. But fortunately Grams hadn't had a say in whether or not her parents would marry each other.

Rachel watched as the coffee drinking began. First, Kerem's parents brought the little cups to their mouths, and Leyla watched them as she held her plate in one hand and her cup in the other, paused between the plate and her mouth. Then, very unexpectedly, peals of laughter erupted from Zümrüt Teyze. Leyla quickly tried her coffee, then stood up and exclaimed in horror, and quickly reached to collect everyone's coffee cups from their hands to return to the tray. Zümrüt Teyze jumped up and hugged Leyla, who started to cry, and then Kerem and Efe Amca also gathered around Leyla and seemed to comfort her while Bahar Teyze and Timur Amca looked either stunned or horrified, Rachel was not sure which, and she couldn't imagine what on Earth was going on. Then Zümrüt Teyze started explaining something, and Aylin, sitting next to Rachel on the balcony, gasped so loudly that surely she would have been heard downstairs if there hadn't been so much commotion.

"What's happening? Is this normal?" Rachel asked. Aylin didn't answer immediately. She watched as if it were the crucial scene of a movie, which in some sense, it was. She didn't respond to Rachel; she didn't even seem to notice that Rachel had asked a question. A minute later, when the loud, fast, high-pitched talking continued, Rachel asked again.

"What is going on down there, Aylin? Is everything ok?" This time, Aylin laughed and opened her eyes widely in an I-can't-believe-it expression.

"Leyla put SALT in the coffee." Aylin said it as if it explained everything, but Rachel was still confused. Granted, she didn't think salty coffee would taste very good, but she didn't know if it was part of the ritual or if it was really bad or something else.

"Why did she do that?" Rachel asked innocently. Aylin giggled happily and shook her head at Rachel's ignorance.

"Actually, some families do it on purpose to test the reactions, but our family does not... for us this was an accident! Rachel, this is a nightmare to put salt in the coffee. My mother is telling her "I told you to taste your coffee before you serve them" and Leyla is saying "I was so nervous that I forgot" and after that, Zümrüt Teyze explained that she did the same thing when her parents met the parents of Efe Amca and she thinks this is a good sign. Wait wait, they are quiet again," Aylin turned her ear towards the quieter conversation, and soon began to smile and then squeal.

"Now, Efe Amca said to my parents, "We will be happy to accept any coffee from your daughter, even salty coffee. She is so sweet that we will forget the salt. Will you give your daughter Leyla to marry our son Kerem?" and my parents smiled and they said something quietly to each other and then they said, yes, we will give our daughter Leyla for your son Kerem.

"Wow! So now they're engaged!" Rachel said, feeling once again as if she were watching a movie.

"Congratulations! Hayirlisi olsun, may it be for the best!" Aylin shouted down through the bougainvillea, revealing her hiding place behind the pink flowered vine. Then, to Rachel, she made a clarification. "They are not engaged yet, Rachel. They are promised." Rachel thought for a moment before responding.

"Well, promised sounds even nicer than engaged."

"Oh, that is a really nice thing to say, Rachel! Now we can relax a little."

Once Zümrüt Teyze and Efe Amca had left, Aylin and Rachel grilled Leyla for the details. Leyla was glowing and calm, in spite of, or maybe even because of, the salty coffee incident.

"When will you have your engagement, Leyla?"

"We will have it the first week of September, in Izmir. Unfortunately, you will miss it, Rachel. But we will share the photographs with you." Suddenly, Leyla looked more like a woman. Rachel was disappointed. She'd only known Leyla a week, but she had been made to feel like such a part of the family that she couldn't imagine having to miss an important family event.

"Maybe I can change my ticket?" Rachel said, before thinking. How could she do that? The first day of school was September third. It would mean missing the first week of her senior year.

"That is really nice of you, Rachel," Leyla said, kindly but she clearly had other things on her mind than whether or not Rachel would attend her engagement.

"That would be soooooooo fun, Rachel! We must change your ticket, you must talk to your parents," Aylin said. Rachel was grateful for her enthusiasm, and thought she might actually consider it seriously. Why not. Life is short, right? "Dear sister, when will the wedding be?"

"It will be in October or November, in Denizli. I think October will be nice, but of course November will give some more time for planning."

"Of course you have to get married as soon as possible so you don't change your mind, right?" Rachel said, glad she finally had some knowledge of how things worked in Turkey. Leyla laughed and stared at her hand, where a new ring shone on her finger.

"Well, for us I know we will not change our minds. We just want to hurry and be married as soon as we can, so we can begin our life together."

"Did he give you a promise ring, Ablacim?" said Aylin, only then noticing the circle of diamonds around Leyla's finger.

"Actually, he gave it to me before you picked me up in Denizli, but we kept this secret and he gave it to me again in front of our parents," Leyla said in a whisper. "Shhht, don't tell anyone!" she said animatedly.

"Congratulations, Leyla. Kerem seems totally nice, I think you'll be really happy," Rachel said, as usual not knowing the right Turkish expression for the situation, and she was sure there was one.

That night, Rachel finally got a chance to post to her blog.

You probably all think I've been kidnapped or something, but the reality is that I am just having such a great, and busy, time, that I don't have a minute to even turn on the computer. Actually, it's kinda nice to not be online all the time. The people here are awesome, I don't know where to begin. There are two sisters in this family and they totally welcomed me into their family. The parents are great, too. We're in this little town here on the water, they call it a summer village because people pretty much only come here in the summer. It doesn't have any shops or anything, but it has a disco-type thing and kids are allowed to go, and it's safe and everything because pretty much all the families know each other. Leyla, the older sister, got kind-of engaged today, but it's not called engaged, it's called promised because they have to have a ceremony to be engaged. It's so different here! The engagement is in September and it's like a big party, from what I hear. So should I change my ticket to attend? I'm totally not joking, it would be awesome.

Chapter 10

That which is false troubles the heart,

But truth brings joyous tranquility.

- Rumi

Didim, Turkey

July 22, 8 p.m.

The thermometer on the wall in the living room said it was still 33 Celsius. Rachel wasn't sure exactly what that meant except that it was hot, but not as hot as it had been earlier in the afternoon. The sun had almost set into the ocean, and a gentle breeze had started wafting through the evening air. Ten minutes earlier, everyone had carried supplies up to the rooftop terrace for a barbecue. Aylin and Leyla carried trays with the plates, silverware, glasses, and bottles of beer. Rachel's plate had the vegetables: tomatoes, onions, peppers, eggplants, and leeks.

"We don't trust you, things can break," Bahar Teyze joked.

"If you want to scare away the evil eye, you know who to call," Rachel joked back.

"Oh, don't remind me," Leyla whined. "I miss Kerem,"

The view from the roof was much better than the view from downstairs. From the tiled rooftop terrace, they saw the entire bay as its water changed from orange to red as the sun lowered itself into the Aegean Sea. They could see stragglers on the road coming home late from the beach, and others who had already taken their showers and dressed, perhaps on their way to dinner invitations with friends. In Didim, everyone seemed to know everyone else, and they all kept inviting each other over for meals. It was no wonder there was not a single restaurant in the neighborhood. Aylin's family had been invited over to many homes already since Rachel had arrived, but they had refused them all, first to let Rachel get over her jet-lag, and then to prepare for the meeting with Kerem's parents. The next day, they were invited to Emre's parents' house. Timur Amca was not happy about it.

"Hakan Abi will just talk the whole time about England, as always, and how perfect England is and how much English Emre learned and how his wife had tea with English ladies and now her English is perfect, too, and how they now always drink their tea with milk and they don't like the Turkish beer anymore, they must drink English beer. The last two times we met with them, this is what they told us. And now we can hear it again."

"They are not bad," Bahar Teyze said. She seemed to be trying to speak English more often the past few days. "We will speak English and practice. You don't want them talk about England England England then you say something interesting."

"For example, what will I talk about?" Timur Amca asked, quite seriously. Aylin, Leyla, and Bahar Teyze laughed.

"If you don't say interesting thing then you don't complain, Timur Bey!" Bahar Teyze said. Rachel smiled, knowing that her parents would like her host family as much as she did. She felt a little bit guilty, having so much fun with this family as if it were her own. She wished she had a brother or sister, but felt badly for wishing it, knowing it wasn't possible. She wondered what mom and dad were up to. Probably at work.

Timur Amca was in charge of the grill. It was the first time Rachel had seen him doing anything with food other than eating it, unlike her dad, who liked to make Chinese food a few times a week. The vegetables and meats came off the tiny charcoal grill slowly, so they couldn't all just sit down and eat, like they usually did. Instead, they nibbled a bit every time something was ready. They all spoke English tonight, perhaps in anticipation of the dinner with Emre's family. It turned out that Bahar Teyze understood pretty much everything in English, and she could say almost anything she wanted, too. She managed to make perfect sense, even though she clearly had no respect for grammar.

"You want drinking Turkish national drink, Rachel?"

"Uh, sure," Rachel answered, wondering what it was.

"This drink name rakı. Make from grapes and anise. You know anise?" She poured a small amount of the clear, colorless liquid into tall, straight glasses. It looked like, well, water.

"I've heard of it, but I don't really know what it is." There was a tea at the coffee shop, anise-green tea or something, but Rachel hadn't tried that one.

"Rachel, do your parents allow you to drink alcohol?" Timur Amca asked. Oops, I didn't expect Turkey's "national drink" to be alcoholic, Rachel thought. Is this a test? What is the correct answer? It was like a pop-quiz she couldn't possibly have studied for.

"Actually, they do, Timur Amca. But not every day. Just on special occasions. They say they want me to respect alcohol and not think it's a forbidden fruit." Except, Rachel didn't add, she wasn't allowed to drink any alcohol when Grams was around. Nor was she allowed to drink more than two ounces. And it felt excitingly wrong to be accepting alcohol tonight, without asking her parents' explicit permission.

"Your parents sound very reasonable," Timur Amca replied, nodding his head with approval. Aylin beamed a conspiratory smile at Rachel.

"So you will let me travel to visit Rachel in America, Babacim?"

"You don't miss any opportunities, do you, Aylin'cim? Godwilling," Timur Amca chuckled. "I saw on television that drinking alcohol is a problem in America. For teenagers, for college students. Is this true?"

"Unfortunately, it is pretty true," Rachel said. Dad would have had lots of statistics to back up the statement, but Rachel had no idea how big or small the problem was. Her own friends weren't the type to get drunk or anything, but lots of kids at school did, and one girl from her school had actually drunk some alcohol and drove and killed a pedestrian last year. But she decided not to share this information, in case it prevented Aylin from visiting one day. She couldn't imagine what Aylin would think of her boring life in Olympia. She'd have to figure out some cool new life before Aylin came over. "Anyway, just so you know, I'm not into that. I mean, alcohol is not my thing. But I would like to taste your national drink."

"I know, Rachel. I can understand that from your actions. Children think that parents don't know anything, but we know more than you think.

"Now," Bahar Teyze said, drawing attention back to the rakı. "You watch this Rachel. This our national drink." She poured water from a plastic bottle that was normally kept in the refrigerator to keep the water cold. The clear liquid in the glass immediately turned white, and the result looked like milk. One glass looked more like whole milk and the other four looked like fat free. And two of the glasses were only a quarter full. Bahar Teyze then put a few tiny cubes of ice in each glass and handed them around, giving Timur Amca the "whole milk" one, Rachel and Aylin the partially-full ones. She lifted up her glass, and made a toast. "For healthy and happy together."

"*Serefe*," Timur Amca, Leyla, and Aylin all said.

"*Serefe*," Rachel said, late but not unappreciated; everyone smiled every time she tried to say a Turkish word. She wasn't sure if they were laughing at her or glad she was trying to speak their language. Maybe some of both. They all lifted their glasses up to clink them together, just like at home. Amazing, Rachel thought, how people always did that. Before anyone had sipped their rakı, Bahar Teyze spoke.

"No, no, no, I teach Turkish style. Timur Amca old man here, so his glass high. After Timur Amca, Bahar Teyze. Bahar Teyze glass, here," she said, showing that her glass was lower than Timur Amca's glass. "After Bahar Teyze, Leyla. Leyla glass here. And who more old, Aylin or Rachel?" Bahar Teyze looked at Aylin.

"Rachel is older than me, Annecim. I am the baby here, so Rachel, your glass will be higher than mine," Aylin took Rachel's hand and moved it so that Rachel's glass was lower than Leyla's but higher than Aylin's.

"Do you do this every time?" Rachel asked.

"Yes, it is nice, don't you think?"

"Nice, but then you have to know how old everyone is."

"You always must know. If no, you make you glass low," said Bahar Teyze. "Now you drink."

Rachel took a sip of the milky liquid and decided it tasted nothing like milk. She wasn't a huge fan of milk, but in this case, milk would have been the preferable option. This national drink was awful. It tasted like black licorice. Hanna would have loved it. Her whole family was full of black licorice nuts. Rachel, however, would have preferred just about any other flavor. But she decided to drink it anyway. Not because she didn't want to offend her hosts, not because she didn't want to be rude. Rachel drank the cold, nasty beverage because it felt extremely grown-up to be drinking a cocktail on a rooftop in Turkey, the air filled with the scent of grilling meats and vegetables, watching the sun set. The more she sipped, the less repulsive it became, and before she knew it, it was gone.

"You like rakı," said Bahar Teyze, more of a statement than a question. "You drink more?" Rachel was feeling slightly dizzy from the first one, or maybe it was from too much sun. She had gotten used to the taste, but decided to refuse the second one.

"No, thank you. I think one is enough," she said. If it had been good, she might have gone for a second, but one was all she could tolerate.

"Bravo. I give only one. One enough. I make only very very not strong rakı for you but no more. I only want you taste this. Only tonight, you understand?" Bahar Teyze shook her finger. It had been a test. Whew, she had passed. Bahar Teyze and Timur Amca continued to sip their rakı. The evening air was cool, but the smoke from the grill was warming as a gentle breeze blew it towards Rachel and Aylin.

"After dinner, we can go night swimming," Aylin suggested as she dipped a piece of bread into grilled tomato on her plate. "It will take away the smoke smell. Right, Leyla? Will you come?"

"No, I will let the young people do night swimming. I will write a long e-mail to Kerem. We will talk about organizing our engagement ceremony." Leyla blushed as she said the words, and looked down at her ring. Just then, the call to prayer began. It sounded like a cross between a chant and a song, in a foreign language of course. Rachel had heard it four or five times a day since her arrival. She had read about it in a world religions unit in history. One of the calls to prayer was in the middle of the night, or really early morning. Rachel couldn't even see her watch to know what time it was, but she wondered who was praying at that time. At first, she heard it because she was jet-lagged and awake at random times. But now it only occasionally woke her up. Aylin didn't seem to move a muscle as she slept in the next bed during the early morning call. She was probably used to it. Rachel had never seen anyone in the family praying. But she noticed that Bahar Teyze and Timur Amca put down their rakıs when the call to prayer sounded.

Just then, the telephone rang. With the houses so close together, they were never sure at first that it was their telephone, but Aylin ran downstairs to check. Rachel heard Aylin speaking in English on the phone, and then her footsteps as she ran back up the stairs.

"Rachel, it is your parents on the phone!"

It was weird. Like a call from another world. One second, she was on a rooftop on the Aegean coast, and the next she was back in Olympia.

"Mom? Dad?"

"Hi baby, how ARE you?" Mom sounded so excited.

"Hi Mom, how is everything? What's up, is there news?"

"What news? No, everything is the same as always, I just miss you so much, just hearing your voice makes me want to cry. Are you really having fun? Is the family nice to you? Are you taking lots of pictures? We bought a phone card to call you."

110

"Mom, I've only been here a week. I'm sorry, I guess I haven't written enough messages. Everything's fine, great. I don't even know where to begin. It's so fun here, I'm so glad I came. How is everything there? How's Dad?"

"Hi Pumpkin, I'm listening on the other phone, everything's great here. House is so quiet without you. We got approval for a rework of the highway 101 to I-5 interchange, so that's a big deal around here. How is my camera working for you?" Dad was way more talkative than usual. It felt really good to be missed, even though Rachel felt kind of bad for her parents. Things were boring for them, exciting for her.

"Hi Dad, that's great about the interchange. Your camera is great – I've taken like 500 pictures or something already. They're actually planning on getting a high-speed Internet connection next week. Maybe I can send some pictures then. The family is totally nice. I wish you could meet them, I mean you'd love them."

"What have you been up to, Rachel? How do you spend your time? How's the food?" Rachel's mother asked.

"Oh, the food is different but good. Breakfast is totally big, lots of stuff we wouldn't really think of eating like raw tomatoes and olives and cheese. We go to the beach every day. It's really different from the beaches in Washington, really small and crowded here, but still lots of fun because there are tons of kids our age and nobody has summer jobs so they're all out swimming and playing volleyball and hanging out."

"Are there any good-looking guys, Rachel?"

"MOM! Ugh."

"Well, I'm just asking, can't I ask?"

"No. I mean yes. I mean, Mom, why do you always ask that kind of question? I don't have a boyfriend. I don't have anything to tell and you keep asking me and putting pressure on me." Then there was silence on the other end.

"Rachel, I'm sorry. I really just missed you and I'm curious about your life there. I just don't know what else to ask really. I

111

won't ask again. I just want you to share with me, you know? So I'm in on your life. I won't judge you or tell you what to do, I just want to know what's going on. I, I,"

"That's ok now, dear," Dad chimed in. "Let's not all argue here. We all understand the situation now let's move on."

"Thanks, Dad. Sorry, Mom. So anyhow, things are great here. I'm having so much fun and I have great friends here. I wish you could be here and see everything and meet everyone. How are things at home?"

"Same old, same old," said Mom. Honestly, in a week nothing has changed. I really miss you. We really miss you, I mean. I'm thinking of going to visit Aunt Celia in Vancouver to help the time pass quicker."

"That would be cool," Rachel said, secretly glad that she didn't have to go. Except that she would like to tell her flaky aunt about reading coffee grounds. It would probably become her latest passion or something.

"Now, what's this about extending your stay?" Dad had read her blog posting.

"Oh nothing, just a thought. Leyla, the older sister of this family, she's getting engaged and I wanted to attend the ceremony. But whatever, they don't even have a date set yet, and school starts the first week of September so I'm sure it wouldn't work out. It was just something to write, you know?" Was it? Rachel would have liked to stay longer, but after just a week away, her parents were already sounding lost, even though she was the one who should have felt homesick.

"Well, honey, we'd really miss you if you stayed. Just keep sharing, we're always looking forward to news from you. I must check your blog 20 times a day to see if you've posted anything." Mom must have said the right thing, because Rachel felt a twinge of homesickness. Aylin, Leyla, Bahar Teyze, and Timur Amca were nice and fun and different, but they were almost like a fantasy world. Mom and Dad were all hers and they were real.

"Make good choices, Rachel," Dad's signoff was comfortingly repetitive. In a week where everything had been unexpected, exciting, and new, a little bit of boring was soothing.

"Good night, Mom and Dad. Thanks so much for calling."

"Good morning from Olympia, we love you, please send our greetings to your host family there," Mom said, and they hung up.

When Rachel walked back up the stairs to the rooftop terrace, she felt suddenly homesick, wishing that it were her parents and Hanna who were waiting for her.

"How are your parents? Everything ok?" asked Bahar Teyze. "You say hello from us, yes?"

"What are they saying?" asked Aylin.

"Not much," Rachel said, deciding it was an honest answer.

"I think they missing nice daughter," said Bahar Teyze.

Rachel wiped her moist eyes.

"Are you ready for night swimming then?" Aylin stood up and started gathering plates and silverware.

Rachel and Aylin walked down to the beach wearing their bathing suits under their terrycloth cover-ups, which were still slightly damp from the afternoon swim, in spite of being hung out in the sun. It had been a humid day. Some people were all dressed up for their nightly beach hangout, dressed to impress each other, perfume and makeup, cologne and hair gel. A small group, most of whom Rachel already knew, had gathered for the night swim.

One of the boys made a quick, excited announcement, which of course Rachel did not understand, and then everyone rapidly started removing their cover-ups and t-shirts and running into the water. Rachel did the same, and the water that had felt so cold after the blazing sun of the day now felt warm compared to the cooled night air.

"What did he say?" Rachel asked Elif, whom she noticed was beside her after the chaos had abated.

"He said that the last person who was in the water must remove their bathing suit. After they are in the water, of course. That was Emre talking, is it so dark you did not notice? Perhaps he thought you will be last because you don't understand." Elif said with some disapproval.

"As if. I wouldn't have done it. I get exemption because I don't understand Turkish."

"What is exemption?" asked Aylin, who had just found Rachel and Elif.

"It means like, oh how do you explain it. It means that the rule doesn't count for me. So, who was last?" The three girls turned to look towards the beach, where the last one in was surely closer to the beach than them. Emre stood on the beach, smiling and slowly untying the string on his bathing suit. Then he ran into the water, splashing as much as possible and making the girls squeal.

"Do you guys always do this kind of thing when you go night swimming?" Rachel asked. This was not the kind of thing she'd ever done before and that she wouldn't have expected to witness here. "I mean, wouldn't your parents be mad if they found out?"

"Why would they find out?" Asked Elif. "You won't tell them, right?"

"Who, me? Of course not. I just figured, you know, everyone here knows everything."

"We are only night swimming. Enjoy it and don't ask too many questions," Elif warned.

"Allah Allah, what is he doing, he is crazy!" squealed Aylin with a combination of pretend-shock and pleasure.

Rachel turned her head to see Emre waving his orange bathing suit above his head like a victory flag. Rachel felt her cheeks flush and was sure Aylin must be blushing, too, but she couldn't tell in the moonlight. It was almost a full moon and the moon's reflection was broken in the ripples of the water as the night swimmers flirted with each other in the relative obscurity of the darkness and distance from the shore.

"Where is Emre?" Aylin asked, and then he appeared, as if on cue, behind Aylin.

"Jay-Ay!" he said after bursting from the water.

"Aye!" she squealed. "Shame on you, I am glad you behave now and put on your bathing suit."

"Who says I'm behaving now?" he said with a naughty grin.

"Eeeeeeeeeh? What?"

Emre lifted his suit from the water and quickly pulled it under again. He knew better than to risk getting Aylin into trouble.

"Shame on you, Emre, go go go!" Aylin said, covering her eyes with her hand. "Don't do things like this, what is your problem?" This time, she seemed seriously annoyed, not just pretending as before.

"You should try it, Aylin'cim, it feels really good."

"Try what?"

"Take off your suit, come on then, the crowd is far enough out, nobody will spot you. Elif and Rachel will protect you, right?" Neither Elif nor Rachel could find an answer to Emre's question. Rachel felt that she didn't know Aylin well enough yet to know what she would want Rachel to do in this situation. Did she want to give in to Emre's temptation or not? Even if she wanted to, would she? Rachel wondered what she herself would do, if it had been her boyfriend. Probably not, she thought, but everyone said it's different when you have a boyfriend. They have a way of getting you to do things you didn't think you'd do. That's what Mom said. She couldn't imagine Dad pushing Mom to do anything at all. But Mom said things are different when you're young.

"I won't do it," Aylin said, awakening Rachel from her thoughts. "Please, put on your suit," she continued, her hand still over her eyes.

Emre fidgeted in the water. "Ok, it's on now. I didn't realize you were so dull, Aylin. I'm sure Rachel and Elif aren't such bores, are you? Which one of you will take off your bathing suit? Just for a second?"

Quick, quick, Rachel thought. Think of something smart to say.

"We've already taken them off and put them back on again. You're too late," Rachel managed.

"Yeah, sure. See you later, prudes." Emre swam off to the larger group of boys.

"Am I dull?" Aylin asked once Emre was out of earshot. "Should I have taken off my suit? I mean, I think I should not but maybe I am wrong? I should ask Leyla, the boys always like her, maybe I am too boring and he will find someone else. But he shouldn't even ask me this, he got too influenced by English girls. They ruined him. Last year, he never asked me this kind of thing."

"You are not dull, you are correct," Elif said. "He will only like you more now, just wait. If the fish jumps on the hook in the first minute, then fishing will not be fun, my father says. Then he has no excuse to sit in the boat for hours and have peace from my mother. Then he will go in the boat for five minutes and already come back with dinner. Then he must clean the fish and take off the skin and start the grill. And with his extra time he must find something else to do the rest of the day. That will be dull. The fun part is trying to get the fish."

"Oh, Elif, you are right! This is why you are my best friend! She is so smart, right Rachel?" Rachel was quickly reminded of her status: exchange student, not best friend. For a brief second, she felt sad. Why couldn't she have thought of something smart to say?

"I like your analogy, Elif. I should remember that one." Rachel decided she'd use the analogy to sound smart another time, with someone who didn't know it was a borrowed idea.

Suddenly, someone burst out of the water, and before Rachel could register what was happening, she felt herself being dunked under the water. The salty Aegean water entered her mouth and nose, and she came up coughing. She wiped her eyes and saw that Aylin had been dunked, too, but that Elif had been spared. Rachel looked into the water and saw a naked and un-tanned rear-end glowing in the moonlight, swimming away.

"It was your stupid boyfriend, Aylin. It is good that he didn't push me under, or I would ask my cousin to beat him."

"He knows I don't have any cousins to beat him up," Rachel added.

"Elif, why did you say that? He is not stupid."

Elif didn't answer, and the night swimming ended with a strange silence that nobody knew how to break.

Chapter 11

Let the lover be disgraceful, crazy, absent-minded.
Someone sober will worry about events going badly.
Let the lover be.

- Rumi

Didim, Turkey
July 23

Rachel decided to post a blog entry after breakfast.

Greetings from Didim

I've been here a week now – in some ways the week went by really quickly, but in other ways I feel like I've been here forever. So much has gone on, I don't even know where to begin. So I feel like a lot must have gone on at home. But in a week at home, not much usually changes so maybe I shouldn't expect much news from you all. Last night, we had a barbecue on the roof – the roofs are mostly flat here – and we watched the sun set. After that, we went night swimming. I wish you could all have been there. The water was warm and it the crescent moon was up. One kid took his bathing suit of in the water and teased the others and tried to make them do it, too. Don't be shocked, Mom and Dad. I didn't do it. I've decided that people are complicated. This is only just occurring to me now, for some reason. I guess I just so want to understand what everyone's thinking, and it's not always happening. Part of is the culture and part is not knowing the language, I'm sure. But I think the important thing is that these are all new people. At home, it's the same people all the time. Here, there's new people I don't know, and I haven't figured them out yet. And I care, so I'm trying to. Maybe going to college away from home would be a good thing? Because the challenge feels pretty exciting. Love you all.

When she checked her e-mail, there was a long one from Hanna and a short one from Grams.

Hey Achelray,

What's up? How's it going there? You're not really keeping in touch much. I guess you just haven't been there long. Or you're having too much fun. Or they have you locked in the kitchen with a veil on. Haha, just joking. I did some research on Turkey after you left, sounds like it's nothing like what I thought. I guess I had Saudi Arabia in mind or something. Olympia's still the same. Eric Porter and Alyssa started hanging out a lot. My mom says Eric's mom's pretty upset since Alyssa is black. Who knew what a racist Eric's mom was? Ever since that whole thing started, Alyssa doesn't want to hang out with anyone but Porter anymore so I'm pretty much alone. But there is this um, this guy at work, Andrew Ehrstrom. He is totally blonde with whitish skin and blue blue eyes, I swear he makes me look like I have a tan. Anyhow, he's helping out his dad for the summer at the doctor's office next door. His dad is an OB/GYN. Which is kind-of creepy for a man, if you ask me. I am all for gender equality, but I don't get men being OB/GYNs. Andy is pre-med. He wants to be a plastic surgeon. I wasn't sure how I felt about that because, you know, I think people should be happy with what they're born with, but he wants to work in the burn unit, which is totally respectable, you know?

What are YOU up to? Any cute guys there? I bet there are. If you don't tell me now, you WILL tell later. Have you thought any more about what you're going to major in? I know, I know, we're not even in college yet, but you have to pick out the right college according to what you want to be. Anyhow, write back and let me know what's up. I know you won't really share what's going on in your blog, but you'd better share with me.

Hanna

Yep, who needed parents telling you what to do when you had a friend like Hanna? Rachel decided to write back to Hanna before reading Grams' e-mail.

Merhaba Annahay,

First off, who the heck is this Andy guy? All you say is "there is this one thing…", so what's up with him? Does he just kind of exist next door and barely know you exist and you learned all this stuff by snooping on Facebook, or is something going on there? I need more info, girl. Your e-mail totally reminded me of something, which is that not a single person here has talked about what they want to be or what they want to study or asked me what I want to be or what I want to study. Good thing you're keeping me in line! It's kinda weird though, I should ask my host sister at least. To be totally frank, none of the guys here do anything for me. My host sister, Aylin, has a boyfriend who I think is a slime. He's cute, but I don't know, there's something I just don't like about him. And the other guys we hang out with are ok, they just don't all speak English well so you know, I haven't gotten to talk to any of them. Some are cute, some aren't, but I don't know. No sparks yet, but there are still 3 weeks to go. I figure if I don't have any juicy stories to tell, I'll just make something up when I get back. It's not like anyone would know! Aylin, my host sister, jokes that she's gonna marry me off to her cousin. I'll just tell people at home that a marriage was arranged for me. Given they know nothing about Turkey, they'll probably believe me. How's your internship going? I am so glad I didn't end up working at the coffee shop this summer. I swear, I've learned more in the week here than in like 6 months at school. I totally sound like a study-abroad brochure, but it's really true. You should definitely go for it next summer.

Achelray

Next, Rachel read the e-mail from Grams.

Dearest Rachel,

I miss you so much, you have no idea. Once upon a time, I was furious at your mother and father for being irresponsible and going off and getting pregnant too young and unmarried and before finishing college. But now that you're so far away, I realize you're one of the brightest stars in my life and I miss you and I'm so glad your parents had you. I'm not sure whether or not I should tell them so, but I'm telling you. Not that I want you to run off and do such a thing, I pray every day that you follow the Lord's way and teachings and stay pure until marriage. But I am also not stupid, and life has shown me that people don't always do what their parents and grandparents wish for them. So please be careful in that foreign land, don't fall in love there, and come back safely to tell us all about it.

No news here, just wanted to say I miss you.

Love,

Grams

Wow. Grams was never that emotional. If she got nothing else out of the trip, Rachel was glad that she had come to Turkey so Grams could miss her and realize that maybe her parents hadn't done the wrong thing after all. Maybe Grams would actually tell them and then things would finally be ok at home with her. Every time they all got together, there was so much tension.

"Let's go swimming for a long time today," Aylin suggested once they got to the beach. The water is shallow for a long way, then we can swim by the boats." There were a few dinghies and one small sailboat anchored a few hundred yards from the shore.

"Don't you wanna wait for the others?" They did everything as a group – Aylin, Elif, Rana, Ela, and Rachel. While it was possible to do things without Ela and Rana, Elif was always around.

"No, it's ok. This time I just want to swim with you. I want to tell you something I can't tell Elif."

"Oh, ah, sure." Rachel was worried that Elif would be jealous. Actually, worried was not the right word. Sure was more like it. When she got to the beach and saw Rachel and Aylin swimming together, Elif would be mad. It was like Aylin belonged to her.

Rachel and Aylin waded in the water from one shallow sand bar to the next, never getting deeper than their waists. The water was clear and turquoise, and there wasn't any seaweed to obscure the view of the soft, white rippled sand below their feet.

Since Aylin didn't seem ready to talk about whatever it was she was going to talk about, Rachel decided to open the college major topic.

"You plan to go to college, right?" Rachel asked as they walked slowly over the silky sand bar in knee-deep water.

"Of course, don't you?" Aylin answered with little enthusiasm.

"Yeah, I mean my parents both went, even though my mom didn't finish, so I'll go, too. But my best friend, Hanna, she knows what she wants to be. She wants to be a doctor. So she's spending the summer working at a doctor's office. She's only applying to colleges that have good pre-med programs. Stuff like that. I just don't know what I want to major in. Do you know?"

"I don't know. We have to take the qualification examinations next June and then I can learn what my options are."

"What do you mean?"

"We must take an exam called ÖSS, and if we get high score we can choose almost anything to study and if we get lower score, we can only study certain things. For example, with the highest scores we can study engineering, but with a lower score, we cannot study it. Don't you have these exams in America?" Rachel thought about the SATs and ACTs. But it didn't seem to work the same way here.

"We have some tests. But they're just for getting into college. Like, if you want to get into a better school, you have to have higher scores. But once you're into a school, you can study anything you want."

"Wow, that is nice. Except that then the stupid people can be engineers and doctors and lawyers, too." Rachel didn't know how to respond to that one.

"No, you have to go to grad school to be a doctor or a lawyer. And there are different exams for that. And if you're really stupid, you couldn't pass tests in college, right?"

"I guess." Aylin didn't seem interested in the subject, but for once, Rachel was. It was somehow better talking to Aylin about it because, unlike Hanna, she wasn't trying to tell Rachel what to do. Maybe that was why Aylin wanted to talk to Rachel instead of Elif. But Aylin didn't seem to want to open the topic.

"If you got the highest possible score on the tests, what would you major in?" Aylin was silent for a few seconds before she replied. The sun felt hot on Rachel's back, but they were walking into deeper waters and her shoulders would soon be submerged as they swam towards the boats.

"My parents want me to be a teacher or you know, a professor like my father. Guys here like to marry teachers, for some reason. But I want to do something more exciting. Like be a journalist or international business or something. But my parents say no to journalism. They say it's too dangerous. That if you have the wrong opinions, you get arrested. It was not always like that in Turkey, but that is true now. What do your parents want you to be?"

"Oh, my parents don't care. I mean, they do care of course, but they don't tell me what to be. They say I'll figure it out. And I know I will. But my best friend keeps pressuring me, telling me I have to figure it out now. I think I'll figure it out once I am in college already, you know?"

"You mean you can decide after you start university in America?"

"Oh, yeah, definitely. A lot of people go in with an idea of what they want, and then they change their minds their second year."

"Maybe I should go to university in America," Aylin pondered.

"Oh, that would be so cool! We should go to the same one!" Rachel said. If Aylin came to college with Rachel and Hanna, there was hope that college could be fun, after all.

"Well, Babam would never let me."

Rachel, having momentarily genuinely considered it a possibility, was disappointed.

"Then at least you should try to do something exciting. Don't be a teacher if you don't want to be," Rachel said, realizing how much like Hanna she sounded. Gotta stop that!

By now, Rachel and Aylin were swimming in cool, deep blue water. It was salty, and every time a few drops splashed into Rachel's mouth, she was shocked by the taste.

"Rachel, I want to ask you something serious."

"Go for it." Oh my God, Rachel thought, I sound like Dad. Why do I sound so much like other people today?

"What does that mean?"

"Oh, it just means go ahead and tell me. Like, I'm listening."

"I understand." Again, silence. Aylin's rapid-fire chatter of the previous week had been replaced with a string of awkward silences.

"What do you want to ask me?" Rachel said, hoping to hear the question that had been building for twenty minutes.

"You never had a boyfriend, right?"

"Right." How embarrassing. Maybe I shouldn't have admitted it. Should have made something up from the very beginning. Too late now.

"This means that you never, um, spent time alone with one."

"Well, I have guy cousins. I've spent plenty of time alone with them."

"Rachel, you are clever. You know what I want to say." *Uh, yeah. So why am I pretending not to understand? Why am I avoiding the topic, just like Dad?*

"Yeah, I guess. You mean sex, right?"

"What! No! What do you think of me!? No!" Aylin was not being specific, assuming Rachel knew what she meant. But Rachel's guess was obviously not right.

"Sorry, I just, I just don't know what you're trying to say, you're not telling me, like you just want me to read your mind or something." Aylin was quiet again for a minute, but didn't look angry. She just didn't look like she knew what to say. Or maybe what to think. "What do you mean, about being alone with a guy?" Rachel said, trying to sound gentle (like Mom) and hoping to break the silence.

"I think I don't even know myself what to do alone with a guy. Even when I kiss Emre, we are hiding somewhere in the Gazino or on the beach. Or we hold hands under a towel so that nobody can see. But now his parents and brother will go to check on their rental apartment and he will stay here and he wants me to come to his parents' house alone. I told him of course I cannot come alone, so he says you must also come with me, and we will enter through the back door so neighbors do not see, and then you can watch a movie and we can be alone. But he doesn't tell me what we will do and I am afraid. I don't know what I want to do or not to do."

Rachel decided to listen quietly rather than say anything, mostly because she didn't know what to say.

"He told me that if I do not come, it shows him that I do not love him. Is this true?" Oh, no. A question Rachel would have to answer.

"I don't know, Aylin, I really don't. I mean, it sounds like the kind of thing a guy would say just to get you into bed. But maybe it is true. I mean, you've been with him like a year, right? Maybe after a while it's just something you do. Why are you asking me? Why don't you ask Leyla, she should know."

"I cannot ask Leyla, not this time. I don't know why, but I cannot tell her."

Rachel thought about what to say. Silence is ok, right? It takes time to come up with a good answer.

"What are you afraid of?" That's what psychologists do, Hanna had said. Instead of telling you anything, they keep asking questions until you answer your own questions.

"I'm afraid that I will make a mistake. I am afraid that he will make me do something I do not want to do."

"Like what?"

"Like sex."

"Do you love him?"

"I think so."

"Do you trust him?"

"Maybe."

"Do you want to go to his house and be alone with him or not?"

"Will you come?"

"Of course I will," Rachel said, feeling like a conspirator to a crime. "I'm going to sound totally like my dad now, but I'll say it anyway. Everything you do will be your choice. Make good decisions."

The girls swam towards the rope marking the boundary of the swimmers-only area. The water was completely calm; not a single wave or ripple broke its mirror surface.

"I think it is very annoying when my parents always tell me what to do and what to not do. But now, I think sometimes I just want someone to tell me what I should do."

* * *

Back at the house, Rachel posted a new blog entry:

College Majors

I learned something new today, which is that you don't really get to choose what you major in here. You have to take a national exam, and if you do well then you can pretty much choose anything, but if you don't do well then you have more limited choices. So like if you get the top score, you can become an engineer or something like that. If you get a bad score, you can study Sociology or something, which doesn't seem fair to me. On the one hand, it kinda limits your options, helps you find something you might be good at. On the other hand, if you suck at tests, you don't have many choices. I wonder what the system would tell me I could study. So nobody here talks about what they want to major in. Weird, huh? I guess it's just all different in different places.

"You have a Facebook account, don't you?" Aylin asked out of the blue, as Rachel posted her blog entry.

"Yeah, I do, but I don't look at it much. I only have like 5 friends on it, and I already know what they're up to, so you know, it's useless."

"Well, in Turkey it is very popular. Let's send a friend request to Cem so you can meet him."

Suddenly, Rachel felt very warm and queasy.

"I thought you were joking, Aylin. C'mon, he's like hours away, right? Why should I meet him online?"

"You are lucky you can meet him at all! Our great-grandmothers did not have this option!" Aylin said, laughing. "This will not hurt you, I promise. It is possible that you can meet, you never know. And if you meet him online, that will be good. I already told him about you and sent him your picture so he wants to meet you."

"What!" Rachel was simultaneously embarrassed and pleased. "So, he saw my picture and liked me?"

"Why are you so surprised?" Aylin asked. "You are very pretty and natural, and that is what he likes. I know my cousin well. Log into Facebook."

Rachel did as Aylin asked. She somehow remembered the password, even though she hadn't logged in for months.

"First, you must make a friend request for me, because of course you are my friend. And then you will have six friends. And now let's put a friend request for Leyla, so you will have seven friends. And now, for Cem. Rachel watched as Aylin typed Cem's name into the search field. His first name was easy and short, but his last name? Dogakaganoglu? It was so long that she didn't even attempt to pronounce it.

"How do you pronounce that?"

"Do-ah-kan-olu. Sorry, it is a little hard to write, but not too hard to say, right? All the "g"s are silent. "

"Can I keep my last name when we get married?" Rachel asked, playing along with the game.

"I will try to negotiate that in the contract," Aylin answered, with a pretend stern look. "But I will not make any guarantee."

"Thanks for trying, anyway."

"Ok, I sent the friend request. After he accepts it, perhaps he will send you a message."

"Doesn't he have his picture on his profile? You showed him my picture, don't I get to see his?" Before this went too far, Rachel wanted to make sure that he wasn't a troll.

"Actually, he put a cartoon that he drew as his picture. Sorry."

Rachel looked at the tiny image. She recognized it. It was the double helix of DNA she had studied in Biology. She didn't know what to think of that, so she decided not to think too much about it.

Chapter 12

Within tears, find hidden laughter

Seek treasures amid ruins,

Sincere one.

- Rumi

Didim, Turkey

July 24

    Phones and alarms always seem so much louder when they are so rude as to wake you from a deep sleep. And Rachel was sleeping very deeply, perhaps as a result of the longer-than-usual swim the day before, when the phone's ring pierced the morning air. She sat up in bed, suddenly confused as to where she was (in her dream, she had been jumping through fire hoops at a circus and trying to balance on an alligator's tail). Aylin turned over, put the pillow over her head and mumbled something that Rachel didn't understand, either because of the muffling effect of the pillow or because Aylin was mumbling in Turkish. I hope it's not for me, somebody forgetting the time difference, Rachel thought to herself. She looked down the hall and saw Leyla sitting on the hallway floor, her back leaning against the wall. She wore a pink nightshirt, and was speaking in hushed tones that Rachel somehow understood. She realized Leyla must be speaking in English, maybe in hopes that her parents would have less of a chance of understanding. But the house was otherwise completely quiet, and Leyla's half of the conversation echoed down the tiled hallway straight into Rachel's ears. A glance at her watch revealed that it was 8 am, and everyone else was still asleep, or at least trying to sleep.

"Good Morning, Canim, why did you not call my cell phone?"

"Yes, that is true."

"Tell me."

"No!"

"When?"

"Can they wait maybe just one or two more months?"

"But did you ask them?"

"Babam will not be happy."

"No, I do not think he will cancel, he will just have an angry mood for some time."

"No, of course my love, I am happy, it is ok, I am just surprised."

"Yes, you told me before, but I didn't think about it."

"We must change the dates of everything. Today is 24 July, right? Oh, we have so little time."

"May everything be for the best."

"I am shocked, I think. I never expected this, not this soon."

"Ok, ok, I will think now about what to say."

"Have a good day at work."

"I send you many kisses."

Leyla looked down the hall as she hung up the phone, and noticed that Rachel was sitting up in bed. Oh, no, she knows I was listening, that is so not cool, Rachel thought, feeling her cheeks blush. But Leyla smiled a weak, not-upset smile, and motioned for Rachel to get dressed and come downstairs. Looking over at Aylin, who didn't show any signs of waking, Rachel slowly and quietly slipped into the clothes she had worn the night before, which were piled at the end of the bed.

When she got downstairs, Leyla was in the kitchen, writing a note on a napkin.

"I told them we are going to walk to the beach, so they will not worry." She put the note on top of the chrome Turkish teakettle and motioned for Rachel to follow her. She turned the key quietly to unlock the door (the doors all locked with keys from the inside and the outside, which on the one hand felt really safe, and on the other hand you couldn't get out if someone took out the key).

It felt really early, but there were a few people walking towards the beach for a morning swim. Most of them were older people who, Rachel guessed, hadn't stayed up late dancing or talking or playing card games. Rachel decided to let Leyla speak first. Somehow, so far away from home, she realized how much like Dad she was.

When Leyla spoke, it was with a quiet, unsure voice.

"Kerem called me this morning."

Silence.

"You don't want to know what he said?"

"Yeah I do, but if you don't want to tell me that's ok, too."

"Of course I will tell you. But here, we always ask questions. If you don't ask questions then I think maybe you don't care or something." In trying not to pry, I had offended Leyla.

"Sorry, I don't mean that at all. It's just that at home, people usually don't like it if you ask too many questions." Leyla was still quiet. Better think of a question to ask.

"What did he say?" Brilliant question. Rachel really felt like she was prying, but Leyla seemed relieved to be asked.

"Kerem will move to Japan."

"What? What's wrong, why is he moving to Japan? You'll go, right?" Suddenly interested in the drama, Rachel quickly forgot her instinct to not pry.

"Godwilling. I hope my parents are not so upset that they break the promise.

132

"They can do that?"

"Yes."

"But couldn't you argue? If they don't want you going to Japan, could they really stop you from getting married?"

"No, I could of course do whatever I want. But I would not want to do that. Then they would be so upset and they would be embarrassed and people would talk about them. Our friends, our relatives. I should not disobey them. But I hope everything will be ok."

"Why is Kerem going to move?"

"It is a big honor. Kerem was invited by the Japanese government to work for two years with Japanese architectural engineers to design safer buildings. It is a special project, Kerem cannot say no. This project is so good for his career."

"Wow, Japan. That's closer to Olympia than Turkey is, though!"

Leyla laughed, her tension easing.

"Then you must visit us in Japan."

"So you think your parents will be ok?"

"Yes, I feel positive. At first, they will be shocked like me, but all will be ok. The difficult thing is that now we must be married sooner. He said that the project will start the first day of September. If we are not married before that, then we must wait six more months before he has a vacation break. And they will only pay for a tiny apartment if he is not already married. This part will make my parents upset. Today is July 24th. We have only one month and one week before we must marry. Wow."

"Maybe I can actually come to your wedding, then!"

"Every cloud has a silver lining you say in English, isn't that right?"

* * *

Breakfast was a rush of rapidly spoken Turkish, none of which Rachel understood except for the occasional Kerem and

Japonya. The conversation was animated but hushed, tense but not angry, with Leyla looking uncomfortable and nervous, and Aylin fighting back tears. Afterwards, on the way to the beach with Aylin, Rachel couldn't decide whether to follow her instinct to let Aylin talk when she was ready, or to ask questions as was apparently expected here in Turkey. Funny how what was obvious and good manners at home, was not the best choice – maybe even offensive – here. You're not in Olympia. If they expect you to ask questions, ask questions, Rachel told herself.

"Is everything ok?" Even that question would have felt ok at home. If Aylin hadn't wanted to answer, she could have gotten away with of course.

"Everything will be ok. I am sure. May everything be for the best. Kerem will start to work in Japan in September, and Leyla wants to be married before so she can go with him. She is so excited, she does not want to wait. Of course, my parents want her to wait. If she waits only seven months then they can organize a beautiful wedding and she can spend some nice time with us while she prepares to move to Japan. But Leyla says she wants to begin her life together with Kerem at the start of his trip and she will not wait until March. So my father is upset. My mother is upset. And I am upset because Leyla will go so far away."

"Maybe you can visit her in Japan." Rachel thought it was an exciting idea that might cheer up Aylin.

"This is maybe easy for you, Rachel. You have no sister, you cannot understand. For me, Japan is so far away, I cannot imagine Leyla so far away, far from her family and friends and culture. I am sad for me and also sad for her. She will be alone there. We have nobody in Japan, no friends, no family."

"You're right, I don't have a sister. I'm sure it's hard for you. Sorry, I just don't know what to say."

"It is ok. Leyla is happy so I think maybe this is the important thing, you know? I must remember that. She must love Kerem so much if she wants to go to Japan with him."

"I wonder what I would be willing to do for a guy. If I ever find one."

Aylin giggled her infectious laugh and the mood lightened.

"You will find one, and I am sure you will do crazy things for him. Maybe that is what love means. Did Cem accept your friend request on Facebook?"

"I haven't checked yet," Rachel said, at once curious and nervous.

"We can check later."

While Rachel and Aylin played volleyball in the afternoon, Leyla and her parents came up with alternate wedding plans, and called Kerem and his parents to discuss them. By the end of the day, the tension that had permeated the balcony at breakfast was mostly gone.

"What did Annem and Babam say, Leyla'cim? What will happen? Will you really go to Japan?" Leyla was helping Rachel and Aylin with their hair and makeup before dinner at Emre's parents' house. Leyla took a deep breath before answering.

"I will go to Japan. Wow, it feels funny to say that. We must of course marry before we go. So we will make the *nisan* ceremony and the wedding together. Mother really wanted to make the nisan in Izmir, but it will be too complicated, so it will be in Denizli, and Ilkay Teyze will help to organize it. The same night, we will have kına gecesi and the next day we will have the wedding."

"Sorry, I forgot what all those things mean," Rachel said, wishing she didn't have to ask for translation during such an important conversation.

"No problem. I love to translate!" Aylin had been acting nervous all day because of the dinner with Emre's family, but she temporarily returned to her normal, lively self. "Nisan is engagement ceremony."

"Wasn't there one more thing there? The night of the nisan?"

"Kına gecesi," Aylin said, looking at Leyla for translation help.

"Sorry, I do not know how to call that in English," Leyla said, shrugging her shoulders.

Rachel reached for Aylin's large Turkish-English dictionary.

"Can you write it down so I can find it?" Aylin wrote it down. K, I without a dot, N, A. Rachel looked it up, and read the entry out loud.

"Kına means henna in English. Ok, I've heard of that. I even saw it on a documentary once. It was an Indian family, they were drawing designs on the girls' hands. I didn't realize Turkish people did it too."

"We don't draw designs usually," Leyla explained. "We just put a small amount in the center of the hand and some people put it on the ends of the fingers. But on this night, only the girls get together and sing and cry."

"Cry, why do you have a party to cry right before your wedding?" It just didn't make sense to Rachel, but Leyla and Aylin burst into laughter.

"What's so funny this time?" Rachel said with a smile, no longer self-conscious about being laughed at.

"I don't know," Leyla said through her happy tears. "It's just like that. We cry here before weddings. You know, in villages girls live with their parents all their life until they get married, then they will live with their husband's family. So it is a big change. And the kına gecesi is the last night a girl will live with her family so she will cry. And of course the mother will cry because she will lose her daughter. And the sisters and cousins and aunts will cry to support her. And everyone will sing sad songs. But the wedding day should be happy and no more crying. Maybe I won't cry on my kına gecesi. I already went to university and lived away from my family."

"I will cry," said Aylin in a small voice, not laughing anymore.

* * *

Emre's mother, Derya Teyze, had prepared numerous dishes for the dinner. The entire table was covered with platters of food. Rachel didn't know whether she would like Derya Teyze and Hakan Amca. Timur Amca didn't seem to like them, and Rachel didn't like Emre, though she couldn't admit it to Aylin. But they had gone to all this trouble to invite them over, and they spoke English well, so Rachel was looking forward to a whole meal understanding the conversation. It was getting tiring to listen hard at every meal, trying to pick up a word she understood here and there and still never understanding what was being said. She couldn't expect Aylin and Leyla to translate every conversation, because that would have been tiring for them, too. So she usually sat quietly at meals, sometimes listening for familiar words and other times just zoning out and focusing on the food on her plate, the flowers in the garden, and the bees that flew between the brightly colored flowers and her food.

Derya Teyze had very short, spiky auburn hair. She had green eyes and pale skin, and Rachel thought she had probably been pretty when she was younger. Hakan Amca had graying black hair and dark brown skin and was a handsomer version of Emre. Emre's brother was staying with his Aunt in Izmir, preparing an application to study abroad.

Within the first half an hour of the evening, Rachel was thinking that maybe it wasn't all that bad to silently eat her meals. In fact, it was relaxing. Tonight, she felt like she was being interrogated. She was being interrogated. The questions were never-ending, and every time she answered, Hakan Amca and Derya Teyze acted like they already knew the answers and then went on and on about England and how superior it was to pretty much anywhere else in the world. It was just like Timur Amca had predicted.

What do you think of the US government? At what age do children drive in the United States? Do they take a gap year in the US? Do children wear uniforms to school in America? How do you drink your tea in America? Do they not teach you the REAL English accent at school in the States?

Every time Rachel answered a question, Hakan Amca or Derya Teyze would go on about how it was better in England and how maybe the US would be better if it had never gotten its independence. Dad would have said they were people who felt they had something to prove. Rachel just found them irritating. At the end of the dinner, when they were leaving, Rachel couldn't take it anymore; she had to say something.

"Have you ever been to the United States?"

"No, we haven't felt the need to go," said Derya Teyze. It felt like a stab in the back. Any remaining good feelings about Emre and his family were gone. Rachel had been hoping this evening would show her a side of Emre that she liked, but she only saw more sides that she didn't like. How could Aylin, funny, sweet, happy, smart Aylin like him? Rachel had no idea. But she was glad that Aylin's parents would have to approve of him if he ever asked to marry Aylin. And she was sure that they would never approve of him.

On the way home, Rachel thought about the strangeness of the evening. What could she have said in response to their comments? She couldn't come up with anything smart. Finally, Bahar Teyze spoke up.

"You are right, Timur Bey. They are changed after England. Like new people. Is this possible? They were our good friends. Now they think they are better than us."

"What can I say? This situation is very uncomfortable," answered Timur Amca. Aylin didn't say anything, and looked at her feet as they walked.

* * *

Later that night, Rachel, Aylin, and Leyla sat on the rooftop terrace and looked up at the sky as they talked about Leyla's upcoming engagement ceremony and wedding. Haunting, melancholic music floated in the air from the house next door. It was folk music, Aylin explained. From the house facing them came the cries of a baby who couldn't fall asleep, from the house behind theirs came German rap music, and from the streets came the barking of street dogs. Above all the sounds came the evening call to prayer over the loudspeaker, which Leyla ignored as she explained the plans that had been made that morning.

"We decided to organize our wedding for August 16th. It is a Saturday. So our kına gecesi will be on Friday the 15th. We won't have a nisan anymore. Only three weeks from now. And then we will spend a week in a hotel. Then we go to Japan on August 28th already. We cannot go later because we must move into our apartment before Kerem begins his job." Aylin didn't say anything, so Rachel felt obligated to break the silence. Well, not silence exactly, as there was plenty of sound all around. But Aylin's thoughts were somewhere else, who knew where. Was she thinking about Emre or about Leyla?

"That's exciting," Rachel said, really meaning it. "I bet you can't wait!"

"I'm scared, excited, nervous, maybe also stressed. There are so many things to do! I have to organize my dresses for the events. I think our aunt will design them and I will just go a few days before and they will make them fit me correctly. I already gave her my wedding dress ideas and measurements. I must also collect all of my things and pack them to send them to Japan so they arrive before we arrive."

"What about the place for the wedding? And the invitations? You didn't already figure that out, did you?" Rachel remembered when one of her cousins got married. They planned for eleven months and were still rushing around at the last minute, trying to get the flowers and place cards and caterer in order.

"Kerem's parents will organize that. They will already go tomorrow to look at the places and then they will explain everything to me. And they will print the invitations when they know the place where everything will be, then they will give us some and my parents will deliver them. But we will also call them because there is not a lot of time. They must also organize. Tomorrow, we will call everyone to explain that my wedding is August 16th in Denizli and later I will give more information."

"What will you do in Japan?" Aylin finally spoke up. She had been so ecstatic when Kerem had come to ask for Leyla's hand, but now she looked as if she were about to cry at any moment. Leyla paused before answering.

"I will write you e-mails."

Aylin smiled for the first time in hours, practically the first time all day.

"Oh, Leyla, I will miss you so much!" Aylin's tears finally poured out. "You will move so far from us. I never expected this. I thought I would be the one to go far away, to America."

"Life is not always as we expect," Leyla said. "Believe me, I also never thought I would move to Japan!"

"But what will you do there? You do not speak Japanese. You cannot work there, right?"

Leyla breathed in deeply before answering.

"Everything is happening so fast, I have not thought about it yet. I have too many things to do now, I cannot think about it. I will go there on August 28th with Kerem and we will arrive there and begin our new life together. I do not know how this life will be, but I will tell you everything. And you will tell me everything about your life. Promise?"

Aylin wiped her tears away with the back of her hand and nodded.

"Use a tissue, Aylin'cim. You must not act like a child!" Leyla's gentle scolding brought another smile to Aylin's lips. Rachel noticed a star flying slowly through the air.

"Is that a shooting star?" Rachel asked. "We should wish on it!" Leyla and Aylin looked in the direction that Rachel pointed and then Leyla laughed.

"It is not a star, it is a satellite! We can wish on the satellite."

"Sounds like it makes sense in the modern world," Rachel said, looking at Aylin.

"I wish that you come home soon," said Aylin, fighting back new tears.

Chapter 13

Words are a pretext.
It is the inner bond that draws one person to another, not words.
- Rumi

Didim, Turkey
July 25

Dear Achelray,

You're totally right, all the way. At first, Andy pretty much didn't know I existed. I didn't look him up on Facebook, but that would have been a good idea. I should've. Anyhow, I kinda just watched him and once I pretended to bump into him and we just chatted. So long that his dad came out looking for him. Next day, same thing except that I didn't have to pretend to bump into him. He was all I could think about. I couldn't concentrate on my work at all. It was getting on my nerves. I mean, I have to take this internship seriously. I need to concentrate. So I decided to put an end to it. I thought about what to do, and then I decided I just had to go for it, like I do with everything else. The third day, I asked him out directly. I asked him if he wanted to go to lunch with me, as in on a date. He totally turned red, I mean not blushing pink, but red. But he said yes. We go to lunch every day now and I think I might be in love, but I don't want to be in love. It would mess up all my plans. Andy is so perfect, but I was supposed to meet him later, like in med school at the earliest, maybe even during my residency. This is probably your fault for being gone! I don't know what to do, what do you think? Oh, and by the way, how are things going there? What's up with the cousin?

Signed, Annahay in love, maybe, probably

Dear Annahay probably obviously in love,

One word: OBSESSED. You're totally crazy about Andy. I just thought I'd tell you, in case you didn't realize. You're 17 years old. I'm sure he's way nice, but c'mon, do you really think this is it? The man you're gonna spend the rest of your life with? You've known him like, what, a week? Can't you just relax a little and slow down, enjoy it? No, I guess not, it's not you. Besides, who am I to give love advice? Just do what my dad always says: make good choices. I give that advice all the time now. I'm becoming my dad.

Things are good here. A little weird with my host sister, Aylin. She's moody these days. Not sure if it's about the boyfriend or about her sister. Her older sister, Leyla, is getting married on August 16th. Then she's moving to Japan a few days later to be with her husband. They only just got engaged like a few days ago. Things seem to move so fast here. Maybe that would work well for you. The fiancé, by the way, is Turkish, but he has a job in Japan. Cool, huh? Aylin doesn't think so though. Anyway, it's all complicated family stuff, just like at home, I guess. Everyone has family stuff.

I'm still not married. Haha. No word from the cousin. I'll let you know.

Signed, never in love Achelray

Rachel remembered her friendship request to Cem. Had he accepted? Rachel quickly logged into Facebook. He had accepted her request and sent her a message.

Hi Rachel, nice to meet you. How are you enjoying Turkey? Aylin says you're great. I'm glad you guys are having fun. You need to post a profile picture. I'm in Antalya for the summer. It's a city on the southern coast of Turkey, on the Mediterranean. It's really hot here, perfect for surfing. Too bad I can't surf. Oh, and there aren't any waves. What are you guys up to? Say hi to Aylin for me. Cem

Now that they were "friends" on Facebook, the program let her view his photos. 50 photos! Rachel couldn't resist. She flipped through a few of the photos. He had wavy, shoulder-length hair in some pictures, short hair in others. He had nice eyes, but you couldn't really tell much because he was pretty small in most of the pictures. He had a really handsome smile, though. Rachel felt herself starting to like him. It wasn't just the pictures – he was definitely not a troll – it was his message, too. This is silly, she thought. He was hours away, and they'd probably never meet. This was their first interaction. Why let a crush form? She decided to write back anyway. After writing and erasing at least 20 different sentences, Rachel settled on a laid-back, non-committal message.

Hello Cem, Nice to meet you, too. Turkey's great, I'm having a lot of fun, and learning a lot, too. It's really different here. Aylin and Leyla, Timur Amca and Bahar Teyze are all super. You're lucky to have such awesome relatives. Too bad you can't surf. Maybe you should get a kayak instead. Have fun in Antalya. I'll put up a profile picture later. Rachel.

That sounded casual, right? Like makeup that is supposed to look like you're not wearing makeup, the entry was supposed to look like it hadn't been a major effort. And Rachel hoped there was no indication of her developing crush as she clicked "post".

Didim, Turkey

July 26

"Yesterday, we called 300 people," Aylin said. "And today some of our uncles and aunts will come to congratulate." The previous day, Aylin had helped Leyla call their friends and relatives, and was finally in a better mood after hearing their excitement and congratulations. Rachel could not imagine having 300 people to call.

"That's nice." Rachel couldn't think of anything more interesting to say, as usual.

"You will meet some of our cousins, too," Aylin said. " They are all nice, especially Cem." Cem seemed cool, but how can you really tell from some pictures on Facebook and one short message? She hoped he wasn't anything like Emre. Rachel didn't know what to expect, and not knowing what to expect had become the norm. By now, she knew that if she didn't ask questions, nobody would think to explain anything to her, because it was all very normal to them.

"What time will they come? What will we do?"

"They will come in the afternoon, for tea. And we will also have some cakes and fruit and pastry. And then maybe the young people will all go for a walk together and the old people will talk. And you can get to know Cem!" Aylin was sounding like her bubbly self again. Rachel knew Aylin was serious about the pairing when, half an hour before they were supposed to arrive, she dragged Rachel upstairs to supervise her preparation.

"Maybe you should wear this white shirt, Rachel. Now you are very tan and so white will look super. And you can wear hmm, you can wear shorts because you have nice legs. And we will ask Leyla to put on your makeup because still you did not learn." Rachel felt nervous about meeting Cem, even though she thought the whole situation was slightly ridiculous. How would Aylin know what she was looking for in a guy, when she didn't even know herself?

"What's Cem like?" Rachel asked, hoping for a little more information, even though she knew it was hard to describe a person.

"He is natural. He is my favorite cousin. He is very smart. His heart is very clean." Rachel didn't know exactly what that meant, but she was pretty sure Aylin wasn't referring to his grooming habits, so it sounded good.

144

The table was set with plates and forks and knives and spoons and tulip tea glasses. Bahar Teyze and Leyla had prepared three different pastries and potato salad, and had ordered multiple pides from the seaside restaurant where Rachel had eaten with Aylin and Leyla. In the kitchen were a juicy watermelon and a bowl full of ripe peaches, ready for later.

"I thought they were just coming for tea!" Rachel said, not to anyone in particular, when she saw the spread. She thought of the times her aunts and uncles and cousins came over. "There's OJ in the fridge, should we order a pizza in or go out for pizza?" Mom would say. It was no big deal.

"They are only coming for tea," Aylin replied, in a celebratory mood again. "But they are coming to congratulate Leyla for her promise to Kerem and her coming wedding. They will come all together. We must offer them something to eat, right?!"

"Of course, but this is really formal, don't you think?"

"This is Turkey, Rachel. This is how we do it here. I think it must be different in America, right?" Before Rachel could explain how casual things were at home, the first three of an eventual five cars drove up and parked in front of the house. Aunts, uncles, and cousins filed out of the cars, dressed as if they were going to a chic restaurant. One cousin was way more dressed up than the others. While most of the cousins were in jeans paired with dress shirts, this one was wearing a light grey suit, a white shirt, and a grey tie. His hair was cut way too short and it made his ears stick out. And in spite of his fancy outfit, Rachel noticed that one of his shoelaces was untied. I hope that's not Cem, Rachel thought. I don't know why. I just...

Rachel had imagined the relatives coming over to hang out, congratulate Leyla and a say quick "hello, nice to meet you" to Rachel. In fact, the tea was perhaps the most formal event Rachel had ever attended. Like a meeting of foreign dignitaries or royals, Rachel imagined, even though she had obviously never been to one herself. That's just how it felt. Bahar Teyze and Timur Amca greeted everyone at the top of the stairs, and they came in one by one, kissing cheeks and exchanging greetings. When the cousins filed in, they kissed Bahar Teyze and Timur Amca on the hand, then brought the kissed hands up to their foreheads, as Rachel had seen done a few times before. The Aunts all wore jewelry and smelled of perfume, and every Uncle wore dress pants and shirts with neatly tied neckties. One wore a blazer. Next, Leyla kissed the hands of each aunt and uncle and both cheeks of each cousin. Then Aylin did the same, and introduced each one to Rachel.

"This is the sister of my mother, and her name is Hediye, so we call her Hediye Teyze. And this is her husband and his name is Ibrahim, so we call him Ibrahim Eniste. Teyzem, Enistem, this is Rachel, our exchange student."

Just as Leyla and Aylin had done, Rachel kissed each of them on the hand and then brought their hands up to her forehead. Both Pinar Teyze and Haluk Eniste laughed and said something which Rachel guessed had something to do with her, and they seemed happy, and Pinar Teyze even pinched Rachel's cheeks. Rachel went on to kiss the hands of the remaining aunts and uncles, who all gave her similar reactions.

"This is the brother of my mother, Ali, so we call him Ali Dayi. And his wife, Ayca, who we call Ayca Yenge. This is another brother of my mother, Omer Dayi and his wife, Filiz Yenge. This is a brother of my father, Haluk Amca, and his wife, Pinar Yenge. This is the husband of the sister of my father, Soner Eniste, and the sister of my father, Gulsah Hala. This is Ilkay Teyze, we told you about her before. She is the daughter of the sister of the mother of our mother. Do you remember?"

Rachel racked her brain, but it was slowed by the traffic of the calculation of what it meant to be the daughter of the sister of the mother of Bahar Teyze.

"Oh, yes, of course!" said Rachel. "Nice to meet you!" Rachel really had no idea how she was supposed to know who Ilkay Teyze was, but she decided not to make that public. Who's who appeared to be extremely important in Turkey, and she got the impression that it was really good to pretend you understood who everyone was if you couldn't actually remember. Ilkay Teyze was the last of the parent-generation to enter, and Rachel took a moment, after she had kissed her on the hand and before she moved on to kissing cousins' cheeks, to ask Aylin to remind her why she should know Ilkay Teyze.

"How can you forget?" was Aylin's whispered answer. "She is the one who introduced Leyla and Kerem!"

"Aha!" said Rachel, in a brainstorm. "Your mom's cousin! Oh, she seems really cool!"

"She is the most cool of all the relatives, but we must make all of them feel that they are the best ones and then everyone is happy."

Next, came the procession of the cousins, led by Cem. By the time Aylin had introduced him and Rachel had shaken his clammy hand (which Rachel thought might have also been slightly trembling), it was too late to go back. She already liked him. She wasn't sure why she hadn't wanted to like him. Maybe because she had to tell Mom and Dad and open up a whole new conversation that she'd never had before and didn't know how to have. Or forget about knowing what to say to Mom and Dad – they were Mom and Dad. What about knowing what to say to Cem? She didn't even know what you were supposed to say to guys you liked at home, how could she know what to say to a guy she liked in Turkey? Why hadn't she asked Aylin earlier? She just hadn't seen this coming. How on Earth could she have been expected to know that she could see some guy and ten seconds later be asking herself all these questions that were rending her speechless?

"Merhaba. Oldum Memnun. Nice to meet you." The words were etched in her brain from the Teach Yourself Turkish book and from saying them about two hundred times in the previous ten days. Cem smiled a huge smile, almost laughed, and then said with a slightly shaky voice.

"Hi, nice to meet you." Great, he spoke perfect English. No excuses now not to like him. His eyes were dark brown and were framed by long, dark eyelashes, the kind girls would kill to have. He looked into her eyes and bit his lip. He looked like he wanted to say something else, but he didn't.

Aylin would tell her later that she had messed up the second and third words she said to Cem. She had said them correctly hundreds of times, but in her nervousness, she had reversed them. Kinda like saying meet to nice you instead of nice to meet you.

There were, of course, other cousins to meet, too. They were all warm and friendly, kissing Rachel on the cheeks as if they were old friends. They all spoke English and wanted to practice speaking with her. She could not, of course, remember any of their names because, for one thing, they were foreign names she'd never heard before and they were hard to remember. But that was just an excuse really – she was too busy thinking about Cem to even retain a single name as Aylin introduced them.

"This is the daughter of the brother of my father, and this is the daughter of the sister of my mother, and this is the daughter of the sister of my mother, and this..." Aylin was wasting her explanations on Rachel, whose knees were feeling weak and whose ears heard only the hum of many voices speaking a beautiful foreign language. Rachel tried not to be obvious about watching Cem as he moved about the room, chatting with his fellow cousins, laughing, and every once in a while looking back at Rachel. They were more than glances. Their eyes locked until Rachel couldn't take it anymore and looked down, sure she was blushing and hoping that it would be less obvious because of her tan.

The "tea" must have been the longest tea in the universe. Each of the aunts brought something sweet – syrupy cakes, meringues, cookies, and chocolates.

"They want Leyla's married life to be sweet," explained Aylin. "So they are bringing sweet things to her."

Rachel was sure she had never eaten so much in her life, indulging in the pide and then following up with dessert after dessert. Even though she politely refused more dessert, nobody paid any attention to her, and her plate was filled with second helpings.

"In Turkey, you always have to refuse. No doesn't mean no," said a male voice from behind her. It was Cem. Rachel felt her cheeks heat up. And her toes, and just about everywhere in between. How could someone she had only just met have such an effect on her? What was Cem referring to, anyway?

"Excuse me?"

"Food," Cem clarified. "You always have to refuse food. It's rude to accept the first time. It's like a dance. They ask, you refuse, they ask, you refuse. If you refuse two times, you still receive the food. If you refuse three times, they might accept your refusal, or perhaps they'll give you less food than they had planned. It's a battle of wills. If you really don't want to eat, you have to keep refusing until they leave you alone. Or, you have to accept the food after a while, and just don't eat it."

"Wow. I've probably seemed really rude up to this point. I always said yes the first time when I was hungry," Rachel said, trying to remember if anyone had seemed offended.

"Don't worry," Cem said. "You are foreign, everybody knows you can't know all the rules yet."

"So is it just food, or is it with everything?"

Cem looked thoughtful before answering.

"Come to think of it, it's with other things, too. I guess we Turkish people don't like to accept no for an answer. We want to convince the other person every time."

"Hmm, that's interesting." Rachel said. "By the way, your English is perfect. How come you speak so well? Did you live abroad?"

"I go to MIT."

"What does MIT stand for?"

Cem smiled before answering.

"Millî Istihbarat Teskilâtı. It means National Intelligence Organization. It is like your CIA."

"Oh my God," Rachel couldn't stop the words coming out of her mouth. Cem was a spy. She was falling for a Turkish spy. There has got to be something illegal about being in a relationship with a foreign spy, she thought. This could not be happening, finally she finds a guy to like and he's a spy.

"I'm only joking," Cem said.

Rachel wondered how long she had been standing there with her mouth open.

"Huh? I don't get it, why did you say that?" Rachel wasn't feeling nervous anymore. Just irritated that Cem had made her feel like an idiot.

"I go to the Massachusetts Institute of Technology, you know, MIT? Haven't you heard of it? It's a really famous college in the US. Come on, I couldn't help myself – you asked what MIT was, how could you not know?"

"Oh, yeah, duh," Rachel felt her red cheeks coming back, but this time it was embarassement, not nervousness.

"I'm sorry, it was a cheap shot."

"No problem, I asked for it, I guess. Is MIT really the Turkish CIA?"

"Yes, it's pretty fun to tell people in Turkey that I'm "working" at MIT. And it's not a lie; I have a lab job at school."

"I bet. Are you too old for me? I mean, um, sorry, what year are you?" Rachel was trying to calculate whether or not Cem was too old for her by asking how long he'd been there, but she accidentally thought out loud.

Cem gave her a huge smile, and this time she thought she noticed him blushing, too.

"You're really direct, huh?" he said after a chuckle.

"Uh yeah, that was a total accident, I just completely embarassed myself, can I hide behind the sofa now?"

"I'm 20. I'm gonna be a Junior. I've been there for two years."

Rachel didn't know what to say next. She was still embarassed, and she also didn't want to get into the what's-your-major conversation, since she still didn't know what she wanted to study, and knew it would come up. She was saved by a prayer.

One of the uncles announced something, then everyone came together and looked down as the uncle said a prayer out loud. Rachel took the opportunity to say her own prayer.

Dear God, I don't ask you for help often, so maybe you'll consider that this is really important. Of course, I pray for the health and happiness of my friends and family and I pray that Leyla and Kerem are really happy. But can you also do something about Cem and me? I just have this feeling, you know? Of course you know, you're God. You probably planned this whole thing, made the Mexico exchange full so that I could come to Turkey and meet Cem. And thank you for not making him a spy. Amen.

After the prayer, the aunts and uncles and cousins started the long process of leaving. Kissing of hands and cheeks, preparing of plates of food for everyone to take home, everyone refusing to take the plates home, a few times, before eventually giving in, then more kissing of cheeks and have a safe trip and pass along my regards to so-and-so. Half an hour later, everyone had left. Everyone except Ibrahim Eniste, Hediye Teyze, and Cem.

After they helped clear away the dishes from the table, Aylin whisked Rachel upstairs and shot a barrage of whispered questions at her.

"Well? What do you think? Do you like him? What were you guys talking about? I think he maybe likes you. This is so great. You see, you can marry him and then we can become family, right?"

"Whoa, I just met him, Aylin!" Rachel said, not revealing what she was really thinking, which was, if we get married, I'll be the wife of Aylin's cousin. But Aylin will call me the wife of the son of the sister of her mother. Or something like that.

"Oh, no. How is it possible for you to not like him? He is so perfect!"

"Aylin, I do like him, but you know, we, I, um, I don't know what to say. I don't want to jump into this too fast. And I mean, I'm only here for like 2 more weeks, right? I'll be heartbroken if I do like him and then I never see him again, right?"

Rachel was trying to be practical, but she was hurting Aylin's feelings.

"What do you mean you will never see him again? You must believe in fate. You must believe or you will always be alone."

"Is he a Pisces?"

"What? I don't know that word."

"You know, the horoscope. It's the fish, you know, February and March, I think."

"Ah, *balik*. Yes, his birthday is February 29ᵗʰ."

"Leap day! That is so funny. I definitely don't know anyone else with that birthday!"

"We used to tease him about it and he would get really upset. How did you guess that? Or maybe you saw it on his Facebook page?"

"No, I just, it's weird. I'm Pisces. My birthday is March 17ᵗʰ. And I don't believe in astrology at all, but I have this Aunt in Vancouver, Canada. Anyway, that's beside the point. But she always tells me I'll marry a Pisces. And then when Leyla read my coffee grounds, she saw two fish looking at each other. I didn't say anything then, but I didn't forget it."

"It's meant to be!" Aylin said with bubbly excitement.

"Maybe," Rachel agreed, warming up to the insane idea. For once, she wished Aunt Celia could read her Tarot Cards. Right now. "By the way, why is he still here? Did you organize this, Matchmaker?"

"No, I don't have to be Matchmaker right now. God is being the matchmaker for you, I think. Their summer house is in Antalya, and that is like 6 or 7 hours from here, so it is too far for them to stay only for tea. They will stay here for two nights."

Since the tea had been more like food with tea on the side than tea with a little food, nobody had any interest in dinner. Aylin suggested to her parents that she, Leyla, Rachel, and Cem go to Altinkum to get ice cream. None of the adults mentioned that there was ice cream in the freezer, because they all knew that it was just an excuse for the young people to get away and hang out.

"What is Altinkum?" Rachel asked, wishing that she didn't have to ask so many questions all the time.

"It is the town. We are staying in a summer village, but this is not a real town. Altinkum is a town with restaurants and discos and bars and shops. It used to be a tiny village, and now it is an ugly town with tall apartments. Leyla and my mother went to the hair salon there, do you remember?"

"Oh." After spending so much time in the village, Rachel had almost forgotten that there were actual towns here.

"What should I wear?" The usual question.

"Whatever you want. But look nice, don't forget that Cem is coming."

"Yeah right, like I'm gonna forget that," Rachel replied. Her skin was tingling and her cheeks felt warm.

Rachel chose a purple sundress, even though the sun had already set, because she had heard (from Hanna, of course) that guys liked sundresses. She brought along a cotton sweater because she was sure somebody would ask her about it if she didn't.

When the girls went outside, Cem was already waiting by his parents' car. He had changed into jeans and an MIT shirt.

"Nice shirt," Rachel commented. "Don't you think people here will be a little freaked out by it?"

"I hope so," Cem said. His eyes sparkled, and he didn't take them off of Rachel, who wondered when she should look away. Would Cem think she didn't like him if she looked away? Was there some sort of rule in Turkey about looking away? Was there a rule in the US? She'd have to ask Hanna. And Aylin. Rachel smiled and finally looked down at her feet because she couldn't take it anymore.

Chapter 14

At night, I open the window and ask the moon to come

And press its face against mine.

Breathe into me.

Close the language-door and open the love-window.

The moon won't use the door, only the window.

- Rumi

Rachel, Aylin, Leyla, and Cem sat down at a restaurant next to the waterfront boardwalk. Most of the people walking by on the crowded walkway spoke in heavy British accents that sounded more foreign to Rachel than the Turkish she was now accustomed to hearing. The summer village where they were staying had seemed busy and noisy compared to Olympia. People of all ages went for strolls all evening and into the night, arm in arm, hand in hand. Teenagers gathered on the benches and ate sunflower seeds as they gossiped and teased each other. Women (grandmothers and mothers alike) pushed babies in strollers while older children wove their bicycles between pedestrians; street cats and kittens competed for crumbs thrown from terraces, and whenever there was a moment of silence, a dog barked to fill it. The tiny village pulsed with non-stop energy, but in spite of the fact that it could have been chaotic, it wasn't. The residents of the summer village flowed through the cobblestone streets like streams that knew their way.

Altinkum made the village seem quiet in comparison. There were some Turkish families, but mostly British tourists. It felt frantic as groups of people stopped in front of restaurants and bars, trying to decide where to go, interrupting the crowd. Everyone bumped into everyone else. Sleazy-looking men stood outside of the bars, trying to attract the attention of the older women tourists, who were dressed in mini-mini-skirts and heels, low-cut tank tops revealing their sun burnt and wrinkled "tan" lines and heavy makeup adorning their red faces. It wasn't as Rachel had imagined it, and she wished they had instead gone to the local pide restaurant. She felt uncomfortable and out of place, but as they made their way through the crowd, Cem put his hand lightly on her shoulder, and Rachel felt... safe. Once they were sitting down at the restaurant, the conversation with Cem quickly and easily made Rachel forget about the new surroundings.

"What's your motto?" he asked out of the blue once they had sat down. Nobody answered.

"Whom are you asking?" Leyla said, keeping the conversation alive.

"All of you."

"What do you mean?" Aylin said. "What does that mean, motto? Now that you study in America, your English is better than ours, but do not embarrass us!"

"You have nothing to be embarrassed about," Rachel said, assuring both Leyla and Aylin. "If I could speak any language as well as you speak English..." Rachel couldn't finish the thought because she didn't know what would be different, but she did wish she'd been able to study Turkish before coming to Turkey. "Anyway, even I don't understand what Cem's asking."

Cem smiled and looked into Rachel's eyes again.

"I'm not trying to embarrass anyone. But this is my new thing. I think that everybody should have a motto and live by that motto. It helps make decisions easier when you do, really." Cem then looked at both of his cousins, who were looking frustrated.

"Cem, I am glad you have a motto. I do not know what a motto is, but congratulations to you." Aylin said, looking genuinely annoyed. "But I will not have one because I do not know what a "motto" means."

Rachel thought about how to answer the question, feeling responsible since it was her language that they were all trying to communicate in.

"A motto is like a slogan, a saying. Companies have them. Like, um, let me think… Nike, you know Nike shoes?"

"Yes," Aylin said.

"Their slogan is Just Do It. Have you heard that before?"

"Yes, I have, I know what you mean. But people don't have slogans, do they? This is a silly idea. What is your slogan, Cem?"

"My motto is Why?"

Silence. What was that supposed to mean? Rachel thought.

"So you mean like you will just do anything because life is short, why not, something like that?" Rachel was starting to wonder if maybe Cem were a little reckless, with a motto like that.

"No, mine is much more thoughtful," Cem answered intensely, as he put his arms on the table and leaned in closer to Aylin and Rachel on the other side. "I think so many people do things without thinking about them, just because that is what is expected of them. They don't take risks because they don't think about how those risks might be good for them, and they sometimes take risks that are too big because they don't think enough about it. I think that when we make decisions, we need to really think about why we make those decisions."

"You've thought about this a lot," Rachel said.

"America made me do it," he replied.

"What?" Rachel felt defensive, having lived in the US all her life and having never been asked to come up with a motto for herself.

"When I applied for a scholarship this year, I had to write an essay about what my motto was, and why. So I thought a lot. America is such a different culture for us, I had to suddenly think about why we do things a certain way in Turkey and how I should make myself comfortable in America without forgetting who I am.

When you are in a new culture, you have to make so many more decisions. Because when you are in your own culture, you just already know how things work. You know? So I really decided to live by my motto."

"What do you mean more decisions, Cem? Are you saying we don't have decisions to make in Turkey?" Aylin asked defensively.

"No, of course we have lots of decisions to make, but many times, our answers are automatic. We already know what we want on our pide and which clothes are the appropriate clothes here. In America, for example, they ask you paper or plastic at the grocery store. So I have to think about what kind of bag I want, but here we just have plastic. Or salad sauce. In the US, they give you so many choices, like 10 choices or something and you know how it is here, there is only one possible salad sauce. Going into a new culture forces you to think about everything."

"I don't know," Leyla said, finally entering the conversation. "But I guess I will need to learn something from you, dear Cem, since very soon I will be living in Japan."

"Maybe you're joking, but it's true, I might be able to help you," Cem said sincerely.

"I was not joking, you are right. I don't know what my life will be in only one month."

Rachel thought about her motto. She didn't have one. Dad's motto would probably be "make good choices." Hanna's motto would be "plan, plan, plan."

"Let's not talk about it," Aylin said. "I don't want to think about you being gone in only one month." After this comment, silence reigned. Rachel was almost too busy thinking about her own motto to notice that Cem was looking at her. Aylin was playing with her necklace and looking at Leyla, while Leyla watched the crowd walking by.

"How's your Emre doing, Aylin'cim?" Cem asked, perhaps hoping to get Aylin's mind off of her sister's imminent departure. But he hadn't picked a wise subject. Aylin shot him daggers with her eyes, and this time it was Rachel who tried to change the subject.

"So, what are you studying at MIT?"

"Biological Engineering," Cem answered, seemingly excited to explain.

"That sounds pretty cool," Rachel said after a pause, when neither Aylin nor Leyla spoke up. "What exactly is that?"

"Well, the simplest way to explain it is that we fool with nature. We manipulate the genetic material of plants and animals to create better versions of them."

"It really sounds like you try to be God," Leyla said, laughing.

"If God didn't want me to use my brain, he wouldn't have given me one," he said with a smile, and sipped his beer.

Rachel had ordered a Sprite. When the waiter had come around to take their orders, she had thought quickly what the appropriate thing might be. At home, there wouldn't have been a choice between an alcoholic drink and a non-alcoholic drink. But here, nobody seemed to be carding. Everyone was just expected to do what was appropriate. Rachel decided that she didn't want a beer. Her parents had let her try them at home, and she hadn't liked them. Maybe Cem would think she was childish. Then again, did she want to impress a guy by drinking? She wasn't sure.

"We learned a little about that in Biology," Rachel said, hoping that he might be impressed by what was in her head, not what was in her glass. "Like you create corn plants that don't get bugs and stuff, right?" Aylin and Leyla both looked at Rachel with what Rachel thought was approval. The corners of Cem's mouth turned up in an almost smile."

"Exactly!" he exclaimed. "That's exactly the kind of thing I want to work on. I have an assistantship in a lab where they're working on creating fungus-resistant banana trees."

Wow, Rachel thought. While I'm in high school trying to keep my grades up so I can go to college to study who knows what, texting Hanna during study hall, and wondering if I'll ever meet a cool guy, Cem is saving bananas from fungus. How did I ever think he would like me? He is so in another world.

"That makes me feel kinda boring. My life consists of going to high school and working at a coffee shop; you're a superhero to banana trees." Everyone laughed, but Rachel had been serious.

"Don't feel bad," Cem said, looking concerned. "I'm only an undergrad, so I don't get to do cool stuff. All I really do is enter findings into the computer and label Petri dishes."

"Aha!" Aylin said, poking Cem in the side. "You talk like you are such an important man in the laboratory and really you are a secretary!"

Cem didn't appear offended. He grinned widely and said something that made Rachel blush.

"I am trying to impress Rachel, and you are an obstacle! Why don't you go and find something useful to do while I tell Rachel about my exciting work labeling Petri dishes."

Everyone laughed, including Rachel, who was glad they had sat in a dark part of the restaurant because she was sure she was as red as the British tourists sitting at the next table. She had no idea what to say. Cem wasn't hiding at all that he liked her, but she couldn't help but try to hide that she liked him. Fortunately, Leyla seemed to understand Rachel's embarrassment, and she started up a new conversation.

"Why were you wearing a suit at tea, Cem dear? And why is your hair so short?"

"About my hair, it was a communication problem. I think. The barber did what he wanted and not what I asked him. My hair was quite long, and I did want it to be shorter because I only cut my hair one time every year, but this was extreme."

"And the suit?"

"Why?" Cem's motto was coming in handy.

"I can offer an answer to why not, which is that it was very hot, and you are young and nobody expects you to wear a suit to a summer tea at your aunt's house. That is why not! You tell ME why?! You are a strange man!"

Cem was up for the challenge.

"Did I look nice?"

"Sure you did, but you also looked a little weird. You stood out."

"Maybe I wanted to stand out. You all noticed my clothes, right? Did you notice anyone else's clothes?"

"No, that's true, but why do you want to stand out?"

"There are some times when a person does not want to stand out, but there are other times when a person does want to stand out," he said, effectively ending the conversation because everyone seemed to know what he meant, but the flirtation had gone far enough, and even Cem realized it. He took another sip of beer and then looked down at the menu. When he looked up again, he looked directly at Rachel, with a sweet smile. Rachel smiled back, unaware of whether or not Aylin and Leyla had noticed.

* * *

It was at least one in the morning before everyone went to bed, including the adults. They were sitting on the veranda laughing and playing cards when Aylin, Leyla, Rachel, and Cem got home. Rachel crawled under the covers, exhausted but unable to sleep. Even when she closed her eyes, all she could see was a replay of the day's events. After a few minutes of silence, she learned that Aylin couldn't sleep, either, when she whispered loudly from her bed.

"He really likes you, Rachel, I can understand it from his smiling at you. He is not like that with every girl, you know."

"Really? I mean, you never know, right. I kept thinking maybe he did like me, but then I kept doubting myself. He is so cool, Aylin, just like you said... I mean, why would he like me? I feel really boring and plain compared to him."

"I don't know why you say that, Rachel. You are so nice to be around. You are very pretty. You make other people feel good. You like adventure. And you make other people feel confident."

"Nobody's ever said that to me before, Aylin, wow, that's so nice. It's weird, though. I'm not even self-confident, but I make other people feel confident. How can that be?"

"I don't know, dear, but you do. And if you marry Cem, then we will be relatives, which is so exciting, right? And you can be a Turkish bride and we can have a henna night for you and Leyla can come back from Japan to attend your wedding!"

Rachel was excited too, but she did feel as though Aylin was getting slightly carried away.

"Maybe you should wait until we get engaged before you plan our wedding," Rachel said jokingly. Aylin didn't seem to find any humor in the situation.

"If you are not serious about Cem, then do not make any games with him. He is a very important person for me and I don't want you to hurt him."

"Aylin, I have no plans to hurt him. And he may like me, but be realistic, we only get a few days together and then it's back to being really far away again. I wish I didn't even like him because this is not even rational."

"I know the word rational," Aylin said, no longer in a whisper. "And tell me, when is love rational? When you love somebody, you find a way."

Rachel knew better than to let Aylin doubt her intentions, because her intentions were... she didn't have any intentions. She didn't know where this was going, but she didn't want to hurt anyone, especially Aylin.

"Start planning my henna night, then Aylin. I would be really glad if we could be related," she said, and meant it. And both Aylin and Rachel had sweet dreams.

* * *

Rachel's mother was not as happy as she had expected her to be, when she told her parents she had a boyfriend.

"But you're in another country! What if you marry him!? He'll make you wear a veil!"

"No, he won't."

"But he lives so far away!"

"Well, if you don't like him, you should think that's a good thing!"

"Does he speak English?"

"Of course he does, how else could I talk to him?"

"Don't let him make you sleep with him, Rachel. Sometimes, guys can be pushy, but don't give in."

"Mom, if you hadn't slept with Dad, I wouldn't have been here, right?"

"Don't you dare bring Dad into this. We were in a long-term relationship and we were in love."

"How do you know I'm not in love?"

"How could you be in love, you're only seventeen?"

"Anyway, Mom, it's too late. I already slept with him."

As she was talking on the phone, Cem came up behind Rachel and put his arms around her waist. He kissed her on the neck, sending shivers to her sweating palms.

"What are they saying?" he whispered into the ear that didn't have the phone held up to it.

"Make good choices," Rachel's dad said, after a long silence. "Make good choices. Make good choices."

Rachel gasped. She was drenched in sweat. She opened her eyes. It had been a dream. Or had it? Rachel touched her stomach with one hand and her neck with the other. Had Cem touched her? Had she slept with him? She looked around the room. Aylin was asleep in the next bed. She remembered the day, the evening, and her chat with Aylin. Rachel couldn't decide if it had been a nightmare or a dream.

Chapter 15

Out beyond ideas of wrongdoing and rightdoing, there is a field.
I will meet you there.

- Rumi

Didim, Turkey

July 27

Rachel said very little at breakfast. She listened to the Turkish conversation, trying to understand, paying special attention to every word Cem said. She understood a little more than nothing. Just a word here and there, not even enough to know the subject of conversation. She had told everyone not to translate everything on her behalf all the time, because she felt awkward having everyone go out of their way for her. Cem wasn't staring at her as much as he had the night before, in Altinkum. Did he change his mind about me? Rachel was sure he had, and she felt like crying. What had she done wrong?

After breakfast, they all got into their bathing suits and cover-ups, and met on the terrace before walking to the beach together. Rachel didn't look at Cem, and avoided walking next to him. But once they were out of view of the house, he bumped into her, the warm, bare skin of his arm touching hers. Rachel automatically looked up at him and apologized.

"Sorry," she said in embarrassment.

"You don't have to apologize," Cem said, with his characteristic smile and sparkling eyes. "I bumped into you on purpose. What's wrong, Rachel? You seem distant."

"Sorry," Rachel said. "How am I supposed to be acting? I mean…"

"Stop saying you're sorry!" Cem exclaimed, bumping into her again. I wonder if he noticed that my arms have goose bumps, Rachel wondered.

"Sorry," Rachel said, completely by accident, and then laughed, finally feeling better, and reassured that Cem still liked her.

When they got to the beach, Ela, Rana, and Elif were sitting on a towel eating simit, even though breakfast had just ended. One thing here that never seemed to stop was eating. Rachel wished she could have just sat alone with Cem with nobody around, not even Aylin. But here, she was never alone. At home, she had so much alone time, she sought out her friends in town, or went to a coffee shop to read just so she wouldn't be by herself. Here, she had no idea how anyone organized a way to be alone… or to just be with maybe one other person, for example, Cem. When they put down their towels and said their merhabas, Elif gave Rachel the same smile-with-evil-eyes that she'd been giving her recently.

"Elif, Merhaba, Ela, Rana, *ne haber*?" Cem said with his usual friendliness.

Rachel felt her heart sink. Cem knew them. Maybe he had already dated them. If he ever dated Elif, I'm not interested anymore, Rachel told herself, knowing she wouldn't lose interest in him that easily, but feeling jealous nonetheless. I bet they have dated. Cem is handsome, in his own way, and Elif is pretty, in a witchy way. And she wears a red bikini. How do they even know each other? Cem lives so far away. Maybe Aylin introduced them. I bet that's it. Oh, please, say it's not be true.

"How do you know each other?" Rachel asked, trying to keep herself in the conversation.

Elif answered. "Cem has come here every summer since we were babies, for one or two days at least. He used to stay for a few weeks, but then they bought a place where the girls aren't so pretty, so he still has to come and see the beauty here, right Cem?" It was irritating that Elif knew so much.

Cem smiled comfortably and looked straight at Rachel.

"That's right," he said. In spite of, or perhaps because of, Cem's unabashed crush on Rachel, Rachel started to doubt herself. This guy who she met yesterday, who was from another culture, whose name was hard to spell, who was cool beyond belief, and smart, and so together that even her parents would approve of him if she ever told them about him, who was getting hotter by the minute as he tanned in the hot late-morning sun, was making it completely obvious to Aylin and now to her group of friends that he liked Rachel and thought she was pretty. It was just all too easy. Rachel couldn't trust it. She was sure she liked him, but maybe he was one of those guys who flirted with all the new girls. Maybe he had a reputation as a player but Aylin had failed to mention it. She had said that he had a clean heart, but who knew what that meant.

"Who wants to go swimming?" Cem asked the group, looking around at everyone but ending his laser gaze on Rachel's face.

"Ela and I are both a little sick, we won't swim today," Rana said, looking slightly disappointed. "Sorry, Cem."

"Why not?" said Elif, flipping her long hair over one shoulder and tightening the tie on her red bikini.

"Aylin?"

"Um," Aylin looked at Rachel, but Rachel wasn't sure what her eyes were asking. She looked for a sign, but wasn't sure what she was supposed to do or say, so she shrugged her shoulders. "Sure, I will swim with you. Rachel, you must come, too."

"Ok," Rachel said. She didn't need any convincing.

The morning water was clear and cool. By the time Rachel was knee-deep, her smooth, tanning skin was covered in goose bumps. She crossed her arms over her chest to keep warm, but still visibly shivered.

"Are you cold?" Cem asked. Nothing seemed to slip by his observant eyes.

"Um, yeah, just a little," Rachel said, embarrassed.

"Of course I'm not," Elif replied at the same time. Rachel wondered whom Cem had meant the question for.

"You'll be ok once you're swimming, but you have to get in fast," Cem advised. He had already submerged himself in the icy water (surely the Pacific was significantly colder, but nobody expects me to actually enter the water there, Rachel thought). Rachel looked up at him and noticed drops of water dangling from his earlobes. "I'll help you," he offered. Before Rachel could figure out what he could possibly have meant by that, he was racing up to her, splashing so much that there was no escape. Rachel covered her face with her hands and yelped. She expected to be pushed into the water, but instead, Cem was splashing her from up close.

"Grow up, Cem!" Elif shouted, and started to swim away.

"Stop!" Rachel squealed, taking her hands away from her face and trying to figure out where Cem was in the chaos of splashing water. She had forgotten the cold temperature of the water, and just wanted to, to... she didn't know what she wanted to do. But as soon as she found Cem, she would figure it out. Cem was, in fact, hiding behind her at this point, and as fast as Rachel could turn around, Cem swished further around and remained behind her. The game of catching him was exciting, unexpected, and warming. Finally, Rachel decided to be strategic. She stopped moving, took a deep breath, and then after a few seconds, turned around as quickly as she could. She expected Cem to continue his game of hiding behind her, but he had changed strategies as well, leaving Rachel without a plan. She had thought she was going to keep chasing him until she could get a hold of his arms and dunk him in the water, but there he was, standing calmly in front of her, smiling, disarming her on her warpath.

"If we weren't standing here in full view of everyone, I'd kiss you right now," he said.

166

Who knew how long it was before Rachel realized her jaw had dropped and she was standing there with her mouth hanging open, salt water dripping into her eyes from her soaked hair. Think of something smart to say, think of something witty to say, think of ANYTHING to say went through her mind, but she had no answer for Cem. She had never imagined that this was how things could work. She had thought you went on a date, then the guy brought you home, then you kissed on your parents' front porch, blah blah blah, get caught by your father, whatever.

"Sorry, did I offend you?" Cem's expression had changed from confident to concerned.

"What?" Rachel was so busy thinking about how this was supposed to have happened to hear Cem's question.

"Did I offend you? I'm sorry, I,"

Rachel interrupted. "Oh God, no, I mean, I'm sorry, I just didn't know what to say, nobody's ever said anything like that to me before and I didn't have an answer ready, you know?"

"Well, I never said anything like that to anyone before," Cem said, suddenly seeming shy. "And I was being spontaneous, so I didn't have time to apply my motto to it. I didn't think about the why or why not part. But now I can think of a few things. Why not, well, for one, I might make Rachel feel uncomfortable and in an awkward position."

"No, it's ok, spontaneous is supposed to be good, you know? I'm just really bad at thinking on my feet. I think about everything too much."

"They say it's good to be thoughtful," Cem said, putting a positive spin on what Rachel was sure was a bad trait.

"No, in my case it's no good. I think too much about everything and in the end I can't make decisions because I can always think of just as many cons as pros. You know? My best friend is always irritated with me for not thinking about my future. The reality is that I have thought about it a lot, but I can't come up with any decisions. There are too many options. So instead, I don't make any decisions and life ends up making decisions for me."

"So, then how did you decide to come to Turkey this summer?"

Rachel had to think before she could answer Cem's question. But after what felt like a minute of thinking, she couldn't come up with a response.

"I'm not sure, it's weird. It just sorta happened, like everything else in my life, I guess. My mom didn't even want me to come. But my guidance counselor had this scholarship and I felt like I couldn't turn it down, he was so excited about it. I didn't have much time to think. Maybe that's better for me, not having too much time to think. But then in theory, it's probably better to think about stuff before you make big decisions."

"Wow," Cem said, his eyes wide open.

"Oh crap, what am I doing, psychoanalyzing myself here in the middle of the sea, scaring you away?" Rachel was sure Cem regretted his kissing comment now.

"No, it was awesome," Cem said, sounding like he meant it. "Finally, you talked about you. And actually, you sort-of make me second-guess my motto. Because you are probably a... how do I say it nicely, an example of overdoing my motto, if you are how you say you are, generally unable to make decisions. But I like to be challenged, and now I want to kiss you even more. So here's your chance to make another quick decision without thinking too much, without asking why or why not. If we were not here in the view of the entire summer village, would you kiss me back?"

The water still felt cool on Rachel's legs, but the sun was quickly evaporating the salt-saturated droplets on her back and arms, making her skin feel parched and papery. Rachel heard a word roll off of her tongue before she could think of a witty response.

"Yeah."

"You see! You just answered quickly, without thinking too much!"

"That's why my answer was so lame," Rachel said, still shocked she had answered.

"So, we've had a virtual kiss," Cem said.

How weird, Rachel thought. "This is totally not how I expected my first kiss to go," Rachel said, then wondered if she should have admitted it was her first kiss. Well, it wasn't actually a kiss. "My first kiss was a hypothetical kiss," she said, repeating the embarrassing fact.

Cem didn't laugh or say anything about Rachel having never kissed anyone before. Rachel was glad, because at home it was an awkward detail that she had often been teased about, though she had never wanted to kiss any of the loser guys at home just to drop the uncomfortable title. She figured that they would eventually find something else to tease her about. She wondered if this hypothetical I'd kiss you if we were under the right circumstances could count as being kissed.

"So, did you enjoy your hypothetical kiss?" Cem asked.

Rachel could not believe she was so comfortably having this bizarre conversation. "It was definitely, um, different than I expected, but less technically challenging. I'm still worried about the real deal and what you're supposed to do with the noses. Don't they get in the way?"

"There's nothing to worry about. We'll find a better place and take care of that soon, so your worrying doesn't last much longer. And so you can't change your mind."

"I don't know what to say," Rachel said. "Um, thanks?" Everything that is coming out of my mouth sounds foolish, but Cem doesn't seem to care. And I don't care either, I guess. Because Cem just keeps on liking me, for some reason. "Where are Elif and Aylin?" Rachel had forgotten that her quasi-sister and her moody friend had entered the water with them.

"They're right over there, swimming, pretending not to watch us," Cem said, waving towards them. Aylin waved back while Elif's sulking was even obvious from a distance.

Rachel and Cem swam towards Aylin and Elif. When they were all together again, Aylin looked concerned.

169

"Did you argue or something? You were standing for a long time talking after Cem made Rachel wet. Cem was only joking, to make you go in the water faster, Rachel."

"Oh, no, everything's fine," Rachel said, wondering when would be the right time to tell Aylin about the virtual kiss. If Cem weren't Aylin's cousin, the answer would have been as soon as I'm alone with Aylin, but since they were cousins, Rachel felt strange about telling Aylin, even though she was the one who had approved the match in the first place. Aylin didn't say any more on the topic, but Rachel knew she would be asking questions later.

"I was wondering," Cem began, changing the subject, what does your last name mean? I mean, I never met any Americans with the last name Guo."

"I think I'll go back to the beach now and get some sun," Elif interjected.

"See you," Aylin said with a nervous crackle in her voice.

"Your name?" Cem reminded Rachel of his question.

She knew the answer thanks to the family tree project she had done in fourth grade. "My father is Chinese," Rachel explained.

"Yes, Aylin told me that already on e-mail."

"She did?" Rachel replied, wondering what else Aylin had told him.

"Yes, I think she told me everything she learned about you."

"Hmm," Rachel said, hoping that was a good sign. Both that Aylin had wanted to tell him everything and that he knew everything and still liked her.

"What did she say about me?" Cem asked.

"Not that much, actually," Rachel said, wishing Aylin had been more forthcoming. She felt like a movie star or something – everyone knew her but she didn't know them. "She told me that you have a clean heart and that you're her favorite cousin."

"Isn't that enough? I'll tell you the rest," Cem said, winking at Aylin.

Rachel worried that Aylin would get bored of the constant flirting with Cem, so she got back to the question of her last name.

"So anyway, my dad's ancestors are from an ethnic group in China called Daur. They live in Inner Mongolia."

"You could be Turkish!" Aylin exclaimed. "The original Turkish people came from Mongolia!"

"Really?" Rachel felt instantly more connected to this country, to this town, to Aylin - to Cem. "I'm pretty sure I'm not, though. The Daur people still live in China."

"Well, maybe, somewhere really far back, we're related," Aylin said, hopefully and warmly.

"Let's just say we are," Cem said. "What else do you know about the Daur people?"

"Not that much," admitted Rachel, wishing she knew more. "My dad's ancestors moved to Beijing hundreds of years ago. My grandfather doesn't even speak Daur. He speaks Mandarin. And he's obsessed with it. Every time we're together, he tries to teach me new words in Mandarin and how to do Chinese calligraphy. When I was little, it used to annoy me, but last year I started to think it was interesting, so I've learned a few words."

"But you don't know about Daur people?" Cem asked.

"Well, I started doing a research project once for an assignment at school, but I couldn't find that much information and I did it on something else. But I found out that Daur people invented field hockey."

"What is field hockey?" Aylin asked.

"It's like ice hockey, but on grass," Rachel said, wondering if Aylin knew what ice hockey was.

"Maybe I sound stupid, but I don't know ice hockey," Aylin said.

"Yes you do, don't you remember, Aylin'cim? We saw it on the Winter Olympic games together?" Cem to the rescue again.

"Oh, yes, I remember. Hm, we don't play this in Turkey."

"Anyway, the only other thing I know is that the original religion of the Daurs is Shamanism."

"Ah! I know that! You are Turkish!" Aylin said with excitement, but Rachel was entirely confused.

"I'm sorry, could you explain that?" Rachel asked.

"The original Turkish people also were shamans. You see! Our ancestors come from the same place and both were shamans, so they must also be Turkish! But they did not migrate to Anatolia, they stayed in central Asia."

Rachel thought about it. It could be true. Maybe her ancestors were Turkish. After all, she did feel comfortable here. It was flattering that Aylin wanted her to be Turkish, but it was a little far-fetched. Rachel decided not to reject Aylin's suggestion.

"At the very least, our ancestors came from the same place," Rachel said. "By the way, what does your last name mean, Cem? I can't even pronounce it. Sorry." I must feel really comfortable with him if I'm admitting I can't pronounce his last name.

"I'm sure you could pronounce it, but the spelling confuses people who aren't Turkish because you don't have the silent "g". Do you remember when you saw my name, it had a "g" with an accent over it?"

"To be honest, no. I just remember that your name was really long."

To Rachel's pleasure, Cem laughed.

"I like your honesty," he said, and splashed her. Rachel had almost forgotten that they were swimming. She was no longer cold, and she didn't even feel tired. "My name is pronounced Doh-oo-kan-olu."

"Doh-oo-kan-olu. That is still pretty long. What does it mean?"

"It means the son of the eastern king."

"Wow. That is pretty awesome. It's like something from a movie. Was your ancestor a king?"

"My grandfather was a king, so I am a prince. Don't tell anyone." Cem looked serious. Rachel couldn't tell if he was teasing her or not. Either way, she didn't know what to say, so she looked back and forth from Aylin to Cem, neither of which said anything.

"And we of course have the same grandfather, so I am a princess," Aylin added.

"Doesn't anyone know?" Rachel asked, beginning to believe them.

"Just you," Cem said.

"Why is it a secret?"

Aylin started to laugh. Then Cem dunked her in the water. When she came up, she giggled uncontrollably and motioned for them to swim to shallower water. Cem began to laugh, too, and Rachel felt humiliated. This time, it didn't feel funny. She wanted to cry, and felt tears building up in her eyes before she could stop them. She swam freestyle with her head in the water, hoping that they wouldn't see her tears. Why am I so upset? They were just joking. She wondered. But she knew. She had felt like they had ganged up on her. She was the outsider and was being made fun of for her faith in them. Hanna had also pointed out how gullible she was, but this was the first time it had hurt so badly. It must be because I like Cem so much. I feel embarrassed that he made a fool of me. She had swum so far that her knees were hitting the soft sand of the sand bar. She stood up and opened her eyes, the salt water stinging them as she looked around for her friends.

"You ok?" said Cem's voice right behind her.

"You guys just made a fool of me," Rachel said, and to her horror, she broke down into tears. He'll never kiss me for real now, she thought. But to her surprise, four arms, Cem's and Aylin's, wrapped around her.

"Sorry, Rachel, we were only joking, of course you are not a fool," Aylin said in a soft, worried voice.

"I'm sorry," Rachel said, crying harder. "I feel so lame, I don't know why I was so sensitive this time, I just, I don't know, I mean, I guess I just feel like I don't know stuff and you, you just picked on me or something. But it's stupid, you didn't do it in a mean way, I don't know, I should just stop talking."

"It's my fault," Cem said finally. "It was my stupid joke. Listen, I'll tell you the real reason I have this name and then you will understand this joke a little. Before the time of Ataturk, the creator of the Turkish Republic, Muslims in Turkey did not have family last names. Christians and Jews did, but not Muslims. In 1934, Ataturk said that everyone must register a last name. Our grandfather's father was a very popular, social person who was important in the high society of Denizli. He was liked by everyone, and everyone called him Dogu Kagan, which means Eastern King, as a nickname. We don't know why, but everyone always called him this, even family. He died in 1932. So, in 1934, when our grandfather had to register a family name, he wanted to relate this to his father. So he took Dogu Kagan and added "oglu" which means son. So, our name is now Dogukaganoglu."

"That's a totally interesting story," Rachel said, her tears now dry and the salty streaks they would have left on her face were camouflaged by the salt layer left on her skin by the water of the Aegean sea.

"Should we go back and relax on the beach?" Aylin asked, exaggerating fatigue by panting. "I swam longer than you two, I am tired now."

"Sure. Sorry about the crying, I don't know what got into me," Rachel said, with a deep breath.

"What crying? I don't know what you're talking about," Cem said. "Let's go and get some ice cream from the Gazino."

Chapter 16

The heart has its own language.
The heart knows a hundred thousand ways to speak.

- Rumi

At the summer village, there was one thing that everyone seemed to do, and which nobody seemed to do back in Olympia: nap. Rachel's parents certainly didn't nap. When could they? They both worked full-time, and weekends were the only time for them to go shopping, do their hobbies (bowling, hiking, oyster digging for the whole family, antique car restoration for Dad, knitting, gardening, kayaking, and beading for Mom), and go to the movies. When they did go on their Pacific coast beach week every summer, it was only a week, so they barely slept at all day or night, to take advantage of the vacation.

"It's weird," Rachel reflected out loud. "I've been here almost two weeks, and I haven't gone shopping once, or bowling or hiking or to the movies, and I just noticed it. At home, we fill every weekend with all these activities, and here you don't do any of that stuff. Don't your parents have any hobbies, you know, in their free time?"

Aylin was lying in her bed, trying to take a nap, but she answered anyway.

"This is the summer," Aylin said without opening her eyes. "In the summer, our life is so different. It is just eat, sleep, cook, swim, play games, and then eat some more. Do not think that this is our life in the rest of the year."

"So, what are your parents' hobbies?"

"My father's favorite hobby is watching football – you say soccer in America – on TV, and he also writes songs. Actually, they are poems, but he thinks that he will get a famous singer to make a song from his poems one day so he says they are songs. They are beautiful."

"What about your mom?"

"She designs clothes for her friends."

"What, really?! Why didn't you ever mention that before? I mean, she dresses so well, but I didn't know she was a designer!"

"Well, she does not work for a fashion house or something, but she wanted to when she was younger. So she designed clothes and then she chose the fabric and she brought them to a dressmaker to make for her because she didn't want to make them herself. And her friends liked those dresses, so they asked her to design dresses for them, too. So she always is drawing pictures of dresses and other clothes for her friends and they choose the fabrics together and go to the dressmaker. I saw that she is designing a wedding dress for Leyla, but she did not mention it yet."

"That's awesome," Rachel had no idea that her host parents were so talented, having only seen them cook, eat, and relax since she had arrived. "So, is it a business? Does she charge her friends?"

"No, but I think she should. But she says it is fun and it is no cost to her, so she does not want to charge her friends. She is happy, they are happy, so it is good. I want her to design a dress for me, to wear to Leyla's henna night and wedding."

Unable to sleep, Rachel decided to go downstairs and check her e-mail.

Dear "never in love" Achelray,

You are so SLOW! Give me some news, already! Great that the sister's getting married, but what about the cousin and YOU! I don't want to be the only one with news here. And yeah, I DO have news, but I'm not telling you until YOU give me some news. Ok, that's a lie because I just can't wait to tell you. Andy told me he loves me. And I told him I love him, too. And yeah, it hasn't been that long, you're right, it's not much time at all, but yeah, I know I'm in love and yeah, I think I could spend the rest of my life with him. This was totally not my plan, but right now I'm thinking maybe the plan was a little too rigid. I mean, if I happen to meet THE ONE at seventeen, then fine, right? After all, your parents did, right? And you're also right about the make good choices thing, but how do I know what the right choices are? I mean, right now maybe the right choice is to not date the man of my dreams because it could ruin my dreams, but then what? I also want love in my life. I hope I don't have to choose between the two! Well, right now, we are planning on me going into the same pre-med program as him. And we'll apply to the same medical schools and hope that the med school placement lottery treats us well. I wonder if they'll place us together if we're already married before we apply? Hmm, I'll have to find out. So, sorry, just blabbing here, but anyhow, I totally miss you but I'm glad you're not here because I would probably be ignoring you if you were, and then you'd get irritated with me, so this is working out well. You see, this is predestined. You were sent to Turkey so I could find the love of my life. Thank you Rachel, thank you God.

So, any news on the cousin or are you gonna bore me to death with news about the sister's wedding and national exams?

Signed, totally and completely head-over-heels Hanna.

p.s. – how does Dr. Hanna Ehrstrom sound to you?

Scrolling down to the message Hanna had replied to, Rachel cringed at what she had written just a few days before. "C'mon, do you really think this is it? The man you're gonna spend the rest of your life with? You've known him like, what, a week?" She had so much to tell, but didn't know where to start. If she hadn't had anything to say, this would have been an easy e-mail. Easier to just talk about Hanna first.

Dear Dr. Annahay Stromehray,

Your potential future last name makes an excellent Pig-Latin alter-ego name. Definitely score on that one. I'm really glad you like Andy so much. Maybe you're getting ahead of yourself a little you know, planning the rest of your lives together already, but maybe not. Maybe that's what love is. Look at my parents. Who says it has to be this huge struggle that lasts until you're 30 and desperate, right? My parents knew, maybe you know. Sorry, I was a little cynical in my last message. I don't know what that was about. Maybe I was jealous or something...

So anyhow, things here are great. It's sunny and hot every day. I'm getting totally used to the food, but I do miss some things from home. I miss the coffee from Batdorf and Bronson. I miss the Japanese restaurant on Harrison, I miss hanging out at the marina. And hiking. But you know, lots is going on here so I don't have a lot of time to think about it, and my trip here is already half over. So hard to believe. I mean, I've only been here a couple of weeks, and in some ways it feels like I've been here a really long time. Like, I have all these new friends who I feel like have known me a long time and I've known them a long time. But on the other hand, the time has passed really quickly. It's weird. You'll see what I mean when you go to Finland next year. Oh crap, what are you going to do now that you have a boyfriend? Will you still go next year? Maybe your parents would let you take him! Yeah, right.

So anyhow, you asked about Cem, "the cousin". Yeah, so he's, um, AMAZING. Perfect, anyone?! There is not a single word that exists to describe him, he is so awesome. Every time I'm with him, I feel nervous, but in a good way, and I sometimes get in embarrassing situations and he always says the right thing. And if you believe the magazines we read, guys are experts at saying the wrong thing, so I don't know which planet he comes from but anyway, I feel so good when I am with him. He goes to MIT (yep, the one in the US) so I guess we're at least in the same country most of the time. But he's staying like 7 hours away from here or something, so we only get a few days together. Oh my God, now that I said that I feel like crying, it sucks so bad, he got here yesterday afternoon and he leaves tomorrow evening. So, ya see now why I apologized for doubting your love of someone you'd known a week? I have known him like 24 hours and I am going crazy, all I can think about is him, and I'm already thinking now how we can make this work, because I can't imagine my life without him. Already. I must sound so pathetic. And we haven't even kissed, but he wants to. I know, it sounds so fifth grade or something, but it's kinda sexy, adds to the excitement. I can't believe I just said that. But I'm not going to erase this because I need to send it now before something happens to the connection and I lose this email.

The only reason I'm spending time on the internet while Cem is here is that he is currently sleeping (and I doubt anyone would approve of me going to sleep with him).

Love, eating her words, Achelray

p.s. – please DO NOT mention anything to my parents – I don't want to tell them yet. I'm afraid they'll freak out and think I'm not coming home or something.

Rachel clicked send before re-reading her e-mail, afraid she'd be too embarrassed to send it. Now, the harder e-mails. Mom and Dad, and Grams. Mom and Dad had written an e-mail together which was pretty long, but contained very little information other than the weather, what they had eaten for dinner, and that they missed her even more than they expected to and that they couldn't wait for her to come home. She felt guilty about not missing them at all. Sure, she looked forward to seeing them again, but she didn't think she missed them as much as they missed her. What should she tell them? Once she had started writing to Hanna, it just all started coming out. But the words didn't flow in the e-mails to Mom and Dad and Grams. She decided to send one message to all of them.

Dear Mom, Dad, and Grams,

Thanks for your messages. Things here are going great. I'm having a good time and learning new things every day. The people here are mostly really friendly and warm, and I feel like I've made friends faster here than at home. I'm used to the food now, but I still miss all of your cooking. I haven't had Chinese food at all here, so Dad, maybe you can plan on making me some when I come back.

They had an afternoon tea yesterday to celebrate Leyla (the older daughter)'s engagement. A bunch of aunts and uncles and cousins came over. They prepared tons of things and it was really formal, totally different from the pizza/popcorn parties and potlucks at home. Not better or worse, just different. I'm thinking about that a lot here, that nothing's better or worse here for the most part, just pretty different from the way we do things. Thankfully, everyone tries to explain it all to me so I'm not totally lost. One interesting thing is that they have special names for every aunt and uncle depending on which side of the family they're on. Dad, didn't grandpa say there was something like that in Mandarin? Now I sorta remember, but at the time he told me, I thought it was dumb so I ignored him. Oops. I should ask him about that next time he visits. Anyhow, it was really fun, we all got a little dressed up and there were really nice things to eat, and we were so stuffed that we didn't eat dinner. The "tea" foods were dinner. Maybe we can do that when I come home, you know, invite everyone over and get everyone to dress up and make lots of cool things we don't usually bother making, you know? Think anyone would go for it?

So, I was wondering, not for me, but because a friend here brought it up, how long does it take to fall in love? You know, some people believe in love at first sight and other people say it takes years. Who am I supposed to believe? I was just wondering what your perspective was, since I've never asked before but I think it's important to know. Don't you think?

Well, I gotta get going. Everyone's napping now, but they'll be up soon and then we'll probably go to the beach again or something, who knows. Life is tough here, let me tell you. Oh, and thank you for letting me come here. I think I forgot to say that before. It's been a great experience. Actually, it's been amazing, and I still have two weeks to go.

Love,

Rachel

"*Merhaba, kizim,*" came Bahar Teyze's voice from behind Rachel as she clicked "send". With all the wedding planning, Rachel hadn't chatted with her for what felt like a long time.

"*Merhaba,* Bahar Teyze," Rachel said, turning around and smiling, glad to have company in the sleeping house.

"You drink coffee with me?"

"*Lütfen,*" Rachel replied, proud that she could respond in Turkish, even if all she said was please.

"Come and I... I show you, good?" Bahar Teyze headed toward the kitchen, and Rachel followed her. Once they got there, Bahar Teyze took out a tiny little pot and two tiny coffee cups. By now, Rachel recognized the little cups, which would have been called espresso cups at home, but of course here were not. Funny how something can have a different name, even though it's the same thing, because it's used for something different. "This called *fincan,*" she said, picking up a cup and showing Rachel, as if she hadn't seen one nearly every meal for two weeks. Bahar Teyze was correct, however, in that Rachel hadn't known what it was called. "This is called *cezve,*" she said, pointing to the little pot, which didn't look big enough to hold enough coffee to fill two espresso cups. But Bahar Teyze was experienced in this matter. She filled one of the cups with water and poured it into the little pot. She then did it again, and all the water fit into the pot, with a little room to spare at the top.

"Now, we make this middle sugar. Ok? You can make no sugar or much sugar, but we make middle sugar. Many peoples like middle sugar, ok?" Bahar Teyze didn't wait for Rachel's answer before dropping in two small cubes of sugar, which quickly began to melt at the bottom of the tiny copper pot. "Two cup, two sugar. Ok? Now, two small spoon coffee. Special coffee. Very small, very small coffee like powder. You see?" Bahar Teyze took a heaping teaspoon of the coffee, which looked exactly like the powdered cocoa Grams used to make flourless chocolate cake. It looked very much different from the coffee grounds she had sold the previous summer. Even finer than the espresso grounds. "You put two sa-poon like this in *cezve*."

"We call that a heaping spoonful. I understand."

"Heap sapoonful. Good, you understand. Now, put sapoon in and mix this."

"Your English is really good, Bahar Teyze. How do you know so much English?"

"I study English of course in University, but I never use, I forget. Now sometimes I watch American cooking show on Turkish television. I sometimes understand."

"That's great! I can teach you some more if you want," Rachel felt like she needed to give back to this family somehow.

"You speak English with Aylin and Leyla, enough. You busy with them, with love, no time for teach me English. No problem. I don't need."

Rachel couldn't ignore that she had said Rachel was busy with love.

"Love?" she asked before she could stop herself.

"My eyes see."

Rachel looked at Bahar Teyze, speechless at the admission that she had been so obvious.

"Now, you watch me. Maybe one day you need make Turkish coffee." Bahar Teyze had said enough to show that she knew exactly what was going on. She didn't appear to approve or disapprove, she simply winked and continued her tutorial. "Mix this coffee and water and sugar only now, not later. You must make good foam."

The rest of the instruction was mostly visual. The cezve was placed onto the smallest gas burner, which was turned on to medium heat. And then they watched and waited. At one point, Rachel looked at Bahar Teyze as if to say "what are we waiting for?", but Bahar Teyze just pointed back to the coffee.

"You stop watch then coffee boil too much then no good. Watch. Small bubbles come now. Little bit more little bit more. Ah! Little boil. Now." Bahar Teyze removed the cezve from the flame, but didn't turn off the burner. She poured a little of the thick foam in to each *fincan*, and then put the cezve back onto the flame until the coffee came to a strong boil. She divided the remaining coffee into the tiny coffee cups, and the foam floated to the top." She motioned for Rachel to drink. Rachel sipped the perfectly sweetened, hot coffee, and wondered why they didn't have this back home. I'll definitely have to introduce this to the coffee shop, she thought.

"Tomorrow, you make." Said Bahar Teyze. Not a question, but a command.

Cem and his parents insisted on taking everyone to the Pide restaurant for dinner. Bahar Teyze insisted that they were the guests and that she would make a nice home-cooked meal. Timur Amca insisted that he would treat everyone. Rachel thought about offering to take everyone out, but she had no idea how much it cost and was afraid she didn't have enough money. They probably won't accept. Maybe I should offer so they don't think I'm rude, she thought. But she was too afraid they would accept. In the end, an arrangement was made, though Rachel was unsure what it was. In any case, she was glad to go back to the restaurant where she had shared such a nice meal with Leyla and Aylin.

Rachel remembered how gusty the breeze had been there and decided not to wear a dress, to avoid potentially embarrassing wind-under-skirt situations and, of course, goose bumps. Instead, she wore jeans and a black tank top. She was in good company, as both Aylin and Leyla also wore jeans.

"You need something," Leyla said when she saw Rachel exit the bedroom. Leyla somehow managed to look glamorous even in jeans; Rachel was grateful for any advice from her. Leyla produced a turquoise and silver necklace and put it on Rachel. As she arranged it, she whispered to Rachel. "Somebody gave this to me. I won't mention his name anymore. It is a beautiful necklace, but I do not want it in my new life. It is my gift for you. I hope you will have memories of your trip to Turkey with this necklace. Now, the old memories I had with this necklace are washed away."

Rachel couldn't see the necklace well, as it was already around her neck, but she touched it with her left hand and felt the cool silver chain and smooth turquoise beads.

"I can't take it, Leyla, it's yours."

"No, Rachel. It is now yours. And it is more beautiful on you than it is in a bag in my room. Because I would never wear it again."

"Oh, thank you so much."

"Wear it happily," Leyla said with a genuine smile. "I am very happy that it is now yours. But you do not need to tell anybody where you got it. Nobody in my family saw this before, so no problem. It is our secret, ok?"

Rachel held her finger up to her lips, indicating that they were sealed, and went downstairs.

Chapter 17

I want to sing like the birds sing,

not worrying about who hears or what they think.

- Rumi

They walked together along the rocky road that led to the other side of the hill, and through the older neighborhood with winding roads lined with olive trees. The adults walked first, followed by Leyla and Aylin, who walked arm-in-arm and conspiratorially left Rachel and Cem to walk together behind them.

As usual, Rachel didn't know what to say or how to open the conversation. Not surprisingly, Cem knew.

"We've already had a virtual kiss," he said, sending hot blood rushing to Rachel's cheeks. "Now, let's virtually hold hands. On the way home, it will be dark, and there are no lights on this road, so we can really hold hands."

"Something to look forward to," Rachel replied, amazed at her ability to come up with a decent remark when it was actually needed.

"In the US, everything is so easy. My parents aren't there, none of my family is there. Everyone's separate from my family. I can do whatever I want. I could hold you and kiss you right here in the middle of the street if we were in the US."

"And here you can't?" Rachel was surprised; Cem seemed like the kind of person who pretty much did whatever he wanted wherever he was.

"I can do that here, but I won't. Here, it doesn't seem right. Maybe Bahar Teyze and Timur Amca will be upset. They will want to protect you, like you are their daughter."

Rachel felt irritation and warmth at the same time. As in, it would be nice of them to be protective of her, but she only had limited time with Cem and protection wasn't exactly what she wanted.

"So, is that what you do in the US? Whatever you want with girls?" Rachel was trying to scope out what kind of guy Cem was. There was a pause before Cem answered. Rachel hoped she hadn't offended him.

"Rachel, I am a guy. I look at girls. I like girls. I kissed some girls in high school. I admit it. And I did try to kiss a girl in the US. I was obsessed with her all year. She is from Turkey, too. She reminded me of home. I was homesick. But she slapped me."

"Seriously? Is that what Turkish girls do when you try to kiss them?"

"Haha, don't make generalizations. No, she had a serious boyfriend and I didn't know it. She never mentioned him, it wasn't my fault. I later learned that the reason she didn't mention him was that she was really afraid that her parents would somehow find out, so it was a complete secret. I had been flirting with her for months and I thought she was flirting back, but I guess she was just being friendly or something."

"Just so you know, I'm not just being friendly." I can't believe I just said that, Rachel thought. It was as though Cem had a spell on her, enticing her to say all these things that betrayed her usual reserve. She couldn't look at Cem, having made herself feel shy.

Then she felt his warm skin graze her bare arm.

"That wasn't an accident," he said. "I'm not just being friendly, either."

"Ok, so this is all really romantic, but I'm totally going to have to ruin it now," Rachel said, unable to stop herself even though her brain was flashing neon STOP signs at her.

"How?"

"I just have to ask you, why do you like me? I mean, I'm just having a hard time believing this is happening to me. Nobody I like ever likes me back. And you're this handsome, smart, funny, nice guy and you seem to like me. And we met each other like, what, a day ago? So how is this possible?"

"I'll answer your question with a question. Why do you like me? You've admitted that you do, but you've only known me the same time I've known you. And thanks for thinking I'm handsome, smart, funny, and nice, but, you know, not everybody thinks that. I don't have good luck with girls. Actually, I must say I have bad luck with girls." He actually sounded irritated.

"I'm sorry, I'm so sorry," Rachel began.

"Don't be, I don't know how this happened, either. I am shocked, too. But please don't think I am a bad guy or I am flirting with every girl or anything like that. You want to know why I like you? You are sweet. You like adventure. You challenge me. And, by the way, you are beautiful."

"Can't you just kiss me quickly now? Nobody's looking!" Unbelievable things are spilling out of my mouth.

"No."

Unexpected answer. Ok, I've finally scared him off.

"No, because I don't want our first kiss to be like that."

"That's romantic, I think."

"Thanks. And by the way, why do you like me?"

"Exactly the same reasons you like me. I also like that you almost always make me feel comfortable. And you make me say things that I usually only think."

Rachel looked at Cem. His ears stuck out and the sunset behind him made them glow. As he walked, he kicked up dust from the road. Then, he looked at Rachel, smiled, kissed the air in her direction, and kept on looking until Rachel smiled and looked down at the stones on the road.

Throughout dinner, Rachel had a hard time following or participating in any conversation, but nobody seemed to mind, or to notice. The few times that Aylin translated for Rachel, it was some story about the past, and no matter how good Rachel's Turkish was, she wasn't going to be able to reminisce with this family she hadn't grown up with. Cem managed a few stolen glances, but as Rachel now understood, he was being discreet. The promised hand-holding on the way back didn't pan out, either, as Timur Amca monopolized Cem, asking him about his studies. Rachel walked back with Aylin instead.

"I think Cem likes you," Aylin told her, almost in a whisper.

"Um, yeah, I know, I mean, I think so, too," Rachel responded to Aylin's statement of the obvious.

"So, do you like him?"

Rachel, who had thought that her infatuation with Aylin's cousin was completely obvious, couldn't keep her obsession from her friend-sister anymore.

"Aylin, I've never, ever felt like this about anyone before. Ever. Like never. I feel so, I don't know, light or something, like I kinda have a headache but not really, and I just don't know what to do or say and I'm so sad that he's leaving tomorrow."

Aylin went silent. They had been walking arm-in-arm, as girls often seemed to do in Turkey. Aylin removed her arm from Rachel's.

"What's wrong?" Rachel asked, taken aback by Aylin's reaction.

"I don't know, it is just weird, I feel strange that you like my cousin and I know you like him. Please do not break his heart. He has always bad luck with girls."

"Aylin, don't worry, I have no plans to break his heart. I can't even think about it. All I can think about is how I can see him again after tomorrow. Thinking I should apply for colleges close to him or something. I mean, this is crazy, I've known him for a couple of days and I'm thinking this stuff. I'm scaring myself." Instead of being speechless, Rachel's feelings for Cem were giving her the confidence to say what she really thought.

"Please promise you won't hurt him," Aylin's worry was genuine.

"I promise." Rachel's intentions were, too.

Once back at the house, the adults decided to drink coffee and play cards. Cem suggested night swimming for the cousins. It was another hot evening, more humid than usual, and night swimming was the perfect antidote to the heat.

The currents that day had kept the water warm, and nobody got in slowly. Aylin, Leyla, Cem, and Rachel weren't the only ones who had chosen the activity tonight, and Aylin was quickly swept away by Emre.

"I'm just going to swim around a little," said Leyla knowingly. She winked at Rachel, or was it at Cem, and then swam through the still water, towards a group of women her age.

Rachel, feeling bolder than ever, thought about encouraging Cem to keep his promise of a kiss, but she was wise enough to know that she would only ruin the moment if she did. Plus, she was nervous. What if she couldn't kiss? And maybe this wasn't the right place, anyway. Maybe too many people were around. They were standing on the soft sand, but the water reached the top of Rachel's shoulders. She felt Cem's hand reach around the small of her back. She looked around to see if anyone was watching them.

"Don't worry, nobody can see this," Cem said, apparently reading her thoughts.

She wondered what else he was going to do that nobody could see. Please, please don't do anything that I'm not ready for, Rachel thought. Wait, what am I not ready for? I'm 17. Cem likes me, he really likes me. I'm probably the least experienced 17-year-old girl in the world with guys. But that doesn't mean I'm not ready, right? Ready for what? Ok, stop thinking, Rachel, just enjoy... Before she could think any more, Rachel felt Cem's other hand hold hers. The water hadn't seemed cold at first, but Rachel wasn't moving much, and she was starting to feel a chill, followed by a heat wave and shivers. Cem's hand was warm.

"You're leaving tomorrow, Cem. What's gonna happen then?"

"I don't know."

"Starting something with me totally doesn't match your motto. I can think of more why not's than why's." Why am I saying this? Why can't I just enjoy it? I always just let everything happen to me, why am I suddenly interrupting a beautiful moment?

"I think I'll have to forget about my motto, at least related to you. Sometimes, you just like someone because they make you feel really good. You make me smile, Rachel. Really smile, from the inside."

"Even when I say stupid things and ruin the mood?"

"Moods are for movies. You challenge me, even my motto. You keep my feet on the sand. Auf! A fish just bit me!" Suddenly, the confident, increasingly handsome Cem was jumping and splashing around, arms flailing, looking in the water for the fish that had bitten him.

"Stop moving!" said Rachel, herself unable to stop frantically turning around, looking into the moonlit water for the fish that dared to bite her darling Cem. "How can we see the fish if you're jumping around like crazy?"

Cem and Rachel then both slowed their movements enough for the water to become still again. It would be impossible to see a fish in the darkness, Rachel thought, but then a white flash the size of her pinky finger darted up and nipped her in the stomach.

"Ouch! It bit me, too!" Rachel said, laughing. "It was so tiny, though! We're being attacked by a sardine!"

And then, at a moment when she was thinking about nothing but the assault of the piranha-sardine, she felt Cem's lips pressed into hers. And then, they were gone. Her lips tingled where they had touched her. There was Cem, looking at her,

smiling, his lips clearly not on hers anymore.   And that was it.
They had kissed.   Over as soon as it had begun.   Nice, but...
already over. Rachel was thoroughly speechless.

"I didn't expect that to happen just now," Cem said,
looking a little surprised, himself.   "But I'm glad it happened
finally."

Words came back to Rachel.

"You're talking like it's not in your control or something."

"You're talking like it's in my control! I feel like somebody
pushed me into you, but," Cem looked behind him, one direction
and then

the other, and came back to face Rachel, "Nope, nobody
else is here."

Chapter 18

What you seek is seeking you.

- Rumi

Didim, Turkey

July 28

When Rachel woke up, she still felt Cem's lips on hers. She had woken up numerous times at night, wondering if it had all been a dream. But in the morning, she felt sure that it had really happened. And then her heart dropped when she remembered that Cem would be returning to Antalya that evening.

"What do you miss about home?" Cem asked her at breakfast, in English, in front of everyone, who patiently waited for Rachel's response. But home was simply not on Rachel's mind at that moment.

"Um," Rachel began. She couldn't think of anything. "I'm sure I miss something, but I'm having a lot of fun right now, I'm not thinking about missing home," Rachel said. Everyone looked pleased with her response and smiled, but Cem didn't relent.

"There must be something," he said, winking at her. She hoped nobody had seen his wink. But they probably hadn't – all eyes were on her.

"Well, ok. I miss... I miss... I miss my mom and dad. I wish they could be here to meet you all. And the trees, I guess I miss the green trees. Olympia has really tall fir trees everywhere."

"Like Black Sea region," said Bahar Teyze. "We have these beautiful trees also in the north part of Turkey," she said with a smile. "Very beautiful. You come again, and we go together to Black Sea part of Turkey, ok?"

"Ok," Rachel said. "And you can all come to Olympia to visit, too," she offered. Especially Cem, she thought.

This is torture, thought Rachel. For the first time in seventeen years, I really, really like a guy and he likes me back. He's going to be here for a few more hours, and then who knows if I'll ever see him again. And I can't even get any alone time with him. I want the whole world to know. But I also want it to be our secret. If we were in Olympia, we could go for a walk in Tumwater Falls Park and hold hands and talk about anything and everything until he had to go. And maybe we could try that kiss again.

But Rachel wasn't the only one who wanted time with Cem; everybody did. Aylin asked if he'd come and talk to her on the rooftop terrace, probably about Emre. Leyla made him coffee and offered to read his coffee grounds in exchange for advice on living far away from home. Timur Amca had questions about academia in the US. And Bahar Teyze even snatched him away for a little while. They went to the grocery store together and were gone for an hour, but only came back with a few things. Rachel was irritated.

Not knowing what else to do, Rachel sat down on the swing-bench on the front terrace and brooded. I pretty much have no right to be annoyed that Cem's family wants to spend time with him, but I am anyway. She was so busy in thought that she barely noticed the children playing soccer with a beach ball in the street, the family in the facing house drinking tea while playing backgammon, or Leyla's phone conversation with her soon-to-be husband, Kerem. What am I doing? I'm in love, well, maybe I am, I think I am, with a guy who comes from the other side of the world and goes to college on the other side of my country from me. How is this ever going to work? We're in the same house right now, and I still can't talk to him today, how on Earth is this going to work once we're thousands of miles apart? On the other hand, I really, really like him. When I see him, my heart races. Is that love? When I talk with him, he makes me feel like I'm the only person there, and I feel completely comfortable when we're together. And he's so cute. But still, how could this ever work? It's not like my parents are going to let me hop on a plane to MIT and visit him. But then again, I'll be graduating in a year and then I could go to college near him. But could this last a year after only being together for 3 days? I wish I could talk to Dad or to Grams, because they always have good advice, but maybe in this case they would just be afraid because he's from so far away and they have all these wrong ideas about Muslims. But you never know, Dad's open-minded. Grams would want him to convert. Oh my God, this sucks. Where IS he? The whole time I've been here, I've rarely had a chance to be alone, even if I wanted to be, and now I just want to spend every second with Cem and here I am sitting on a cushioned swing bench with pink bougainvillea flowers above me and a warm breeze BY MYSELF.

"What are you thinking about?" asked Cem's smooth voice, as if summoned.

Rachel looked around to see who was listening, and when she saw nobody, she told Cem the truth.

"You."

"Good things or bad things?"

"Huh?"

"You look upset or something."

"I just, I, I don't know, I haven't been able to see you all day and I," Rachel looked around again. "I wonder if this is going to work."

Rather than replying, Cem just looked sad or scared or maybe a little bit angry, or perhaps all three. Rachel had to fill the painful silence.

"I just haven't been able to see you all day. I missed you. I just wonder if I'll be able to handle the distance."

"Well, if you feel that way, maybe you're right?" It wasn't the answer Rachel had expected or wanted. She had hoped he'd try to convince her that everything would be ok.

"Cem, I really really want everything to work out, but I guess, maybe I'm afraid."

Against all social expectations and precedents of secrecy, Cem walked over to Rachel and sat next to her. He didn't hold her hand or even sit close enough to touch her, but she could hear his almost-whisper without straining.

"Do you like me enough to try? Because believe me, there are plenty of girls at school who like me, who hit on me, who make it clear that they're interested in me. But I reject them because so far, none of them was interesting enough to me at all. You break my motto. There are so many more reasons why not to. But I can't stop thinking about you. It makes me a little scared. But fear is exciting. If you want to run away, tell me now."

Is this a fight? Is this what it feels like to be in a fight with a boyfriend? Can I call him a boyfriend? What am I doing? Am I breaking up with him? What's wrong with me?

"Sorry." Of course she didn't want to run, but she didn't know how to undo what she'd suggested.

"So that's it?" Cem asked, moving further away from her on the bench. "You don't want to try?"

"Oh crap, no, that's not what I meant at all. I mean, sorry I freaked out for a second. I totally want this. I guess maybe I just wanted to make sure that you did. I'm afraid that you're gonna leave tonight and change your mind."

Cem smiled and Rachel felt the afternoon sun on her knees.

"You don't know me very well. Yet. So I forgive you. I am a person who doesn't give up. Once I decided to go to MIT, I applied and they rejected me. So I took extra classes here, and then applied the next year. And I got in."

"So basically, you want to say that you don't give up when you believe in something."

"Yeah, that's the short way of saying it." Cem chuckled.

"And you believe in us." Rachel wasn't laughing yet. She just wanted to be sure.

"Very much. Do you?"

"It feels a little crazy, but yeah, I do."

"Don't worry, I'll find a way to visit you in the US. I have holidays that are too short to come back to Turkey. Maybe, now I'll have someplace to go."

Rachel blushed, and smiled, and even her ears felt warm. She wondered what her parents would think, what they would say. They had always been so open with her, but Rachel had made it easy for them. She wondered if they'd be able to not be overprotective if their little girl had a boyfriend. Especially one who wasn't from Olympia.

Bahar Teyze came onto the terrace and motioned for Rachel to come with her. Does she know? Is she trying to get me away from her nephew? Rachel wondered. Bahar Teyze then said something in Turkish to Cem, who quietly listened. Oh, no, this is not good, Rachel thought. Cem's getting scolded for sitting alone with me or something. Then Cem turned to Rachel and spoke to her, as Bahar Teyze watched.

"My Aunt wanted me to translate something for you," Cem said calmly. How can he be calm? Rachel wondered. "Tonight is a holy night. I don't really know how to explain it because I don't think you have this in the US. But anyway, on the holy nights, we bring sweet things to our friends and neighbors, and they bring sweet things to us. We get together with our families, if they are nearby, and we have maybe a meal together, and our prayers on this night are even more important than the prayers on the other nights. Also, we don't drink alcohol on holy nights. Basically, we try to be very good on these nights."

"Shouldn't we always try to be good?" Rachel wondered out loud.

Cem laughed and translated for Bahar Teyze, who also laughed and said something in Turkish back to Cem.

"My aunt says that of course we should always try to be good, but usually it's not possible, so we just focus on the holy nights."

"I like that idea." Rachel was starting to feel comfortable, and dropped her worry that Bahar Teyze was intentionally trying to separate her from Cem.

"Bahar Teyze will make a traditional Turkish sweet now, to share with the neighbors. She wants to know if you want to help her and learn how to do it."

Whereas she would normally have loved to help and learn, now it meant time away from Cem, and she paused before answering. Bahar Teyze, perhaps noticing her hesitation, spoke again, this time in English.

"Cem, you come. You help to tell how we to make *irmik helvasi*."

Before Rachel could answer, Cem stood up and offered Rachel his hand, to help her get up off of the bench swing. As her hand touched his in front of Bahar Teyze, she felt like she was breaking some sort of rule. Her hand tingled at the excitement and wondered if it was bad luck to (almost) hold hands on a holy night.

When they entered the matchbox kitchen, Rachel was shown the large saucepan on the stove. In it was a fine, beige-colored grain.

"In the US, I found that you call it cream of wheat," Cem explained.

Bahar Teyze turned on the gas burner and added olive oil to the wheat. She also added pine nuts. She told Cem something, at which Cem laughed.

"My Aunt wants me to translate things for you, but I don't know the cooking words in English!" he said, laughing. "Only the science words!"

"I guess I better learn more Turkish, then."

"I guess so," Cem said, and seemingly intentionally bumped Rachel with his hip. "So my Aunt says you must mix this all the time, mix mix mix. It cannot burn. Mix mix mix until these things, I don't know what you call them in English because you don't use them in American food," Cem said, pointing to the pine nuts.

"Those are pine nuts," Rachel said. "My mom uses them sometimes, in a special salad she makes."

"Good, I am glad you know them. They will start to become brown in color. Then we are ready for the next step."

"How long will it take?"

Cem translated for Bahar Teyze, then came back with the answer.

"About half an hour," Cem said.

After only two minutes, Rachel's arm was burning.

"Wow, no wonder nobody seems to go to the gym here," Rachel said.

Cem translated for Bahar Teyze, who flexed her muscle for Rachel. Rachel wouldn't have minded if she and Cem had been left alone to stir the wheat, but as always, Bahar Teyze had lots to do in the kitchen. She heated water and milk in another saucepan, and added sugar to it. While that was happening, she prepared a pastry with spinach and large pieces of flat bread that looked like giant flour tortillas. She also managed to make a soup with rice, yogurt, egg, flour, and mint. It looked a little strange, but she gave Rachel a taste, after which Rachel asked her to explain again how to make it so she could make it for Mom and Dad who, she was sure, would like it.

Rachel diligently stirred the wheat, and Cem used every opportunity to touch Rachel. His hand grazed hers as he helped her stir, he bumped into her more than he needed to, and once, when Bahar Teyze had left the kitchen to get something from the refrigerator under the stairs, Cem pushed Rachel's hair out of her eyes, and pinched her cheek. Then he glanced up to make sure that nobody was looking, and kissed Rachel on the corner of her mouth. If Cem hadn't reminded her, Rachel might have forgotten to stir the wheat, and the holy night dessert would have been burnt and ruined. After half an hour, when her arm was sore and exhausted and she was sure that she couldn't stir it any longer, the pine nuts finally started turning brown.

"Look, look, Bahar Teyze," Rachel said, impatient to be relieved of her job, but disappointed that Cem wouldn't have an excuse to be close to her.

"Good!" said Bahar Teyze, who quickly turned off the gas, picked up the pot, and put it onto newspaper that she had placed on the floor. "Now, very important, I tell Cem what you must do, very important, do not burn you." She then explained to Cem, who happily translated.

"My aunt will pour the hot milk and sugar into the wheat and you must stir. They are both very hot, so they can jump on you so you must stand back and stir at the same time. Ok? Or perhaps you want to pour the milk?"

"No, I can do it," Rachel said. Maybe you can help me stir?" Rachel said, feeling bold.

"My pleasure," Cem replied.

They stirred the wheat together, which splattered as Bahar Teyze poured in the hot milk, one side of her mouth smiling slightly. I wonder if she knows and is pretending not to notice that we like each other, Rachel pondered. Once all the milk had been added and stirred in, Bahar Teyze put the cover on the pot. Rachel's arm felt like it was going to fall off, but her lip tingled where Cem had kissed her.

When the sun started to set, Leyla and Aylin put small portions of the crumbly dessert, which had absorbed all of the milk-sugar syrup, onto white plates with pink flowers, and Rachel dusted each with a sprinkling of cinnamon.

"Before we bring these to the neighbors, you should taste it," suggested Aylin.

Rachel took a bite of the odd-looking dish. She couldn't categorize it or compare it to anything she'd ever tried, but it did taste good.

"It's weird, but I like it."

"That is a strange compliment," Leyla laughed, "but I'm glad you like it."

And then the girls set off, each with a tray holding four or five plates, depending on the size of the tray. Cem didn't come, as he had been employed by Timur Amca to grill *köfte*, miniature hamburgers spiced with cumin, for dinner.

"If I drop my tray and break all the plates on the holy night, is that an extra bad thing?" Rachel wondered out loud. She was half joking, but also half serious. Neither Leyla nor Aylin seemed to notice the serious part, and they both laughed.

"No, I am sure Allah would forgive you," Aylin said. "We will say that the evil eye left. Do you remember that?"

Rachel felt relieved, and joined in the laughter. She was feeling superstitious tonight. She didn't want anything to get in the way of her and Cem. Not God and not evil eyes. Still, she decided against intentionally breaking something to release the evil eye, since she didn't want that eye to think she was trying to cheat it.

The sun was low in the sky and Rachel occasionally noticed a faint breeze, but she could still feel the warmth of the cobblestone road, which had baked in the sun all day, through the thin soles of her flip-flops. Other young people, both girls and boys, were also carefully carrying small portions of desserts on trays, prepared lovingly by their mothers, aunts, and grandmothers. They greeted people they knew as they passed them in the street, the beaches having emptied out slightly earlier than usual. Rachel recognized many faces, and wondered if she would recognize as many people at home in Olympia if she walked through her neighborhood. Maybe, but they wouldn't necessarily have said much to each other.

When they got back to the house, Cem had finished grilling the *köfte*, and the table was set. Everyone sat down to eat a meal of yogurt soup, spinach pastry, *köfte*, a salad of tomatoes, cucumbers, cheese, onions, and dill, and an assortment of ever-present sides such as homemade pickled cabbage, fresh anaheim peppers, and even whole cloves of peeled, raw garlic.

Bahar Teyze indicated where everyone should sit, and Rachel felt fortunate to be sitting next to Cem. I think Bahar Teyze might be scheming something, Rachel thought. The soup was better than Rachel had expected, but she didn't register the flavor of any of the other foods because Cem had removed his slipper and was stroking Rachel's foot with his. This must be what they call "footsie" and I can't believe I am playing it here at a table full of people. Then again, maybe that's the whole point.

"You don't like the food, Rachel?" Cem's mother, Hediye Teyze, asked. She was much different from her younger sister, Bahar Teyze. She was quiet and reserved, and perhaps even shy. She didn't speak too much when they were all together, though Rachel had seen her chatting a lot with Bahar Teyze. And though she wasn't always smiling, when she did smile it was warm and genuine. Rachel saw some of herself in Hediye Teyze.

Suddenly, Rachel looked around and realized that, while everyone was already going for seconds, her food had was mostly still waiting on her plate. What have I been doing? It's like I was in a time warp or something. This is dangerous....

Once dinner was finished, it was time to sample the holy night desserts that had been brought.

"Come, Rachel, you help me make coffee," Leyla said with a wink.

Once they were in the kitchen, Rachel protested.

"Leyla! I only made coffee once, and that was pretty much 90% your mom, 10% me. I can't make coffee!"

Leyla's eyes sparkled with mischievousness.

"I know what is happening with you and Cem, Rachel. Don't worry, I will not put salt instead of sugar. But you will carry the coffees and serve them to Cem and my aunt and uncle. This means something, you know. They will find it very charming if you serve them coffee. I already heard my aunt tell my mother that she thinks you are a very nice girl and she thinks Cem likes you. Maybe you don't know it, but this is very important."

Suddenly, Rachel felt as if the water was deeper than she thought.

"What did I get myself into?" she asked out loud.

"What do you mean?" Leyla asked, as she distributed the foam from the top of the coffee so that each cup would have some.

"I mean, I'm not ready to get married or anything! Does she think that?"

Leyla stifled a laugh.

"Of course not, Rachel! You won't return to the US married! But you can tell your parents that, it might be funny. I just mean that if she did not like you, that would be bad, maybe she would convince Cem that this is not a good idea. But she likes you, so that is all. She just will not stop it."

Rachel felt both relieved and humiliated, but the suggestion that she tell her parents that she was getting married was, well, tempting. Or would it be mean? Her parents had always offered their support and encouraged her openness and honesty, but somehow it felt hard to tell them she had a boyfriend. Well, she thought she had a boyfriend. She wasn't sure of the terminology. When do you start to call someone your boyfriend? Is it a time thing or a seriousness thing? Or do you discuss it? Rachel realized that there was a lot of stuff that she didn't know. Stuff she'd never even thought about before.

When she served the coffee, everyone acted like it was a miracle and pretended to be very impressed. Or maybe they really were impressed. Rachel didn't bother reminding them that she had worked at a coffee shop before and that this felt like no big deal to her. But when she handed Cem his coffee, his eyes pierced hers with their smile, and she almost fainted right there and then, with one last cup of coffee, her own, on the tray. That crashing cup would have sent the evil eye running, but she caught it, spilling hot coffee all over her hand and her khaki shorts and the tiled patio floor. Cem jumped up to help her, and, in doing so, spilled his own coffee.

"I guess we cannot read your futures tonight!" Leyla said with a grin, diffusing Rachel's embarrassment.

Rachel didn't know whether to laugh or to cry. And then, to her horror, she started to cry.

Chapter 19

I am your moon and your moonlight too

I am your flower garden and your water too

I have come all this way, eager for you

Without shoes or shawl

I want you to laugh

To kill all your worries

To love you

To nourish you.

- Rumi

For the first time, Cem didn't seem to care who saw them. "Come," he said, placing his hand on her back and collecting her now-empty coffee cup from her. "We can go for a walk." He kept his warm hand on her shoulder as they walked down the marble steps to the cobblestone street.

Rachel couldn't help but feel superstitious about the coffee.

"So, this is like a bad omen or something, isn't it?"

Fortunately, Cem was less serious.

"Yes, spilled coffee. It's unthinkable to be in a relationship with a girl who spills coffee," Cem laughed. "Oh, come on. We're not that superstitious, are we?"

Oh my God, he just said we're in a relationship. In a relationship. I'm in a relationship.

"If you want to be superstitious, think of it this way. Maybe the evil eye just got away,"

"That's a very convenient use of the evil eye," Rachel instantly felt better, as if the evil eye really had left her body.

"It's gotta be good for something!" Cem said, and then quickly looked behind them before whisking Rachel into the branches of a patch of fuchsia Oleander by the side of the cobblestone road not in the view of any houses. He proceeded to kiss her, really kiss her, far longer than he had managed to kiss her before. Then he stopped and looked her in the eyes.

"How come you're so beautiful?"

"Um, I don't know what to say," I never thought anyone would say something like that to me.

"That's ok, I wasn't expecting an answer," he said, and kissed her again, only stopping when the call to prayer started sounding from the mosque's minaret, as if it had caught them doing something wrong. "We'd better stop, you know, the holy night is starting and everything."

"Do you really believe it's bad to kiss your girlfriend on a holy night?" Oh my God, I just called myself his girlfriend, please don't be scared away, Cem!

"No, but I don't want to mess up, just in case. My Why? motto doesn't hold up when it comes to the mystical world of religion."

"Good idea," Rachel genuinely felt relieved. "I don't mind breaking human rules, if they don't make sense, for example. But I don't want to go breaking any supernatural ones." Things were just going too well to risk messing it all up.

"It's hard to know which ones are supernatural and which ones are human, but I also think that if I kiss you any more, your cheeks are going to be supernaturally pink and we'll have some explaining to do." Cem laughed and grazed her cheek with a light kiss.

"Let's see if we can find a way to meet up again before I leave Turkey," Cem suggested.

"Really!?" Rachel couldn't contain her surprise. She had thought it would be months, if not years, before she saw Cem again. Suddenly, she didn't feel as sad anymore. This must be love, or something, she thought, wishing someone could define it for her.

Once they got back to the house, before the sky had darkened enough to see any stars, Cem and his parents started to say their goodbyes. Cem kissed the hands of Bahar Teyze and Timur Amca, while Leyla, Aylin, and Rachel kissed the hands of Cem's parents. Then, Cem kissed his cousins once on each cheek. And finally it was Rachel's turn. The kisses were not especially strong or drawn out; that would have been too obvious. Even though everyone probably already knew what was going on, they all had to pretend that Rachel was nothing more to Cem than his dear cousins' exchange student. Rachel had learned her role in the drama.

Maybe it's better that we don't have a drawn-out goodbye, Rachel thought. Then I might cry and that would be obvious and weird and uncomfortable. It's better this way.

Bahar Teyze gave Rachel a glass of water as Cem and his parents got into their car. "You throw this on the car and they will come back," she said with a wink.

"Just the water, not the glass!" Leyla added with a giggle. Rachel did as she was told, and they honked their horn as they drove away, waving through the open windows as Rachel and her Turkish family stood in the dusty road, waving until they couldn't see the car any longer.

The rest of the evening, the house felt strangely empty and quiet. Rachel was sad. She didn't feel like crying, but didn't feel like talking either. Nobody seemed to notice, as Leyla and Aylin listed the names of the people they would prepare invitations for once the invitations arrived, Bahar Teyze read over Leyla and Aylin's list, and Timur Amca smoked a cigar.

"Is it ok if I write some e-mails?" Rachel asked anyone who would answer.

"Of course!" Leyla answered.

There were e-mails from Hanna, her parents, and Grams.

Dear Achelray,

OMG, you are so in love, or in lust, I guess I haven't learned the difference yet. I hope he kissed you already. I mean, come on, you're not 11. And I look forward to the juicy details, which I have a feeling you're not going to tell me in an e-mail. But you know, I have to be me and tell you to be responsible and think about your future and don't do anything stupid. And I know I am totally talking like a parent, but I can't help myself. You have weird parents. When you tell them you have a boyfriend, they will freak out, in a good way, and will want to know all the details because that's just how they are. At least your mom. My parents found out about me and Andy, and my mom promptly gave me a sex (read: abstinence) talk. And also bought me condoms. Mixed message, eh? As if!

I guess we're in a similar situation. Aren't you glad you went away? I was a little doubtful about you going to Turkey of all places, but if you hadn't gone, we both wouldn't have had boyfriends this summer. That would have been tragic. Seriously, I am having so much fun. Too much fun, probably, but whatever. It's not affecting my grades, and right now I'm thinking it's good for all of this to be happening right now, before med school, so I can focus once I'm there.

Since you're not handing out details, I'm not either. But if you can tear me away from Andy for an evening once you're home, we can compare notes.

Even though I'm glad you're gone, I miss you because I have nobody else to TMI with. I'm feeling like talking to your mom. Would that be ok with you?

Hannah

Next, the e-mail from Grams, which probably wouldn't say anything interesting and would be easier to answer.

Dear Rachel,

I hope this e-mail finds you well. I'm sorry I haven't written to you recently. Please don't take it personally. I hope that your trip is going superbly. Your parents have told me you're having a great time, and I am really glad about that. I miss you more than you can possibly understand, but you are having experiences most people only read about and you need to do those things when the opportunity arises.

There's something I have to tell you. I wish I could have told you in person, but I guess I was acting a little like a coward. And now, I just have to tell you, get this off my chest and I can't wait until you're home. Or maybe this is just easier to say in an e-mail when you're thousands of miles away.

I'm getting married. Your grandpa was never a bad man, but I didn't love him. We got married so quickly, because he was drafted to go to Vietnam. I don't know what I was thinking. Well, I suppose I do know. I was already 30, thought I'd never marry, thought I'd never find anyone. And on our second date, he asked me to marry him. Maybe, in some sense, I thought he wouldn't come back. Maybe he thought he wasn't coming back, either. Your mother was born when he was gone, you know that much. But when he came back, he seemed different. I'm sure the terrible killing that went on changed him. But I also didn't really know him before he left. And then your aunt was born, and he was just not interested in your mom at all. Maybe because he wasn't around for the first few years with her. He was crazy about your aunt for a while, but then he just started fading away into his own little world until he just disappeared when your mom was around 10. And once he had been gone for ten years, I was able to get our marriage ended. I know you knew your mom's side of this story, but I never felt it right for me to tell you mine. I'm not even sure why.

But now, I feel like I should tell you because you are almost an adult and I am getting married. I've been seeing this man for a year. In secret. I just told your mom yesterday. The whole experience taught me a lot about why your parents kept secrets from me. Sometimes, you're afraid of what other people will think or say, and you don't want them to make your decisions for you, you don't want to be judged. Live and learn. It took me 17 years to understand why your parents deceived me. All I could think about all those years was how I had done everything for your mother and how dare she not listen to me and how dare she keep things from me. She was wrong to keep her secret from me and I was wrong to be so judgmental of her. And I was wrong to keep my relationship a secret from you all. Now, I plan to marry him and none of you know him, so I guess I can't expect to get your approval, but I'm not asking for it, either. I'm starting over now. No more of these useless secrets. I hope you're ok with this news. In some sense, I shouldn't have told you when you're so far away, in case I upset you, but I just couldn't keep it in anymore and I guess I wanted you to hear it from me, rather than from your mom.

I look forward to hearing all your stories when you get back. I can't wait to see you and for you to meet my fiancé. His name, by the way, is Bob.

Love,

Grams

Shock was not a strong enough word to describe Grams' e-mail. It almost felt like it was written by somebody else. Grams never shared any stories, not even about mom. And what a weird time to be getting it. So, Grams only knew my grandfather for short time before they got married. And it didn't work out. Does this mean it can't work with Cem?

Dear Grams,

I don't know what to write. Congratulations? I guess I have a lot of questions. Do you love Bob? What was mom's reaction? I'm really glad that you understand mom and dad now, though. That always created so much tension in the family and I hope that'll be gone now.

So the moral of the story is that sometimes, people have reasons for doing certain things. And maybe we don't understand the reasons and maybe sometimes they're right and sometimes they're wrong, but it's good to understand the reasons at least. I'm shocked. But I'm not mad at you for not telling me. And maybe there will be times that I can't or don't want to tell you everything, but I hope you can understand that now. All I can say is that I hope you love Bob and I hope he loves you. Whatever that means. Whatever love is. Not that I know. I'm just full of wisdom, aren't I?

By the way, everyone likes the clothes you picked out for me. You can be my personal shopper when I come home :)

Love,

Rachel

Now, the e-mail she had been avoiding. Did Grams just kind-of give her permission to not tell mom and dad about Cem? She decided to read the e-mails from her parents before making the decision

First, an e-mail from dad.

Dear Rachel,

First of all, you are very welcome for being allowed to go to Turkey. It was your hard work and the scholarship that got

you there, not us. I am really glad that you're having a good time.

Mom and I decided to write you separately this time. We discussed it, and we thought it would be interesting for you to hear from us separately on the issue of love (and then we're going to share what we wrote. Is that strange of us?) My thoughts are as follows:

Love is impossible to define

Love changes with time and experience

Loving someone in the romantic sort of way is wanting to spend your life with them more than wanting to spend it with anyone else. And, yes, about attraction. And it's about wanting that person by your side when things are bad. Because anyone can be around when things are good.

I wish I had a better idea of what to say, but as you already know, I am not good with words. Also, love is not really definable and I am a person who does better with things that can be defined. Maybe that's why guys are known for taking a long time before telling a girl they love her. Since they don't know really what love means, they're afraid to say it.

With regards to your mother, all I can say is that once we got to know each other, I knew that I wanted to be with her. After the initial glow of our relationship wore off, I noticed that there were a few things that maybe I didn't like about her, but love is about accepting those things as part of the package, rather than trying to change the person. If you feel like you want that person to be something they're not, then it's not love. A few years into our relationship, we faced a pretty large challenge, which was your mom's pregnancy. It was not an expected event, and it was not easy. There were some very tense times. But we made it through that. It was a test and we passed it.

I don't know if this e-mail has been helpful to you, or to your friend. I'll leave you with a quote from Mark Twain. He is known for having a way with words, so maybe you'll like what he said:

*When you fish for love, bait with your heart, not your brain. -
Notebook, 1898*

*Perhaps you're sad that more than half of your trip is over, but
for us we're on a countdown until you're home.*

Love,

Dad

Rachel was happy about the Mark Twain quote. Maybe
Dad guessed that Rachel's question wasn't really about her friend.
He sounded like he only sort-of understood what love meant, too.
Or, perhaps, love was as confusing for dad as it was for Rachel.
What would mom have to say?

Dear Rachel,

*We're not writing as often as I thought, so I miss you even
more than I expected. I can't wait until you're home. I want to
see your pictures and hear the stories and so many things have
been going on here since you're gone, did you hear about
Grams? I'm sure you did because she told us that she wrote to
you. But it is bizarre. She is so nice to your dad now, she's like
a new lady. I bet she didn't tell you she changed her hair. After
she told us, she went out and got a new hair cut and dyed her
hair auburn, like it was when she was young, and she bought a
bunch of new clothes, she's dressing much younger, which
doesn't mean you should freak out because she used to dress like
someone way older than she is, she's not dressing like a
teenager or anything now, but it's still weird to me. It's all
good stuff, but it's still weird. Bob is a nice man, we all like
him. Actually, Aunt Celia hasn't met him yet, but you know
her, she did some kind of psychic telepathy I-don't-know-what
and got good vibes. Anyhow, she's going to come down when
Grams gets married, so you'll get to see her soon because it
sounds like the wedding will be in September or October.*

*So, you asked about love. Dad and I decided to write
separately. To tell you the honest truth, I do not believe for one*

minute that you are asking for a friend. What do you think, I was born yesterday? Was I never a teenager in love? But this completely freaks me out because you are so far away, I just do not know what to think. Is it another exchange student or is it a local? I am not going to say things like don't make the mistakes I made or whatever because like I always say, I made choices, not mistakes, and I am really happy with the way my life turned out so you know I'm not going to tell you that kind of stuff. But I still have rules, and you MUST finish high school. And obviously, it would be better for you if you finished college, too. Then you wouldn't have to have a boring job like me and go back to college in your 30s. But actually, I went to an orientation session for the nursing program last week and it was exciting and there were plenty of students in their 30s. But that's not the point. The point is, it's fine to be in love, just don't forget about your life back home.

The main thing I wanted to do was answer your question, but look at me. I'm just giving you all this advice you didn't ask for, but it's like that happens to you as soon as you give birth, you can't just let your kids live their lives. It's like a weird disease that you know you have but you can't get rid of it. Fortunately, it's not lethal.

So, honey. You've been there two weeks. Maybe you met the guy the first day you were there, but even so, I can tell you that you cannot love anyone there yet. Unless, that is, there is someone you've been seeing here for a long time that I don't know about. As I'm writing this, I am trying to imagine how you're going to take my ideas. And I just re-read what I wrote and if my mother told me these things, I'd probably never ask her anything again. I can't tell you what love is. But the thing is, if you really like someone a lot, and you want to spend all your time together, and they like you back, and want to spend all their time with you, then enjoy it. Because, in my opinion, it can't be love yet, but it could turn into true love.

Hope you still want to talk to me after this e-mail!

Love,

Mom

Dear Mom and Dad,

You are awesome. I kinda regretted asking you about love after I sent my e-mail before, but it was too late. And now I'm really glad I sent it. Mom, you're right. I wasn't asking for my friend. There's a guy here who is, simply put, the most awesome guy I've ever met in my life. And he happens to like me back. There's no way I could describe him to you in an e-mail, so you'll have to wait until I get back. But I can tell you that you have nothing at all to worry about. Ever since I've been making decisions, you've been reminding me to make good ones. It got really annoying. In reality, I was usually avoiding making any decisions in part because I was never sure whether they were good or not. But now, I'm starting to feel good about making decisions. And I'll try to make good ones. Right now, I'm making a decision to try my best to make this thing work with this guy. I'm sure I'll screw up sometimes, but hopefully not too much.

That's all for now.

Love,

Rachel

Chapter 20

When someone beats a rug,

The blows are not against the rug,

But against the dust in it.

- Rumi

Didim, Turkey

July 29

Naptime came at around two or three in the afternoon, right after lunch. Calling it "nap time" made Rachel feel far too young to have a boyfriend, but the only other name she could come up with for it was siesta, which she had learned in Spanish class. But siesta basically meant nap time, and using a Spanish word because the English word makes you feel like a baby didn't seem reason enough to start using Spanish in Turkey. Nobody forced anyone to take a nap, but everyone would be asleep, and without a nap, Rachel found it difficult to stay awake past midnight every night, talking and playing card games and walking and hanging out with the other teenagers on the concrete bench under the carob tree on the beach. So she lay on her bed and happily let herself drift into sleep every afternoon on a full stomach, sometimes sleeping for forty-five minutes, other times for three hours.

On this particular day, just as Rachel was drifting off to sleep, Aylin awakened her with a whisper.

"Rachel, I must tell you something."

Without opening her eyes, Rachel responded with an unenthusiastic, sleepy "Hmmmm".

"Open your eyes please, this is very important and I cannot tell anybody else."

Unable to ignore Aylin's plea, Rachel propped herself up on her elbow.

"What is it?" she whispered back.

"Tomorrow, my parents will be gone. They will go to deliver invitations for Leyla's wedding. Emre knows this. Actually, I didn't tell him, he learned from his parents. But his parents and brother will also be gone. Remember, I told you they will go for one day and one night to check their rental apartment because the tenant is not paying his rent. Of course Emre does not want to go, it is boring work. He wants me to come over tomorrow night."

Not too naïve to miss the implications, Rachel was worried for Aylin. Mostly because her dislike for Emre increased every time she saw him. Even Aylin only seemed moderately impressed with Emre. Maybe that was the bigger problem. Rachel decided not to comment.

"Leyla will not go with my parents to deliver the invitations because they do not want to leave us alone. Actually, they trust us to not do anything wrong, of course, but they think it would look bad to your parents. So Leyla will stay. But of course she will not let me go to Emre's house at night, so you must come."

Rachel felt queasy. She wasn't sure if it was the fatigue or disgust, but she had a feeling it was the latter. She didn't want to be Aylin's accomplice in anything related to Emre the slime.

"Why do you have to go at night? Why can't you go in the afternoon?" Rachel tried to remove herself from the situation if she couldn't prevent it.

"Emre's parents will not leave until after lunch. Their meeting with the tenant is the next morning so they have no hurry."

Aylin's answer confirmed Rachel's suspicion that the point of the thing was for them to be together, alone. And that it would be more obvious to Leyla at night.

"Also," Aylin continued, "Leyla is not stupid. She knows about Emre and she knows the dangers when the parents are all gone. So you must come. Then she will not think anything."

"You think?" Rachel questioned, still hopeful that she would be spared the awkward situation. What was she supposed to do anyway, while Aylin and Emre were alone and doing whatever it was they had planned. And then, as her brain woke up from its near-nap, she realized that perhaps she should try to talk Aylin out of being alone with Emre. "What are you planning to do?" she boldly asked.

Aylin looked uncomfortable, and blushed. The usually chatty Aylin looked as though she was trying very hard to prevent herself from speaking.

"I don't know. You know. He won't make me do anything I don't want. I won't do anything wrong."

A moment of silence.

"I think. Rachel, I know, it sounds wrong, but I am sure nothing bad will happen. Especially if you are there. You can be my reason not to stay too long. I can always say Oh, Emre, I heard Rachel, I think she is bored and we should go home."

"If you're so nervous, why did you agree to this?" Rachel asked.

"How can I say no?" Aylin questioned, as if she had no say in the matter. "He is my boyfriend, he won't do anything wrong. But if I will not go, maybe he will think I am boring or I don't like him."

"Aylin," Rachel said, thinking that her host-sister was playing the part of the naïve girl in the after-school specials about saying no to guys. But before she said anything else, she remembered that she had no experience in the matter herself and didn't really know what she would have done if she and Cem had managed to be alone together for a few hours. Actually, she knew. She would find a way to be with him, whatever that meant. And she'd think about her decisions as they presented themselves... and she felt sure that Aylin would have covered for her. "Of course I'll come with you. But please promise me you'll make good choices."

"I promise," Aylin said in an uncharacteristically quiet, soft voice. "Thank you."

"I know you'd do it for me."

Didim, Turkey

July 30

The morning started out with an argument between Leyla and Bahar Teyze. Until this point, there had not been any raised voices at the summer house, but Rachel had watched enough movies about weddings to know that they were stressful.

"What's wrong?" Rachel asked Aylin as they waited on the stairs, afraid to go down into the living room.

"Nothing is wrong really. My mother complained that the wedding is at the wrong time of year and they will have a difficult time to find everyone in their summer houses and on vacation. And Leyla became insulted and said that she should not invite anybody if it is too much trouble for her. And then my mother became offended and so on."

"So, are they delivering the invitations personally because there isn't enough time or something?"

"No, it is always this way here. We try to deliver the invitations by hand if we can. It is more personal than by mail. Also, perhaps we do not trust the mail. Do you send them by mail?"

"Yeah, actually I think people think it's better to get something by mail. It's more official or something."

"Strange. It is the opposite of here."

The argument ended with Leyla going upstairs in tears. Aylin and Rachel went downstairs into the living room, where Bahar Teyze was writing the last few names on the envelopes. There were no addresses, no fancy calligraphy, no stamps. Just the names of the invited. In an attempt to break the tense silence, Rachel asked a question.

"Where will you drive to deliver these invitations, Bahar Teyze?"

"Where we will not drive!" Bahar Teyze replied with a hint of exasperation. "We will drive to Izmir, to Kusadasi, then to Denizli. I hope we have time. We will not have time for sit with friends and drink tea, just to bring invitations like deliver person."

"In the United States, we just send invitations by mail," Rachel offered, hoping that if the option hadn't occurred to Bahar Teyze, it might help her.

"Here, we deliver with our hands," she answered, apparently not seeing the mail as a possibility. Only for people very far away in Istanbul and in Ankara, we will send by post, but with hands is better." There was no way to continue the conversation, so it ended. By the time Timur Amca and Bahar Teyze drove off in the car, Leyla was feeling slightly better, and kissed their hands as they left.

"In the end, this stuff won't matter too much. I will be married to my love and that is the important thing, right?" Leyla said as her parents drove off with a box full of invitations.

"How many invitations are there?" Rachel asked, slightly changing the subject.

"Oh, I think about two hundred invitations from our side and perhaps three hundred from Kerem."

"Wow." Mom and Dad probably didn't even know two hundred couples they'd want to invite to a wedding. This was going to be huge.

* * *

The plan was to go to the gazino disco first, with Ela, Rana, and Elif, as usual. Emre and his friends were going to be there, too. Then, instead of joining everyone for sunflower seeds on the beach, Aylin and Rachel were going to go home with the excuse that Leyla was all alone and they didn't want her to feel lonely. In reality, Leyla's college friend Meryem had driven over from Kusadasi, a large summer town, to spend time with Leyla before the wedding. They would be having so much fun that they wouldn't think too much about Aylin and Rachel's whereabouts. That was the plan. Every time Rachel thought about it, she felt nauseous and dishonest. Leyla had always been so sweet to her, wasn't she being disloyal by going along with the plan? But not going along with the plan would be disloyal to Aylin. *I hope that the plan gets messed up and Aylin doesn't go through with it.* Rachel thought. Later, she would remember to be careful what she wished for.

The gazino was the same as it always was. Dim, hot, humid, too loud to converse quietly, and full of people under the age of twenty. They had gone multiple times a week since Rachel's arrival, and she hadn't minded until tonight. *If Cem were here, I wouldn't notice the noise or the darkness or the other guys staring at me.* As usual, Ela, Rana, and Elif were there first and had occupied a table next to a lanky philodendron plant like the one Grams had in her white-carpeted living room. They were dressed up and their makeup was done expertly. They all smelled of the same perfume. Rachel hadn't bothered with her clothes, makeup, or jewelry today. After all, Cem wasn't going to be there and she had no desire to attract anyone's attention. A clean black t-shirt, jeans, and brushed hair were all she had the strength for tonight.

"*Merhaba arkadaslar,* hello friends" Rachel said, her Turkish improving daily.

"*Merhaba* Aylin, Rachel," they said in unison as everyone kissed everyone on both cheeks. Elif looked at Rachel disapprovingly, as always. Rachel didn't blame her. She probably felt like Rachel had taken away her best friend, which was true, even if it were only for a few weeks. Maybe Rachel would feel the same way about Hanna's boyfriend once she got back.

"We heard that Cem likes you a lot," said Ela. "That is so good! Now you have a Turkish boyfriend! But now he is far away. What will you do when you are home again? Will you forget him?"

As if I didn't already feel bad enough, Rachel thought.

"I miss him a lot. He's a great guy. He goes to college in the US, so hopefully we can figure it out," Rachel answered. She didn't want to talk about Cem because it made her miss him more. The conversation turned to boys in general, long-distance relationships, and Leyla's upcoming wedding. Apparently, Elif, Ela, and Rana's families were all invited and planned on attending.

"What will you wear?" Elif asked Aylin, who had been looking around, probably for Emre. She didn't answer the question, probably not having known it was directed at her, which irritated Elif. "Aylin, are you awake? Are you sleeping? What will you wear to Leyla's wedding?"

"Oh, sorry," was Aylin's half-hearted response. "I guess I'm a little tired. I don't know yet. Normally, my mother would have a special dress made, but we don't have time now since we are not in Izmir, so Rachel and I are going to Denizli next week to find something with my aunt."

"Really?" Rachel asked, not having remembered hearing about that plan."

"Oh, yeah, sorry, I forgot to tell you. It will be fun," Aylin replied, her mind seemingly elsewhere. What will you wear, Elif?"

Elif had been trying to beg the question.

"My mother bought me a red dress with silver beads on it. It is long and has a silver color shawl with red beads. She found it when she went to Izmir last week. I hope you will have time to find something at the last minute!" It sounded more like a threat than concern.

"Oh, it will be fine. My aunt already went shopping and asked the shops to hold some dresses for Rachel and me, and my mother designed the dresses for Leyla and herself. They will go early to the dressmaker so she can make them fit perfectly at the last minute."

"Really?" For a moment, Rachel forgot her discomfort. "She set dresses aside for me, too? But won't I be back in the US already? I'm supposed to leave on August 15th."

"But the wedding is on August 16th. Of course you will change your ticket, right? How can you miss Leyla's wedding?"

"You're right. I should talk to my parents." How did I not think of this before? Cem will be there. I'll get to see Cem again before I leave! Rachel's mood went from perfect storm to spring day with a warm apple-blossom-scented breeze. The room didn't seem as dark, the music wasn't as loud as it had seemed, and the crowd was less oppressive. Thirty days have September, April, June, and November… Sixteen days until I see Cem again.

The arrival of Emre and his friends only slightly dimmed Rachel's mood. Emre wore jeans and a wrinkled green Bob Marley t-shirt. Wheras Aylin had spent an hour prepping herself, Emre looked as if he didn't really care how he looked tonight. His hair was gelled and he had used cologne, but he didn't look like he considered this a special night. When he greeted Rachel with a light kiss on each cheek, he put his hand on her waist. Ugh, take your clammy hands off of me, she thought, this waist is for Cem's hands only. She cringed at the thought of him touching her host sister tonight. Aylin looked nervous as Emre greeted her. He pressed himself up against her, looked around to make sure nobody important was looking, and kissed her boldly on the lips. Rachel heard Elif gasp. Almost immediately, Aylin pushed him away.

"Ssht! Shame on you, Emre!" she said. She didn't look like she was teasing, but that she meant it.

When Emre disappeared to get himself a Coke, Rachel decided to say something to Aylin. She felt protective of her newfound sister.

"Aylin," she whispered so that the other girls wouldn't hear. "Are you sure about what you're going to do? I just have a bad feeling.

"Don't change your mind, please," Aylin whispered back. "I have been waiting for this moment for a long time and Emre has, too."

"Do you love him?"

"Of course."

"Please make good choices, Ayiln. I don't want you to get hurt."

Aylin pulled away from Rachel and looked irritated.

"I already have a mother," she said, ending the conversation.

* * *

An hour later, Emre suggested that they all go to the beach.

"I thought we weren't going to the beach tonight," Aylin said in a confused, rejected tone.

"I have something I want to share with you all," Emre said, winking at Aylin and pinching her cheek.

They sat on the sand below the retaining wall instead of on the usual bench under the carob tree. Passerby on the sidewalk and benches above could hear, but not see the small group. Emre pulled a bottle of whiskey and another of Cola-Turka, a Turkish brand of Coke, out of out of a bag Rachel hadn't previously noticed he was carrying. He had so thoughtfully brought plastic cups for everyone.

"Ladies first," he said as he offered each of the girls a plastic cup with a warm rum-and-coke mixture. Rana and Ela nervously accepted and tried not to wince as they tried the concoction. Aylin held hers, but didn't drink from it.

"I won't drink," Elif said, which brought great relief to Rachel, who had no desire to drink the potion.

"Oh, come on, are you a baby still?" Emre teased.

"Actually, I am grown-up enough to refuse," Elif said haughtily. For the first time, Rachel felt some respect her. Even though she didn't have anything against alcohol, the situation was weird, and she didn't like the pressure.

"No thank you, Emre," Rachel said, glad she wasn't the first to reject his hospitality. "I don't feel well."

"Oh, come on, I know you girls drink willingly in America."

"Well, some people do and some don't, just like here. Free country and everything." Good comeback, Rachel, she thought.

"Your loss," Emre said. Then he served the other guys and lifted his drink to them. *"Serefe,"* he said with a self-impressed smile. The boys proceeded to down their drinks in one gulp while Rana, Ela, and Aylin sipped theirs. The conversations warmed up over time, but Rachel was in another world, thinking about Cem and what they would have done if he had been there. She wondered if he would have dared hold her hand in front of the others, even in the dark and out of sight of the sidewalk.

Half an hour passed before anyone said anything to Rachel.

"Rachel, I need to go back to the house, to the bathroom, do you want to come?" Aylin asked.

"I need to go, too!" said Rana in a loud, shaky, alcohol-fueled voice. "Can I come?"

"Sure," said Aylin. "Rachel do you want to come?"

"No, thanks, I'm feeling kinda tired, I don't know if I have the energy to walk the hundred yards!"

"What is a yard?"

"Oh, never mind. It doesn't matter, it's a distance. I'm ok, I'll just hang out here until you're back."

With Aylin and Rana gone, the group fell quiet. Just the sound of crunching sunflower seeds broke the silence, until a guy in his twenties came up to the group.

It turned out it was some other friend's older brother, who was in college. His father and Ela's father worked together, and Elif looked very happy to see him (Rachel would later learn from Aylin that Elif had had a crush on him ever since she had noticed boys). Rachel didn't pay attention to his name as he was introduced.

"We will be back soon," Elif said as she and Ela walked off with him blissfully, leaving Rachel alone with Emre and three of his friends. They only stood 20 feet away, and Rachel could hear Elif giggling and flirting.

How long has Aylin been gone? I hope she gets back any minute because the creep factor in this group is increasing. Rachel thought.

With all of the other girls gone, Emre boldly addressed Rachel.

"Turkish girls are difficult; they make us work so hard for what we want. But British girls and American girls, you live to please us."

"I don't know what you're talking about," Rachel said, hoping she misunderstood what Emre was implying.

"Oh, come now, don't play shy with me, I know you all want it."

"I don't want anything right now except for Aylin to come back. And why do you think you know so much about Americans, anyway?"

"I watch TV, movies, you know, they tell us a lot. And I spent a year in England, after all."

"Where? At charm school?" Rachel was pleased with her sarcastic comeback, but it did her no good.

"You have something on your cheek," Emre said, and before Rachel knew what was happening, he had leaned in to brush the probably-imaginary "something" off of her cheek and his lips then rapidly approached hers. Rachel leaned back as quickly as she could, and Emre's attack kiss landed in the air between them. What Emre hadn't realized was that Elif had come back to get her cell phone and had seen the whole thing, perhaps even heard it. She gasped, and seconds later there was a faint, almost voiceless shriek - nothing loud enough to attract the attention of passerby. It wasn't from Rachel or Elif or Emre. It was Aylin's pained cry as she had arrived to find her boyfriend kiss Rachel. That was how it looked from the unfortunate angle from which she watched the scene.

"I cannot believe you, Rachel, stealing my boyfriend and cheating on my cousin! May God curse you, you, you, I don't even know the words in English to call such a person as you!"

And with that, she turned around and walked quickly, instead of running, which would have attracted attention, back to the house.

"Come with me, Rachel," Elif said, thinking quickly. "Rana, Ela, you go home and do not stay near this stupid idiot." Together, they walked up the concrete stairs to the street above. Neither talked as they walked to Aylin's house, and Rachel wondered what Elif was going to say or do.

"I don't know why he did that, maybe it was the alcohol," Rachel began. "I tried to move away, I wasn't expecting it." Rachel wondered if Elif had seen what had really happened. She opened her mouth to say more, but Elif finally spoke.

"I saw everything, and I will tell Aylin. Emre is such an idiot. I always hated him but Aylin will not listen to me. And I tell you now that I was jealous of you because you are now close to my best friend, but I am very sorry. I was wrong. You are a good person. I heard you try to defend yourself. Aylin does not understand what happened. And I hope you do not have a wrong idea about Turkish boys. Emre is a bad example. I am sorry you experienced this bad night."

"You don't have to apologize," Rachel said, finally coming to. "I didn't like Emre from the beginning, either, but I only met Aylin a few weeks ago so it wasn't my place to interfere. And I knew you didn't like me, but I understood that you were jealous. I would have been, too."

"It is not that I do not like you, it was only envy. Now, when I think about it, I was being stupid. Anyway, let's go talk to Aylin."

Leyla and Meryem were on the porch trying to calm Aylin when Rachel and Elif arrived. "What happened?" Leyla asked Elif, not looking Rachel in the eye. The conversation between Elif and Aylin was in rapid-fire Turkish. Aylin was sobbing and angry. As the conversation went on, the crying and sobbing continued, but Aylin's tone got softer and she started looking at Rachel, as did Leyla and Meryem.

"Can you forgive me?" Aylin finally said to Rachel. It wasn't what Rachel was expecting her to say, but she was able to answer without thinking.

"What are you talking about? For what?"

"Because I did not trust you. I said that you took my boyfriend and cheated on my cousin. I am so sorry, Rachel, please forgive me."

"Aylin, I don't know what Emre was thinking, I didn't lead him on or anything, he just threw himself at me. I think he might be drunk. He started telling me that American girls want to please guys and he implied that I wanted him and I just tried to ignore him, but he just wouldn't let it go. That's never happened to me before, ever, and I really wasn't expecting it. I mean, I have to tell you the truth, I never liked Emre, but still, he's your boyfriend, I never thought he'd do something like that."

"He was my boyfriend," Aylin corrected.

"I think that maybe we still have many things to learn about boys."

"For sure, I do," Rachel said, feeling sorry for Aylin. Aylin walked up to Rachel and hugged her, then brought Elif into the hug.

"Emre is finished for me. I cannot believe what I was about to do."

"What were you about to do?" Leyla asked in a motherly but not-shocked tone.

"Oh, um, nothing. Just I didn't um know he, um," Aylin didn't know how to explain herself to her sister, who was wiser than she thought.

"Whatever it was, you won't do it for a very, very long time, will you?" Leyla was making a statement, not asking a question. Aylin looked down as Leyla gently scolded her.

"I am sorry, Abla. Rachel also always tells me to make good choices. I almost made a very bad choice. I even knew it was a bad choice, but I ignored myself. Thankfully, God stopped me. God sent Rachel to stop me. But I knew I was wrong, why did I do that?" Perhaps Aylin wasn't expecting an answer, but she got one.

"I also knew that I was making a bad choice when I almost got engaged to..." she didn't speak his name. "And when I was saved from myself, I learned a lesson. To listen to myself and to make good choices."

Suddenly, Aylin looked panicked.

"Please don't tell our mother! If she finds out, she will never trust me again."

"Of course I won't tell her, silly!" Leyla said, throwing Aylin a pillow that she had been leaning on. "I am so happy with the way today has ended. Now, you two, go to bed."

"Can I just write one e-mail? Ok, two e-mails?" Rachel asked Leyla, who was clearly in charge tonight.

"No!" Leyla said, laughing, pleased with her newfound power. "You go to bed and think about the day, then you will write a better e-mail tomorrow. *Iyi geceler*! Good night!"

Chapter 21

Be like the sun for grace and mercy.
Be like the night to cover others' faults.
Be like running water for generosity.
Be like death for rage and anger.
Be like the Earth for modesty.
Appear as you are. Be as you appear.

- Rumi

Didim, Turkey

July 31

Hi Cem,

I miss you. How are you? Yesterday sucked. For one thing, I missed you. Did I already mention that? I don't even know where to begin. Basically, Aylin's now ex-boyfriend, Emre, came on to me. He was saying things like American girls want it, don't they, crap like that, and I was backing away from him and then he tried to kiss me. Fortunately, he missed. I think he was drunk. Aylin saw it from a weird angle, so she thought he actually did kiss me and she (wrongly) assumed that I was actually asking for it and she got mad and ran back home. I forgot to mention we were on the beach. But Elif, who I always thought hated me, saw what really happened, and she told Aylin. So everything's ok with Aylin now. And with Elif, too. Actually, better than ok because she's not with that creep anymore. But seeing what a complete jerk he was just made me think about what a great guy you are and so now I'm feeling sorry for myself that you're so far away. Actually, there's good news, too. Maybe. I was supposed to go back on August 15th, but now the wedding's on the 16th, so obviously I have to extend my ticket. Are you going to the wedding? I assume you are. Aylin and Leyla said you are. So I'm going to ask my parents today whether they can change my return date and then I can see you again. I know, it'll be in front of all your relatives so you won't want to hold hands or whatever, but still, if I could at least see you and talk to you, that would be enough. Well, not enough (hee hee) but good enough. I'll let you know.

Love,

Rachel paused. She automatically signed e-mails to her relatives and friends "love", but it felt... premature with Cem. They hadn't told each other "I love you". And after some thought, Rachel was sure that she didn't love Cem. Yet. She could one day. Not that she loved every friend to whom she signed "love, Rachel", but it was just a formality. With Cem, maybe it would mean something. I don't want to freak him out, but I don't want him to think I don't care. I better decide quickly, before the electricity goes out like it does all the time and I lose the whole e-mail. Rachel deleted "love," and decided to sign off in Turkish, as she had learned the Turkish word for I kiss you, which also made her blush, but "take care" felt too distant.

Öptüm,

Rachel

She clicked send, and held her breath until she was told her mail had been sent. Now, one more e-mail before the guaranteed power outage (the weather was very hot, and everyone who had AC had it on full-blast).

Not surprisingly, there was an e-mail from her parents:

Dear Rachel,

We are so proud of you. You are an honest, smart girl and even though you had us pretty freaked out about this guy you like, especially about him being foreign, your e-mail reassured us that we've raised you right and that at some point, you have to make your own decisions. We admit that we are still kind-of nervous about the whole thing, but we're not losing sleep over it. Well, ok, kind-of. We can't wait until you get home so that we can hear all about your trip and also about this guy that is so special. We are now on the countdown to August 16th.

Love,

Mom and Dad

As usual, Rachel felt guilty for not missing them as much as they missed her. She wasn't looking forward to going back. Hanna would probably be spending all her time with her boyfriend, and Cem would be at MIT.

Dear Mom and Dad,

Thanks for your confidence. So, I'm gonna test it now: I have a favor to ask you. I was supposed to leave here on August 15th, arriving there August 16th. Well, my host sister is getting married on August 16th, and I really can't imagine missing her wedding. Plus, it would be hard for the family to get me to the airport the day before the wedding. So, I wonder if you could change my return flight to August 18th? I say the 18th because you know, everyone will be tired the day after the wedding, and the airport is 3 hours away, so I don't want them to go to so much trouble when they're so tired. Think of it as a cultural experience. I'll get to see a Turkish wedding. My host sisters' aunt actually reserved some dresses for me to try on to wear to the wedding. How cool is that?! By the way, how is Grams? She hasn't written me for a while.

Love,

Rachel

As she clicked send, Leyla's cell phone rang. Rachel heard Leyla say a few things in Turkish, and then she came into the living room from the patio and handed the phone to Rachel.

"Cem," she whispered, with a wink and a smile.

Rachel's heart flipped.

"Hello?"

"Rachel, it's me."

"Hi!" What do I call him? Honey? Baby? It's all so weird.

"I'm sorry I didn't call before. I ran out of credits on my phone and I had to get some more."

"No problem, since I don't have a cell phone here, I got so used to e-mail!"

"I miss you, too."

"Did you read my e-mail?"

"Yes, I just did. And I think I have to come over there and beat up Emre."

"No, I don't want you to ruin your reputation as a nice guy."

"Well, maybe this is what nice guys do when somebody hurts both their girlfriend and their cousin."

"Actually, the whole thing was uncomfortable for me, but I think he did Aylin a favor. She can do better than him. He was trying to make her do stuff she didn't really want to do."

"I see. Well, in that case, I won't beat him up."

"On the other hand, if you come to beat him up, I'll get to see you."

"But then again, Bahar Teyze and Timur Amca might want to know why I'm beating up this guy and then we have to tell them."

"Oh, I didn't think about that."

"So maybe we just have to see each other at the wedding?"

"I still have to find out if my parents will change the ticket."

"Of course they will."

"What color dress should I get?"

"I have no idea. That is not my department. Let Leyla give you advice on that."

"True. But do you have a favorite color?"

"Green, of course."

"Why of course?"

"Bioengineering student, it just seems appropriate that I prefer the color that most plants also prefer."

"I miss you."

"You didn't mention that before. Thanks."

"Just wanted to make sure I didn't forget to tell you."

"I have to go, I'll run out of credits on my phone again. I can't wait to see you. 14 days."

"It seems like so long."

"Have fun and it will go fast. I'm sending you a virtual hug and a kiss,"

"Me too."

August 3

Dear Rachel,

Mom and I are looking forward to seeing you. It's lonely around here with you gone. But I guess it's good practice for us, for when you go to college. I checked with the airline, and changing your return date is no problem. We just have to come up with a hundred dollars to cover the change fees. Don't you worry about that, we'll take care of it. You just take care of yourself over there and enjoy the wedding. Send our best wishes to the girl who's getting married.

I want to share with you something from Chinese culture that I guess I had no reason to talk about before, and that's weddings. As you know, your mom and I had a small ceremony at home. My parents bought your mom a red silk Chinese dress to wear. You already know that, since Grams has complained so much that mom didn't wear a white dress, and you've seen the picture. Anyway, red is considered a lucky color in Chinese culture, and it's also supposed to keep away evil spirits. Mom looked so beautiful in that dress. My parents gave us a traditional Chinese blessing when we were married. I can't remember everything that they said, but something I'll never forget is that they said may you respect each other like honored guests. I think about that one often, because it's sad how we sometimes treat strangers nicer than we treat our loved-ones. Finally, nine is a lucky number in Chinese because it means "forever". Chinese people usually give gifts of money, placed in a red envelope, often $99 or $999. So there's the lesson of the day, even though you didn't ask for it. Thing is, I just figured you're going to a Turkish wedding and learning all about it, and I never put much effort into explaining my parents' culture to you. Now that you're older, and I'm older, I feel like it's more important. Hope you'll tell us all about the Turkish wedding when you get back. No more dilly-dallying, though. Your new flight leaves same time as your old one, but on August 18th. I don't intend on changing it again because we miss you too darn much.

Love,

Dad

I'm definitely gonna try to get a red dress now, thought Rachel. It felt weird but pleasant to be so sure about things recently. She was sure about Cem, sure about staying longer, and sure about wanting a red dress.

Dear Dad,

Thanks for changing my ticket! Don't worry, I won't ask you to change it again. I'm so excited about the wedding. We're going to get dresses in a few days. Aylin's aunt set some aside for us at a dress shop in a bigger city called Denizli. I hope there are some red ones, because after your story I think I want a red one. After all, who could turn down luck and chasing away evil spirits? Does Aunt Celia know about that stuff? You know she'll start dressing in red from head to toe if she does! Thanks for telling me a little about Chinese weddings. Maybe you can tell me some more when I get home.

Love

Rachel

* * *

Dear Cem,

Just got an e-mail from my dad. See you on August 16th. I'll be in a red dress.

Öptüm,

Rachel

Chapter 22

Be grateful for whoever comes,
Because each has been sent as a guide from beyond.

- Rumi

Didim, Turkey

August 7

In the morning, before Rachel and Aylin left on the noon bus to Denizli, Bahar Teyze baked pastries filled with parsley and cheese and topped with sesame seeds. She also fried meatballs (these ones do not become bad if not in refrigerator, she explained), and washed some giant peaches.

"Annecim, it is only a 3-hour trip! You do not have to send so much food with us!"

"But bus is at lunch time! You must eat. If you arrive in Denizli so hungry, Ilkay Teyze will say I do not feed you." Bahar Teyze smiled and pinched Aylin in the stomach. It was a joke, but only sort-of. Bahar Teyze went to a lot of effort so that everyone who came through her door had enough to eat and drink.

"Is everyone here like your family, you know, always trying to get everyone to eat?" Rachel asked.

"Is your mother not the same?" Aylin asked, stunned at the thought that she might not be.

"Um, no. For one thing, I probably wouldn't be sent on a bus by myself in the US, even for three hours, because most people just don't travel by bus. But, in case I did, my mom would probably tell me to make a sandwich. Or she'd give me some money to get something at McDonalds or something."

"I would be very happy if my mother would give me money for McDonalds," Aylin reflected. "But no, she insists on making something. Anyway, I am glad she is a good cook because at least she makes delicious food!"

"True," Rachel said, in complete agreement.

The bus looked nothing like a Greyhound. It was a shiny Mercedes tour bus, and the interior was clean and spacious. The seats were blue velour, and as soon as everyone was seated, a man came around offering drinks. From tea, coffee, Coke, and water, Aylin and Rachel both chose Coke. Aylin looked around at the passengers, and was pleased that she didn't know anyone.

"We're safe to talk," she said with a wink. "I don't know anyone on the bus." As the bus pulled away from the rickety bus station, Aylin waved to her mother through the window. Rachel waved too, feeling like a big deal was being made over an overnight trip. Her own parents would probably have done the same thing, but she always told them not to, that it was embarrassing.

The main road was only two lanes, and seemed rather narrow for such a large bus, but the cars coming in the other direction passed by just fine. Rachel watched quietly out the window as hills dotted with olive trees passed by. Then there were some fields of tobacco as they descended into a flat valley, which had nothing cotton fields and a few clothing outlets. Just after passing the outlets, Aylin started unwrapping the food Bahar Teyze had packed for them, starting with the pastries and the fried meatballs.

"These are delicious," Rachel said, biting into a savory cheese pastry.

"Yeah, they are. They're traveling food. Sometimes, we stop at the rest stops and eat at the restaurants there. They are usually pretty good. But if we do not want to stop, then she makes these for us to eat."

"So, we're staying with Ilkay Teyze. She seems nice."

"She is the best. I can tell her anything and she will not tell my mother or anybody else. Also, she gives good advice. She found Kerem for Leyla. If I cannot find somebody by myself, then I will ask her to find somebody for me."

"You mean you would ask her before you'd ask your mom?"

"Yes. I love my mother so much, but I think this is a better job for Ilkay Teyze. She knows me better than my mother does because I am more honest with her."

"I see what you mean. My best friend at home, Hanna, is closer to my mom than to her mom. All my friends like my mom."

"I hope I can meet her one day."

"Me, too! It's weird that I know your whole family but you don't know mine."

"Well, you talk about them a lot, so I can imagine them, I think. But I hope that one day I can go to America to visit you."

"I'm sure you will. But I have to warn you, Olympia isn't as fun as Didim."

"Izmir is not as fun as Didim either, Rachel. This is the summer village. It is a dream, that is over every September."

* * *

The three-hour trip passed quickly, and Ilkay Teyze was waiting for them at the bus station. Aylin kissed her hand and brought it to her forehead, so Rachel did the same. Ilkay Teyze was an English teacher, so her English was nearly perfect.

"Welcome to Denizli, girls! I am so glad I get to have you to myself for a day," she said as she pulled both Rachel and Aylin to her for a tight hug. She kissed them both on their cheeks and squeezed them until it almost hurt. "I've planned a full program for you, so you won't have a minute to be bored. Have you eaten? I prepared some things for you at home for later, but we have an appointment at the dress shop at 4:30, so we don't have time to go there now. We can get some *kebap* or *döner* or maybe just get some dessert?"

"Annem sent us with *kizartma kofte, pogaca,* and Sirince peaches, so we are quite full," Aylin offered.

"Then we have dessert," Ilkay Teyze suggested; apparently, being full was not a deterrent to eating dessert. "I love dessert, and I cannot find an excuse every day."

They walked to a shiny café whose walls were mirrored, and sat at a table for four. Rachel and Aylin placed their overnight bag on the fourth seat. A waiter dressed in a black formal pants, a starched white shirt, and a black bow tie, approached with a pad of paper. He seemed very formally dressed for the café, but the unexpected and out-of-place had stopped surprising Rachel. They were handed menus full of names that Rachel had never heard of. There were pictures of ice cream sundaes, but no pictures for many of the other items.

"I will order a few different things and we can all eat them, so Rachel can try some of our Turkish desserts," said Ilkay Teyze, relieving Rachel's nervousness. She just realized that she had only been to two restaurants in three weeks, and had no idea what to expect.

"I did try a lot of desserts on the holy night," Rachel offered, wondering if any of these would be the same.

"Have you tried *asure* then?" Ilkay Teyze asked.

"Um, which one is that?"

"It is translated as Noah's pudding. It is made from wheat, and it also has some beans in it, and dried fruit, sesame seeds and pomegranate seeds, sometimes orange peel."

"Rachel hasn't tried that one," Aylin answered for Rachel, knowing what she had tried and what she hadn't.

"You must try it. One *asure,* and we'll also get some baklava, of course you have tried that already, I am sure, but it is very good in this shop. And what else should we get?" Ilkay Teyze asked, more to herself than to Aylin, who knew that her aunt wasn't actually expecting an answer. We will have also one *kabak tatlisi* and one *sütlaç.*"

The desserts arrived, and Rachel tried them all. The *asure* was odd – a cold, sweet pudding with garbanzo and navy beans. It was refreshing once Rachel got over the unusual ingredients. *Kabak tatlisi* was chunks of sweet poached pumpkin sprinkled with ground walnuts. Also unusual, also good once Rachel got used to the idea. *Sütlaç* was almost exactly like the rice pudding Grams made, except that it was eaten cold and with cinnamon on top. Over peculiar desserts and hot tea in tulip glasses, they talked about dresses and weddings and boys. Within an hour, Rachel wished Ilkay Teyze were her own aunt.

The dress shop was a short walk from the café. Denizli was a big city full of concrete apartment buildings in various states of disrepair. Some were new, others were falling apart, and there was one that was unfinished and didn't look as though it had any intentions of being finished. The sidewalks were crowded. Despite the heat, which was more oppressive than in Didim, nobody wore shorts, though many women wore capri pants. Some women were veiled and some were not.

"Denizli used to be so beautiful," Ilkay Teyze said with a sigh. "There were Ottoman-style wooden houses surrounded by trees and gardens. The streets were lined with small canals with flowing water, and the peaceful sound of the water kept us all calm. Now, they are trying again to make it beautiful, increasing parks and planting new trees. But it will never be the same."

The shop Ilkay Teyze led them to was small and full of dresses in every color and type. As soon as they walked in, a short, stocky woman in a green suit greeted Ilkay Teyze warmly, and led them to the back, where there was a small sofa. She motioned for Aylin, Rachel, and Ilkay Teyze to sit down.

"Emel Teyze and I went to school together," Ilkay Teyze explained. "She always copied my English lessons, so she is now unable to speak to you in English," she continued, winking at Emel Teyze, who said something else in Turkish. Ilkay Teyze continued to translate. "Would you like some tea?"

Rachel had never been offered a drink in a shop before. And she'd already had more tea than she could handle.

"*Tesekkur ederim*," Rachel politely refused in Turkish. Emel Teyze looked rejected and said something else.

"What can she get you then, Rachel dear?" Ilkay Teyze asked. At this point, Rachel had been in Turkey long enough to understand that she had to accept something or she would continue to be asked.

"A water would be great," Rachel said. Emel Teyze looked pleased. Aylin also asked for water.

Ilkay Teyze and Emel Teyze chatted for a few minutes before Emel Teyze motioned for Rachel and Aylin to stand up. She measured them and then smiled, apparently pleased.

"She says I was correct when I told her your sizes. Of course, what does she expect? I am an amateur dressmaker!" Ilkay Teyze explained, laughing. Emel Teyze went into a back room and came back with at least five dresses on each arm. She hung the dresses on a rack.

"You are to try these dresses on, girls, and we will go from there." Rachel scanned the dresses. None were red.

"All of Emel Teyze's dresses are original, so you can be sure that nobody will have the same dress as you at the wedding, right Ilkay Teyze?" said Aylin.

"That is correct. Now, start trying on dresses! Emel Teyze will make any adjustments tonight so that you can try them on again tomorrow before you leave."

Rachel and Aylin went together into a corner of the shop that had a green linen curtain hanging from the ceiling for privacy.

"Aylin," Rachel whispered. "I've never tried on an original dress before. I mean, a regular dress is fine for me. How much do these cost?"

"Don't worry about it right now," Aylin said. "I have no idea, but we can negotiate with Emel Teyze. She is Ilkay Teyze's friend, so I am sure she will give us a good price."

"Ok, but good meaning what? I don't have that much money and I want to get a gift for Leyla and Kerem. I'd rather spend more money on their gift than on my dress!"

"Rachel, how many Turkish weddings will you attend in your life? Plus, Cem will be there. Just enjoy right now. Try on some dresses and we will figure out the money later, ok? If you don't have enough money, maybe we can give you some and you can pay me back when I come to visit you in Olympia, ok?"

Rachel liked the offer. It was like some sort of guarantee that Aylin would really come all the way to Washington. Still, she hoped the dresses weren't thousands of dollars or something.

"I really wanted a red dress," Rachel whispered again, trying to decide which dress to try on first.

"Stop worrying, Rachel!" Aylin said. "You saw how many dresses were in this shop. I am sure there is a red one for you. I really must choose the right dress to wear to my only sister's wedding now. Will you help me?" Rachel felt embarrassed. She had been focusing so much on herself that she had forgotten that this wedding was even more important for Aylin than it was for her.

"Sorry, Aylin. I'm really sorry. I think you should try on this navy blue dress." Rachel picked up a navy silk dress with silver sequins and a turquoise and silver design embroidered on it. It was a knee-length a-line dress and had a matching transparent turquoise and navy tie-dyed shawl.

"*Aman Allahim*, that is beautiful," Aylin said. She tried on the dress. In spite of having spent countless hours in the sun, her skin was relatively light (due to diligent use of SPF 40, necessary because she burned so easily), and it seemed to glow against the navy silk. Her blue eyes seemed bluer, and her medium-brown hair, which now had some blonde streaks from the sun, shined like the silver embroidery. Aylin no longer looked like the teenager who was about to do something stupid with an idiotic jerk named Emre. She looked like a strong girl about to enter her last year of high school, whose sister was about to get married and move far away. A girl who would and could now take care of herself.

"Wow," Rachel said. "I think this is your dress. You don't need to try on anything else."

"I think this is it. You're right," Aylin said. "Now you try one on and we can walk out together."

"Which one should I try?" Rachel asked, unable to make the decision herself because none of the dresses were red.

"I will try and think like Leyla. She has such good taste. What would she pick for you?" Aylin said, thinking out loud. "Hmm, your skin is getting very dark and your hair is also dark. I agree red would be good. This purple one, no. This black one, no. This green one, blech, no. What about this turquoise one? Oh, look, it has a red sash. And the inside of the dress is red, see? It is lined in red fabric. It is a little bit like a traditional Turkish wedding dress I saw in a museum." It wasn't the red dress Rachel wanted, but she tried it on anyway. The dark turquoise silk had an embroidered silver tulip design along the edges. It was more like a robe – a kimono, kind-of. It went on like a jacket, but it almost reached her ankles. She tied on the wide sash. Unlike a kimono, the dress had slits on the sides up to just above her knees. At least it was comfortable.

"Should we go out?" Rachel asked, hoping to move the process along so that she could ask for a red dress.

Ilkay Teyze and Emel Teyze gasped when the curtain opened. Emel Teyze exclaimed in Turkish, and Ilkay Teyze fussed in English. Mostly.

"*Masallah*, you two look gorgeous, unbelievable, may the evil eye stay far away, are these the first dresses you have tried on? Aylin'cim, *aman Allahim*, you are fabulous. Don't try on any more dresses, *canim benim*, this is the one. And Rachel, this is a very different dress, and you look perfect." Rachel and Aylin looked at each other, and could find no words, just smiles.

"Ilkay Teyze'cim, is there not a mirror so we can see ourselves?"

"Oh!" Ilkay Teyze exclaimed, realizing that the girls hadn't seen themselves. She said something to Emel Teyze, who jumped up laughing, and pulled back another curtain, revealing a large mirror. Rachel turned to the mirror and looked at herself. Forget about a red dress, she thought. This is the most beautiful dress I've ever seen. I don't even care what it costs anymore.

"I have never seen a dress like this one, Rachel. It looks a little bit like the style of wedding dresses women wore during the Ottoman times, one or two centuries ago." Ilkay Teyze then translated for Emel Teyze, who said something back to her, nodding in agreement. "Emel Teyze said she hopes you choose this dress because as soon as she heard that an Aylin and Leyla's American exchange student would be coming to the wedding, she designed it in the hopes that you would like it and show your friends and family back home. It is based on different traditional Turkish designs, but not exactly. In the old times, this dress would have been worn with salwar pants underneath, for example. And there are quite a few other differences. It is not meant to be a replica."

"I was hoping for a red dress, because in Chinese culture, oh, my dad is Chinese, maybe you don't know. Anyway, in Chinese culture, red is for good luck and keeps away evil spirits. But this dress is so beautiful, I forgot about the red dress thing. But it has red inside of it, so I'm really happy about that. It's gorgeous. Thank you, Emel Teyze. I wasn't expecting an original dress!"

When Ilkay Teyze translated, Emel Teyze had tears in her eyes. She approached Rachel and hugged her. She then said something to Aylin, who looked at her aunt.

"Ilkay Teyze, you designed my dress? Wow! Thank you so much! How did you know I would pick this one?"

"I didn't. I just hoped you would. And if you hadn't, I would have encouraged you to get it anyway. Actually, Leyla and I designed it together. So I'm glad you like it. Well! This has been much faster than I expected. Emel Teyze will just have a look and make some marks where she will make a few adjustments tonight, so that the dresses fit you perfectly. Then shall we go home? I have prepared a special dinner for us. I invited Emel Teyze and her husband, but they have another invitation, so it will just be us girls."

"Wait, I need to pay first," said Rachel.

"I'm sorry, that is right, I already bought the materials for Aylin's dress. Let me ask Emel Teyze the cost for yours."

As they spoke, Rachel waited nervously, hoping she had enough money for the dress, with enough left over for a wedding gift for Leyla and Kerem, and maybe for some snacks at the airport. And of course, she should get a few souvenirs for Mom and Dad and Grams and Hanna.

"It will cost one hundred and seven dollars," Ilkay Teyze explained. "Emel Teyze is only charging you for the materials. Her labor is a gift to you. You just have to promise her you will wear her dress in the US, too."

"Oh, of course I will!" Rachel said. It was the most expensive dress she had ever had, but she knew it was worth way more than a hundred dollars. How nice of her to basically make this for me for free, Rachel thought. I should send her something when I get back home. "Do you have a business card or something, so I can have your address?"

After some translation by Aylin, Emel Teyze provided a business card for Rachel and thanked her as she gave it to her. I'm the one who should be doing the thanking! She handed over a hundred and ten dollars. It was so much money, but it was very easy to give to this kind lady.

Chapter 23

A mountain keeps an echo deep inside. That's how I hold your voice.

- Rumi

Rachel imagined Cem seeing her in the dress and hoped he would like it. She couldn't wait to see him again, but the thought that they wouldn't be able to hold hands or even just hang out with each other the whole time was starting to bother her. It's weird. At first, I thought I wasn't going to see Cem again before leaving Turkey. And I was ok with it. Now, I'm going to see him, but basically no PDA. And that feels worse. Having a boyfriend is complicated.

When they got home, Ilkay Teyze changed out of her elegant clothes and put on beige Bermuda shorts, a sleeveless shirt, and an apron and then made lamb chops and french fries for dinner.

"What would you girls like to do tomorrow?" she asked as they ate at a small kitchen table

"Look at jewelry!" said Aylin with much enthusiasm. She was getting back to her old, chatty self. The shock of Leyla's upcoming move combined with Emre's life-sucking tentacles seemed to have worn Aylin down for a while. But now she was morphing back into the bubbly being she had been the first week that Rachel was there. "I plan to buy Leyla and Kerem something as a wedding gift. I don't know what to get them, though. But I will look, perhaps I will find something. And Rachel wants to buy her something gold, too, of course. Right, Rachel? Because we usually give gold in Turkish weddings as a gift."

"Why do you give gold, actually? Does it mean something?" Rachel felt like she might be asking a stupid question, but was curious about the answer. She was mentally collecting information to tell everyone back home.

"No, gold doesn't mean anything special, but it is like giving money. Everybody gives gold and then if the couple needs money for something, they can sell the gold. Most people give gold coins. They are on little pins, and we pin it to the dress and the suit of the bride and groom. Of course, gold is also easy to store. What type of wedding gift do people give in American culture?"

"Well, people have registries. They sign up at a store and say what they want. Like they want a set of porcelain plates or a mixer or a vase or silver or whatever. Stuff they wouldn't actually buy for themselves. And the wedding guests go to the store or look online and pick out stuff to give. My Aunt Celia got married two years ago. She didn't want a registry, she wanted cash, but a lot of guests got mad, so she made a registry anyway."

"But a set of plates might be so expensive for somebody to give! Here, the girl's family must buy plates and furniture and these things."

"Really? So it's expensive for the girl's family here!" Rachel was surprised by how different things could be.

"Well, the boy's family should buy an apartment and pay for the wedding."

"Oh. Well, anyway, about your plate question, it's possible to just buy one plate. They say the ones they want and how many, and people just buy what they can. And hopefully, by the time they're married, they have all the plates or whatever. And if they don't, they can buy them themselves. My parents don't have much fancy stuff, though, because they didn't have much of a wedding. They just got a few silver things from family friends. And they got money from my dad's parents and their friends. In China, they give money."

"Almost like here! You see, Chinese culture and Turkish culture are similar!"

"So, we will go and look at jewelry tomorrow," confirmed Ilkay Teyze. "I have no complaints there. What else should we do? Of course, we must pick up your dresses. And we should find you shoes. I know. In the morning, we can go to the jewelry shops. Then we can pick up your dresses. Finally, I can bring you to our new shopping center where we can find the perfect shoes for you both. Your bus back to Didim is at four o'clock in the evening."

"Our plan is made, we have eaten our dinner, and now the good part," said Ilkay Teyze. Her eyes sparkled. I think we have eaten enough sweets today. But we will eat some fruit now and drink coffee, and I will read your fortunes."

Fortune reading was a lot more interesting to Rachel this time around. On one hand, she really wanted to know what was going to happen with her and Cem. On the other hand, she was afraid things wouldn't work out the way she wanted them to.

The coffee was delicious; neither bitter nor weak, it inspired Rachel to decide she would get Turkish coffee sets for everyone as gifts. And she'd teach them how to make the coffee. And she'd ask Leyla for tutorials on how to read the grounds via e-mail. When she had finished and only the grounds remained in the bottom of the tiny porcelain espresso cup, she put the plate on top and swirled it around three times before quickly flipping it over.

Once the cups had cooled to the touch, Ilkay Teyze's fortune-telling session began.

"Aylin, I start with you this time," she said as she put on her pink-framed glasses and looked into the cup. She rotated it a few times without saying anything. She pursed her lips and clucked in disapproval, shaking her head. "Aylin, I see a very big evil eye. There is a path that keeps turning and turning. It looks like a very difficult path to travel. But this path ends. And then there is another path over here, well many paths, actually. They are all clear paths. There is a fish over here. And a bird. Good, good. But Aylin dear, tell me about this turning path. Do you know anything about it?" Aylin and Rachel looked at each other. To Rachel's surprise, Aylin actually told her.

"Oh, Ilkay Teyze, it was awful. You know, my boyfriend Emre from last summer? Things ended after the summer, and he was in England, but he came back and so of course I wanted to be his girlfriend again this summer. Everyone was envious of me. Emre is handsome and a good student and now he has lived in England and everyone is fascinated. But he is a different person now. And I just went along with it. He made me uncomfortable, but I didn't know how to get away from him. And, well..."

"Go on," Ilkay Teyze said, with more concern than disapproval.

"He tried to convince me to go to his house when his parents weren't there, and I convinced Rachel to come with me and she didn't want to, and my parents were delivering the invitations at the time. And then we went to the beach and I had to go back to the house quickly and I left Rachel there, oh I am so sorry, Rachel, why did I leave you there? What was I thinking? And then stupid Emre, he was probably drunk, he threw himself at Rachel, and I arrived then at the same moment and I didn't understand what I saw, I thought..."

"Aylin, you've already apologized to me," Rachel interrupted. "It's ok."

"My dear," Ilkay Teyze jumped into the conversation. "It sounds like you almost made a mistake. We all make mistakes, some bigger than others. You could have put your your future at risk, but in the end, you did not, am I right?"

"Yes, Ilkay Teyze. And now I never want to see Emre again, although unfortunately I will, every summer in Didim."

"With time, you will move on and it won't bother you so much anymore. Now, stop worrying about what didn't happen and focus on what did happen. You chose a clearer path. And because of that, there are many clear paths available to you. It is a good fortune. Rachel, shall I read your fortune? Do you know about this Turkish tradition?"

"Yes, Leyla actually explained it when I first got here. But at the time I wasn't that into it. Now, I'm really into it. I want to learn how. But also I, um, I want to know my fortune. I think."

"Let me see," said Ilkay Teyze as she examined the patterns in the grounds of Rachel's tiny porcelain cup. "Hmm, I see a large bird with what looks like one person on each wing. You are traveling with somebody. And there is a wide road that leads to a mountain. It looks like the mountain is where you are heading. There is only one path here. There are lots of small paths leading from the wide road, but none of them are very long. It is an interesting fortune, my dear. Everything else is very clear. I hope it pleases you."

"Oh, yes, thank you very much, Ilkay Teyze," Rachel said, hoping that the person on the bird's other wing was Cem.

Denizli, Turkey

August 8

It rained that night. Denizli was at the base of a large mountain range, and the weather changed rapidly. The previous day's humidity had passed, and through the open window Rachel could hear the rhythmic sweeping of sidewalks punctuated by the occasional car horn.

The breakfast Ilkay Teyze prepared was much simpler than what Bahar Teyze made every morning. There was a tray with small bowls of jam, black olives, and honey; a plate with tomatoes, cucumbers, and parsley; a plate with feta cheese; and a loaf of fresh white bread. It was still much more complex than the cereal she usually ate at home. This is a beautiful breakfast, but I'm actually in the mood for cereal. Am I finally succumbing to homesickness? Rachel wondered.

Once the breakfast dishes were cleared, they were off to buy gold. The jewelry stores were all tiny, the storefront windows crowded with shimmering stones and precious metals, every space filled with as many items as possible. There was a mosque opposite the narrow jewelry-store-filled street, and the plaza was bustling with people. Many more women were veiled than in

Didim, but there were still plenty of unveiled women. Children chased pigeons, groups of young girls ate ice cream, and a pack of young boys watched the girls eating ice cream. There must have been fifteen or twenty different jewelry stores. It was a surprising place for jewelry stores to be, Rachel thought, because despite the relatively modern main streets of Denizli, this was an old, dusty area with narrow streets suitable for pedestrians but not cars.

"What kind of thing were you thinking of?" Ilkay Teyze asked Rachel.

"Actually, in Chinese culture, people usually give money. And nine is a lucky number I guess, because it means forever, so they like to give 99 dollars or 999 dollars. But I'd rather give an actual gift, so I was thinking maybe like a bracelet that has the number nine on it or something?"

"And you, Aylin dear, what would you like to buy them?"

"I was also thinking of a bracelet, but now it seems unoriginal. Maybe I should buy a set with earrings and a necklace. Or just earrings. Or maybe I should just get them a big gold coin? I can't make up my mind."

"I'm sorry Aylin, I took your idea. Leyla is your sister. You get her the bracelet, I'll get something else."

"No, Rachel, I like your idea, you thought about it a lot. I will find something."

"Let's go in here, this is a nice shop," Ilkay Teyze said, pointing to one of the shops ahead, which looked no different from any of the others. "I know the owners, they will be helpful."

They looked at the jewelry in the window before walking inside. A man seemed to recognize Ilkay Teyze and walked up to greet her.

"This is Huseyin Amca," she said, introducing a handsome man with graying hair. He wore a grey suit in spite of the heat, but no tie. "Would you girls like something to drink?"

"*Memnun oldum,*" said Rachel and Aylin in unison. Aylin asked for *ayran*, a salty yogurt drink. Rachel asked for coffee.

Being offered a drink made her feel special, and also made her feel like she should really buy something there.

Ilkay Teyze explained what Rachel was looking for, and Huseyin Amca smiled and went to one of the windows to pull out a velvet-covered tray. On it, he put a thick snake chain bracelet and a few rows of slide charms. Fortunately, he knew English. As usual, Rachel felt strange that everyone knew her language and that she didn't yet know theirs, but they were always happy with the few things she said in Turkish.

"This is a charm bracelet. You can buy the chain and some charms. And the bride can then collect more charms as time passes, for special occasions. It is a very nice gift. What kind of symbol charms would you like? These are only some that we have. There are many more in the safe."

"I was thinking about the number nine. Is there a charm with the number nine on it?"

"Yes, we have all of the numbers," said Huseyin Amca. "I will bring you number nine. And what else?"

"Well, I'm part Chinese. So I want something Chinese. Red is really important, it brings good luck and chases away the evil spirit. Are there any red charms?"

"Of course, there is a beautiful gold and red glass charm. There are also some charms with Chinese characters. Those are popular these days. There is one that says "love" in Chinese. I think we have one left. I can bring that. What else?"

"Let's see how much that costs," Rachel said.

"I understand, of course," he said as he turned around and walked down some stairs to another part of the store, where he disappeared behind a curtain to retrieve the charms.

"I have an idea," Aylin said. I could get some charms, too, and we can give this bracelet together! We can share it! Then Leyla has something bigger than if we both just get something smaller. I can also get three charms and we can divide the cost."

"That would be great!" Giving a gift to Leyla together. Aylin is really making me feel like I'm her real sister. Sometimes I forget that I'm not. It's going to be weird to go back and be all alone.

Huseyin Amca came back with the nine charm, the love charm, and the red glass charm. They were beautiful. Exactly the right gift. Aylin then spoke to him in Turkish, presumably telling him that she wanted to get three charms. After a short exchange, he went back behind the curtain and returned with a gold charm shaped like an eye, with a diamond in the center and two blue glass charms.

"I think this is a perfect gift for your sister," he said. Rachel and Aylin agreed. "I will now calculate the cost."

Having never bought gold jewelry before, Rachel had no idea what the cost might be.

"One thousand, eight hundred and sixty three Lira," said Huseyin Amca. But your Ilkay Teyze is my special client, so for you I will make the price one thousand, six hundred Lira." Not having bought much in Turkey, Rachel needed to calculate the price in dollars. She took out a paper and calculated it. One thousand and thirty dollars. Even split with Aylin, it would be $515. Each. More than she had. With just $343 left, Rachel didn't know what to say or to do. Certainly, the bracelet was beautiful, but she couldn't spend all her money and not bring home gifts to her family. And not buy shoes to match her dress.

"That is more than we can spend," Aylin said sadly. Rachel was glad that Aylin felt the same way. "I had only planned to spend 300 Lira. Even if we both spend 300 Lira, we will not have enough. Not even close to enough. We must find something else."

Chapter 24

God turns you from one feeling to another
and teaches by means of opposites,
so that you will have two wings, not one.

- Rumi

Rachel looked at the beautiful bracelet they had created and sighed. It would have been perfect, but there was no way they could come up with that much money. Ilkay Teyze picked up the bracelet, which Huseyin Amca had put together with the charms, and made an offer.

"I like the idea of this bracelet," she said in an aloof tone. "But the price is far too high. Rachel and Aylin can each contribute 300 Lira and I will pay the rest, for a total of 1,400 Lira. And I would like you to give me one extra charm of my choice."

"I am sorry, Ilkay Hanim, you are a dear friend, but I cannot do that."

"Perhaps we can take our business elsewhere then, and find a different appropriate gift? I would like to buy from you, Huseyin Bey, but you know I am not such a rich lady."

Rachel was enamored of the idea of the bracelet, but it looked like Ilkay Teyze was about to walk away from it.

"May I suggest something?" Huseyin Amca said, wiping sweat from his brow with a white handkerchief. "This bracelet chain is quite expensive, but the charms would also fit on a more standard chain. This one, for example, which is a very stylish and comfortable necklace chain. I could give you this one plus the six charms for 1,300 Lira. And Ilkay Hanim, I can offer you a simple charm for 100 Lira."

"Let me see the charms you will offer me," Ilkay Teyze said, without appearing convinced or overly interested. She quickly spotted one of a gold coffee bean. She picked it up and turned it over in her fingers. "Is this supposed to be a coffee bean?" she asked.

"Yes, Ilkay Hanim. It is. Do you like that one? I could give you that one for one hundred Lira."

Ilkay Teyze held it in her palm as if to weigh it.

"I do like it," she said. "It is very cute, and an appropriate addition to this bracelet. Girls, do you agree to each pay 300 Lira each, as I will pay the rest and it will be a gift from us all?"

"Yes, thank you Ilkay Teyze, that is so cool to give a gift together with you, what a good idea! You are the best aunt ever, but you already know that. Here, I will give you my 300 Lira now. Thank you thank you thank you!"

Ilkay Teyze flashed a restrained smile.

"Huseyin Bey, please assemble the bracelet and put it into your best box for us, please. And don't you have gifts for these girls, who helped you sell some very nice charms?"

"I do, my dear. I mean, Ilkay Hanim. Let me see," he said as he cleared his throat. "You may each choose one of these silver charms."

"That's so nice of you, thank you very much," Rachel said.

"My pleasure. Thank you for your business. Now I will wrap this lovely necklace."

Aylin and Rachel sorted through the charms looking for something that appealed. Rachel settled on one that had a sun, a moon, and a star.

"This one would remind me so much of Didim," she told Aylin. "I like that, too. You're right. Is there another one?"

"Yeah, here's one," Rachel said, picking up an almost identical charm.

"Then I want it, too."

Huseyin Amca returned with the bracelet in a box lined in black velvet.

"*Buyurun*, ladies," he said, holding the open box to show them all. "And are those the charms you would like?"

"Yes, thank you, Huseyin Amca," Aylin said.

Aylin and Rachel each handed over 300 Lira. Rachel had calculated it as $192, but even though it was the most expensive gift she had ever given, it didn't feel too bad because she paid in Lira, which felt like Monopoly money to her \. It meant that she had $151 dollars left. She still had to buy four coffee sets and a pair of shoes. Hopefully, they wouldn't be too expensive.

Once they were a few blocks away from the store, Aylin nudged Ilkay Teyze with her elbow.

"Well, you never told me about Huseyin Amca before!"

"I don't know what you're talking about," said Ilkay Teyze, blushing and barely concealing a youthful smile.

"Yes you do! I did hear him call you my dear. I tell you everything, now you have to tell me!"

Ilkay Teyze stopped and pulled both girls into the entrance of an apartment building.

"He likes me," she whispered. "He is trying to get me to marry him, but I am not sure."

"Were you ever married?" Rachel asked in a whisper, and immediately afterwards wished she could take back what she had said, which was probably nosey.

"No," said Ilkay Teyze, who was not visibly offended. "My parents didn't approve of the men I chose and I didn't approve of the men they chose. So here I am. It is not so bad, actually, I go where I want, I do what I want. But many times, I am lonely. There are lots of people around me, but I need romance, too. I have wonderful nieces, but no children of my own. I am in a different world from my married friends. And as my parents grow older and I grow older, I realize that I don't want to be alone forever. Huseyin is very nice and respectable. But maybe a little predictable. I have to decide if I can live with predictable. Love is not so easy to find," she said with a sigh. "As usual, you will not say anything to anyone, dear Aylin."

"Of course, Ilkay Teyze! I am so excited, he seemed like a nice guy! Don't keep secrets from me again, though."

"I promise," said Aylin's fabulous Aunt. "And you don't keep secrets from me either, young lady."

"Deal," said Aylin. Rachel wondered if she should try harder to be friends with Aunt Celia. It would be fun to have a good relationship with a cool aunt. It's just that she couldn't decide if Aunt Celia was cool or just strange.

Rachel looked across the street and noticed Turkish coffee sets like those she had seen in Didim.

"Those are exactly what I was hoping to get as gifts for my family back home!" Rachel exclaimed. Each set contained a copper or brass coffee pot, two white porcelain cups and saucers painted with blue and red flowers, and a bag of coffee ground into a fine powder. The sets were nestled in baskets and covered in cellophane. "How much are they?"

"Tell me how many you need," Ilkay Teyze said, "and I will negotiate for you."

After some haggling, and pretending to not be interested and almost leaving and walking away, Ilkay Teyze said that the man would sell us four sets for ten dollars each.

"It is his final offer," she said.

"I'll take them, thanks!" Rachel said with a sigh of relief. The shopping spree continued.

The mall was large and new. The interior was decorated in polished marble, chrome, and glass. It was much fancier than the mall in Olympia, and larger. There were numerous shoe shops, but Ilkay Teyze had a favorite. They had picked up the dresses from Emel Teyze and brought them to the shoe shop.

Upon showing the dresses to the salesman, he measured Alyin and Rachel's feet and brought five pairs of shoes for each.

Rachel had expected to get a simple pair of black or red shoes, but all of the shoes he brought out were silver or gold or beaded. All had very high heels.

"I can't walk in heels," Rachel said with embarrassment. "Do they have any flats?"

Aylin translated and the man looked frustrated as he packed up the five pairs of heels. He came back with five more pairs of shoes. The second pair was a pair of red flip-flops with a half-inch heel. They had some gold sequins, but weren't flashy – at least not compared to the others.

"How much are these?" Rachel asked, dreading the answer.

"They are 40 Lira," Aylin said. "I think it is an ok price."

Rachel calculated it on paper. 40 Lira was about $25. She breathed again.

"Perfect, I'll take them," Rachel said. She was down to $86, but had everything she needed.

Aylin chose a pair of strappy silver high heels. She looked like a movie star.

After the mall, it was already time to rush down to the bus station. With their dresses, shoes, coffee sets, overnight bags, and the necklace, Rachel, Aylin, and Ilkay Teyze hopped onto a *dolmus*, a van that was a cross between a small public bus and a shared taxi.

"I could have kept your dresses and shoes here, since you'll be staying with me for the wedding, but I know Bahar is excited to see them," Ilkay Teyze said, her eyes tearing up. "I'll keep the necklace here in my safe."

It was hard to say goodbye to Ilkay Teyze. There's so much I didn't get to say to her, to ask her, Rachel thought.

"Have a safe trip and see you at the wedding," said Ilkay Teyze. "It is only one week from now. Until then, have fun and don't do anything I wouldn't do."

"Which is, for example?" asked Aylin.

"Well, it's wide open! Just don't tell your mother I said so."

Didim, Turkey

August 13

"Hi Rachel," Cem's voice said nervously over the phone. He had called on the main phone this time. Bahar Teyze already knew he was interested in Rachel, so there was no need to hide.

"What's up, Cem?" Rachel worried. Cem sounded upset. Or anxious. Or something. I don't know him well enough yet to know what his voice is telling me. I hope he's not calling to break up with me or something.

"I can't wait to see you in your red dress," he said, reassuring her that she needn't worry, at least not about their relationship status.

"Oh, it's not red after all. It's like a dark turquoise color. Ilkay Teyze's friend, Emel Teyze, she designed it especially for me. It's sort-of based on an Ottoman Turkish dress. Cool, huh? It has red inside, though."

"Well, I'm sure you'll be beautiful. You should wear your hair down, though."

"Huh? How else would I wear it?"

"I'm sure you'll get dragged to the hairdresser. Who knows what they'll do to it."

"Really? Nobody's said anything about it."

"They probably assume you know. All the ladies here go to the hairdresser before any event, big or small. There are tons of excuses to go the hairdresser. And the hairdressers are insane. Like there's some contest to make the biggest hair."

"Oh, well I'll try to end up with regular hair, but no guarantees. I'm going for an authentic experience here."

Cem laughed. There was a fluttering in Rachel's stomach. He thinks I'm funny. Even I don't think I'm funny.

"If I don't recognize you, I'll look for the dress. It sounds like you'll be the only one wearing one like that."

"Good strategy. I can't wait to see you. What will you be wearing?"

"Maybe I should dress up like an Ottoman sultan or something."

"Um, yeah, you'd probably be unique, unless that's usual. What do guys usually wear at Turkish weddings?"

Cem laughed again.

"Are you serious? What do you think we wear?"

"Who knows! Don't laugh at me, this is all new to me!"

"We wear suits, Rachel dear. And while I think it would be cool to dress up like an Ottoman sultan, my sultan costume is at the cleaner's so I will probably wear a suit. I'm thinking of wearing a tuxedo, actually. What do you think?"

"You'll look great in anything," Rachel said, embarrassed at herself for saying something so direct to a guy, even though he was apparently her boyfriend, even though she had kissed him.

"In that case, I'll be the one in the orange suit," Cem said.

Rachel laughed, hoping that Cem was joking. She was pretty sure he was, but you never knew with him, it seemed.

"When do you get to Denizli?"

"August 15th. But I hear you guys are doing a henna night, so I won't get to see you until the 16th, at the wedding, I guess."

"Why won't you be at the henna night?" Rachel asked, sure it was a stupid question, but she had already accepted that she either asked a lot of those or she was in the dark.

"Ladies only. But will you spy and tell me what happens at those things? I'm curious."

"Sure. What are the guys going to do?"

"We'll sit around and drink rakı and smoke cigars and watch the game. Besiktas and Sivas are playing that night."

"Soccer?"

"Yep. Of course. So anyway, I should probably let you go, but I wanted to let you know that I'm going skydiving tomorrow."

"What!" Rachel suddenly felt angry and scared. Do I have a right to tell him not to? Not really. "Please don't! Why are you doing that?"

"Why should I not go? A friend is going, so I thought I'd try. Just once. It's pretty expensive, I don't think it's something that's going to become a hobby. My mom is furious, but I will just do it one time and I have promised her I won't do it again."

"Here you go with why or why not again." Rachel was upset. And now, Cem was irritated, too.

"Please don't tell me what to do," he said. "I already have a mother."

Cem isn't the first person to tell me that, Rachel reflected. She didn't know what to say, so she stayed silent. Cem had to have a flaw, and here it was. He liked to try things if he couldn't find a reason not to.

"I asked myself *why or why not?* and I did the research. The bottom line is, skydiving is safer than riding in a car."

"Really?"

"Yes. So don't worry. I'll be fine."

"Will you please call or write me when you're done? So I know you're ok?"

"Of course."

"What time are you going?"

"First thing in the morning."

"Make good choices," Rachel said in a last-chance plea for Cem to not jump out of an airplane.

"I do," was Cem's confident response.

Chapter 25

Silence is the language of God,
All else is poor translation.

- Rumi

Didim, Turkey

August 14

Rachel checked her e-mail right after breakfast, at nine. There were messages from home.

Dear Rachel,

I'm glad you were interested in the information about Chinese culture. Did you get a red dress after all? If not, don't worry. It's mostly for the bride! One day, if you choose to get married, we can get you a red Chinese dress. If that's what you want. Four more days until you're home. Can't wait.

Love,

Dad

Wow. Dad was already planning her wedding. Weird. And Mom was, well, Mom.

Dear Rachel,

Wow! You're getting a fancy dress from a dress shop and I can't be there to shop with you? I am so upset. Please promise me that you'll go to your senior prom and we'll go dress shopping together! Oh, I have an idea, we can get you a new dress for Grams' wedding! Since you've been gone, Dad and I haven't gone out to eat at all and we've been eating a lot of sandwiches. We're jut not that motivated to cook without you. Pretty sad, huh? What are we gonna do once you go off to college? Eat sandwiches every meal? Anyhow, we've saved some money. So you and I can get ourselves some nice dresses and still have enough for my tuition and books. I know I'm jealous of whomever you went shopping with. Don't mind me. I'm not a psycho mom, I just miss you. See you in four days!

Love,

Mom

What is it with weddings and dresses this year? Rachel pondered.

Dear Rachel,

OMG, I have so much to tell you. I don't know where to start and it's not happening in an e-mail. Anyhow, can't wait until you're back. You have so sucked at sending pictures. Hello! Where's the picture of this guy of yours? I'm withholding all pictures unless you send some. You better come home. No more extending this trip. I may have a boyfriend now, but I still need you. Especially since he's going back to medical school in a few weeks. I know, that sounds bad. But I actually want you to meet him and get to know him before he leaves. That's what I mean.

Annahay

I bet she had sex. I just have a feeling. I hope she's ok. If she screws up her future, I'll blame myself for not being there to prevent it. Here I am in Turkey, saving Aylin from stupid decisions and Hanna is probably at home changing so much that I'm not going to recognize her and I'm going to lose my best friend.

By 11:00, there was still no e-mail from Cem.

"Don't you want to come to the beach?" Aylin asked. She was already wearing her bathing suit and yellow cover-up dress.

"It's just that Cem hasn't written me yet. How could he go skydiving? I'm just totally scared that something happened to him."

"That is Cem. Do not worry, my almost-sister. Cem likes adventure, but he is not crazy. And he will not hurt you. Come to the beach with me. We can talk with the girls. We are going tomorrow morning, this is your last day on the beach! I can't believe it, actually. The time is passing so quickly."

"You're right. I can't spend the whole day at the computer. I'll just check one more time."

Rachel clicked on "check mail" and her heart skipped a beat when she saw an e-mail from Cem. He was alive. Thank God.

My Dear Rachel,

I jumped from an airplane. I was attached to the instructor, who opened the parachute at the right time, and I am just fine. Except that all my clothes flew off because of the wind and I had to go home naked. Just kidding. It was ok. It was not as fun as I expected. It was pretty fast. The view was nice, though. In the beginning, before the parachute was opened, I felt like a bird. Except that I had to keep my mouth shut or I literally couldn't breathe. But when the parachute opened, it HURT a very sensitive area. And then when we landed, I twisted my ankle somehow. I don't think that I will do it again. It always seemed interesting, but honestly there are other things that are much more exciting. Like kissing you. Now, delete this message before somebody finds it.

Cok öptüm

Cem

Rachel knew there was no way she was going to delete the message.

"Ok, he sent a message, he's fine," Rachel said, unable to contain her excitement. "I'll be ready in five minutes for the beach!"

Dear Cem,

I am so glad you're ok. And I'm also pretty psyched that you didn't like it that much. Good news that your clothes didn't fly off, too. Kissing me is more exciting than skydiving? What can I say? Thank you.

I'm going to enjoy my last day on the beach now.

Öptüm

Rachel

Didim, Turkey

August 15

The day that Rachel was originally supposed to leave Turkey had become the day that they all left Didim for Denizli. The car carried Rachel's suitcase and duffel-bag carry-on, multiple dresses with matching shoes, Timur Amca's suit, overnight bags, Aylin's laptop, and containers full of stuffed grape leaves, and cheese pastries that had yet to be fried, the latter two which would be served at the henna night. Ilkay Teyze had organized most of the food because she was already in Denizli, but Bahar Teyze had wanted to contribute to her own daughter's special evening. Leyla had already been in Denizli for a few days, for the final fittings of her dresses and last-minute preparations. Rachel had packed up her clothes, which somehow didn't fit into the suitcase as well as they had when she had come, even though she had only added one dress and a pair of shoes. The coffee sets were even already in a separate duffel bag. Breakfast wasn't as elaborate as usual, as they had to use up the fresh goods before closing up the house for a week. Bahar Teyze, Timur Amca, and Aylin would be coming back after the wedding for two more weeks, before packing up for the summer and returning to Izmir.

"It will be weird to come back here in a week without you," said Aylin. "I can't believe I only met you a month ago."

"It was a pretty intense month," Rachel said, hardly believing it herself. A month at home would have simply meant four weeks at the coffee shop, two paychecks, and lots of quiet evenings at home, watching TV and playing board games with Mom and Dad, especially since Hanna had a boyfriend now. "If it weren't for Leyla's wedding, I would be leaving today."

"Ach, I know! At least we can be together for three more days! Thank God."

"So, what's the plan for today, once we're in Denizli?"

"Leyla's henna night will be at Ilkay Teyze's house, and of course we are already staying there, so we will help her set up. My mother will go to the hairdresser this afternoon, but we will go tomorrow morning. I think the henna night will begin at five o'clock. It will not be too many people. Just Leyla's closest friends and our female cousins and aunts. Maybe twenty ladies. Or fifteen, I am not sure."

"Too bad Cem can't come," Rachel thought out loud.

"He would probably agree to wearing a dress just to get closer to you, Rachel, but the others won't allow it, I am sure."

"Yeah, I know. I'm sure this distance just makes it more exciting, but it still sucks," Rachel said, wondering how different things might be if they both lived in Olympia.

"Well, you will see each other at the wedding, don't worry."

Rachel was slightly worried, but she tried not to let it show.

Children were riding bikes up and down the cobbled streets, old people were swinging on porch swings, and teenagers, many of whom were now Rachel's acquaintances, were just starting to make their way to the beach. Flowers fluttered in the gentle breeze. It almost felt as though autumn were coming. It was hot, but not as scorching as it had been four weeks earlier. Everyone continued their summer routine, but summer was over for Rachel.

Elif, Rana, and Ela came to say goodbye. They were already in their beachwear, but each carried a glass of water. Elif hugged Rachel, a big, genuine hug followed by a kiss on each cheek, Rachel was glad that their conflict had ended.

"It was great to meet you, Rachel. I hope that you come back next summer and we can become better friends," she said.

"Me too, Elif. I saw you accepted my friend request on Facebook."

"Of course, you're my friend!."

And then they piled into the car. A number of neighbors had come to the house too, and waved. Elif, Rana, and Ela threw water on the car as they drove away, and tears came to Rachel's eyes.

"You cried when you arrived and now you are crying when you are leaving! What am I going to do with you?" said Aylin, crying herself. "Clearly, you are Turkish, too! We show our emotions proudly."

Aylin and Rachel hugged across the middle back seat, and when Rachel looked up, she saw Bahar Teyze smiling at them. She said something to Aylin through tears, and then Aylin translated.

"My mother says that when she knew that an American was coming, she thought she knew what to expect and she did not think she would like you. But now she likes you so much and feels like you are her almost-daughter."

"You come again next summer," said Bahar Teyze. "I promise, I will study English. And you promise you will study Turkish."

"I promise," said Rachel, and meant it. She wondered how that would be possible in little old Olympia where she wasn't even sure there were any Turkish people, but she would find a way.

Once they arrived at Ilkay Teyze's apartment, Rachel and Aylin helped Timur Amca bring everything up from the car while

Bahar Teyze hurried off to the hairdresser, where Leyla was apparently already having beauty treatments done. Timur Amca also disappeared to a barbershop.

"All of the men are gathering later at another apartment to watch a soccer game on TV. So we will not see them until late," Aylin explained.

"Will Cem be there?" Rachel asked.

"Of course!" Aylin exclaimed. "It's a really important game."

I think I'd rather be hanging out and watching a soccer game with Cem than at a henna night, but clearly I have no choice. I can't believe that Cem is here, in this same city, somewhere, and I can't see him.

They were soon too busy for Rachel to sulk. They moved all of the furniture in Ilkay Teyze's formal sitting room to the edges of the room. The sofas were stiff and uncomfortable and looked very old-fashioned. They were covered in white sheets, which Aylin and Ilkay Teyze removed and folded up while Rachel was given a cloth to brush off any dust from the sideboard.

"I guess you don't use this room much," Rachel said, thinking out loud again.

"Only when guests come," replied Ilkay Teyze. The furniture is my mother's. Actually, the apartment is my mother's. She was staying with my brother at his summer house when you were last here, but she is back now, and is at the hairdresser."

"You live here, though, right?"

"Yes, of course. I never got married, so I never left. I know, I have learned enough about American and British culture to know that it might be strange to you, but to us it is normal. It works well. We both cook, and my parents are not lonely."

Next was the task of frying pastries and placing all of the food that Bahar Teyze, Ilkay Teyze, and Ilkay Teyze's mother had prepared on platters. There were at least fifteen different kinds of finger foods, both sweet and savory, in addition to many desserts and fruits. A copper platter with handles held twenty tea glasses and plates. One copper bowl was empty, and had a plastic bag with a greenish powder and some candles inside of it.

"What do I do with this?" Rachel inquired, wondering what it could be.

"Ah, that is the henna. We will mix it later. And then put some candles in the paste. You will see."

When everything was ready, Ilkay Teyze, who had already gone to the hairdresser first thing in the morning, looked at her watch.

"Oh, my, they will be here in only half an hour! Let's all get dressed! I almost forgot, Leyla left you each a gift that she wanted you to open before she came. Here they are, now hurry and open them and then get ready. We don't want to be in our dusty clothes when the guests arrive!"

Aylin and Rachel looked at each other and then unwrapped the large boxes. Leyla had given them outfits to wear for the henna night. A red, sleeveless raw-silk shirt with red sequins and black capris for Rachel and a pale blue version of the same shirt with matching blue capris for Aylin. She had also enclosed a silver bracelet with blue glass evil-eye charms for each. Written on plain white paper was a note for each.

Dear Rachel,

It has been wonderful to meet you and spend time with you this summer. I am so pleased that my sister has such a sweet American friend now. I hope that you will come to visit Kerem and I in Japan. After all, it is not so far from Olympia. The last few days that you are here, I will be incredibly busy and I might not get a chance to spend much time with you, so I wanted to say to you now that you are very special to me and I am so honored that you are coming to my wedding. These clothes are a gift to you from both Kerem and I.

With love,

Leyla

Aylin's note was in Turkish, and tears came to Aylin's eyes as she read it. Rachel decided not to ask what it said, but Aylin hugged Rachel when she was done reading it.

"If my sister must get married and leave me, I am glad it is with Kerem," was all she said.

Moments after Aylin and Rachel had finished dressing, applying lip-gloss and mascara, and spritzing perfume on their necks and wrists, the doorbell started ringing. First it was Leyla and Bahar Teyze. Leyla's hair and makeup were done, but she was in sweats and a blouse, so she was rushed off into a bedroom to get dressed. Five minutes later, she emerged from the room wearing white linen pants and a lavender blouse with dark purple embroidery and beadwork. She carried a white linen purse to which many guests would later pin gold coins adorned with red ribbons.

"Some people will give their wedding gifts tonight, and some will give them tomorrow night," Aylin explained. "Some people even give gold at both the henna night and the wedding."

Guests filed in, dressed up and made up, smelling of different perfumes and hairspray. Once they were all there, Rachel counted eighteen women. Some, Rachel recognized as cousins that had come to the tea where she had first met Cem. Cem, what is he doing now? I hope his team is winning. Kerem's mother, Zümrüt Teyze, was there, too, and greeted Rachel warmly. Everyone was speaking rapidly in Turkish, and Aylin was too busy chatting with everyone to translate, but no translation was really needed. Everyone was smiling and chattering, drinking tea and eating. As the food disappeared from the trays, Rachel and Aylin replenished the trays with the stores from the kitchen.

The loud hum of eighteen excited women was then drowned out by the sound of Turkish music from a stereo. The music must have been familiar, because everybody knew the words and sang along as they danced, young and old, round and thin. At one point, Leyla disappeared along with some of the younger women.

"Come with me," Aylin said to Rachel, grabbing her hand. "Now is the time for the henna."

Rachel followed Aylin back into the bedroom, where Leyla had changed into a cream-colored cotton blouse, a wide red, black, and white sash in a traditional-looking fabric, a black vest, and burgundy salwar pants, which were full at the hip and gathered at the ankles. It looked comfortable and special. Nothing like anyone would probably wear on a daily basis.

"This is a type of traditional Turkish outfit," Aylin explained.

The copper bowl that Rachel had asked about before now contained a paste made from the henna powder. Aylin put some candles into the paste and lit them, and one of Leyla's friends kissed her on both cheeks and then put a sequined red cloth over her head.

A cousin carried the copper bowl with the glowing candles in two arms as she slowly walked towards the guests. Leyla's friend and Aylin stood on either side of Leyla, linking arms with her. They then followed the girl who held the bowl with the glowing candles. The music had been turned off, but then somebody with a beautiful voice began to sing the same slow, haunting song. The procession of cousins and friends led Leyla to the other room, where Ilkay Teyze was singing and Bahar Teyze was crying.

Leyla was seated on a chair that had been brought into the center of the room. As Ilkay Teyze sang, Bahar Teyze and Zumrut Teyze slowly danced in circles around Leyla, whose head was still covered with the red fabric. When the song ended, Leyla was uncovered, revealing that her beautiful face was stained with tears. Zumrut Teyze put some henna into each of her palms, and put a gold coin into the henna in one hand while Bahar Teyze put a gold coin into the henna in the other hand. Bahar Teyze closed Leyla's fingers over the henna, and then put a small red cloth cover over each of Leyla's fists. Leyla then stood up and both Bahar Teyze and Zumrut Teyze kissed Leyla on each cheek. The song ended, and the stereo was turned on again. Everyone danced to the music, including Leyla. Rachel, unsure of how to dance like everyone else, stood against the wall and watched.

Aylin noticed that Rachel wasn't dancing, and came up to her.

"Why are you not dancing?" she said loudly, to be heard above the music.

"Oh, I'm totally having fun just watching everyone, I mean, I don't know how to dance to this music, really."

"It's ok, dance however you want. Just celebrate."

And so, Rachel did. She watched the others as they put their hands into the air and shook their hips to the beat. Leyla noticed that Rachel had begun to dance, and winked at her. Rachel was glad that Leyla had given her a sleeveless shirt, as the room was balmy and only got hotter as she danced to the music, quickly forgetting that she didn't know if she was dancing correctly. Nobody seemed to care. Everybody was smiling, and some were simultaneously crying.

What an awesome way to spend the night before you get married, Rachel thought.

Eventually, people started to leave. It had been dark outside for a long time, but the music wasn't turned down until the last guest left. By the time Rachel and Aylin were in their pajamas and curled up on the couch to sleep, it was one o'clock in the morning.

"What was that song about, the one that Ilkay Teyze sang?" Rachel asked before drifting off to sleep.

"That is a song that we often sing at henna nights," she explained. "It is called *Yüksek Yüksek Tepelere*. That means high high mountaintops. I will try to translate for you. Hmm, they shouldn't build homes high up on the mountain tops, they shouldn't give girls to faraway lands, they shouldn't neglect the mother's special one. May the birds carry the message, I miss my mother, both my mother and father, I miss my village. If my father had a horse, he could jump on it and come, if my mother had a sail, she could open it and come, if my siblings knew the way, they could come."

Aylin was sobbing by the end of her translation.

"Now I know why everyone was crying. What a sad song! I thought weddings were supposed to be happy!"

"We are all happy and sad. Happy of course that Leyla is marrying a nice man who she loves, but sad that he is taking her so far away."

"They will come back, though," Rachel said, not knowing why she was so sure.

"Do you think so?" Aylin asked, as if Rachel knew the answer.

Chapter 26

Wherever you are, and whatever you do,

Be in love.

- Rumi

Denizli, Turkey

August 16

Rachel had been sleeping well at night. She usually slept through the early morning call to prayer that she had heard her first night in Didim, but the night before Leyla's wedding she heard it again, the mysterious voice of the imam echoing through the night air, more a chant than a song. Is Cem awake now, too? I wonder if he's hearing the same sounds as I am right now. Where is he staying? If I knew, I would sneak through his window.

She must have fallen back into a deep sleep, because when she woke up Aylin was already dressed and was gently tapping Rachel on the shoulder. In Rachel's dream, it was Cem who was tapping on her shoulder, getting her attention to sneak away from the wedding just long enough so that nobody would notice.

"But Cem, I don't want you to get in trouble, I don't want anyone to think we're doing something wrong," Rachel said. Out loud. Aylin, aware that Rachel was dreaming, played along.

"Oh Rachel dear, we are married, nobody can tear us apart now," she said, mimicking Cem's voice.

But Rachel flinched and suddenly opened her eyes. She looked around the room and saw Aylin, then blinked and realized she had been dreaming.

"Sorry!" Aylin said, not concealing her giggles. "You were talking to Cem in your dreams, I had to answer you!"

"Oh my God, did I say that stuff out loud?"

"Yes, my lovesick friend. But I won't tell anyone. Now, please hurry because we must quickly eat breakfast and then go to the hairdresser. We must be at the hair salon at nine and at the wedding hall at eleven and it is already eight thirty. Wear a shirt that buttons in the front so that you don't ruin your hair and makeup when you get changed into your dress, ok?"

When they opened the door of the salon at 9:05, they were greeted with a burst of hot air that smelled of hairspray and nail polish. Multiple hairdryers whirred, and men worked in pairs on each client. Leyla was just leaving as Rachel and Aylin arrived. She was dressed casually in jeans and a plaid button-up blouse, but her hair was in an up do of dozens of corkscrew curls. She had a few new red highlights, and the whole hairstyle was adorned with silver glitter. Her makeup was heavier than usual, and her lips shone with pale pink glittery lip-gloss. It wasn't what Rachel had expected. Oh my God, this is what Cem was talking about. Maybe I shouldn't let them do my hair!

"Ablacim, you look gorgeous!" Aylin said, appearing to mean what she said.

"What a beautiful bride," Rachel said. She meant it, but Leyla was gorgeous in spite of the makeup and hairstyle, not because of it.

Before Rachel and Aylin could protest, they were whisked off to adjacent salon chairs. A woman dressed in black with burgundy hair and false eyelashes came first to Rachel. She ran her fingers through Rachel's hair and asked some questions. Rachel looked at Aylin in hopes of translation.

"She says she has some good ideas for your hair," Aylin said.

"Ok, like what, for example?"

"She didn't say. I'm sure they will make something nice."

"You mean they're not going to ask me what I want?"

"You can tell them, of course, if you know."

Rachel thought about what Cem had said.

"I want to keep my hair down. Nothing puffy, no curls. I want to look like myself."

Aylin translated and the hairdresser sighed and shook her head as she said something to Aylin.

"She said that your hair should be curled, that if you leave it down you shouldn't come to a hairdresser."

Rachel felt bullied by the hairdresser, but she decided to give her a chance, with guidelines.

"As long as most of my hair is down and straight, maybe they can figure something out."

Aylin translated, and the hairdresser half-smiled. She then brought over two young men and gave them some direction. They started to work on her hair, and the woman with false lashes moved on to Aylin. She tousled Aylin's hair and then called over two assistants, who then began to work on Aylin. The men worked rapidly with a hot iron and a hairdryer, clips and glitter, hairspray and more hairspray. After twenty minutes, the top of Rachel's hair had been pulled back into nine silver clips with rhinestones. There was a scattering of corkscrew curls, but most of her hair was straight. The finishing touch was a sprinkling of silver glitter. Aside from feeling somewhat like a cake, the final result was glamorous. Aylin's normally-frizzy ash-blonde hair had been straightened and then set in loose curls that were iced with just enough gold glitter to make it look like she had gotten her hair highlighted. Next came the makeup. Rachel explained, through Aylin, that she wanted minimal makeup, and the makeup woman complied, sort-of, with a few swipes of mascara and a generous application of matte red lipstick. Aylin was adorned with a small amount of pale turquoise eye shadow, mascara, and clear lip-gloss. She looked surprisingly enchanting. I guess they know what they're doing, Rachel decided.

Back at the apartment, it only took them a few minutes to change into their dresses. Aylin stepped into her navy dress and silver strappy heels, and Rachel into her red-lined turquoise dress and sparkly red sandals with miniature heels.

"This is fun," Rachel said. "We don't get this dressed up for weddings back home."

"Really? Why not?"

"I don't know. I mean, I'm sure there are some people who do, but a lot of people don't. I've been to a lot of my aunt and uncle's weddings and it was never this fancy. I wouldn't like to dress up like this all the time or anything, but I do kinda feel like a movie star."

"You look like one, too. Wait until Cem sees you."

Rachel knew she was blushing.

"What time is it? I took my watch off this morning."

"It's already ten fifteen. We will leave here in about ten minutes."

"Where's Leyla?"

"Oh, she and Kerem are already at the photo studio having their pictures taken. My sister is a bride. I can't believe it."

"I wonder who's next, you or me?"

"I wonder, too."

When they arrived at the wedding hall, they had to wait for the guests of the previous wedding to leave before they could file in. Apparently, the hall was reserved for one-hour blocks. At home, the churches and receptions were decorated from top to bottom, but here, it was more the people that were decorated. On the outside, the wedding hall looked like... a government auditorium. Inside, it was like a high school theater. It had no decorations other than the Turkish flag, and the blue plastic seats had no frills. There was a table on the stage with four chairs. It had some flowers on it, and large floral wreaths stood on easels at the edge of the stage. Each was draped with banners saying "Leyla & Kerem 17-08" and then the name of the person who sent the wreath.

Rachel, Aylin, and Aylin's family as well as Kerem's parents and siblings sat in the front row. Turning around to look for Cem, Rachel realized that while some guests were very dressed up, many were not. She felt overdressed, as quite a few women were simply wearing blouses with slacks.

"Are we too dressed up?" Rachel asked Aylin, wondering if Aylin felt the same way.

"No, don't worry. We are wearing the same thing for the wedding and for the dinner. The people who come to the dinner will change their clothes before they come, see, even my mother is wearing a suit now, but she'll wear a dress at dinner."

"So, not everyone who is here now at the wedding will be at the reception? The dinner?"

"Oh, no. Everyone is invited to the wedding, even people who are not close friends or family, just acquaintances or co-workers that are not close friends. But to the dinner, only close friends and family and co-workers come."

"So that will be pretty small then, right?" Cousins, aunts, uncles, bosses, close friends – maybe a hundred people, Rachel figured.

"I heard Leyla say that there will be five hundred people at the dinner."

"Five hundred!" Rachel gasped. "How could you have five hundred close friends, family, and co-workers?"

"Oh, we don't!" Aylin laughed. "We have about two hundred, and three hundred are from Kerem's side. We would have had more, but they are in Izmir, Istanbul, and Ankara, so they cannot all come."

"Two hundred is a lot!"

"Well, it is not," Aylin said in a whisper. "My mother is upset that so many people cannot come because they are in summer houses or traveling now and are too far away to come, or we could not find them to deliver the invitations."

"How can you have two hundred, though! How many cousins do you have?"

"I have, oh, I don't know, I think eighteen cousins. That means from my mother and my father. And we have my parents' cousins. I have no idea how many. And our aunts and uncles and the parents of our aunts and uncles, Leyla's childhood school and summer friends and college friends, and of course the parents of her childhood and summer friends, and some of my good friends who know Leyla well, and our parents' close friends and their children, my father's colleagues, my mother's colleagues. So many people must be invited!"

"Wow." It was all Rachel could think to say. *If I ever marry Cem, not that he's asked me, or that I expect him to, but if I do, there would be a ton of people at our wedding. If we got married in Turkey. Ok, I'm getting way ahead of myself now. Where is Cem?*

Rachel looked turned around again and noticed Cem sitting six rows back. They linked eyes and he winked so quickly that nobody else could possibly have noticed. He was wearing a tuxedo jacket with a white tie. Rachel's heart skipped a beat and she felt her hands start to shake. *I can't believe Cem likes me. When will I get over it?*

Then, the music started. It was a classical piece that sounded familiar, but it wasn't the wedding march. Rachel turned back around, not knowing where to look for Aylin, since nothing else about this wedding was as she had expected. Then she saw her, wearing a classic white dress with a full skirt, a lace veil draped over her head, and a red ribbon tied around her waist. With the complete ensemble, her hair and makeup didn't stand out much at all. She was a beautiful bride, just as everyone had anticipated. Rather than waiting at the table for her, Leyla and Kerem walked in together.

They walked down an aisle and then up a small set of steps where they sat next to each other at the table, Kerem to Leyla's left. One of Leyla's uncles, Rachel couldn't remember the name, sat next to Leyla and another man sat next to Kerem.

"Who are the men sitting next to Leyla and Kerem?" Rachel asked Aylin, wondering at what point Aylin was going to get tired of answering questions.

"You are testing my English today!" Aylin said with her usual enthusiasm. "They are the um, they are watching the wedding and they will sign their names to say that they saw the wedding."

"Ah, witnesses," Rachel said. "Aylin, if you are all Muslims, don't people normally get married in mosques?"

At this question, Aylin laughed.

"My friend, you are funny. Mosques are only for praying. For men to pray, actually. Women pray at home. Now watch, or the wedding will be over and we will miss it!"

A man in a satin red robe came out and sat down at the table, in front of a microphone.

"He is a judge," Aylin explained before Rachel could ask.

He spoke for a minute and then asked Leyla a question, to which she answered *evet* which, by now, Rachel knew meant yes. He then asked Kerem a question, to which Kerem answered evet. Then they were asked to sign their names to a book and everybody clapped. Kerem and Leyla kissed each other on both cheeks and everyone clapped again. Then they stood up, and walked down the aisle smiling broadly, back the way they had arrived. When the guests all stood up, Rachel stood up, too.

"That's it? It's over?" Rachel asked, looking over at Aylin, who was simultaneously crying and smiling, like when it rains while the sun is shining. Aylin didn't appear to have heard Rachel's question, and Rachel didn't repeat it. She followed Aylin's lead and walked to the side of the building, where Leyla and Kerem, Leyla's parents and Kerem's parents, and Kerem's siblings stood.

"I will stand next to my parents and thank everyone for coming," Aylin explained. "You can sit on the chair over there and relax. When the guests have finished, we will give Leyla her gift together with Ilkay Teyze." Aylin quickly moved to Bahar Teyze's side, knowing the motions even though there had been no rehearsal.

Rachel watched as wedding guests pinned gold coins with red ribbons onto Leyla's wedding dress, like at the henna night. Some gave her gold hoop bracelets as well. Some guests pinned the coins to Kerem's suit. As the coins accumulated, they started to look like red and gold flowers along the neckline of Leyla's white dress and Kerem's black jacket. Leyla and Kerem kissed the hands of some of the guests, and simply shook hands with others. Something they both did consistently was smile, so much that their cheeks were surely sore, but they looked as though they couldn't help it. They were that happy. They were finally together. Once the hundreds of guests had congratulated the newlyweds, Ilkay Teyze motioned for Rachel to come.

Together, Rachel, Aylin, and Ilkay Teyze fastened the necklace around Leyla's neck.

"Each charm has a meaning," Aylin explained. "But we can tell you about them later. *Allah, bir yastikta kocatsin.*"

"Congratulations!" Rachel said. "Am I allowed to kiss you on both cheeks?"

"Well, it might ruin my makeup, but you are the last one to try so I will allow it. I have time to fix it before the dinner. You must learn the Turkish expression we say to newlyweds, though."

"Ok, what is it?"

"*Allah, bir yastikta kocatsin.*"

"Wow, that's a little hard. What does it mean?"

"It means may you sleep together on one pillow. This means basically may you become old together."

"That's beautiful. May you grow old together," Rachel said in English, looking at both Leyla and Kerem.

"I will teach you how to say it in Turkish," came Cem's voice from behind her.

Rachel turned around and looked at Cem standing only a foot away from her. It was the closest they had been for two weeks, but it wasn't close enough. She knew they couldn't, or at least shouldn't show any public display of affection. So she was very glad that kissing cheeks was an appropriate greeting for them. Cem's skin was slightly sweaty as their cheeks brushed against each other, and his breath smelled of mint. I hope my breath smells ok, Rachel thought. Cem first pinned a gold coin on Kerem's jacket, congratulated his cousin and her groom, and then turned to Rachel.

"See you at the dinner," Cem said. "By the way, your hair looks nice."

Rachel had forgotten about her hair. Suddenly, she wondered if Cem was being honest or making fun of her.

"Seriously? I mean, I asked for them to leave it all down, but the hairdresser got irritated. I'm not sure about the glitter."

"I warned you," Cem said with a sly smile. "But you came out without too much damage. I mean, I prefer your natural everyday look, but you still look great. Maybe I should get some glitter for my hair, too. See you tonight," he said with a confident smile as he turned to follow his parents to their car.

Aylin elbowed Rachel, who was apparently staring a bit too obviously.

"Come on lovebird," she whispered. "We should go back and take a nap before tonight."

Kerem and Leyla were driven off by a friend in the back of Kerem's parents' car, which had been decorated with an arrangement of flowers on the hood and large banners that said "Kerem + Leyla".

"Where are they being taken?"

"They will stay at Kerem's parents' house until they go away on their honeymoon. I don't know if I want to smile or cry," Aylin said. "My sister is now married, in a different world from me, not staying in my parents' home anymore."

"I think you should smile," Rachel said. So Aylin did.

Chapter 27

The minute I heard my first love story
I started looking for you,
Not knowing how blind that was.
Lovers don't finally meet somewhere.
They're in each other all along.

- Rumi

After a snack, Aylin and Rachel changed into their pajamas and lay down to rest on the couches in Ilkay Teyze's living room.

"Are you sure our hair won't get messed up?" Rachel asked, never having had such an elaborate hairstyle before and unsure of how delicate it was.

"Ah, no. They used so much hairspray that I am sure our hair will last three or four days if we don't wash it. I know my mother's hair is always good for a long time after going to the salon."

"All right, then." Rachel lay down on the couch, sure she wasn't tired. Three hours later, they woke up, every hair still in place. Just a little glitter marked the spots where their heads had rested; their makeup hadn't even smudged. They put on their dresses and shoes again and were ready when Ilkay Teyze came out in a burgundy and gold evening gown.

On the drive to the reception, Ilkay Teyze mentioned Cem.

"I hear that our Cem likes you a lot," she said with a conspiratory smile.

"Um, yeah, I really, um," Rachel wasn't sure what she was supposed to share or not share, but Aylin took care of it for her.

"Rachel and Cem are supposed to be together, Ilkay Teyze. Fate made them meet, and I am so happy about this!"

"It's only the beginning, dear, but I did see some nice things in your coffee grounds, do you remember Rachel?"

"Yeah, I do. I really, really like Cem. He's perfect," Rachel remembered that secrets were safe with Ilkay Teyze.

"Nobody is perfect, Rachel. But it is a great feeling to think that somebody is. Still, you must allow him to be a human, as we are all imperfect. Always remember that. I made that mistake when I was young. I looked for perfection. Maybe I still do."

* * *

The dinner was at a restaurant that had been designed for special occasions and it looked like an oasis. Tall trees provided a green canopy over small patios that held two or three large tables each and were surrounded by flowering bushes. An artificial stream wove through the whole area, with small bridges crossing over it. The tables had lavender tablecloths and glowed in the light of tiny flickering candles. Bahar Teyze, Timur Amca, and Aylin were ushered to a special table with a yellow tablecloth and golden plates.

"This table is for the family of the bride and groom," Aylin explained. "You could have sat here, Rachel, but I have a surprise for you. You will sit at the table of the cousins on my mother's side. I don't think this will upset you too much. Am I right?"

Rachel was initially upset. And then Aylin kept talking.

"Cem's English is obviously great, so he can explain everything to you. If that is okay with you."

Duh, Rachel, Cem is Bahar Teyze's sister's son, he will be sitting here, oh my God, this is awesome. Rachel patted her hair, an instinct she didn't even know she had (until now). The hairdo was going to be around for a while.

Up on a pavilion that was raised about ten feet above the rest of the tables was a rectangular table with a large bouquet of flowers.

"That is where Leyla and Kerem will sit," said a male voice. Cem had a habit of sneaking up behind her and making her heart skip.

"Hey you," Rachel said. She tried not to smile too widely at him, but she knew her grin was more than casual. I may as well give up trying to be chill at this point. He knows I'm crazy about him. Why hide it anymore?

"I've been appointed as your translator for the night."

"No complaints here."

Once all of the guests had been seated and the oasis restaurant hummed with the excited sounds of friends and relatives who hadn't seen each other since the last event. And then the chatter slowly died down when a classical piece started to play. Finally, Leyla and Kerem appeared, walking from patio to patio and finally up a small stone staircase to their table on the raised pavilion.

After an applause, waiters started serving each guest a plate with multiple small appetizers on each, which Cem tried to explain to Rachel.

"This is eggplant, I think. And this is carrots with yogurt. And this is cheese, and this is potato salad. This is a grape leaf stuffed with something, probably rice and meat, and this is, is, I have no idea what that is. I think it has walnuts in it."

"I'm sure I won't notice any of it," Rachel said. "You're too much of a distraction. In a good way."

Cem didn't answer with words. Just with a giant grin and a deep breath.

The next dish was chicken with a side of rice, followed by a plate of melon and grapes. And then, a band came out and set up next to the pavilion, where there was a large open area, presumably for dancing. It didn't take them long to set up, as all they had was a synthesizer, a guitar, and two singers, one male and one female.

The music they played was all Turkish, and quite remarkable in spite of the unimpressive size of the band. It had a strong beat and everyone seemed to know all of the songs. While some of the songs sounded familiar by now, Rachel wasn't sure if she wanted to humiliate herself. Dancing was definitely not her strong point. But then dozens of people stood up and started dancing near their tables, and dozens more headed to the dance patio. People of all ages danced in circles and in pairs, and children ran around giggling and squealing. Some children held hands in circles and danced as well as the adults, if not better.

After a few songs, the waiters appeared with a giant tiered cake on a trolley. It was decorated with dozens of lit sparklers, and when Leyla and Kerem approached the cake, they both seemed to glow.

"Come over here for a second," Cem said to Rachel, and without touching her motioned for her to follow him.

"Is this ok? Won't someone notice us walking off together?"

"No, everyone is watching the cake. Besides, if they notice us, the world will not end." Cem led Rachel to a patio whose tables had been vacated. "Rachel, I just wanted to get a chance to talk to you one more time before you go back and this is my last chance, I think. Here, I got this for you." Cem didn't waste any time in handing Rachel an oval-shaped silver coin encased in a flat acrylic cover.

"Um, thank you," Rachel said. I don't exactly know what this is or why Cem gave it to me, but I hope he explains, she thought as she turned it over in her hands. On one side, there was an engraving of a flower, under which it said SAKAYIK Paeonia turcica. On the other side, it said Turkiye Cumhuriyeti 7,500,000 Lira 2002.

"Oh my God, Cem, what is this?" Rachel blurted out as she tried to figure out how many dollars seven and a half million Lira were. At about one and a half Lira to the dollar, it was millions of dollars however you calculated it.

"Oh, it's a mint coin. The flower is called a peony in English. This one is native to the mountains near Antalya, where my parents have their summer house. You know, I like plants and girls like flowers, I guess, and so I thought it would be nice. Don't you like it?"

"Um, thank you so much. I just, I don't know what to say, it's, what is it made out of?"

"Silver. Sterling silver. Why?"

Cem is acting very innocently as if this is something he got from a vending machine. I have no idea how to deal with this situation.

"And why does it say seven million five hundred thousand Lira on it?"

A smile flashed across Cem's lips and then they quivered as he spoke the next line.

"Well, you're worth more, but it's all I could afford."

"There's something really weird about this." Rachel said, though she wasn't sure if she was addressing Cem or herself. But then Cem started to giggle.

"I'm sorry, Rachel, I couldn't help it. It's from 2002. The Turkish Lira was devalued in 2005. 100,000 Liras became 1 new Lira. Knock off six zeros."

"Thank God," Rachel said, slightly embarrassed by her own lack of knowledge. "I totally understand, you had to get me on that one," she said, finding her breath and a laugh again.

"Sorry. It's not worth millions of dollars. Do you like it, though? Is it a weird gift? I mean, I'm such a biology geek, I thought it was great. Maybe you would have preferred a necklace or something."

"No, I mean yes, I do like it. I wouldn't have preferred a necklace. It's really beautiful. And I am totally glad it's not worth millions, because what would I do with a flower-stamped coin worth millions of dollars?"

"I got you something else, too," Cem said, seeming pleased that she liked the coin.

"I'm embarrassed, I didn't get you anything," Rachel said, wondering why she hadn't thought of it.

"Well, this isn't worth seven and a half million lira either, but here it is," he said, placing a plastic watch on her left wrist. It was white with images of ladybugs and flowers and leaves. It didn't match her outfit at all, but she was happy to wear it anyway.

"Aww, thank you," Rachel said.

"Notice the time?" Cem asked eagerly.

Rachel looked, and the watch read twelve o'clock.

"Is it really twelve o'clock already?" Rachel asked, baffled.

"No, it's seven o'clock," Cem said. "It's noon in Cambridge, Massachusetts. That's where MIT is. You can keep this watch on Cambridge time and then you'll know what time it is where I am. When you leave, I'm going to set my watch to Olympia time. And then every time I check the time, I'll think of you."

"And then you'll get everywhere at the wrong time."

"And it will be your fault! Just kidding. I'll get used to it. My watch until now was seven and a half minutes fast but I never got anywhere early because I knew precisely how fast it was."

"Wow. I don't know anything about romance, or even exactly what that means, but this seems like a pretty romantic thing to do."

For the first time, Rachel noticed Cem blush.

"Um, thanks. Don't tell any of my friends, I might lose my reputation as a tough guy."

"Yeah, I'm sure you have a reputation as a tough guy," Rachel said, instantly regretting it and hoping she hadn't hurt his ego.

Cem glanced around the patio and then quickly kissed Rachel. On her lips. Her cheeks burned and her lips tingled. She

287

hoped nobody had seen them, but she didn't really care. She looked up at Cem, to make sure that her lipstick hadn't rubbed off on him. It hadn't.

"I didn't think that was going to happen tonight," Rachel said. "I was just thinking how weird it is; at home, having a boyfriend is all about kissing and touching and stuff. Or at least that's they way everyone makes it sound. And we've barely had any time alone together, but somehow you're still my boyfriend. I think. Sorry, can I use that word?"

"Um yeah, I just gave you a coin worth millions, remember?"

"So I guess that's it then, expensive gifts mean boyfriend," Rachel teased. "No, seriously though, without the kissing and stuff, how is this different from any friendship?"

"I don't know. But it is. I want to kiss you, for one thing," Cem said.

The guests started clapping, and Rachel and Cem moved to the edge of their patio, from where they could see the bride and groom tenderly feeding each other cake.

"Let's go back separately, in case anyone noticed we were gone," Cem suggested. "You go that way and look like you're coming out of the bathroom, and I'll go this way."

"Cem?" Rachel said, not knowing what she was going to say, but wanting to stall their departure in different directions.

"Hmm?"

"Nothing, I just, thank you."

Cem smiled broadly and kissed the air in Rachel's direction.

Rachel had no place to put the coin, so she went into the bathroom and put it in her bra. It was less than comfortable there, but Rachel was glad to feel its presence.

When she got back to the table, Cem and all of the cousins were gone, and Rachel noticed them dancing in a circle on the dance floor. Unsure of how to dance in such a group, Rachel wondered if she should just sit alone and watch them, but then Aylin approached her.

"Where have you been, my dear Rachel? I was worried!"

"I was with Cem, of course," Rachel whispered, just in case someone who overheard them understood English.

"He really likes you," Aylin said, looking neither pleased nor upset.

"I really like him, too," Rachel said, worried about Aylin's look.

"Good then," Aylin said with a smile. "He is my favorite cousin, as you know. Only the best for him and only the best for you. Now, come and dance."

"But I don't really know how to dance," Rachel protested.

"With dancing, there is no right, there is no wrong. You just move. Come."

Before she could object, Rachel was nearly dragged by Aylin (good thing my heels are low ones, she thought) to the dance floor. She was swept into a current of cousins and friends, including Elif, Rana, and Ela, who were dancing in a large circle. Every once in a while, someone would be pushed into the center of the circle and would do a solo dance; some of the dances were sexy, some were silly, all were better than what Rachel thought herself capable of. Cem was in the circle, too, and to Rachel's horror, one of the cousins pushed her into the center. She tried the best she could to move to the rhythm, raising her arms into the air as she had seen others do, shaking her hips a little bit, wondering if she was shaking them too much, and afraid that if she moved too much the silver peony coin would fall out of her bra. She left the center of the circle after fifteen very long seconds, and all of the cousins smiled and whooped and generally approved of her solo dance. Rachel looked across at Cem, who winked at her.

A few minutes later, it was Cem's turn. Apparently shy about actually dancing but not about having fun, he bent his knees and stuck his butt out and acted like a duck, flapping his elbow-wings to the beat of the music. When his routine was over, he left the center of the circle, but rather than returning to his previous spot, he stood next to Rachel. Just in time, too, because a new song began and everyone in the circle put their arms over their neighbors' shoulders and kicked their legs to the song, in a sort-of Turkish Can-Can. Right kick, left kick, step step step. The circle broke and became a line, and others joined until everyone who was dancing was a part of the line dance. The beginning of the line was kicking and stepping at entirely different times as the end of the line, some people kicked left when most kicked right, and some forgot to step at all, nearly bringing the whole line crashing down. Both of Rachel's feet were stepped on, both by Cem on her right side and Aylin on her left, and she was sure she had stepped on their feet as well. Everyone was sweating and laughing and worn out when the song ended and the dancing line broke up into individual guests.

Cem then bent down to whisper in Rachel's ear. His cheek was warm and moist as he gently said something to Rachel. In Turkish.

"*Seni çok sevmeye basladım.*"

"Sorry, I didn't catch that," Rachel said quietly.

"I had to say it in Turkish, because it means more to me in Turkish," Cem said. "But I'll say it again in English," he said, bending down to bring his lips so close to her ear that she could feel their warmth. "I have started to love you."

Rachel somehow managed not to faint in the middle of the dance floor.

Chapter 28

Like a sculptor, if necessary,
Carve a friend out of stone.
Realize that your inner sight is blind
And try to see a treasure in everyone.

- Rumi

Somewhere between Denizli and Izmir International Airport

August 18

Leyla and Kerem had departed on their honeymoon to the Mediterranean coast of Turkey, and she had left a vacancy in the family. Bahar Teyze and Timur Amca were quiet on the ride to the Izmir airport to bring Rachel to her return flight.

"It will be very strange when you are gone. I feel like you were always part of my family. But now you will see your own parents, I am sure they miss you so much."

Rachel admitted to herself that she looked forward to seeing them, but she didn't want Aylin to feel as though she was glad to leave. Because she wasn't.

"I miss my parents and my grandmother and my friends, well, one of my friends. But I don't want to leave you guys here, either," Rachel said, thinking what an odd situation it was. She'd never felt this way before. "It isn't this way at home. I don't know what I'm going to do until school starts. I'll probably go and see if I can work at the coffee shop to make up for all the money I spent. My parents are going let me work there during the school year if I can keep my grades up. And if I can't get a job, I guess I'll just read or something. I mean, what am I gonna do? My best friend back home has a boyfriend now, so I'll pretty much be alone."

"I wish I could visit you, but there is not enough time before school begins," Aylin complained.

"I really want you to come, but I have to warn you that it's not as exciting there as here."

"It won't be exciting here now. I will go back to school soon, too. The summer village is not real life, Rachel. It is like our summer dream. We think about it all year and then it passes too quickly. This year will be really difficult for me. I must take the national exams in June, so I need to study very hard. I want a good place in University."

"And I have to figure out which college I want to go to. Assuming I get in. At least your English is better now, Aylin! Hopefully, you'll get a good score on the English part."

"True."

Rachel thought about Cem and wondered how much she should tell Mom and Dad. And she wondered when she would ever see him again. But Aylin and Rachel couldn't talk about boys in the car today. Timur Amca and Bahar Teyze's English had improved as well.

A late summer heat wave had hit Western Turkey, and the air outside was scorching. Timur Amca parked the car and carried Rachel's bags, despite her protests.

"I can carry them, Timur Amca. Please."

"You have a long journey ahead of you," he said with a fatherly smile, and didn't loosen his grip on her suitcase and carry-on. Suddenly, Rachel felt homesick. She longed for Dad and Mom and Grams and home.

Rachel hugged everyone goodbye, and then remembered that she should probably kiss the hands of Timur Amca and Bahar Teyze. They had tears in their eyes as she did, and the sight of them brought out an unstoppable wave of crying in Rachel and

Aylin. They couldn't find any words, but they hugged each other tightly.

Drying her eyes with a tissue, Rachel looked back at her new extended family as she walked towards the passport control window. When she handed her passport to the immigration official, she was too busy watching Bahar Teyze, Timur Amca, and Aylin waving to even look at the officer.

"Excuse me, madam, but I must see your face to match it with your passport."

Rachel looked at the man, who smiled at her.

"*Allah kavustursun*," he said. Rachel had no idea what it meant, but she was sure he said it to comfort her.

"Thank you," she replied.

He gave Rachel her passport, and she walked towards the gate, waving until she couldn't see her Turkish family anymore.

Characters

Aunt Celia – sister of Rachel's mother

Grams – Rachel's mother's mother

Grams Ming – Rachel's father's mother

Hanna – Rachel's best friend at home

Bahar Teyze – Rachel's host mother

Timur Amca – Rachel's host father

Aylin – Rachel's host sister

Leyla – Older sister of Aylin, also Rachel's host sister

Elif – Aylin's best friend

Ela – Aylin's friend

Rana – Aylin's friend

Hediye Teyze – sister of Bahar

Ibrahim Eniste – husband of Hediye

Cem – son of Heidye and Ibrahim, cousin of Alyin and Leyla

Pinar Teyze – sister of Bahar

Haluk Eniste – husband of Pinar

Ali Dayi – brother of Bahar

Ayca Yenge – wife of Ali

Omer Dayi – brother of Bahar

Filiz Yenge – wife of Omer

Gulsah Hala – sister of Timur

Soner Eniste – husband of Gulsah

Ilkay Teyze – cousin of Bahar

Huseyin Amca – love interest of Ilkay Teyze

Hakan – Leyla's ex-boyfriend

Kerem – Leyla's boyfriend/fiancé

Zumrut Teyze – mother of Kerem

Efe Amca – father of Kerem

Derya Teyze – Emre's mother

Hakan Abi – Emre's father

Emre – Aylin's boyfriend

Emel Teyze - dressmaker

About Rumi, whose quotes begin each chapter:

Rumi, whose real name was Jalal ad-Din Muhammad Balkhi, was a 13th-century poet, jurist, theologian, and Sufi mystic. He was of Persian origin and was a Muslim. Rumi was born in the eastern part of what was then the Persian Empire and is in modern-day Tajikistan. His family then moved west for political reasons, and settled in Konya, which is in modern-day Turkey, where he spent most of his life. His works have been translated into numerous languages, and are famous worldwide.

Thank you

No book can be written without the help and support of a vast network of friends and family. It would be wrong to publish this book without giving credit where it is due.

That said, once I started writing my thank-you paragraphs, I realized that they were too personal and added numerous pages to this book. So, I will do the personal thanking in person. For now, I'd like to just acknowledge that lots of people have supported me in my writing and in this project. Wonderful friends and family have been readers and have given me their opinions, and I am eternally grateful for you all (you know who you are).

I have dedicated this book to my dear husband, whose stories directly inspired this book. He is also the reason I went to Turkey in the first place.

I would also like to dedicate this book to the memory of my dear Aunt Judith Rauck. I wish that she could have seen this book in print. I hope that she is watching from somewhere nice, wherever that may be.

About the Author

Born and raised in Atlanta, Georgia, Saskia E. Akyil, like many writers over the age of 25, began her art by keeping a journal and writing letters to her friends, pen-pals, cousins, and grandparents. After receiving a B.A. in International Studies from Emory University and an M.A. in Teaching English as a Second Language (ESL) from the University of Minnesota, her writing took on a more formal tone as she wrote articles for academic publications. She gained incredibly diverse experiences while simultaneously working three jobs in Olympia, Washington; as a community college ESL professor for immigrants, as a state program administrator for displaced homemakers, and as a Spanish-language medical interpreter. She has also taught numerous cooking classes in the United States and in Germany. As a hobby, she collects languages, and has studied French, Spanish, Italian, Japanese, Turkish, and German. She left her jobs behind in 2005 when she moved to Munich, Germany with her husband and proceeded to have two sons, who inspire and exhaust her, and never cease to make her laugh.

Saskia E. Akyil

Secrets of a Summer Village